Acclaim for Rosslyn Elliott

W9-AJO-945

ELL

"A novelist to watch! Elliott excels at bringing a bygone era to life with all of its charm and its flaws. An unhesitating indictment of cruelty and a celebration of the freedom of spirit which can only be found in God."

— Siri Mitchell,
author of *A Heart Most Worthy*

"Rosslyn Elliott weaves a gripping story full of fascinating historical details. She creates realistic and poignant characters who touch your heart with a message of true grace and forgiveness. *Fairer than Morning* is the kind of book you'll think about long after you read the last page."

— Jody Hedlund,
best-selling author of
The Preacher's Bride

"*Fairer than Morning* is a fabulous debut! Rosslyn Elliott has not so much written a story, but crafted a tale with a dedication to depth and detail equal to that of the artisan she brings to life. With two very real people at its core, the story unfolds with characters and intrigue reminiscent of a Dickens novel, bringing the reader face-to-face with the heartbreak of bondage and the sweetness of freedom. Rosslyn Elliott is a welcome new voice, almost luxurious. Readers deserve this indulgence."

— Allison Pittman,
award-winning author of *Stealing
Home* and *Lilies in Moonlight*

"*Fairer than Morning* is a book to savor. As you read this exquisitely written story, the present fades and you are drawn into a tale of cruelty, honor, love, and deliverance. When you reach the last page you close the book wishing for more. However, Rosslyn Elliott's characters will go with you, forever embedded in your heart."

— Bonnie Leon,
author of *Touching the Clouds* and
the Sydney Cove series

SWEETER
THAN
Birdsong

Wapiti regional library

SWEETER
THAN
Birdsong

Book Two

THE SADDLER'S LEGACY

ROSSLYN ELLIOTT

PAPL
DISCARDED

THOMAS NELSON
Since 1798

NASHVILLE   DALLAS   MEXICO CITY   RIO DE JANEIRO

© 2012 by Rosslyn Elliott

All rights reserved. No portion of this book may be reproduced, stored in a retrieval system, or transmitted in any form or by any means—electronic, mechanical, photocopy, recording, scanning, or other—except for brief quotations in critical reviews or articles, without the prior written permission of the publisher.

Published in Nashville, Tennessee, by Thomas Nelson. Thomas Nelson is a registered trademark of Thomas Nelson, Inc.

Published in association with the literary agency of WordServe Literary Group, Ltd., 10152 S. Knoll Circle, Highlands Ranch, CO 80130. www.wordserveliterary.com.

Thomas Nelson, Inc., titles may be purchased in bulk for educational, business, fund-raising, or sales promotional use. For information, please e-mail SpecialMarkets@ThomasNelson.com.

Scripture verses are from the King James Version of the Bible.

Publisher's Note: This novel is a work of fiction. Names, characters, places, and incidents are either products of the author's imagination or used fictitiously. All characters are fictional, and any similarity to people living or dead is purely coincidental.

Library of Congress Cataloging-in-Publication Data

Elliott, Rosslyn.
  Sweeter than birdsong / Rosslyn Elliott.
     p. cm. — (The saddler's legacy ; bk. 2)
  ISBN 978-1-59554-786-6 (trade paper)
1. Fugitive slaves—Fiction. 2. Underground Railroad—Fiction. 3. Ohio—History—1787–1865—Fiction. I. Title.
  PS3605.L4498S94 2012
  813'.6—dc23   2011043180

Printed in the United States of America

12 13 14 15 16 17 QG 6 5 4 3 2 1

For Gwen Stewart, a true friend in my hour of need,

and for Meredith Efken, an editor in shining armor

One

WESTERVILLE, OHIO

1855

HER CUSTOMARY WALK ACROSS THE COLLEGE QUAD-
rangle had become an executioner's march. Kate's heeled shoes
clunked over the flagstones. Her full skirt and horsehair crinoline dragged from her waist, too warm even for this mild May
morning.

She climbed the stone steps of the whitewashed college
building and laid hold of the black iron door handle with a
clammy palm. The dim foyer led to the lecture hall. Her breath
came faster and her corset squeezed her lungs—it had not felt
so tight when the maid laced it an hour ago. Ahead loomed the
dark rectangle of the hall's oaken door, which stood ajar.

At the threshold, she paused. A baritone voice lifted in
clear, well-balanced phrases inside the hall. The speaker's per-
suasive power carried even here. Ben Hanby. He was the best
orator in the class. She laid a hand to her midsection to quell
the pulsing nausea there. If she did not go in now, she would
not go in at all.

At her push, the door swung open to reveal rows of masculine shoulders in dark coats, all heads turned toward the speaker. Each gentleman's neat coattails fell open over his knees, black against the polished wood floor. Each white collar rose to the sweep of hair worn according to the current vogue, longer than a Roman's but never past the collar.

On the raised platform beyond them, Ben Hanby stood, as natural and poised as if he were alone in the room, his dark hair thick over his brow. His eyes were intent, his face alive with interest in his subject, but his words floated past Kate in a wash of sounds her jumping nerves could not interpret. Of course speaking came easily for him—his father was a minister.

He finished with a question to the audience, and even her disrupted attention caught the subtle humor in the lift of his eyebrow as he delivered his line straight-faced. A chuckle rose from the young men, echoed in the lighter laughter of the small party of young lady scholars seated with their chaperone on the end of the front row.

Ben Hanby descended the stairs, the barest smile appearing as he exchanged glances with his friends.

"Miss Winter." Professor Hayworth's bass rumbled across the hall.

Heads turned toward her. Her skin tingled in waves of heat, her heart kicked in an uneven cadence. Could it stop from such fright? The thought made it worsen, like a stutter in her chest that could not move on to the next beat.

"I am glad you choose to join us today." Professor Hayworth spoke to her from the dais beside the podium, full-bearded in his formal black robe. "You have arrived just in time to give the first of our ladies' speeches."

She avoided their curious stares as her pulse quickened and her mouth dried.

"Please proceed to the podium," he said.

She produced a bare nod and started down the aisle. Her skirt swept an arc so wide she had to brush against the wall to ensure it would clear the chairs.

The chairs scraped as the young men stood up. They always rose to acknowledge the entrance of young ladies into the hall. But to have them do it for Kate alone, to be the sole object of their interest—she had to fix her gaze on the far wall and its carved paneling as a chill rippled over her shoulders and spread, bringing a layer of cold perspiration after it. She must have blanched even whiter than her usual paleness, and moisture had settled on her upper lip, on her forehead. How ghastly she must look. They would all see her fear. A pain cramped her chest.

It seemed something terrible would happen if she stepped on that stage—the pain in her chest might spread into a full, searing arrest.

She turned the corner to the platform. Ben Hanby looked at her and gave an encouraging nod. The compassion in his brown eyes made it worse. Did he know that she was ill, that her tortured breathing threatened to constrict to nothing?

One foot at a time, only three yards to the podium. She stepped behind its flimsy refuge and gripped the raised lip of the stand with both shaking hands.

The room was silent—a horrible, waiting hush like the moment before a cat seizes a rodent. Into the silence came the pounding in her ears. The whole room pulsed to its beat—her mouth was so dry.

A score of faces turned toward her, expectant. Kate braced against the podium and pulled in one tremulous breath.

She looked over the students' heads, past their neat rows of coats and ties to the small cluster of women off to one side with their chaperone. *Help me, help me, please.* But the women could not hear her—did they not see she was not well?

The thrumming in her ears rose to a rushing like water.

The first words were "On the Purpose of Friendship: An Argument Drawn from Aristotle and Cicero." She would say the title, now, by opening her mouth.

A quiet rasp escaped her throat before it closed with a gulping sound.

Kate inhaled again and forced it out. "On the Pur—" Her throat clutched once more.

Professor Hayworth was only a dim figure in her peripheral vision. Now her lips and tongue would not work at all. Her will had brought her this far, but her voice would not obey her.

Kate released the podium and stepped back on wobbly legs.

She turned and fled, down the steps of the platform, past the blur of young men, out the door of the recital hall, through the hallway, out to the free air where no one was watching. Her heels caught at the light green lawn. Where should she go so no one could find her?

She hurried around the white-planked corner of the building. She must hide herself behind the bulge of the chimney, for someone might come in pursuit, and she did not wish to speak. Too late for words to be of any use.

In the safety of the corner where chimney met wood, she leaned against the cool brick, heaving for breath through her tight throat, wheezing as barely any air came through. She had not died, but her heart still beat erratically, a pain with every skipped beat. She must slow down her panicked breathing; she was light-headed. The sides of her bodice were soaked through.

Now they would send her away. No one could remain at university without giving orations. She had failed herself and disgraced the small band of young women who had been permitted to enroll at Otterbein.

More cramps seized her chest and abdomen, burning, pinching.

Her dream of graduating from college and leaving Westerville was over.

Two

WHEN A YOUNG MAN HAD SEVEN YOUNGER SIBLINGS, IT was only natural that one of them would be a pox on his very existence. Ben supposed he should count his blessings that the other six brought him such joy. But none of the joys had come to the general store today—only Cyrus, the pox himself.

"Do you suppose the college will ask Miss Winter to leave?" Cyrus asked. He picked up a new hat from its box and adjusted it with care over his wild mass of light brown curls. "Rather a scene she made in class yesterday."

"A gentleman would not speculate on her situation." Ben picked up a sheet of music and did his best to ignore Cyrus. As his eyes followed the black lines of notes across the staff, he hummed the melody under his breath.

"It would be a shame to lose such a beauty from the college," Cyrus murmured. "With hair and eyes such as hers, who needs a voice?" Cyrus adjusted the hat to a sharp angle over his brow and gave himself a burning stare in the small looking glass on the wall.

The effect of his seventeen-year-old playacting was not as impressive as he imagined. Ben suppressed his dry comment.

Their father was holding a list of supplies up to the light. "And cinnamon, and ten pounds of flour," he read aloud to Mr. Bogler, the store owner.

"How's your trade in harnesses been, Mr. Hanby?" Mr. Bogler lifted a flour sack to the counter.

"Brisk of late," Ben's father said. The gray streaks in his dark hair did not detract from his still-vigorous appearance—in his midforties, he could keep pace with men a decade younger. "The railroad has helped. What's good for Columbus is good for Westerville."

He folded the shopping list and glanced at Ben. "Are you finished, son?"

"Yes, sir." Ben kept hold of the sheet music and walked to the front, fishing in his pocket for coins. He would pay for it himself—his father had enough mouths to feed, and Ben's seasonal work as a schoolmaster paid for his Otterbein tuition and any small luxuries like music.

A man shouted outside, then another. His father stiffened, and Ben followed his gaze outside through the checkered panes of the wide store window.

A small group of black men shuffled down the street, their shoulders hunched. Chains linked their ankles through iron cuffs so heavy they would grind away flesh within a mile's walk. And from the mud-streaked, bare feet of the slaves, it was clear they had come more than a mile. Behind them strode four white men in broad-brimmed, dusty hats and travel-worn clothing. One propped a long whip over his shoulder as if it were a fishing pole while two others dogged the heels of the slaves. One yelled for them to hurry it up, and the other laughed and shoved the hindmost prisoner forward. He stumbled into the slave ahead,

7

weaved and staggered, then tripped on the chain and fell prone in the dirt. The bounty hunter kicked the fallen man in the belly, hard, again, and he doubled up in pain. Ben's gut clenched in sympathy.

With three swift steps he made it to the door and grasped the handle.

"Ben." His father's call carried a command.

Ben paused, struggled to unknot his clenched fingers—it was too much, he could not tolerate it. He turned his head. "Must we stand here and do nothing?"

"Yes. I'm sorry, son. We've spoken about this before." His father's deep-set eyes said more, reminded him that they could not discuss such things in public.

The smug expression on the bounty hunter's face made Ben want to slam his fist against the door. "But they're taking them right down State Street. Throwing it in our faces."

"It's the law, Ben. That's enough." Beneath his words lay a warning.

Ben gritted his teeth and walked back to the counter. He grasped the flour sack in one hand, stuffed the sheet music under his arm, and snatched his hat from the courtesy peg on the wall. He jerked the door open and stormed out, gaze averted from the spectacle in the street. Cyrus would have to help his father carry the rest. If Ben saw any more, he could not answer for his actions, law or no law.

Three

THE DIMNESS OF THE HALL OUTSIDE THE PRESIDENT'S office did not soften the rigid face of Kate's mother. Her tight mouth and narrowed eyes augured ill for what might happen once she and Kate returned to the cold formality of the house behind the gate.

Kate sat on the edge of her chair and kept her posture as perfect as the young ladies had been taught. It was habit. She would not win her mother's approval through proper deportment, especially not after the debacle of the oration day.

Professor Hayworth opened the door and stepped back. "Ladies, if you would be so kind as to join us." The effort behind his genial tone made it all the more ominous.

Her mother glided past her and onto the dark red carpet with its pattern of blue looping vines. President Lawrence had risen to greet them at his desk. After Kate and her mother seated themselves in the two velvet wing chairs, the president and Professor Hayworth resumed their own seats behind the wide, ebony expanse of the desk.

"Mrs. Winter, thank you for accompanying your daughter this morning," President Lawrence said.

Her mother nodded without reply.

The college president, Mr. Lawrence, had a kind, open face, clean shaven to reveal ruddy health across his cheekbones. His eyelids drooped at the edges with the onset of middle age, but his eyes were bright. He wore the traditional light black robe over his navy waistcoat and tie. The president took a piece of paper from the drawer below him and laid it on the desk, a lone ivory island in the sea of black. He stared down at it for a moment. "I trust you are aware, Mrs. Winter, that your daughter has a delicate sensibility. It prevented her from giving an oration before her classmates. And orations are required for the completion of an Otterbein degree."

"Yes." Her mother pressed her lips into a line.

The sharp smell of the freshly painted walls turned Kate's stomach. If they wished to be merciful, they would do it quickly and without ceremony.

Professor Hayworth perused a sheaf of papers he held in his hands. "You may also be aware, madam, that your daughter is one of our most gifted students."

Her mother's lips twitched but she said nothing, still as a plaster bust beneath her architectural twists and coils of black hair. What had she almost said? Certainly nothing complimentary.

"She is at the top of her class in Latin and Greek, as well as mathematics," the professor added.

Mr. Lawrence leaned forward, interlacing his knuckles on the desk's smooth surface. "Because of her prodigious gifts, we are unwilling to dismiss her at this time. Oration is not as vital for a young lady as it would be for a gentleman."

She must have misheard. They were not going to dismiss her?

"However, we cannot simply ignore the requirements of

Otterbein College," Professor Hayworth said. "And so we wish to give you more time, Miss Winter. After the new year—in eight month's time—you must be able to deliver an oration to the entire class. Until then, you may present your assigned recitation to me, in the company of the ladies' chaperone."

"Do you wish to continue under these conditions?" President Lawrence asked.

Kate murmured, "Yes, sir."

"Very good." The president sat back in his chair as if released from a string. Professor Hayworth looked relieved, though his bushy brown beard made it hard to tell for certain.

"Thank you, President Lawrence." Her mother rose to her feet, a silvery beaded handbag dangling from her wrist against the lilac silk of her dress. She had dressed as if to meet in the Oval Office with President Pierce himself, not with the president of a small college. The gentlemen rose with her and Kate followed suit, stepping forward to allow her skirt its room.

"Kate, you will wish to thank them as well, I am sure." Kate's mother flashed her a steel-blue look, then assumed a milder aspect to the men.

Kate lifted her head. "I am grateful to you, sirs." Her answer was too soft, she knew—they would hardly hear her, and her mother would take her to task for it later. Her words slipped out, artificial, manufactured by her mother's will, not her own. Perhaps they thought they were kind, but a summer and a semester would make no difference. She had done her best to speak, but her body had refused her will. The faculty's stipulation would not change her weakness. It was simply a stay of execution.

"You have great promise, Miss Winter," said Professor Hayworth. "We wish you to fulfill it."

Her mother clutched her silver handbag in one tight fist. "Thank you, Professor. Good day, gentlemen." She inclined her head and swept out the door in a puff of powdery lavender scent.

Kate followed her down the hall. The tightness of her dressed hair pulled into a dull ache at her temples. She could not bear to go back through their iron-gated yard into the Winter residence, but she had no other place to live.

As soon as their maid Tessie let them in the front door, Kate's mother sailed across the foyer and threw an order over her lilac shoulder. "Come to the parlor."

Kate avoided Tessie's sympathetic look as she trailed in her mother's wake through the double doors. She had never liked the parlor's blue-and-white formality, punctuated by spiny-legged chairs and hard upholstery.

Her mother rounded on her, and Kate suppressed a start.

"I suppose we must count our blessings that President Lawrence is so magnanimous." Dry, papery-fine skin pulled into deep grooves around her tight mouth.

"Yes, Mother." If Kate did not argue, it would end sooner.

Her mother peered at her. "Clearly, you have a brain somewhere in your head. You do well enough in your studies. So why do you stumble over a simple declamation?"

"I don't know." Resentment pricked deep beneath her meek response like a burr under a saddle.

"And you won't speak to the few eligible suitors I have brought to you."

"It is not deliberate, Mother. I am not gifted in social discourse."

"You are too intelligent to be incapable of conversation. Something in you wishes to defy me, Kate."

"I don't intend to displease you." But that hidden spikiness within her belied her polite response. Her mother was so determined to be dissatisfied.

Her mother picked up her embroidery frame from a lace-topped side table, but then set it down again. Her lips drew into a taut smile. "Young Mr. Hanby is directing a musicale for the college, I hear. Is he not holding auditions soon? Mrs. Bogler told me so. I believe this performance would be a perfect opportunity to overcome your flaw. You must audition."

"Mother, I have proven I cannot speak in public settings." Kate stared at the parquet below the full hem of her sea-green dress. This did not seem just, to be controlled by the dictates of so many others, never given a choice. She must be very calm, though beneath it all her will thrashed like an animal in a trap. She pressed her hands together and counted in Greek.

"What did you say? I can't abide this half-audible murmuring of yours." Her mother walked away a few steps to pretend to examine the clock above the fireplace. "President Lawrence's daughter will appear in this musicale. And why is that? Because her parents know their daughter must be poised and articulate if she is to make an enterprising match, beyond this small town."

"I do not have any poise, Mother. I am certain to—"

"Speak up, I tell you!"

"Ruth, you leave that girl 'lone." Her father's slurred voice came from his study, at the other end of the parlor behind her mother's back. Sickly sweet fumes drifted to Kate, as if the bourbon on his breath spread throughout the house.

Her mother turned her head a fraction, like a duchess in

her stiff-bodied gown. "Stay out of it, Isaiah. You're hardly in a position to judge social niceties. She will do as I bid her and go to the audition."

Her father's figure loomed in the doorway, his beard rumpled, a dark, wet stain on his lapel. His reddened eyes fixed on her mother as she fell back a step. "You'll let her do as she wishes."

"It is all right, Father. I will go." Fair or not, it did not matter. She must bring this interview to a close before her parents flew into one of their battles. Her scalp tingled and she took a deep breath. "But I would like to sing instead of read."

Her mother raised her thin-plucked brows. "Singing is less abhorrent to you?"

"Yes." If she sang, she might arrange to sing with others and blend into the group. She could avoid a solo performance.

"Ruth, tell her she may sing. Don't be so hard-hearted." Her father's voice was always too big for the room. Liquor must affect one's hearing.

Her mother stared back at him with cold dislike. "Very well."

Kate bowed her head. She must not show the struggle inside. "May I go to my room?"

Her mother did not answer, but only jerked her head, as if she had pricked herself with the embroidery needle. Her eyes were shadowed, her still-beautiful cheeks looked pinched.

Kate's father lumbered back to his den without comment. A glass clinked. She hurried away from the sound—she loathed it now.

At the top of the stairs, her sister's door was closed. Kate did not want to be alone just yet—even Leah might provide some company. Kate tapped on her door, turned the handle, and stepped in.

Leah swiveled away from her vanity with a start, and her ivory brush tangled in her long dark hair. Her wide eyes gave her the look of a little girl still in the pinafore and pantalets Kate remembered from their nursery days.

"In the future, please knock." Leah's attempt at a worldly expression did not sit well on her girlish features.

Kate shut the door behind her. "I must leave. I will not live here anymore."

"You have no choice. Neither of us does." Leah extricated her hair from the brush and began to style it again as she gazed in the mirror. "I'll be married as soon as I turn eighteen, and if you had any sense, you'd already have done the same. You could have been out of this house a year ago." She curled one lock with fastidious attention, then pinned it up.

"I won't go from one prison to another. I will find some other way to sustain myself. One doesn't always have to marry."

"But the alternatives are hardly respectable. Will you choose one of them nonetheless?" Leah shot a look of disdain over her shoulder but continued arranging her hair.

A burn started at Kate's collar. "I will find a decent way. You will see." She withdrew from the room and disciplined herself to close the door with a gentle turn of the knob.

When would she learn? She did not have a family like other families. Leah's character had altered in a peculiar way in response to the harshness of their parents. But her superficial hardness was not of her own making—Kate would not blame her for it. In happier days, Leah had been quick to giggle or offer a sisterly embrace.

Kate's own room was hardly a haven, with its black mahogany armoire looming over her and a heavy four-postered bed dominating the floor. Still, it was such respite as she could get, and she closed the door and fled to her reading corner. Here was her solace. Her bookshelf, her chair turned to the wall, so she could look only at the books and out her window. She sank down into the welcome embrace of the chair.

She would not think of the oration anymore, or her shame, or how she would face the students again in the classroom. She leaned forward and plucked a book at random from the shelf. *Rasselas*, by Samuel Johnson. She had already read the prologue about the prince who finds a secret tunnel out of his isolated valley kingdom and ventures into the real world to find the meaning of happiness.

A wild idea struck her, and she stood up and gazed out the window, the book folded over the back of her hand.

Otterbein was not her only path to freedom. She did not have to endure the humiliating, inevitable failures her mother pressed upon her. There might be another way to secure a living, if she could find the right woman to teach her an honest trade. Her mind raced as if she had taken three cups of tea. She must not continue to think of teaching as her only route to independence and college as the only way to attain it. Teaching required public presentation, and thus would be unpleasant and perhaps impossible, even to an audience of young ladies.

It would not be so hard to leave. No one would know her plan, no one would stop her. She imagined herself far beyond the trees that surrounded the house, and her mood lifted like white smoke from a watch fire, liberated from ground to air.

But Prince Rasselas had not found happiness.

Still, he had made his own choice. She would risk anything for the chance at a choice. She would be a quick study at a trade— perhaps even millinery. She had always liked hats, and as a girl she had drawn them in many styles according to her fancy. A city milliner might be willing to apprentice her in exchange for room and board.

The future rose up in her imagination, so light and open and full of promise, nothing like the cramped dimness of her life here. What a joy to escape! Even the thread of fear and the "what-ifs" could not weigh down her buoyant heart. She tucked her book close to her bodice and smiled.

She could leave and make her own way. It was not as fool-hardy as it sounded. She might escape this sad house after all, and sooner than she had thought—but first she must think of how and when to do it.

Four

NEITHER THE NOTES NOR THE WORDS WOULD ANSWER his call tonight. Ben dipped his pen in the ink and wrote another line: *Poor Nelly never saw her man again*. No, that wouldn't do. He drew a precise line through it, to match the ten previous phrases already struck through on this page.

The oil lamp guttered and a shadow wavered across the page to climb the walls of the parlor. The clock ticked, steady as a metronome, the only sound at two in the morning. Still, the presence of his sleeping family filled the house, the warmth of their breathing steady and strong for his parents, quick and light for his three smallest brothers and sisters. A house full of sleepers did not feel empty.

A floorboard creaked in his parents' bedroom. He turned from the piano bench to see his mother tying the peach ribbons of her housecoat as she walked into the parlor.

"I thought I heard someone out here." The faint lines of middle age on Ann Hanby's forehead deepened into concern.

"It's all right, Mother. I'm finishing some work."

"In the wee hours of the morning?" She padded up behind him and looked over his shoulder, the ruffle of her cap framing her still-pretty face. "Oh, Ben—the Nelly song again. If it robs you of sleep, lay it aside. You've written so many fine songs." She seated herself in the nearest padded armchair, graceful and petite even after eight children.

"I can't. Not until I've written this song as it should be."

"You only torment yourself by writing it over and over. I've heard scraps of it before—it's quite good. Just finish it." She laid her hands in her lap and tucked her feet up under herself in the chair, like a girl.

"Are you cold?" Ben rose and retrieved the crocheted blanket from the top of the piano, then brought it to her.

"Thank you, son." She settled it over her knees. "Now if only I could persuade you to care for yourself as well." She gave him a smile full of memory of a boyhood of scraped knees and snow-frozen limbs.

"A few hours' missed sleep won't harm me. Especially in a good cause." He kneaded the tense spot in the middle of his forehead.

"But I worry for you with this song. You mustn't gnaw at yourself about Joseph—you were too young to see such things. I told your father so at the time."

Joseph—an image flashed in his mind—the brown skin of the sick man turning gray, the last rattle of breath through his chest, the pain and hope in his eyes turning to an empty hole in his pupils. Even after so many years, a bitter aftertaste of his boyish horror remained.

"I was nine years old, Mother. Father couldn't shield me from the fugitives forever."

"But had you not been so young, it wouldn't haunt you now."

"Perhaps there's a reason for it, something I'm called to do."

She sighed. "You are so like your father, which is why I love both of you so." She bunched the lap robe in her arms and stood. "You cannot free every imprisoned soul in our country—you can only do the best that one young man may do. And I admire you for it."

Joseph's voice hoarse with fever still echoed in his ears, *"Nelly . . . Nelly."* It vibrated through his bones, a low groan of dismay, both Joseph's and his own. Ben blinked, picked up the pen, and dipped it in the ink again.

His mother laid the blanket back on the piano, crossed behind him, and laid her hands on his shoulders. "Go to bed, son." Her kiss fell on the top of his hair and she laughed softly. "I can't do that anymore now you're so tall. Good night . . . or good morning."

"Good night, Mother."

She rustled away and left him alone in the shadows again.

He scratched a few more words on the page, stared at them, counted the meter. His choices were never good enough for this song. The ideal lay always out of reach, goading him, irritating in its abstract perfection. He rubbed his eyebrows and stood. It would not come tonight—he muttered a few impatient and self-accusing words as he turned away from the piano.

Wait. What about that relic Joseph had left with them so long ago? Ben walked to the curio cabinet, opened the glass door, and groped behind the little oval portrait of his mother's mother, long passed away. His fingertips brushed latticework. There it was—he pulled it out. He had not opened it in years.

The basket was so tiny and neat, with its hinged lid, that one of his sisters would have taken it as a plaything long ago had not Ben and his father protected it. He lifted the lid. Inside was a single lock of hair, black and shiny, in a spiral curl against the woven reeds. His heart twinged—here was proof of Nelly's existence, her sad state, the real woman who would suffer when the man she loved and trusted never returned for her.

Was it all that was left of Nelly? Or might she be still waiting, somewhere, in her enslavement, for her bridegroom who would never return?

He did not have to sit like a nine-year-old boy and wonder. He knew many conductors on the Underground Railroad. One of them might be able to trace the whereabouts of Joseph's Nelly.

Perhaps it wasn't the unwritten song keeping him sleepless all these years. Maybe a different task lay ahead.

Because if he could find Nelly, he could steal her away to freedom.

Five

THE THOROUGHBRED GATHERED HER LEGS UNDER HER and cannoned out into the fallow field. Kate's hat would have blown off but for its chin strap, which tightened in the sudden gust of wind.

She clenched her knee on the horn of the sidesaddle as the fence rushed toward them, larger with every stride. Her breath shortened and her vision narrowed to only the top of the fence. Four strides. Three. Two. One. Garnet's weight shifted back. Kate leaned forward and pushed the reins up her neck. The mare's front legs left the ground and she soared upward.

Kate flew, weightless over her horse's back, time suspended. The mare's feet thudded hard on the ground and Kate sat up, correcting the balance as they surged forward. Pounding hooves echoed the wild thump of her heart as she let Garnet canter on at a good clip. Finally, Kate slowed her to a trot. On the slope ahead, a grassy checkerboard of fields lay in patches of spring green outlined by white fences. She would like to ride on and on, over every fence, far from her parents and their misery.

But that would not do. Not yet, anyway. She could not leave town without money or a bag packed. It was difficult enough to get permission to ride alone, even to a nearby neighbor's fields. A valise slung over her mare's haunches would not pass her mother's inspection. But Kate would find her opportunity.

She reined Garnet along the fence and passed a clump of white birches in full, bright green leaf at the corner of the field.

Oh no. Two gentlemen, there, on horseback. She had not seen them through the trees, but they must have seen her wild ride. Then she must avoid them—it was not ladylike to gallop pell-mell across fields like a steeplechaser. Her mother must not hear of it, or she would be forbidden even this small freedom. She turned Garnet's head to cut across the field to the gate on the far end.

The first man urged his mount along the fence at a brisk walk, then a trot. He appeared to be moving to intercept her.

The three horses converged on the gate. She could not elude them—she slowed Garnet to a walk for the last few yards. The man on the black horse halted at the gatepost, and his companion pulled up beside him on his white mount.

"Miss Winter?" The first young man tipped his hat, not at all out of breath, revealing hair the color of bronze. It waved over his strong-planed face. She knew him—he was one of the young men from the literary society.

"Frederick Jones, at your service. Though you hardly seem to need it, with such daring." He grinned. "And you know my friend, Mr. Hanby."

The dark-haired young man lifted his hat as well, dispelling the shadow it had cast over his deep brown eyes. His thoughtful, quiet manner made him seem every inch the reserved gentleman. In person, he differed from the impassioned young orator she had seen in class.

The memory of her oratory thundered back into her consciousness. A hot tingle crawled over her cheeks. She must get away before they attempted to discuss it.

She inclined her head to them. If she remained silent, they might take the hint and ride away.

Ben Hanby maneuvered his horse to the gate and unlatched it, then cued the white gelding to swing its hindquarters around so he could open it for her. Kate pressed her leg to Garnet's side and moved her ahead through the opening. "Thank you." A moment more, and she would be trotting away without further incident. She kept her gaze between Garnet's ears.

"I saw you jumping," Frederick said as she passed within a few feet of his sidelong horse. She looked up to find him smiling at her. "That was admirably done. I don't know many riders who can keep their seats over four-foot fences."

She halted Garnet and stared into Frederick's greenish-hazel eyes. Easy enough for him to be blithe, with all his friends and no burden of secrets. "I pray you won't mention it to anyone."

"Of course not," Ben Hanby said. His defined dark eyebrows drew together as if he were making a study of her. "You have our word, Miss Winter. Does she not, Mr. Jones?"

"To be sure," Frederick said. His black horse tossed its head, spraying droplets of foam from its bit into the grass. "You see, even Bayard agrees." He chuckled.

She must close this conversation—her palms were damp against the braided reins. Her tongue threatened to tie itself for lack of an idea, so she said the only thing that occurred to her. "I understand you will have auditions for your musicale tomorrow."

"Yes." Ben Hanby eyed her, plainly puzzled.

"I will attend."

"You wish to audition?" He seemed pleased. Frederick's eyebrows rose to his hat brim.

"Yes." She was making the conversation awkward by her monosyllables. Of course they would find it amusing that such a shrinking violet would dare to audition. But she would depart Westerville before the musicale took place. Until then, she would go along with her mother's command and convince her nothing was amiss.

Enough was enough. She had satisfied the demands of bare courtesy, and her fingers gripped the reins too tightly, as if she could rein in herself instead of her mount. Garnet stepped sideways, sensing her unease. "Good day, Mr. Hanby, Mr. Jones."

"Good day, Miss Winter." Frederick cued Bayard to move away and give Garnet more room.

"Until tomorrow then," Ben Hanby said.

She cued Garnet to walk, then trot, easing into the rhythm of her mare's gait. Their eyes were on her back—she could feel it. After what felt like an eon, Garnet trotted to the privacy of the tree-lined road.

If Kate had to bear the torture of a public audition this once, so be it. And she would only sing a few bars, no speaking, no personal words required. She might manage it if she did not look at the audience. She would not think of it any more today—she had only a few minutes remaining to enjoy the peace of the pastel sunshine, the warmth of spring. In the treetops, a bird trilled random notes like a broken flute. A breath of wind stirred Garnet's forelock.

She would hate to leave her chestnut mare. She leaned down to stroke her smooth neck, the hair glossy over Garnet's fine skin as her hooves clopped along the gravel embedded in the dirt road. Should she really leave this creature who trusted her? But Kenny, their groom, would take good care of Garnet, even if no one else in the family was fond of animals.

Kate would never again have to smell the bourbon wafting from her father's unconscious form slumped in his chair, or suffer shame at her mother's will. And Leah would not miss Kate, consumed as she was with her own image in the looking glass. The pain of the truth singed Kate like a lit match, setting her thoughts aflame.

Her family need not be pierced by barbed words and blasted by liquor-laced rage—if only her mother and father would choose otherwise. But she must not dwell on pointless conjectures. Too many times she had prayed with childish hope for her father's sobriety, only to hear their voices raised again, he drunk, her mother strident. She could leave behind all the pain, like shedding a pile of old garments on the floor. And she would not look back to those who did not care for her and would not miss her.

She would pack her valise tonight and hide it in her armoire. The thought of it sitting there, bulging with promise, would help her survive the audition.

Six

ONE NOTE AFTER ANOTHER SLIPPED FROM THE PIANO into the room, to expand and ring there. The ivory keys resisted Ben's fingertips only a fraction of a second before giving way, the tension before each note released from silence into its mysterious opposite, music.

He should stop and gather his sheet music for the auditions, but the lure of the new song drew him on. Should the melody gather itself like a wave here, or scatter like rain? He tried one, then the other. Not quite right, not yet.

"Hanby, you mad genius! Why are you sitting in the dark?"

He twisted on the bench to look for the voice. Frederick stood on the threshold, framed by the yellow wash of light from the hallway. He removed his hat and hung it.

Ben eyed him, deadpan. "I'm working. But you wouldn't understand. Now be a good man, and go light the lamps. The ladies will be arriving at any moment."

"Very well." Frederick grabbed the long pole with an easy flip of his wrist and brandished it like a saber ahead of him as he walked out into the hall. "We will give them a bright Philomathean welcome."

Ben reached down into the open satchel propped against the bench leg and pulled out a sheaf of papers. Sheet music mixed with his college assignments: Latin, human physiology, higher mathematics. But it was too dark to see which was which and Frederick would be a minute or two in getting the lamps lit. Ben stood and went to the doorway to let the glow fall on the pages. He riffled through the stack, pulling out a page here, a page there.

Here was one in an unfamiliar hand. *To William Hanby, a request for a sermon to be delivered at our abolition meeting, Sunday next.* What was this? His father's paper, gathered in with his own by accident. And here was a piece of paper covered with nothing but Ben's own scratched notes. *Joseph and Nelly . . . taken away, separated forever . . .*

He turned back toward the empty recital hall, papers still sheafed in his hands, his sight drifting beyond the rows of chairs, into the darkness of memory.

Twelve years ago, in an upstairs bedroom, the light had been just like this: a feeble radiance from the hall that faded his father's black frock coat to a ghostly gray as he stood over the bed, his back to Ben.

His father turned. "Ben, come here. I would like you to meet our guest, Joseph Selby."

A match flared in his father's hand as he lit the oil lamp on the bedside table. It threw deeper shadows on the ceiling and revealed the face of the strange man who lay in the bed. His skin was brown, his cheeks gaunt and sharp. He must be a fugitive from across the river. Ben had seen them before, sheltered in his parents' home.

The man parted his lips as if to say something, but a cough

erupted and jerked his body forward. When he could breathe, he spoke, almost as if to himself. "It ain't no good. I don't mind if it's my time." His haggard face drew even tighter, so tight it must hurt him. "But it's gonna be real hard on Nelly. She's still back there."

The notes of Ben's song drifted through his head.

A cloud of light from the lamplighter entered the recital room, and the spirits of the past fled before it.

"Hanby, stand aside." Frederick's friendly order disrupted the reverie, and Ben moved to grant him access to the wall lamps. One by one, the six lamps came to life until the recital hall took on the warm, neighborly glow of a sitting room by night.

"Ben, you didn't wait for me." His brother Cyrus strode into the room, pointing an accusing finger, his hat tilted at a sharp angle.

"Duty called," Ben said. "Had you been more punctual, I would have walked over with you. Where else could I find such witty banter, such sparkling repartee?"

Cyrus laughed. "Nowhere but the Philomathean Society of Otterbein University." He swept his gleaming hat from his curly mop of hair and held it at his waist with a flourish as he bowed. "Pleased to oblige." Two more society members came in on his heels, also hastening to remove hats and brush hair back in place.

"I'm delighted to hear it," Ben said. "Then you fine literary gentlemen won't mind arranging the chairs for our musical gathering. Posthaste. Six on the gentlemen's side, seven on the ladies'."

"Seven? But I thought there were only six in our sister society." Frederick lifted a chair and carried it to one side of the room, facing the piano. Cyrus and the others followed suit.

"You don't think we would be permitted to entertain them unchaperoned, do you?" Ben raised a brow at Henry. "Mrs. Gourney makes seven."

They arranged the chairs just in time as the lighter voices of women floated down the hall.

"Quickly now, a receiving line of sorts." Frederick took a place on the men's side of the hall and the others hurried to stand shoulder to shoulder, Ben taking his place last in the spot closest to the piano.

Mrs. Gourney was first to appear in the doorway, trim in her straw hat, her head held high, an example of conduct for all her lady students. Otterbein's lady principal created a model for how a lady student was to behave. So few colleges in the nation had students of the fair sex, and thus the rules must be strict. Ben understood why, though Cyrus complained of his limited opportunities for conversation with the pretty ones.

The young ladies filed in after Mrs. Gourney and took their position in line across from the men. Each carried a satchel hung neatly from one shoulder—the badge of her unusual scholarly pursuits. The depth of their minds intrigued Ben—they were every bit as well read as their male counterparts.

"The ladies of the Philalethian Literary Society bring their regards to the gentlemen of the Philomathean Society." Cornelia Lawrence's auburn hair was covered by a smart black hat, but her crisp enunciation would have revealed her identity to anyone on campus.

"And we gentlemen of the Philomathean Society are incomparably graced by your presence," Frederick replied. He relished the flowery language of ceremony, and so he had been elected to speak for the gentlemen until the rehearsal started.

"Thank you, Mr. Jones." Miss Lawrence turned to address the room at large. "We now introduce to you our newest Philalethian, inducted since our last gathering. Miss Winter, will you step forward."

The black-haired girl moved a foot or two out from others in the line. A flush passed over her pale, translucent skin, and she kept her gaze on the lamps above the gentlemen's heads. Her eyes were a bright, almost royal shade of blue. Waves of dark hair set off her face like a sculpture, and her stillness increased the effect. Ben felt sorry for her—they should not subject her to scrutiny, not with her painful shyness.

Miss Lawrence smiled with a lift of her chin. "I know you gentlemen are all aware of Miss Winter's intellectual achievements."

The target of the compliment grew two pink spots in her cheeks and looked at the floor.

"We have been pleading with her to join us for some time," Miss Lawrence said. "And now that she has agreed, she will be a star in our Philalethian firmament, no less bright for her quiet demeanor. You gentlemen will need to look to your laurels, particularly in Latin."

It was true. All the students knew that Mary Kate Winter led their class in academic studies, but few had ever heard her speak. Ben had been surprised to hear even a few words from her yesterday, awkward though she may have felt. She had always been a rarefied and enigmatic creature, notable for her beauty, but likely to be forgotten when not in sight. Except by Cyrus, who would occasionally let out a heavy sigh and proclaim the gloriousness of her aspect, or whatever happened to spark his adolescent muse.

Miss Winter fell back into line, her eyes still downcast. Miss Lawrence resumed her stance as proud leader of the Philalethians, holding the gold-painted cane in her left hand. "And we are now ready for our joint musical endeavor."

Frederick nodded toward Ben. "Mr. Hanby, the floor is yours."

"Or the piano bench, as may be," Ben said. He had no intention of playing Philomathean throughout the entire audition—it would be exhausting—so he moved without ceremony to the piano and arranged his sheets on its music stand.

He straightened and turned to face them. "Welcome, all, and thank you for supporting the college's first musicale."

A smattering of applause surprised him. Cyrus and his two cronies clapped their hands, mock-serious faces betrayed by occasional smirks. Ben frowned. They should not act so childish in the presence of ladies.

Giving his brother a stern look, he continued, "Some of you are already aware that the children from my Sunday class will present a rural pageant set to some songs by Schumann. I will need at least two singers to accompany them."

He stole a glance at Cyrus and hurried on to prevent another round of applause.

"We will be reading pieces on the subject of Childhood, and one of us may read a short fairy tale for children. Finally, we will have a few musical selections. May I ask who is interested in singing and who in reciting?"

No one spoke. Perhaps a stronger suggestion would bring forth volunteers. "I would like to hear the singers first." He walked to the piano, seated himself, and played a few chords. "Any nursery song will suffice. Who will sing?"

Frederick stood and walked to the front of the room. "I feel a little foolish, but I'll give it a try. What shall I sing?"

"Any children's song you know by heart. Perhaps 'Twinkle, Twinkle, Little Star'?"

Ben's fingers picked out the opening measures to give his friend the key. Frederick began to sing, *"Twinkle, twinkle . . ."*

Giggles rose from the young ladies' section. They were right—it was amusing to hear a simple nursery song sung earnestly by a strapping young gentleman. Frederick had a light baritone, quite good. He sang through his rhyme and finished with an extra operatic flourish on *"How I wonder what you are,"* which caused more merriment among the ladies. He grinned in response, revealing white teeth, and sat down to chirps of "Well done" from the girls.

Chairs scraped as Cyrus and his friend both jumped up, eager to win similar acclaim.

Ben stopped them with a raised hand. "Perhaps we might allow one of the ladies a turn?"

Rebecca Bogler rose to her feet and stalked to the piano. Sadly, this was one female voice with which he was all too familiar.

"'Green Grow the Rushes,' please." She straightened her stocky figure and cocked her blond head at an odd angle. This would not be pleasant. Ben played as quickly as he dared, to hasten the finish of what was about to emerge from her mouth—or rather, her nose, since that was the place where her screechy soprano voice originated.

"I'll give you one-oh!" she sang, a full octave above the one he had intended. He tried to dispel the image forming in his mind, a horrible old witch flying through the sky on a broomstick. He played louder, adding more chords to protect his ears from the voice.

"Green grow the rushes oh!" She shrilled the melody unbearably

33

high. He banged out a few more bars and brought it to a merciful close.

As Rebecca flounced back to her peers, Ben looked at Mrs. Gourney. "Do you have any other young ladies here who sing, ma'am?" Yesterday Kate Winter had implied she would audition, but Ben did not wish to force her hand—he would not ask her aloud.

The gray-haired ladies' principal wore her high collar buttoned tightly, but despite her prim correctness, her expression was gentle. She scanned the row of girls. "Mary Kate?"

Miss Winter stared at the polished floor as if she wished it would split open and swallow her. So reserved a young lady would not sing, Ben was sure of it. Then again, she was not likely to read either, based on her flight from the recital hall the previous week. What was driving her to do something she found so distasteful?

She rose to her feet and lifted her gaze to his, surprising him again with that blueness, so bold for a silent lady.

"I would like to sing from here, Mr. Hanby, if you don't mind," she said. She stood facing him from the front row a few feet away, her back to the others. Perhaps she was too shy to turn toward them.

"Of course!" he said. "What will you sing? Perhaps 'Mary Kate Had a Little Lamb'?"

Miss Winter looked away and laced her fingers together.

What an idiotic thing to say. He flushed and adjusted his sheet music.

"That song will do as well as any other . . ." The end of her sentence faded so he could not make out her last words.

Ben played the opening bars of the nursery rhyme, finding the notes by touch, watching her. She began to sing.

Her voice was silvery, and though it was not loud, its tone was so pure that it filled the air of the recital hall. It made him think of Christmas bells, and how his younger siblings looked when they were sleeping.

He had stopped playing without realizing it. Kate Winter looked at him with surprise as her voice carried the last notes alone into a hush.

"Thank you, Miss Winter. That was lovely." It truly was. He must overcome his distraction. "Anyone else?"

No one moved. Cyrus and the other young men regarded Kate with interest. The slender young lady smoothed her brown skirts as she took her seat. One of the other girls leaned over and whispered something.

Courtesy of Kate Winter and Frederick Jones, Ben had already found two perfect voices, and no one else wished to volunteer. The singing audition need not continue any further, so he could now move on to the readings. He shuffled through his papers to find the essays.

Someone cleared his throat. Ben looked up to see Cyrus making his way to the piano. As he passed the ladies, he inclined his thin frame in a sweeping bow, but his hair bounced around on his head and marred his intended effect. A few young ladies giggled as he strutted to the front. He placed his hand on the piano like an Italian tenor and struck a pose.

Ben glared at his brother's back. Why must Cyrus make a fool of himself?

He leaned around the piano and addressed his brother. "I believe I am already familiar with your melodious voice, my friend." He pounded out two ominous minor chords for emphasis. The assembled company laughed again.

"Are you saying that I may not have my chance?" Cyrus loaded his voice with tragic melancholy.

Ben shut his mouth and modulated into a major key. Cyrus was not going to go gently. Best to get it over with.

"Very well. You may sing 'Oranges and Lemons.'" He played the first chords.

Cyrus took a step toward the audience and lifted his hand to his ear, as if listening to something. He manufactured an expression of delighted surprise and belted out the first line at the top of his voice. *"Oranges and Lemons, say the bells of Saint Clemens—"*

"That will do, thank you!" Ben snapped, amid peals of amusement from the ladies.

Cyrus stomped back to his friends and a round of applause.

Ben was determined to forestall any similar performances from the others. "Shall we move on to the readings?"

The audition continued, as several of the gentlemen and ladies read from the prose selections. When the readers finished, Ben paused a moment and shuffled parts in his head. Six readers, two solo singers, and the rest for ensemble singing.

He turned to the group. "I thank you for your interest. The piece will benefit from all of your talents, so I will arrange the music and the readings to include everyone here. Mr. Jones and Miss Winter will be our solo singers."

Cyrus raised his fist in the air. "Three cheers for the director! Hip hip—"

"That's quite unnecessary." Ben grew warm around the ears and neck. He fumbled with his music and readings. No one ever had such an infuriating, troublesome younger brother.

The ladies stood and grasped their satchels in their neat line only ten feet away from Ben. They were so delicate in their white lace blouses and full skirts. He rose to his feet to respect their departure, in Otterbein tradition, and the other gentlemen did the same.

As Miss Winter lifted her brown leather case by its shoulder strap, it caught on the wide edge of her skirt. She grabbed for it, but her startled gesture upended it so her papers shot out and slid across the floor. Her face colored deep pink.

His heart went out to her, shy as she was. He could not leave her without assistance. Looking neither left nor right, Ben walked to her and crouched over the papers to collect them. It took him only a moment—he would spare her this indignity. He rose to his feet.

He had miscalculated the distance between them—he was very near her. He smelled something delicious that hinted at wildflowers and fresh fields. She seemed startled at his closeness as well, and took a step back. Her dark hair set off her delicate bone structure, and her deep blue irises were threaded with light.

"Miss Winter," Mrs. Gourney called from the other side of the room.

The young lady turned and started for the door. Ben watched her retreating back until the door closed behind her.

He turned to find his brother observing him from the corner of the room, his eyebrows at a devilish slant.

Ben did not like that look at all. "Come along, Cyrus." He picked up his music. "We have work to do with Father."

"You were very solicitous of Miss Winter, Ben. I don't suppose that has anything to do with those limpid blue eyes." Every word Cyrus spoke was like the jab of a cattle prod.

"Keep your idle fancies to yourself." Ben closed the piano lid and strode to the door.

Jealousy on Cyrus's part, no doubt, but still maddening. Any gentleman with a heart would go to her aid, especially after her recent classroom catastrophe. And yes, she was exceedingly beautiful, but that had nothing to do with it. Cyrus was a heel. The subject of Miss Winter was closed.

Seven

THE IRON GATE HAD BECOME HER ENEMY. KATE STUD-
ied it with dislike through her bedroom window as she sat in her
reading chair. How would she make her way past the gate's forbidding black spirals and twisted poles, but still take her valise
with her? Walking out with nothing but the clothes on her back
seemed monstrous. It was more civilized—and therefore less
frightening—to leave the house with a second dress and some
personal toiletries.

Perhaps her obsession with the gate was the fault of the book
Rasselas, for the prince in that novel lived behind a gate in his
valley prison. Her copybook lay open in her lap with the passage
she had transcribed.

> *The iron gate, he despaired to open it, for it was watched*
> *by successive sentinels, and was, by its position, exposed*
> *to the perpetual observation of all the inhabitants.*

Perpetual observation—an insurmountable problem for
Kate, as well as Prince Rasselas. No means of departure had
appeared, despite her tentative requests sent up to where she

imagined God must be, far away in his heaven. He was too far away to hear, apparently, as he had always been.

The bell rang at the door downstairs. She stood and replaced her copybook in the bookshelf.

The bell rang again, tinny and insistent. Perhaps she would not go down at all. She could stay up here and look out her window and drink her afternoon tea in peace. She did not care for the teatime calling hours, when Westerville's prominent citizens stopped by to visit the Winter family home. Nonetheless, she would have to go downstairs, or face her mother's wrath later.

Tessie's voice floated up from the foyer as the maid opened the front door and greeted someone in her lilting accent.

It might be the gossipy Bogler girls, or Rose Everett, her sharp criticism veiled in sugary compliments. Most of their callers were members of the Methodist church the Winters attended. There were several families there whose company Kate thought she might enjoy. Unfortunately, they were not the ones who paid these formal visits.

Downstairs, a male voice replied to Tessie.

A gentleman—Kate hoped it would not be some awful repetition of last month's visitor from Columbus—the one with whom she had not been able to summon any conversation at all. And whoever it was, let her mother not come home until he had departed.

She hurried to her armoire and took down her second-best gown, a blue silk with flowing sleeves and a neckline perfect for attaching her prettiest collar. Her mother insisted on appropriate attire for every tea. One never knew who might come calling, she said. Kate unbuttoned her everyday dress and drew her arms out of the sleeves. The voluminous skirt tangled around her head. Changing without Tessie's help was a difficult business, but Kate needed to learn. If she left town on her own, she would not have a maid. She finally extricated herself with a gusty sigh of relief, laid the brown dress on the bed, and began the slow process of donning the blue one.

As Kate adjusted the yards of skirt over her arms, drew the gown over her head, and straightened it over her corset, Tessie arrived, out of breath.

"Oh, Miss Winter, not ready yet?" Her middle-aged face tensed with alarm. "I didn't remember you would need to change—I'm sorry, miss." She bustled around the circumference of the dress, pulling the blue skirt into its graceful folds so it cleared the floor by an inch.

The Winters were one of a few families in town with the luxury of an Irish maid. At night, Tessie boarded with another family, but from dawn to dusk she managed the Winter abode. She answered the door, cleaned, cooked, polished silver, and dressed the three ladies of the house. And she kept her position by never, ever displeasing Ruth Winter.

She circled Kate and squinted at her hairstyle. With a disapproving click of her tongue, the maid moved closer and tucked an errant lock behind Kate's combs.

"Who is calling, Tessie?"

"I do not know him, miss."

"And you did not take his card?"

"I'm sorry, miss. He laid it on the table and I was all in a flurry to come up and tell you. I left it there."

Not an ideal situation in the least. But the maid's creased forehead asked for pity.

"Don't fret," Kate said. "Perhaps Leah may go downstairs while I finish."

Leah loved gowns and formalities, but was not sensible enough to play hostess alone. Still, it would only be a few minutes, and Tessie could wait in the parlor as chaperone.

The maid looked dubious, but ducked out of the bedroom. Kate heard her murmuring at Leah's door across the hallway. Doubtless, Leah was dressed and had been ready for the past half hour. She would jump at the chance to be the lady of the house. Their mother had gone out to call on the Whites, but she would expect her daughters to receive guests in proper style until she returned.

Tessie slipped back into the room and bustled over to Kate to fasten the gown's scores of tiny buttons, all the way from waist to neckline.

Leah's heels thumped down the stairs. Tessie and Kate locked gazes, then the maid scurried out once more. Leah had no common sense—she could not go down without Tessie.

Kate walked over to the doorway to listen to the voices rising over the banister. Leah was talking with the anonymous male visitor, and true to form, she was monopolizing the conversation. At least Leah's unending babble was better than Kate's conversational void.

She started down the first flight of stairs as every mute disaster of her parlor history presented itself to her memory, each giving her stomach a turn. As her skirt swept around the landing, the parlor came into view through its white double door frame. The visitor was seated in the French toile wing chair. He had tilted his head to listen to Leah, who chattered at him without pause. That bronze-colored hair was familiar—the young gentleman was Ben Hanby's friend Frederick Jones, the other singer from the audition. She must think of something to say to him, but she was distracted by the beginnings of clamminess at the sides of her dress. Thank goodness the deep blue fabric would hide perspiration, a horror not even to be mentioned in polite company. But her throat felt tight again, and an ache began in the center of her forehead.

Kate crossed the foyer with light step and lingered out of his sight by the door frame. Against the far wall, Tessie waited in her black and white uniform, hardly noticeable, guarding their reputations.

"Where in the world did you get such fetching boots?" Leah said to Frederick.

His even features twitched before he resumed a good-natured smile. She didn't think a man would like to hear the word *fetching* applied to any item of his wardrobe. "I would have to ask our manservant," he said.

A manservant—Kate had never met a young man of her age with a personal servant to buy his boots. Frederick did cut an impressive figure in his frock coat. He sat very straight in the chair, his bronze coloring even more vivid and healthy against the blue and white fussiness of the parlor.

Leah's gaze traveled to Kate. Frederick spotted her and stood up. He was a head taller than Kate and very imposing in the parlor, which did not seem large enough to contain such masculine vigor. "Good afternoon, Miss Winter."

"Good afternoon," Kate said. "And welcome to you, Mr. Jones." An uncomfortable pause followed—only the first of many, she feared. She seated herself beside Leah as her mind scrambled but found no purchase in a solid topic. The musicale was the only subject they held in common, and she certainly did not want to discuss it in her sister's presence.

"Would you like some tea?" Leah asked him.

Frederick murmured a polite thank-you. Kate lifted the pot to pour.

"It comes as no surprise to me that Ben Hanby picked you to sing," Frederick said.

The teapot quivered in the air. She set it down and glanced at her sister.

Leah stared, her cloying artifice dropped. "You are going to sing in the musicale?"

"I don't know." A curt answer would deter further questions. She did not like to lie, for she was not, in fact, going to sing in the musicale. "Mr. Hanby seems to wish me to sing."

"Mother will be delighted." Leah spoke like an actress relishing her role in a stage drama. The long ringlets beside her face shuddered with her dramatic inflection.

Frederick leaned toward Kate, very earnest. "You mustn't go back on your word now. Not with that splendid voice of yours."

She could not flee and could not think of a new subject. Her heart drummed to a faster rhythm. But she could not blame him. He did not know she had been compelled to audition by her mother's iron decree.

Leah jumped in. "I hear you have quite the singing voice yourself, Mr. Jones."

Leah must have been talking to the Bogler girls, with their cooing and gossip about the wealthy, handsome member of the Philomatheans. Though Kate avoided such talk like a noxious odor, Leah lived for it.

"I would so love to hear you sing." Leah sounded like a bad

actress again, drawing out her vowels in her idea of an English accent.

Kate wanted to cringe—she picked up the teapot instead and aimed for a perfect pour into the cup. Her sister had worn her best pink gown in addition to styling her dark hair around her face like Little Bo Peep. Leah was a pretty girl, but she was so forward.

Frederick shifted on the edge of his chair. "I must confess that I came here on a mission. And, of course, I obtained your mother's consent to call."

Kate passed him a cup and saucer.

Leah filled the silence. "Mr. Jones has just invited us to a spring social on his family's farm this Saturday afternoon."

Frederick set his cup on the low table between them and regarded her with his hazel gaze that reminded her pleasantly of the woods. "Miss Winter, I wonder if you might like to ride there with me in my buggy."

Leah's rosebud mouth hung open.

Still no words came.

When Kate finally thought of something and opened her mouth to say it, her tongue hardly worked. "And will Leah be coming with us?"

Frederick hesitated and gazed outside through the filmy curtain over the window. "I fear my buggy is too small for three to fit comfortably. But I would not miss your sister's company for the world, and so I will be delighted to see her arrive with your parents."

"Oh." Kate picked up her saucer and touched the handle of her teacup, examining the milky brown liquid with close attention. "I must ask my parents if I may go in your buggy. I will, if they agree." She had to glance at Frederick then. It was a small room.

He smiled. "I've already asked your parents. They gave consent."

Had he spoken to her father, or only her mother? Please let it be only her mother, who at least would not have reeked of spirits during such an exchange.

"And while I'm delighted to show you my buggy, your company will be the true pleasure," he added.

Kate's face burned. They did not teach responses to such statements at Otterbein.

"Well, I must be off to invite the other families." Frederick bowed slightly. "Miss Winter." He nodded to her sister. "Miss Leah."

Kate rose and followed him to the door, the dutiful hostess. The dutiful, mute hostess. She wanted to kick herself in the shins, if that were not an impossibility. Tessie scurried in front and opened the door to let him out.

He was more solid than Kate had noticed before, his shoulders massive beneath his well-tailored coat. He paused on the doorstep and donned his hat in the afternoon sunlight. Backed by the green lawn, he looked quite the ideal gentleman on a stroll. What if he could somehow sense her thoughts? Her face pulsed hotter.

His eyes rested on her for a moment and he smiled. "I'll await the pleasure of your company." He turned and walked down to the fine buggy that stood at the hitching post.

Tessie closed the door and melted into the dim recesses of the back hall.

"My, my, my." Leah had followed Kate and taken a position

next to the stairway. She raised her eyebrows like a naughty sprite and tapped her fingers on the banister where it curved to an end.

"Oh, do be kind. What shall I do?" Kate murmured. She could hardly go driving with a young man when she could not speak more than five words to him. It would be a disaster.

Leah placed one hand to her forehead in the style of a trage-dienne. "Oh heavens, what shall I do?"

No help would come from her sister. Kate ignored her and crossed to the foot of the stairs.

"Are you really going to be in the musicale? Did you sing for Ben Hanby? Isn't Frederick Jones a catch?" Leah's animation set her long curls bobbing.

Kate fought the urge to press her hands over her ears and started up the stairs.

The doorbell rang again. Leah stopped and looked at the door. Kate paused and then descended the stairs again. Had Frederick forgotten something?

Tessie went to answer the door, but nodded her head toward the parlor. The young ladies of the house must go prepare to receive callers, should it be necessary.

Kate resumed her seat in the parlor chair, arranging her skirt around her. At the door, a young woman's voice drifted past Tessie, her words indistinguishable.

"Please come in, miss," the maid said.

A girl younger than Leah rounded the parlor door frame and stood there, uncertain. Kate rose. How well she understood feeling out of place and awkward. "Good afternoon," she said.

"Good afternoon. I'm not dressed for visiting," the girl said.

"You look quite lovely just as you are." Kate smiled at her.

"I'm Jenny Hanby."

"I remember you," Leah blurted, jumping to her feet. "We were in class together at the academy." The younger division of Otterbein held more students, and they did not always become well acquainted with one another.

"Yes, we were." Jenny Hanby had an open, curious face and hair simply styled in a braid down her back, so much more becoming to a young girl than the fussy ringlets Leah preferred. She turned to Kate. "I have a message for you, Miss Winter."

The front door opened and Kate's mother entered the house, her face weary before she noticed the visitor and brightened into social artifice. "Good afternoon."

"Mother, this is Miss Jenny Hanby."

"I'm sorry to disturb your family, Mrs. Winter." The girl bobbed a curtsy. "But I have a message for Miss Winter."

Oh, this might be unfortunate. For Jenny would only be bringing a message from the director of the musicale, her brother Ben.

"Thank you for coming." Kate's mother gave Jenny a smile too brittle to convince.

"You're welcome, ma'am. Ben . . ."

Kate held herself immobile. She must not react.

"My brother Ben wishes to ask Miss Winter if she will be kind enough to accompany me to a rehearsal for her singing part. He is practicing in the recital hall with my sister and brother."

A rehearsal. So Kate would not get away with one grueling audition, which she had barely managed. The torment of the stage would go on until she left town.

Her mother burst into a genuine smile that wreathed her face in tiny wrinkles across her cheeks. "But of course she will come. Very good, Kate. Off you go. Get your hat."

Her mother's rare unguarded pleasure was almost enough to lift Kate's spirits. But not quite, not when Kate must still march down to a horrible rehearsal like her mother's personal marionette. She envisioned herself jerking on the puppet strings and then reaching up a jointed hand with a little pair of silver scissors. Snip, snip. It would not be long now—with the threat of more rehearsals, she might have to slip through that iron gate and take nothing but her sheer will to escape.

———

The sound of a violin seeped out of the college building before Kate reached the main door. She followed the ascending notes to the recital room. The music soothed the throbbing in her head and steadied her nerves.

She slowed her steps as she neared the room. Around the edge of the half-open door she saw the back of a young woman who played the violin, her chin pressed to its base as her bow glided over the strings. Beyond her, by the wall, a young man with wild, light brown hair removed a cello from its case and set it on the floor. He rested the long wooden bow on his shoulder like a soldier's rifle, then hefted the cello in one lean arm to walk toward the girl. That was Ben Hanby's brother—she remembered him from the audition. And the girl must be their sister.

She stopped in the shelter of the door. She could still turn around and walk away before Ben saw her.

"We have a fair visitor," Ben's brother announced with relish as he seated himself in his chair and positioned the cello against his trouser leg.

Now she would look a fool if she did not enter, thanks to

that rather discourteous greeting. She laid her hand on the door but it pulled away from her fingers as someone opened it wider from the other side. She looked right into the serious brown eyes of Ben Hanby. His dark hair was mussed, as if he had been ruffling it unconsciously while concentrating on his music.

A fractional pause gave away his surprise. "Good afternoon." He made a slight bow, then smiled as if she had brought him a basketful of gifts instead of a bundle of nerves. Extending his arm to invite her in, he stepped back with an old-world courtliness that made her blush.

"Would you like to sit?" He brought a chair from the wall and positioned it a few feet from his own. Then, with a subtle glance at her, he slid her chair farther away to comply with Otterbein standards of decorum. His own awkwardness lessened the burden of hers. She seated herself and he took his own seat, still watching her.

She should mouth pleasant phrases, but her tongue refused to obey the feeble requests of her brain.

Ben seemed to sense her discomfort. "Perhaps you would like to hear us play? Your voice will be beautiful accompanied by the strings." His attention both drew her in and disconcerted her—it was so complete, as if she were a person to be respected and her thoughts of importance. He turned to include the others. "You may remember my brother, Mr. Cyrus Hanby. This is my sister, Miss Amanda Hanby. Amanda, this is Miss Winter."

Kate's greeting in response was too soft—even she herself heard it more as a vibration in her head than a voiced answer.

"We play very well," Cyrus said. He sawed his bow against

the cello strings and a series of tuneless shrieks came from the tortured instrument.

A smile hovered inside her, but the thought of having to sing shattered it. She mustered her will for the inevitable.

Ben rose to his feet. "You will need the music for Miss Winter's song." He turned to the end of the score on the lyre-shaped music stand in front of his brother. "Here it is." He carefully took his sister's violin from her hand and plucked the third and fourth string of the violin several times, listening before tightening one with a turn of the screw.

Amanda paged through her music, then held out a hand for the violin again. He gave it to her and she settled it on her shoulder.

"Let's begin." Ben raised his hand in the style of a practiced conductor. "One, two—" The last two beats were silent and indicated only by the mark of the rhythm from his precise hand.

Cyrus leaned into his bow. Mellow, rich sound filled the room and soaked into the wooden walls like wine in a cask. The melody the cello played was slow, almost regal, but also full of beauty and generosity, like an echo from a more perfect world. It eased into Kate's spirit and lifted her away from herself into its loveliness. Amanda's violin joined in, ascending up the scale in delicate counterpoint to the cello's lower tones.

Ben waved his hand and his siblings stopped, their bows still poised.

"This is where you come in," he said to Kate, a look of entreaty breaking through his intense concentration.

"I'm not familiar with the song." Her throat was tight. She must tell him she would not be singing for him. She could not lie and deprive him of a singer at the last moment by her absence.

"Do you read music?" he asked.

"Not well enough." A good excuse.

He paused, then picked up the sheet music he had been following. "Then I will teach you the first section. You will see. There could be no better song for the purity of your soprano. In fact, I won't do it justice myself, but if this is how to persuade you to try, then so be it." He stepped over to the other side of Amanda, as if to minimize his presence.

So he was also shy, at least in this setting. Improbable as it seemed, this lean, intense young man in a black frock coat and white collar, who could speak to crowds with such confidence—he was reluctant to sing in her presence.

"Lower it by a third." He nodded to his siblings and the cello began again, with the same lovely phrase that caught at her breath, but in a lower key. After the violin, a beat's hush fell, and then Ben began to sing.

His voice was as rich as the cello, though infused with the intelligent spirit carried only by a human voice. It floated straight through her reserve and self-consciousness.

> *Where e'er you walk*
> *Cool gales shall fan the glade*

The lyrics were a lover's blessing. Warmth rushed up her neck, and yet the song was comforting in its promise of protection.

> *Trees where you live*
> *Shall crowd into a shade*

His baritone was so honest, as if it sprang from a bared soul. His gaze traveled to her.

Trees where you live
Shall crowd into a shade.

Her face grew hot, and yet she could not look away from the intimacy of his song.

He stopped. His cheekbones had taken a higher color as he turned to the string players. "Well done. Now we shall let Miss Winter show us how it should truly be sung."

She did not like to refuse his humble request, especially after he had surmounted his own shyness in order to help her. And his dark eyes revealed his sincere desire to hear her attempt the song.

"But I am afraid to be watched," Kate said.

"Then I will not look at you." He was not jesting but considerate. "Please, come stand here, and I'll hold the music for you. Then you won't have to see any of us, nor will we watch you." His plea drew her to her feet. She crossed to him and stood at his elbow, keeping her eyes on the sheet music in his hands.

When the music soared, he pointed to the cello line to give her the place. She opened her mouth—and a squeak emerged.

She covered her face with her hands. He would think her such a fool. A familiar chill shuddered over her—no, it must not happen again. She lowered her hands, her heart fluttering.

"You have a lovely voice," he said gently. "Only remember to breathe. And give it to God, not to us."

An unusual thought. As if God were listening to something as insignificant as her voice. Ben Hanby was so kind, but her mother would certainly think that a fanatical thing to say. She did not turn toward him. He was unsettlingly close as it was.

"I suffer from shyness myself in singing." He looked at the

music stand, his hair falling over his brow in profile. "It helps to imagine yourself in another setting, a place in which you are completely at ease."

That would not help, with her life encircled by the walls of her house, the Otterbein college campus, or, at most, the boundaries of Westerville.

But she did have her view from Garnet's back, her rides through the woods and fields. She envisioned the outdoor scene and summoned the confidence that filled her when she jumped.

"Take a single, slow breath when the violin begins." He must have given the signal, for Cyrus began to play again and Amanda's violin joined in, back in the higher key. Kate inhaled as he had instructed, steadying herself, staring at the lines of notes on the staff. Her voice would be strong, like a horse soaring over a fence. She opened her mouth and the song glided out, buoyed by her breath.

> *Where e'er you walk*
> *Cool gales shall fan the glade.*

She sang in her octave, a light soprano. The strings supported her, surrounded her, helped her feel less exposed.

> *Trees where you live*
> *Shall crowd into a shade . . .*

She ended the last phrase, and the string players let their own notes drift across the room into silence.

"Miss Winter, my brother did not exaggerate." Amanda

laid her bow in her lap, a look of wonder on her oval face. "Your voice is sublime. I could listen to you sing for hours."

Kate lowered her head and muttered a thank-you. Perhaps Amanda was merely as gracious as her brother Ben. But even Cyrus was unusually quiet.

She had waited too long. Now she had done what he wished—he had heard her sing it. She must no longer delay.

"I am sorry, Mr. Hanby, but I must be going." She knotted her hands together in front of her and stared at her knuckles.

"So soon?" His eyebrows rose. "Well, you sang admirably. We can rehearse again next week. May I escort you to the door?"

"Good day, Miss Winter," Amanda said.

Cyrus rose and bowed. *"Au revoir."*

Kate had to hide a smile, especially when Ben sent an annoyed look at his younger brother.

He ushered her out of the recital room and followed her into the hallway.

Now she must tell him, whether she liked it or not. It might be her only chance to do so in private. She turned toward him as they walked, her throat drying out. "Mr. Hanby, I must take you in my confidence for the good of your production."

He stopped in midstride, surprised, and she had to halt next to him to keep her tone low. No one seemed to be around to witness their impropriety of standing unchaperoned in the hall. She must be quick.

"I will not be able to sing in the musicale. You must replace me."

"But you can. You just did."

"My fear of the stage is too great. I would ruin it." It was the truth, or part of it, and it spared her from revealing more. The less said of her family, the better. She must hope he would not reveal a replacement for her yet, so her mother would not hear.

"I believe you can do it."

"No, I cannot." Her voice rose above the heightened thudding of her heart. She turned on her heel and hurried to the door and out.

"Miss Winter, please."

He had followed her into the dim hallway. With a few hurried strides, he stepped ahead of her and turned into her path. She came to an abrupt halt.

"Your voice is a gift from God himself." He moved so close she could see a pulse flicker in his skin just above the collar. "He made things of beauty to help us through the uglier aspects of life. That is what your voice should do for others. It is not meant to be hidden away."

She looked at the floor. She could not possibly articulate to him all the reasons why what he had said was not true. And her thoughts on God were far too private to speak aloud, let alone to a man.

"I will not give up hope that you might change your mind," he said.

She must say something to deter him. She averted her gaze and whispered, "I do not have any courage to spare, Mr. Hanby. I must save what little I have for more serious matters."

She sidestepped him and hurried on, her boots clicking on the polished floor. He kept pace at the edge of her vision and opened the heavy oak door for her. She rushed down the stairs and fled across the quadrangle without glancing back.

Eight

THE HOUR BEFORE DAWN WAS BEST FOR TRAVELING unnoticed—still dim, but providing enough light to see the road. Ben must ride past the luxurious homes on Northwest Street to get to his destination. No one would be awake except the servants, which was ideal. The fewer witnesses, the better.

His white horse picked its way up the dirt road. Some early riser might step to a bay window and wonder at the shape of Gabriel slipping ghostlike up the street. His hooves made little sound on the packed earth.

That redbrick house ahead on the left was Kate Winter's house. Few Westerville citizens had both a barn and a stable as their family did, but how Isaiah Winter made his money was a mystery. He was as much a cipher as his daughter.

The arched, white-framed windows on the second story drew Ben's gaze. Was one of them her room? She had been so enigmatic yesterday at rehearsal, such a study in contradictions. When she sang, the silvery voice issuing from this angelic creature with luminous skin, rich dress, and shining hair had created a moment of artistic perfection. The reverent silence after her song from both Amanda and Cyrus proved that Ben was not the only spectator to feel the mingled power of art and physical beauty. But then came the contradiction—her inexplicable fear, which made her believe she could not share her gift with others. He would never press her to sing against her will, but he was drawn in now, both by Miss Winter's superior qualities and her inability to express them. Perhaps if he helped her through the musicale, he could free her from the suffocating coils of her phobia.

As Gabriel walked past the iron gate in front of her house, Ben stole another look at the upper windows. A curtain twitched aside. She was there, her head and shoulders visible as if she sat for a portrait. Even in the grayish light, he saw a stillness come over her as she registered his presence on Gabriel. He took his hat in one hand and lifted it to her, bowing his head as a courtesy. A faint smile graced her lips.

Behind her, another face loomed high and proud behind the glass. Mrs. Winter, he presumed. She did not look pleased to see Ben at all and fixed him with an icy stare, her black hair and light skin so like her daughter's, but hard and cold as a mask. He settled his hat back on his head, the smile dying from his face and warmth suffusing his neck. Mrs. Winter raised a hand and pulled the heavy velvet drape over the window.

He had done nothing of which he should be ashamed, by a simple greeting to a lady of his acquaintance. But Mrs. Winter's look had accused him as if he were a scruffy Italian serenader asking for coins.

He must keep his mind on his errand, which outweighed the prejudice of a sharp-eyed matron. But he would not return by this road.

A few twists of the rope tied his horse to the tree trunk. Ben stepped over branches flung down by spring storms, careful not to snap any and announce his passage.

He must be quiet now, and approach the dark cabin with alert senses. One never knew who might be watching the free black settlement at Africa Road, and he must not be spotted by hostile eyes. Especially not today, when the man he sought might be inside. He pulled his hat low on his brow to hide his face.

He found the shelter of a tree only yards from the back window. The clearing around the cabin was empty. He could approach.

Something jerked at his neck and lifted him off his feet, knocking his hat off. He fell back, kicked and struggled, clawed his fingers into the rock-hard arm at his throat. He turned his head an inch to the side, all he could manage, the breath whistling in his cramped air pipe. The dark face next to him was familiar. He did not have enough air to speak. Beside his ear, the hammer of a pistol clicked.

He must croak it out. "John!"

The deadly pressure at his throat eased. "Ben?"

Ben staggered up to his feet, gasped in a deep breath, and turned around. "Was that necessary?" He rubbed at the front of his throat.

John Parker's dark brown, severe countenance did not ease. "Yes. I have fugitives with me." He uncocked the pistol and shoved it back in the holster under his arm. "Don't come creeping next time."

"I didn't want anyone to see me or follow me."

John made a skeptical noise in his throat and turned away. "Come in and tell me your business."

Ben retrieved his hat from the ground and dusted it off, then trailed John around the cabin to the front door. John's feet were bare—he must have come out in a hurry.

Inside, the cabin was dark. John opened the shutter over the back window, then sat down cross-legged on the floor without losing one whit of his air of command.

Ben glanced at the sleeping forms under a blanket on the bed. "How many do you have with you?"

"Two girls. I'm taking them to Sinai." Like all Railroaders, John used code to identify his destinations. "One of the freemen gave the girls his cabin, and I bunked with him next door." John was always careful to preserve the womanly privacy of his charges, no matter what degradation they had known in their captivity.

"I have a question for you." Ben must get straight to the point—John had no patience for parlor niceties when he was conducting fugitives. "I'm searching for a woman named Nelly. The last I knew, she lived on the Macrae plantation just over the Kentucky line."

"You want me to find her?" Joseph's voice remained calm, but his head tilted. It was as close as he came to surprise. He had learned stoicism during his youthful enslavement, long before he bought his freedom and became a successful businessman.

"Yes." Ben opened the flap of his knapsack and pulled out the miniature basket. He pulled the reed latch through its closure and opened the lid. "See this?" He showed John the curled lock. "This is her hair. Her promised husband left it at our cabin when he died, twelve years ago."

"So you want me to tell this woman that he died?"

"No, I merely want you to send news if you locate her. I will do the rest."

"Don't do anything foolish. You have my assistance, if you need it. If she's still alive, and still at the Macrae place, it's across the river from my house."

"Thank you." Ben wanted to shake John's hand, but he refrained. John was not one for effusive demonstrations.

"I'll send you a letter when I learn anything." John reached under the bed for his boots and pulled on each with a practiced tug. "Her name is Nelly," he said to himself, as if to seal it in his memory. He got to his feet and moved across the room, his severe, dark face like that of a general at war. "Girls!" he ordered. "Out of bed!"

Two brown girls emerged from the blankets fully dressed, like a rustle of birds flushed from the ground into the air. They rubbed their eyes.

"We must go," John said to Ben. "I heard there was a posse on our trail back in Cincinnati, so we have to stay ahead." He grabbed a pack from a hook as the girls put on shoes. He must have given them footwear, as few slaves possessed such luxuries. John held the door open for them and raised one hand in farewell.

The sleep-dazed girls stumbled out of the cabin as Ben called after them, "God go with you."

John went out, silent and light of tread.

―――――・✦・―――――

In the Hanby barn, Ben unbuckled Gabriel's girth and lifted the saddle from his back. The gelding was not overheated, as he had kept to a moderate pace on the way home. Ben hoisted the saddle to its rack high on the wall and then returned to pull the bridle over his horse's ears and release the bit from his mouth. A horse deserved patience and care for its hard work.

The barn door opened, letting in the dawn light. "Ben?" His father walked in and rested his arms on the half door of the stall. "Did you just ride out somewhere?"

He hesitated. He certainly would not lie. "Yes."

"Might I ask where?"

"To see a friend."

His father's quizzical eyebrows told him of the inadequacy of that reply.

"I rode to Africa Road to see John Parker."

"John? How did you know he was there?"

"President Lawrence told me he would be coming through." The college president was a fellow abolitionist and had secretly aided fugitives many a time to go north from Westerville.

"I wish John had stopped by to greet us."

"He was conducting passengers."

"I see. And what urgent business took you to see him at the crack of dawn?"

"I prefer not to say."

"Indeed." His father watched as Ben rubbed down the horse's back and the mark left by the girth. "That is your right, I suppose, now you are twenty-one. I trust this is business of which I would approve."

"Yes, sir." His father would certainly approve in the abstract of finding Nelly. Whether he would approve of the reality was another question. Ben thrust his hands in the water trough and rubbed them together, dripping, to divest himself of horse grime.

His father turned and walked to the other side of the large barn. Ben left the stall and shot the bolt behind him. "Do you need my help this morning, Father?"

"If you could give me an hour, it would help. I plan to finish this harness commission by evening. The customer may come through town this week."

Pieces of a harness lay over the saddling bench and hung on nails against the rustic planks of the barn. Ben crossed to the straps on the bench and picked them up to inspect them, holding them to the light coming in the door.

By the barn wall, his father unbuttoned his clean shirt and suspended it on the wall peg. Turning to lift his oil-stained shirt from the other peg, he revealed his bare back.

Ben had seen it before, but it still made him wince. Pale scars stood out from the muscle over his father's shoulders, though it was decades since a master's whip had almost taken his life. The whiteness of his father's skin had not spared him from a beating as cruel as any given to a plantation slave.

That map of scars had always made his father reluctant to change his shirt before his children, even now that Ben was far beyond childhood at twenty-one. But his father refused to appear before his mother in shirts stained from his work, not if he could help it. He was careful in his attire, because as he had once explained to Ben, any man who has been forced to live in filth will ever after cherish cleanliness.

But Ben must not brood on it. What was the jauntiest tune he knew? He began to hum "Tim O'Galway" as he checked the bridle straps in his hands.

His father finished dressing and turned around with a faint smile. "Lift those thoughts."

He was never fooled. He patted Ben on the shoulder as he passed and seated himself on the saddling bench.

"Should I do the noseband?" Ben held up the straps of leather.

"If you don't mind."

Ben pulled over the small table and they worked next to one another for a few minutes, his father humming one of the primitive hymns he had collected on his travels.

The humming stopped, and his father looked up. "I told your mother you might accompany her to Columbus next week, if you were willing. Will that interfere with your musical practice?"

"No, Father." Ben aimed the hammer and struck the awl a sharp blow so it plunged into the leather strap. A clean hole for the tongue of the buckle. Three more to go. "Why is she going to Columbus?"

"It's the end of May." His father leaned back and stretched his arm for the two needles lying behind him on the large worktable. He threaded them one by one and began to stitch. "I wish her to make an excursion, to help divert her mind from sad thoughts."

"I see." Ben punched another hole. His mother's father, Samuel Miller, had died in the month of May, and shortly thereafter, she had suffered the stillbirth of her first child. Over twenty years later, his mother still grew mute and sad at the end of May.

"Do you want this browband round or flat?" Ben finished the last hole and moved on to the next piece of leather.

"Flat. Your grandfather always preferred it, and I agree."

Ben crossed to the worktable to get another set of needles and thread. He wished for the thousandth time that he could have met his grandfather. "What would Grandpa Miller have done about the Fugitive Slave Law?"

"Ignored it. And helped those in need. And kept making fine saddles."

"He would not have been afraid to go to jail?"

"He would not refuse to aid a fugitive who came to him bleeding, poor, and hungry, no matter what the law dictated."

Ben pierced the leather with the needle and drew the thread through.

His father bent over his work, speaking with the slow abstraction of the craftsman. "He always said that Colossians 3 applied not only to saddle making but also to how we treat fugitives."

"Which verse?"

"Whatsoever ye do, do it heartily, as to the Lord, and not unto men." With a deft turn of his strong hands, his father finished the row of fine stitches, the unmistakable hallmark of his grandfather's legacy.

The legal work of his legacy.

For the illegal work, Ben must wait upon word from John Parker.

Nine

THE DAY OF THE SOCIAL DAWNED WARM AND FAIR, which was never a guarantee in the unpredictable month of May. Kate spent the morning reading for her classes.

Physiognomy was challenging, even though the ladies had been excused from several lectures out of concern for the potential indelicacy of certain topics related to human anatomy. But she had finally memorized all the bones in the skeleton. She turned to the last page of her notes, the section on the structure of the human hand. *Distal, middle, proximal phalanges, metacarpals* . . . so many pieces. Her gaze fell on her own hand where it lay on the desk beside her papers. The human body gave the illusion of wholeness, with its smooth covering of skin. But underneath, it was a collection of broken fragments held together by strings.

A knock came at her bedroom door, and her mother stepped in. "What are you wearing for the party?" Her voice was always pinched and dry. "Whatever it is, I trust you will select a good sun hat."

"Yes, Mother." Kate could not deny the wisdom of the suggestion. Her mother's iron determination to wear a hat at all times outdoors had kept her skin fair, and only faint wrinkles traced her eyes and the corners of her mouth.

"I haven't settled on what to wear." Little use in stating a preference when her mother would expect to choose her attire for her. "It's just a social, so I probably won't wear the silk."

"Certainly not. The silk would be ruined by any picnicking or the like. Wear your blue linen. It flatters you." Her mother crossed to the armoire, every step a testimony to a girlhood spent in the shelter of fine Philadelphia buildings. She still moved with regal posture and gliding gait from the best deportment classes her family's merchant wealth could buy. She reached inside the wardrobe and fanned out the cornflower-blue skirt. After assessing the dress, she studied Kate with equal objectivity.

"I will wear it, Mother." Kate hoped that would be the end of any discussion of the social. Her mother had been fishing around for days to discover Kate's opinion on Frederick Jones. Kate had demurred each time with noncommittal statements.

Her mother withdrew from the room and Kate began to unfasten her day dress. The buttons were hard to manage in back. She did not want to call Tessie, though, knowing that the maid would also have to dress Leah and her mother that afternoon. And Kate needed all the practice available in managing her own attire. She shrugged out of her pagoda sleeves and hung the day dress carefully in its place before taking down the blue one.

After shifting through yards of material, she found the middle of the skirt and slipped her arms through, swimming up through the piles of fabric to the top. She straightened the bodice over her corset and adjusted the embroidered linen sleeves over her white lace undersleeves. A sigh escaped her. She must go down now and sit with her mother in the parlor.

To the tick of the clock, they waited for Frederick to arrive. Small thumps revealed that Leah was still dressing upstairs with Tessie. Kate's father was out—she dared not ask where. He never accompanied them anywhere, so he surely would not attend this social. The mere thought was too horrible to contemplate. She pushed it aside.

Her mother appeared peaceful in her hard-backed chair. Such serenity from her was always a deception. She picked up her embroidery frame and removed the needle and thread without looking at Kate. "Have you thought any further about Frederick as a suitor?"

"I don't believe I will be thinking of any man in that way for some time yet."

"That would not be a prudent decision on your part. I married at eighteen. The best marriages are made young."

Kate paused, looking at her mother in disbelief. The best marriages, like her parents'? "Really?" she asked aloud. Oh, she should not have said it. Her mother's eyes narrowed.

Kate must cover her hasty response with another comment. She remembered something vaguely from a church sermon. "Perhaps God will choose someone for me if he wishes me to marry."

"Don't talk like a tent revivalist." Her mother jabbed the needle scornfully into the design, then jerked it out again. "That's for the ignorant and the desperate. If you don't make your choices, some other person will choose for you. God has nothing to do with it."

This would be a long lecture. Kate began to count the blue flowers in the wallpaper. If only she could leave this instant.

Wheels crunched on the gravel outside. Her mother looked up from her embroidery. "It appears your suitor is here."

The bell rang, and a minute later, Tessie showed Frederick into the parlor.

Hat in hand, hair burnished, the young gentleman nodded and smiled in response to her mother's pleasantries. Ruth Winter could put on a charming public face.

It would all be the same if Kate lived in Westerville, even if she married. Tea in the afternoons, church on Sundays, and gossip. Then raising another crop of children to do the same thing.

"We'll see you at the social, Mrs. Winter." Frederick ushered Kate out the door.

On the way to the Joneses' farm, he guided his horse and buggy with expertise. He was an excellent horseman, that was clear. The deftness of his gloved hands at the reins was born of long practice. The horse's shoes clicked against the stones in the road, and Kate's tongue stuck fast to her palate.

"Have you finished your essay for Professor Allen?" he asked.

"Yes."

"And I suppose you're a week ahead in Latin as well?"

"Yes."

"You shouldn't admit it." He smiled. "I'll just ask you to help me now."

She considered. "I will, if you need help."

He grinned, taking his eyes off the horse ahead to look straight at her. "You're wasted on Westerville. I've seen your papers. With your mind, and your singing voice, you could be the most brilliant lady of Boston society, leading your own musical salon with scores of Harvard men at your feet."

"That sounds awful." Repellent as it was, she had to smile at its utter impossibility.

He laughed and slapped the reins on the horse's back. "Look, we're almost there. Our home is behind that grove of elms." His face held no secrets—this was a young man at ease with the world and himself. His lips were made to smile, generous but strong.

The odd pulse returned to her ears and made her turn away and focus her attention on the trees beside the road.

They drove down a dirt lane and the trees melted away into jade-green fields. A large home came into view, its proud pillars stretching from ground to roof, a little Parthenon inexplicably transported to the western woods.

The buggy rounded the edge of a glistening ornamental pond and pulled up at the entrance. Frederick left his place to hand her down from her seat. If only she didn't feel so wooden and clumsy.

A Negro servant opened the front door with a deferential bow. Frederick stepped back to allow Kate to precede him through the crystal-transomed doorway.

A small cluster of people stood in the parlor. Cornelia Lawrence, the president's daughter, looked very sophisticated in a pale yellow gown and silk-flowered straw hat. She spoke with an older man, tall, gray-haired, and evidently well fed. She paused at the sight of Kate and beckoned her over. Cornelia had been gracious and warm since her return from a two-year trip to France. If Kate's family were different, she and Cornelia might have become friends.

Frederick offered Kate his arm to escort her in that direction.

"Mr. Jones," Cornelia said to Frederick's father as they approached, "this is my friend Miss Winter with your son."

Despite the older man's girth, Kate saw the family resemblance. Mr. Jones had a friendly face.

"Delighted to meet you." He took Kate's hand with a dip of his head. "Though I must ask what you're doing with this rascal." His speech was Southern and slow, as if he had all the time in the world.

Frederick looked at Kate with open admiration. "I ask myself the same thing, Father." The older man and the younger man grinned at one another. She liked to see their camaraderie. That was how a home should be—harmonious.

As Cornelia and Frederick chatted about his horse and buggy, Kate took in her surroundings with subtle glances to the left and right. The house was new, thickly carpeted and furnished in burgundy and hunter green, with dark wood paneling. In the enormous parlor, a magnificent tapestry covered almost an entire wall. It depicted a white mansion amidst green fields dotted with animals—and slave workers. She turned away, uncomfortable.

"You have a lovely home," Cornelia said.

"Yes." Mr. Jones hooked one thumb in his waistcoat and surveyed the parlor with pride. "Many of the pieces here are heirlooms from my family."

Frederick offered Kate his arm. "May I show you the grounds?"

She laid her hand on his crisp white sleeve, still adjusting to the firm, alien feel of a masculine arm, so solid compared to her own slim wrist.

Frederick called to the uniformed black maid in the dining

room. "Marie, please bring us some bread. We're going to feed the ducks in the back."

He invited Cornelia to join them, and she cheerfully agreed, taking his other arm. He led them past the other guests toward a French door that opened at the rear of the house.

As they crossed the foyer, a servant opened the front door, and in stepped Kate's mother, resplendent in her lilac gown, with Leah just behind her. But to Kate's shock, her father also entered, handing his hat to the servant and waiting to follow her sister in.

Small wonder her mother did not seem at ease. Her smile was tight and she seemed paler than usual as she greeted Mr. Jones. Kate watched her father closely. He did not seem to be weaving as he walked, nor did she smell any bourbon. It might yet be possible to have an uneventful afternoon here.

Then Ben Hanby walked in, only ten feet away from Kate.

She went cold. He must not raise the subject of the musicale. But he would not, after what she had said to him. Her mother had not been at all pleased when Ben greeted her in the window the other morning—she said it was vulgar for Kate to acknowledge him from her bedroom. Perhaps her mother's annoyance would keep her away from Ben, and that would prevent any unintended revelations about the musicale.

Behind Ben came a man Kate recognized as his father, Mr. William Hanby, and a pretty, middle-aged woman who must be his mother. The Hanby men handed their hats to the servant. Why had the room gone quiet?

"Mr. and Mrs. Hanby!" Mr. Jones's voice boomed through the room. He strutted over to them, carrying his extra weight like a suit of armor. "Welcome."

"Thank you, Mr. Jones." Mr. Hanby extended a hand after

a moment, and the two men shook hands, though they looked wary. Mr. Hanby's square shoulders and midlife good looks contrasted sharply with Mr. Jones's bulk.

Ben Hanby was a little taller than his father, she noticed, though they both had the same dark hair and deep-set eyes.

"Ben, come join us! We're going to the pond," Frederick said.

Ben nodded and walked over to them.

The maid brought out a sack of old crusts and Cornelia dropped back to walk with Ben. The party moved through the glass doors and down the wide steps behind the house. A number of guests of all ages strolled across the lawn, the women's dresses like bright flowers in the afternoon sunlight. Cornelia's parents, her two young brothers, and the Bogler girls stood near the house, gazing at the fertile fields that rolled up the hills of the estate. Mr. Lawrence plucked a daisy from a trellis that shaded his wife, Ida.

"Hello, President Lawrence," Frederick said. "Enjoying the view?"

"Wonderful," he replied, handing his wife the daisy without losing a whit of his customary calm dignity. His hair was overcast with gray but retained a faded trace of the auburn hue he had passed down to his children. He did not seem as intimidating, divested of his scholarly robe.

"We're going to feed the ducks," Cornelia said. "Would you like to come with us?"

The Lawrences agreed, as did the Boglers. Soon a host of would-be duck-feeders headed down to the pond.

Kate released Frederick's arm when they arrived at the water's edge. Touching him unsettled her, though it was not unpleasant. She busied herself with feeding the smallest ducks.

"The ducks are lively." What an absolute dunce she was. *The ducks are lively.*

But Frederick smiled at Kate and handed her another small piece of bread. "They're inspired by your beauty." He laughed, which made it more bearable.

Kate took the bread from his warm hand. *They're inspired by the bread.* By the time she gathered the nerve to consider saying it aloud, the moment was past. It was beyond comprehension how Frederick could enjoy her company when she was utterly without conversation. But he continued to smile and say entertaining things about their courses of study.

He stayed only a step away from her, but Ben joined them on her other side as they stood at the pond's edge. Cornelia was still deep in conversation with her parents, halfway around the pond.

Kate fought her rising dismay. The prospect of speaking with two of them at once was so daunting that she wished to be somewhere else—almost anywhere else.

Frederick and Ben tore chunks of bread for her to throw to the birds. Both young men seemed to be tearing bread more and more rapidly. She had trouble keeping up with the morsels being tendered to her from either side. Frederick had a hint of a smirk on his face, belying his air of studied nonchalance. Ben was determined and quiet.

"My friend," Frederick said to Ben, "when I invited Miss Winter to the party, I intended to keep her all to myself, in a most unfair way." He smiled at Kate and handed her another small piece of bread.

"I do not think you have enough food for the ducks. My purpose is strictly humanitarian," Ben said. He flourished a much larger piece of bread toward Kate, with a keen look at his friend. She glanced back and forth between them, then took the bread from Ben, her cheeks warming under their mutual regard.

In another minute, they ran out of bread. Kate seized the opportunity to excuse herself and walked as quickly as she dared to Cornelia, far more out of breath than her exertion would excuse.

"Shall we walk around the pond?" Kate asked her, words tumbling out.

"Of course." Together they stepped through the low grass onto a graveled path that swept a graceful oval for promenaders.

A backward glance revealed that Frederick and Ben had remained at the pond's edge. The two young men glared at each other for a moment, then at the ducks. Finally, Frederick offered to show Ben the horses. They walked away, seeming to regain their easy rapport as they entered the masculine realm.

Cornelia and Kate continued their amble around the pond.

"I've hardly had a chance to speak with you this semester." Cornelia smiled. "Will you walk with me back to the house?"

"I would like that." It would be a welcome respite from male attention.

Cornelia took her hand as if they were bosom companions. Another odd sensation for Kate—she was not accustomed to being touched. But, as with Frederick's arm, it was not unpleasant. "You know," Cornelia said as they walked back, "every girl in town would love to change places with you. The Bogler girls were fit to be tied when you were feeding ducks."

"I will freely give way to those girls. I found it awkward."

"Well, you are certainly making Frederick work for his privilege, as I didn't see you speak more than two words to him." The kindness in her eyes made it a gentle joke between friends, not a reproof.

"I spoke at least four or five."

Ben Hanby was also walking back to the house, about twenty yards ahead of them.

"You did not want to walk with Mr. Hanby before?" Kate asked.

"It was plain that something was on his mind. He was not diverted by my idle chatter, so I told him I wished to stay and speak with my parents. I do like him, but he is sure to be a minister, you know, and the odds of having a decent living in that profession are miniscule. He may not even be able to marry."

"Oh." Kate did not want to say anything on that subject. Discussing men with another young woman was dangerous territory, as Cornelia might ask her something personal. Though it was strange, indeed, that a young man like Ben, with such talent and an appreciation for beauty, would choose something as alien as preaching. It was an aspect of him Kate could not understand. Why did some people have strong faith and others not? Perhaps it was predestined, as some believed. But it would be comforting to have Ben's conviction, his belief that God was close enough to hear. If he was not—if he sat somewhere on high letting the earth spin on through evil and suffering to its predestined end—then a voice lifted in prayer was no better than silence, just as her mother claimed. Kate hurried ahead of her friend across the last few feet of lawn and up into the dining room.

The table was spread with delicious roast meats. There were two giant turkeys and several platters of pork, beef, and venison. Tureens steaming with fragrant corn chowder stood among smaller bowls filled with plump beans and stewed tomatoes. Fresh loaves of bread were sliced and arranged artfully in baskets. It was an impressive display. Her parents had means, to be sure, but they did not entertain, and certainly not on this scale.

Through the open doors to the parlor, she saw her parents and Leah speaking with Daniel Jones. Kate must be a dutiful daughter or she would hear about her shortcomings later at home. She crossed to her mother's side.

Mr. Jones winked at her, but directed his comment to her mother. "I just met your beautiful elder daughter, Mrs. Winter. And I believe my son finds her quite charming as well."

Kate blushed, but pleasure lit her mother's face. Unspoken parental scheming brightened the undertones of her subsequent conversation with Mr. Jones.

The afternoon was deteriorating. To be the target of so much attention and conversation was painful, especially when her mother could observe it. Her father remained silent and probably appeared surly to the others.

If Kate left Westerville, she need never again go out in the company of both her parents.

The rest of the party straggled through the back doors and exclaimed at the feast laid out on the table.

"Where shall we all sit?" Cornelia asked. There were places laid at the grand table, but despite its size, it could only accommodate one-third of the large number of guests present.

Frederick spoke up as he came through the door. "We have arranged some tables in order for some of us to picnic outside, around the side of the house. Please, come along! The more the merrier. The servants will follow with baskets to bring the meal."

As the guests filed back outside, Mr. Jones walked in from

the parlor with a genial grin. "Don't everybody leave just yet," he said. "Some of us will remain here at this table. Frederick, come back and join us when you have seated our guests. Why don't you dine with us in here, Mr. and Mrs. Hanby? And Mr. and Mrs. Lawrence, Mr. and Mrs. Winter, will you stay, with your families? My wife will be here shortly. She has been supervising the cook and servants."

When the four families sat down and the rush of guests subsided, there were twelve at the table, as Cornelia's younger brothers had asked to go outside for the picnic. Frederick sat to Kate's right, and to her surprise, Ben Hanby sat to her left. At the foot of the table was Frederick's mother, whom Mr. Jones introduced as Sapphia. She was petite and blond, as demure in manner as her husband was bluff. She conversed easily with Ben and his parents. At the other end of the table, Daniel Jones spoke to Ruth Winter and the Lawrences about his ancestral home in Kentucky.

The four college students kept silent. Far too aware of the unfamiliar masculine presence of Frederick and Ben only inches from her elbows, Kate gave her attention to her food, which was excellent.

"It's very kind of you to open your new home to guests," Ida Lawrence said to Mrs. Jones.

"Yes, and so many of us," added Mr. Lawrence. "It's good for the community. We appreciate your hospitality."

There was a general murmur of agreement.

Kate's father sat a few places away from her down the table, but his wine glass rose and fell with alarming regularity. A man-servant came to refill it with the decanter four, five times. She lost count. She could not pay attention to the conversation, so distracted was she by the potential disaster looming a few feet from her. Her shoulders were tense and her back hurt.

She avoided looking at the others. But when she reached for her lemonade, she locked gazes with Ben Hanby's mother, whose soft brown eyes were full of sympathy. Wanting to hide, Kate turned away. But that was no better, as she found Ben looking at her too.

Now she must say anything she could to distract him. "You don't seem yourself this evening, Mr. Hanby."

"I apologize. My mind is on other things," he said. The noise of the other guests had risen around them, and the din of talk and clatter of utensils against plates sheltered his response from other ears.

"Oh no, I don't mean to criticize." She stumbled over her words. "I am always poor company, or I would have drawn you out already."

"Miss Winter, I am happy to sit at your side whether you speak or not."

She dropped her gaze and rearranged her food on her plate with her heavy silver fork.

He lowered his voice. "Have you thought further on what I said, about God's gift in your singing, and whether you might share it?"

"What are you two whispering about over there?" Frederick's voice floated over her shoulder and she turned back toward him. She took a breath and hesitated.

"Theology." Ben Hanby spoke across her, his face sober. "But I should not be boring so lovely a lady with the topic."

"Indeed not. So then, Mr. Hanby, tell us about your musicale instead. When shall we perform it?" Frederick was blithe, his hazel eyes merry as he led them to conversational armageddon. He only meant to be a good host and spur talk among the company—she could not blame him.

She didn't dare glance at her mother. *Please, please. Let them all be tactful on this subject.* Her hands clenched together under the tablecloth.

"Mr. Jones, an excellent meal." Her father's voice was noticeably slurred. "Is your cook a slave woman? They have a reputation for excellence, I understand."

All three Hanbys looked at him together, as if pulled by an invisible puppeteer.

Mr. Jones stopped in midsentence of his conversation with Kate's mother. A hush fell.

"Of course, she's not a slave now that we live here," Mr. Jones said. "But she cooks just as well as she did in Kentucky." He picked up a carafe and poured Kate's mother some more lemonade.

No one spoke. Kate glanced at Frederick. He reddened as he stared at his plate.

"You a Southern sympathizer, Jones?" Her father blundered on, oblivious. He flourished his glass as if participating in a vast joke. Even Daniel Jones paused in the awkward silence. It was not done at all, to mention slavery and politics in mixed company, at dinner. Her mother leaned over to him and whispered something.

"No, I'm not ready to go home. I've barely tasted the meal." Her father brandished his fork in his left hand and stabbed a chunk of meat. He missed his mouth on his first attempt to shovel it in.

Kate looked at the gorgeous floral centerpiece, her face throbbing with the sudden rush of her pulse. Her father was too awful and mortifying to watch.

President Lawrence cleared his throat and addressed Frederick. "How are you enjoying your studies thus far?"

"Very much, sir," Frederick said. "Particularly rhetoric."

"Now that's a young man after my own heart," Mr. Lawrence said. "I love to read the old orators."

From there the discussion moved on, and something like peace was restored to the room as Kate's father held his tongue. But an undercurrent of tension remained until everyone finished and the maids cleared the plates.

In the buzz of conversation, Mrs. Hanby stood, walked around to Kate's parents, and leaned down to say something to them.

Kate's father stood, clutching the top of his chair for balance. Her mother also rose next to him.

Mrs. Hanby smiled winsomely at Kate's father. He looked flattered. Mrs. Hanby took his arm and made it look as if he were supporting her, rather than the other way around. Kate's mother took his other arm, and they headed out of the dining room to the foyer. Whatever Mrs. Hanby had said, it had worked. Kate wanted to throw herself on her knees and thank Ben's mother as the three left through the front door.

Mrs. Hanby returned alone. Kate melted nerveless into her chair, finally able to listen to whatever Cornelia had been saying about Otterbein.

The Hanbys rose to leave a few minutes later, making their good-byes to the Joneses. Mrs. Hanby was formal and polite when she spoke to Mr. Jones, but as she turned to leave, she caught Kate's eye and smiled—a lovely smile tinged with sadness. Kate would have to find a way to thank her somehow.

As twilight fell, the outdoor picnickers came back inside the house. Kate listened to the other students chat about the musicale. Thank goodness her parents had departed. As the Boglers pestered Cornelia about their choice of readings, Frederick murmured to Kate, "May I drive you home?"

She paused. That would not be proper, not as darkness drew near.

He must have realized it, for he flushed. "Or perhaps Miss Lawrence has engaged your company already. I have taken you from her for too long."

She nodded.

Cornelia had overheard, for she turned from the other girls. "Miss Winter, you must drive home with us. I have been hoping for it."

Saved once again by another woman's social grace.

"Thank you, Cornelia."

Kate wanted nothing more than quiet from the ride home with the Lawrences. And, with the exception of a few reflective remarks from Mr. Lawrence on the weather, it was quiet. The Lawrences were too considerate to bring up any but the most innocuous of subjects after her father's humiliating behavior.

———————

She let herself in the front door of her house, which was darkened for the evening. A muffled noise of raised voices came from the direction of her parents' bedroom. An oil lamp in a wall niche lit the staircase enough for her to see. She walked up, her skirt whispering behind her. Instead of going to her room, she went to Leah's. Her sister was sitting on her bed, gray-faced and tense.

"Have they been arguing since you returned?" Kate asked.

"Yes, the same things again and again. It's driving me to distraction." Leah did not usually confess such things. It must be the shame of what had happened at dinner—Leah might be adept at hiding her feelings, but tonight had been too much for any fifteen-year-old girl.

"Shall we go downstairs where we won't hear them?" Kate wanted to put her hand on Leah's shoulder, show sympathy, but no one did that in this house.

"Very well." Leah jumped up as if no suggestion could be more welcome. She went to the door with such haste that she outpaced Kate and stepped into the hall before her.

As Kate followed, the door of her parents' bedroom burst open and her mother ran out, one hand held over her eye, her mouth strained with terror. Her father stumbled after her, his face contorted. He reached out, buried his fist in her mother's hair, and jerked her head back, spinning her around and to her knees.

Kate froze.

"No!" Leah ran toward him, reaching for his hand.

His eyes were glassy with rage and liquor. His fist slammed into Leah's midsection. She flew back against the wall with a hard thump, her skirts whipping around her as she slid to the floor. She curled in on herself, clutching at her bodice, her mouth open and gasping for air. Her eyes rolled up and she went limp. Kate's mother still crouched, hands to her head where the tightness of her husband's grip threatened to tear her hair out.

"Father." Kate spoke from where she stood, her voice shaking. "You are not yourself. Please leave before you do damage that cannot be undone." She held her breath.

His bleary eyes blinked and he paused. He released his grip

on her mother, then staggered past Leah and down the stairs. On the first flight, he tripped and had to seize the banister for support. It creaked and held, but his second hand found purchase on a decorative finial and broke it off so it clattered down to the lower level.

He weaved onward, threw himself against the front door, and ran out, leaving it open.

Her mother was already beside Leah on her knees. "Leah," she said, and stroked her face. Leah's eyelashes fluttered and she opened her eyes, disoriented, gazing straight ahead as if waking up from a deep sleep.

"Let me get you into your bed," her mother said.

"I will do it, Mother." Kate put her arms under Leah. It was not the time for tears or hysteria. She had to be certain Leah was not seriously injured, or else call for the doctor.

She half carried her sister to her bed and laid her down. The quilt was rumpled. Kate pulled it up over her sister's body.

"I am only bruised," Leah said. "Go help Mother."

The clarity of her eyes reassured Kate. She went back in the hall, but her mother was not there. Perhaps she had gone back to her bedroom. Kate walked there and opened the door.

Her mother slumped in a chair, her face wet, her beautiful night dress torn at one shoulder.

"Mother," Kate said.

Her mother's eyes opened. "Is Leah recovering?"

"She seems to be."

"Get out of my room," her mother said, her tone flat.

"I only want to—"

"Get out."

"But what—"

"I will not speak to you of it! It's none of your affair."

How could it be none of her affair to see her sister and mother attacked? "You must let me help," Kate said.

"You cannot help!" Her mother's weary face filled with anger. "I won't discuss it further. Leave my room."

Kate walked out into the hall and closed the door with a shaky hand.

If her mother refused to acknowledge it, how could Kate be sure it wouldn't happen again? Leah or her mother might be more seriously hurt the next time.

A wave of trembling passed over her, and she braced against the wall to keep her balance.

This would not do.

She went to her own bed. Despite the lateness of the hour, she did not sleep for some time, alert for the opening of the front door. But her father did not come home.

Kate must ensure his attack did not happen again, and she must act soon. Possibilities tumbled through her mind like pebbles in a brook, until they all washed away into troubled sleep.

Ten

"BEN, YOU NEED SOME DIVERSION. YOU SHOULD COME with us to Columbus. It's quite an honor for Cornelia to play at Neil House," his mother said, cradling a teacup between her hands. Mrs. Lawrence's teacups were silver edged and fine, suited to the expensive elegance of her parlor.

Mrs. Lawrence set her creamer down on the table. "Oh, do come, Ben."

Her daughter, Cornelia, sat behind them at the glossy grand piano. Her agile fingers drew forth liquid notes that flowed through the drawing room. He let the music ease his unsettled state. Witnessing Kate's father's behavior at the social had dismayed him. He could not get the image of Kate's hurt face out of his mind. No wonder she preferred to remain invisible and unheard.

He should show his support for Cornelia's music, even though the journey happened to coincide with a more serious purpose. "I would be delighted."

Cordelia brought the Chopin tune to a soft conclusion and lifted her hands from the keys. "That's so kind of you, Ben."

He had hardly recognized her when she stepped off the

stagecoach last August. It had been two years since the college president's daughter left for France. She departed as a lanky girl and returned as a silk-clad Parisienne, her auburn hair shining in intricate coils. She had always been a good pianist, but now she was excellent—by far the best in town, and perhaps the best in Columbus. He might once have taught her to play scales under her mother's watchful eye, but the tables had turned. This once-awkward miss could now teach him a lesson or two in technique.

She rose from the piano bench, her femininity enhanced by the cut of her green dress. "With your talent, you will notice all my shortcomings." She smiled as she crossed to their circle of chairs and perched gently on the edge of the blue velvet fainting couch next to his seat. "But I'm nonetheless very glad that you will come."

"Nonsense." He smiled. "You know as well as I that there are no shortcomings, not since your return. I can only learn humbly at your feet, Miss Lawrence."

Ben's mother reached for a triangle of buttered toast and set it on a plate, then rose to her feet and brought it to him. He was not hungry, but he accepted it.

"We will depart tomorrow and stay a week in Columbus, perhaps two," his mother said. "After we see Cornelia's recital, we might even visit the circus."

How would their family afford it? He would not ask aloud, of course. There were eight Hanby children, after all. His parents had many mouths to feed and small bodies to clothe. But perhaps his father was bending the rules of practicality for his mother's sake. It was the last week of May.

Mrs. Lawrence lifted her arms in welcome. "You will stay with us, at Neil House," she said.

The woman had an amazing ability to read others—no doubt key to her husband's business relationships with many prominent Columbus men.

"Mr. Neil himself has invited us, and he has offered us three rooms," she continued. "We need a man to escort us, and Teddy is occupied with college business. Your father wants to stay and watch over your brothers and sisters, so you are the obvious choice."

Fortunately, Mr. Neil's hospitality would dissuade the Lawrences from the temptation of offering to pay the Hanbys' way. They had come from Massachusetts, initially, and it was clear there was a family fortune somewhere in their history. That wealth had sent Cornelia to a Paris finishing school and paid for those French dresses that became her so well. Such largesse did not pour from the coffers of Otterbein, for though Mr. Lawrence was president, the college was too new to pay him much for his services.

"What will you play, Cornelia?" Ben asked.

"I will surprise you." She smiled at him, her face pretty and softly rounded, which kept her continental look from becoming too severe.

The windows of the Lawrences' home were open to the cool breeze outside, and the sweetness of spring eased some of his disquiet about Kate Winter.

"Those are beautiful geraniums you found for your window box, Ida." His mother stood and crossed to the window to admire the papery blooms. She and Mrs. Lawrence discussed wildflowers. Ben's attention wandered, and in his distracted state, he said to Cornelia, "Going to Columbus will help me accomplish another errand as well, so it is a providential journey."

That was not discreet. He should not tell her what he intended, no matter how friendly the Lawrences were to abolition.

"And what is that?" Cornelia's delicate brows arched.

"I will surprise you." He smiled.

He must send a letter to John Parker this very evening, while there were yet a few days before the Columbus trip.

"Cornelia, did you hear?" Mrs. Lawrence turned away from the window box and bustled toward the hall. "We are going to pick some geraniums near the creek, so Mrs. Hanby may have some bouquets of her own. Will you come?" She settled her brown silk bonnet over her up-twisted graying hair and tied its large purple bow under her chin.

"Oh yes, please." Cornelia rose and walked to the foyer as well to get her own wide-brimmed hat.

"Ben, I don't suppose you'll come with us?" His mother touched his arm, her eyes bright. "It's a fine day for a walk." Her spontaneous joy made her look almost girlish.

"I regret to decline the pleasure. I have a saddle yet to stitch."

The women departed, still talking about Columbus, and he followed them out, hat in hand. The song running through his mind was melancholy but fierce. *Go down, Moses, way down in Egypt land. Tell Old Pharaoh to let my people go.* With John Parker's help, Ben intended to go down to Egypt. But the Pharaoh Ben had in mind was not amenable to friendly persuasion.

Hot broth spattered everywhere, a few drops stinging the back of Kate's hand. Tessie fluttered over to her. "Oh, miss, I haven't scalded you, have I? I'm so clumsy—I dropped my spoon in the soup."

"Don't worry." Kate resisted the urge to rub her hand. "What has you so nervous?"

"I've forgotten to bring in the potatoes for supper. The box is empty. But now I'm making the soup and I don't want to leave it alone, not with the stove so hot." Tessie poked around in the bottom of the pot with a long fork, searching for the missing spoon.

"I'll go out to the root cellar and get some for you." Kate would not get her bonnet for such a brief errand. The root cellar was behind the house, just short of the tree line. Northwest Street bordered the woods, though if you crossed Alum Creek and walked farther through the trees, the Everett place was only a half mile away.

"Oh, thank you, miss. You're a dearie."

Kate walked out the kitchen door and down the steps onto the spring grass. The trees beckoned, shady and inviting in their promise of refuge. She had sought the solace of the grove more than once rather than stay in the house.

She leaned down and grasped the handle of the cellar door, pulling it open with an effort. The root cellar was a wild pig's paradise, and they would run riot in there unless the door was kept shut.

Steep steps slanted down into the chilly, dim hole in the ground. She descended, minding her head as she passed under the timbered ceiling. The light from the open door was soft, but she distinguished the outline of the potato chest to the right. She raised the lid and rummaged through the sawdust until she had picked out ten cool potatoes to bring back in her basket. The cold bit through her lightweight dress, and she held her arms close to her sides to prevent shivers.

As she climbed up the stairs, the sound of voices drifted from the woods. She craned her neck to see. Laughter rang out, and about thirty feet away, patches of brown and blue silk flashed through the trees. She shouldn't pry, but the women sounded so merry that they piqued her curiosity. She closed the cellar door and set the basket down on it. At the edge of the tree line, she rested her hand on a birch trunk, looking deeper into the grove. She had the fleeting sensation of standing outside a window, watching a party to which she had not been invited.

Cornelia, dressed in flowing green silk, had removed her bonnet and hung it on a nearby branch. Her rich auburn hair was crowned with a wreath of pinkish-purple blooms, and she held out a half-finished blossom wreath to Mrs. Lawrence. "Do wear a wreath, Mother. I missed the woods here while I was abroad. We did not have such wild beauty in Paris." Cornelia skipped like a little girl and jumped over a fallen limb.

"Where is our sophisticated Frenchwoman now?" A woman's voice came from behind another tree. Mrs. Hanby stepped out with her arms full of the same soft blossoms on their green, waxy stems.

"Indeed, Cornelia. A wild changeling has taken your place." Mrs. Lawrence smiled and leaned down to gently remove a whole geranium plant from the soil under the trees.

Kate might not have another opportunity soon to thank Mrs. Hanby for her intercession in her father's drunken debacle. She must overcome her shyness this once. "Good afternoon." Kate's first greeting was too soft, and they did not hear, so she walked toward them a few steps, wending her way around the ground cover and twigs. "Good afternoon, Mrs. Hanby."

"Why—good afternoon, Miss Winter." Mrs. Hanby's surprise

was plain. She laid her flowers in the basket by her feet. Cornelia and Mrs. Lawrence still had not turned around.

"I do not mean to interrupt," Kate said.

"Not at all." Mrs. Hanby moved a few steps nearer.

Cornelia spotted her over her shoulder. "Kate!" She twisted a stem into place between her hands. "As my mother will not accept a garland, I will give it to you." She grinned and held out the circlet of flowers. Kate approached hesitantly. Cornelia lifted the wreath and placed it on Kate's head. The flowers brushed her brow, a sweet scent released by their broken stems.

"There," Cornelia said. "Now we are a couple of wild change-lings together." She took Kate's elbow. "Will you walk with us down to the creek? We're taking the air, as well as stealing nature's beauty."

Kate nodded, and the older women picked up their baskets.

She listened to their gay chatter as she walked through the dapples of sunlight on the woodland path. They did not know what had happened after the party last night, the scene that refused to leave Kate's mind. When they reached the creek's edge, Cornelia went to show her mother a frog beneath a water-side fern.

Kate turned to Mrs. Hanby. "I want to thank you for your kindness last night."

"Not at all," Mrs. Hanby said. "I was glad to meet your family."

Kate blinked and walked to the edge of the creek bank. If only her family were more like these women. The sharpness of the yearning threw her off balance. She sensed Mrs. Hanby behind her, petite but somehow as strong as one of these trees rooted in the riverbank.

"Would you like to accompany me on an excursion to Columbus?" Mrs. Hanby asked.

Kate twisted to face her. "Pardon, ma'am?"

"The three of us are taking a jaunt to the city next week. We will hear Cornelia play at Neil House, and do some shopping and take in the sights. I would like to take you with us. My daughter Amanda does not wish to go, and we will have an extra bed if you wish it."

She struggled against the wave of unreality. She could go with them, have her lodging for free, and then slip off into the city crowd when they were not watching. But what would happen to Leah and her mother if Kate left Westerville now? Perhaps she could get away, establish herself, and then provide for Leah as well with some honest work. She could send for her sister in secret, and at least the two of them would be safe.

"I don't know if my mother would permit me to go." That was the only impediment, and not a minor one.

"Perhaps not, if it were just you and I," Mrs. Hanby said. "She does not know me well. But Mrs. Lawrence is well known to all the townswomen. I believe her presence might influence your mother."

Mrs. Hanby was correct—Mrs. Lawrence would be an asset to any discussion. Her reputation was impeccable. Kate's mother had evinced a desire to impress Ida Lawrence in the past, at charity gatherings and sewing circles. Old money and privilege attracted Ruth Winter's interest as nothing else could.

"But my question is whether you yourself would like to go." Mrs. Hanby tilted her head as if to tease out the real truth like a skein of wool from a spinning wheel.

"Oh yes, that would be splendid." She hoped the other

woman could hear her sincerity, even though she could not look her in the eye. It was embarrassing, for she knew Mrs. Hanby pitied her. But Kate could not let this opportunity pass by.

"Then I will have Mrs. Lawrence speak to your mother, perhaps later this afternoon." Mrs. Hanby smiled and picked up her flower basket.

"Is Kate coming with us?" Cornelia rushed up to them, face glowing from fresh air and her exertions. "Oh, that's wonderful."

"I agree." Mrs. Lawrence huffed a little as she walked up. Her corset was probably binding her breath, what with her round maternal build and the vigorous walk. "It would be more diverting for Cornelia to have another young woman with her."

"Especially you." Cornelia took Kate's hand.

"If I can obtain permission," Kate said.

Mrs. Lawrence waved her hand as if swatting a fly. "I will speak to Ruth myself. She will agree."

"Thank you." Kate remembered the potatoes. "I must be getting back home. Someone is waiting for me."

"Very well. Prepare to enjoy the city!" Ida Lawrence was jovial, and Mrs. Hanby waved her farewell as Kate retreated toward her house.

Her opportunity had come, like a raised window in a musty room. But now she must plan to make a new home for Leah as well as herself if she left. She would need to do so quickly so Leah would not be left at home for too long. And no one must know where they had gone.

Perhaps her plan was too risky—her father might not ever repeat his violent outburst. But as long as he continued drinking in such quantity, she would not be able to predict his behavior.

She laid her crown of flowers on the cellar door, put the potato basket over her arm, and returned to the kitchen. But even as she handed the potatoes to Tessie, her thoughts flew out the window, southwest toward Columbus.

Eleven

THE STAGECOACH BUMPED ALONG THE CITY STREETS, but the women inside were cushioned by yards of their own skirts, muslin and linen jumbled together like a seamstress's basket. Kate drank in all the sights through the dots of rain on the coach window. The damp of early evening did not seem to deter the wagons, men in caps, and women with umbrellas who occupied the streets. In and out they went from a dizzying variety of establishments with signs proclaiming the name of the business owner. A milliner's shop caught her eye—the type of establishment Kate might like to open one day, with its elegant hats on stands in a display window. But she could not stay in Columbus, of course. They would look for her here. Instead, she would go to Cincinnati, close enough to be feasible but far enough to be anonymous.

Such chaos and hubbub would make it easy to slip away from her companions. She glanced at Mrs. Hanby's unsuspecting face as the older woman pointed out a shop to Mrs. Lawrence. Ben's mother might take the blame if Kate disappeared. That would not be fair at all. Kate would have to devise a way to avoid tarnishing the reputations of the Hanbys or the Lawrences. How, she did not know. The plan seemed more complicated now that she had come this far.

"High Street!" the driver called from above. The coach slid in the mud and the ladies jostled shoulders.

"I hope Ben is hanging on for dear life up there." Mrs. Hanby's tone was light, but she clutched her handbag tighter. Ben was riding with the other men up on top. It would not be seemly for any gentleman to squeeze in among so many ladies.

"There are handles. But he may be damp when he comes down." Cornelia closed her book. "Aren't we almost there?"

"Yes, the hotel is near Broad and High." Mrs. Lawrence retied her bonnet. The carriage shuddered to a stop. "You see?"

Outside, men shouted to one another and thumped the roof as they untied the baggage. The door opened, and Ben Hanby looked in. His face was shadowed in the rainy gloom by the dripping brim of his hat, and his coat clung to his shoulders. He extended a hand to help the ladies out. The older women went first, then Cornelia, who thanked him and stepped down with the grace of a practiced traveler.

Kate looked down at the step. It would be easy were it not for the width of her skirt and petticoats, and the corset that kept her back stiff as a washboard.

Ben held up his hand and met her gaze silently. She placed her gloved hand in his steady supporting grasp, and he watched her step down as if alert for the slightest stumble. She found her footing and looked up into his brown eyes. The feel of his hand through their lightweight gloves struck her as different from Frederick's. Ben's was leaner, though no less strong—the hand of a craftsman and a composer. But she should not be thinking such things—they did not seem quite proper. She withdrew her hand and looked away. "Thank you," she murmured.

Neil House stood five stories tall in magisterial gray stone, its name blazoned above tall pillars. A lamplighter passed on the walk with his long pole and ignited a white flame inside the glass. Now Kate noticed a long line of similar flames, unaffected by the drizzle, dancing like fairy lights far down the avenue. She marveled at their eerie beauty.

Cornelia waited for her at the bottom of the stairs. "Mr. Neil's hotel is magnificent."

"Oh yes." They ascended together as uniformed footmen passed them en route to collect their baggage.

"Charles Dickens himself even praised Neil House when he stayed here," Cornelia said.

Another footman held the door, and they walked into the foyer under an enormous gasolier, its crystals shimmering in the steady white light.

"Beautiful, isn't it?" Cornelia said.

"It's extraordinary." In the clear, powerful light, the black walnut paneling gleamed and the heavy carving of the stair posts towered up fifteen feet before disappearing into the high ceiling of the second level.

"Ladies, welcome." A man with heavy sideburns approached.

"Thank you, Mr. Neil." Mrs. Lawrence gave him her hand in greeting, then inspected her valise, which the footman had just set by the stairs. She seemed completely at ease in the presence of the most influential man in Columbus.

"And you must be Mrs. Hanby." Mr. Neil took the small woman's hand in turn. "I have met your husband several times. How is Bishop Hanby?"

"He's quite well, sir, though I should tell you he does not stand on ceremony. The United Brethren call him 'Bishop,' but he prefers the plain 'Mister.' If you call him bishop, he fears he will be expected to sashay around in robes and a pointed hat." Mrs. Hanby's smile grew impish, and Mr. Neil chuckled.

"I will remember to address him as Mister Hanby, then." He spoke to all four of them. "We are delighted to have you. Miss Lawrence, I highly anticipate your performance."

Cornelia made a small curtsy.

A tall, stout man entered the hotel, his boots spattering mud on the mat as he wiped them. It was Mr. Jones, Frederick's father. How odd.

Mrs. Hanby stared and grew still, but the Lawrences seemed unaffected.

"Mrs. Hanby." His voice was as loud and unrestrained as it had been in his own house. "Imagine seeing you here. Where is Mr. Hanby?" He walked over to stand near her.

Mrs. Hanby remained polite. "He is at home, tending the saddle shop. Mr. Jones, do you know Mr. Neil?"

Mr. Neil smiled and the two men shook hands. "Mr. Jones and I are well acquainted. Welcome, Daniel. If you will excuse me, I'll show these ladies to their rooms. They will want to rest before supper."

"Of course." Mr. Jones backed away and gestured for his footman to precede him up the stairs.

He looked at them over his shoulder as he left. Something in his expression reminded Kate of the fox who had just stolen the cheese.

Ben staggered under the weight of Cornelia's small trunk as it fell off the top of the stage and into his arms. Her concert gown must be made of solid gold. She had asked him not to let this trunk out of his sight, as it contained her sheet music. He had assured her he would personally deliver it to her room, though she had protested such care was unnecessary.

He hefted it between his arms, straining to balance the slippery leather in the rain. Finally he found the handle and took Miss Winter's valise in his other hand. Every step up the Neil House front steps was precarious. He could manage it, but he was glad none of the women were there to see him work so hard. Ben's lean build was made for running, not herculean weightlifting feats.

Two more stairs and he crested the top. At the hotel door, a footman offered to take it from him. He refused. He had said he would carry it himself, and he would not go back on his word.

Once through the main door, he had only to carry the trunk and valise up the marble stairs, one flight, he hoped.

"To which floor did the ladies before me proceed?" he gasped to the footman.

"The fifth, sir. Rooms 30 and 31. And I believe you will stay in Room 32, sir."

Of course, five floors. He renewed his grip and started up the first flight of stairs.

By the third floor, the handles were sliding from his fists. He lowered the cases onto the stairs for a breather.

"Mr. Hanby."

He knew that drawl. Descending from the landing above came the gray-haired Southerner, surprisingly light on his feet for a large man.

"Good evening, Mr. Jones. I'm surprised to see you here."

"Frederick told me about your traveling plans when he came home from class the other day. When I discovered Miss Lawrence would be performing, I decided to combine it with a trip to see my old friend Neil."

"I'm sure she will be delighted to have you in the audience." Ben took a deep breath, his legs tense from the climb.

"Frederick is with me. He went to the livery to supervise the horses, but he will join us later."

"That is good news, sir."

"You young bucks might take in the sights of the town. I know he prefers your company to that of any other young friend."

"Thank you, sir. I have a high regard for him as well."

"Well, I won't keep you." Mr. Jones continued his descent, his expensive coat perfectly suited to the rich décor around him.

Ben reached the top floor, his overburdened arms straining the seams of his coat and shirt. Next time he would refrain from promises about personal delivery of luggage.

Just as he reached the end of the hall, the oak door with the brass plate numbered 30 swung open, and Miss Winter stepped out. She stared at him, her blue eyes widening under the brim of her hat.

Miss Lawrence's face appeared over her shoulder, feather-bonneted and equally astonished. "Mr. Hanby, you shouldn't have!"

"It's not heavy," he stated in obvious contradiction to the facts. He bit his lip as he lowered the trunk once more to the ground. "I promised I would see it safely to you."

Miss Winter moved out into the hallway to clear the doorway. Miss Lawrence moved back, and Ben slid the trunk over the threshold.

"I'm sorry you went to such effort on my account," Cornelia said. "But thank you, Mr. Hanby."

"Of course."

The girls dragged the trunk in. Their labor was the price of his chivalry—a porter could have crossed that threshold and carried the trunk in, but a young gentleman could not.

His mother sidled around the girls to draw near Ben. "Here is your key." She pressed a key etched with the number 32 into his hand. "May I speak with you in private for a moment?"

"Certainly." He turned, unlocked the door of his room, and held it for her. After he had come in, she turned to him. "Mr. Jones is here," she said, her expression neutral.

"Yes, and Frederick too. I'm sure they will make our visit merrier."

His mother did not respond. Something seemed amiss, but then again, it was the last week of May. She might be merrier once the entertainment began.

"Does something about Mr. Jones disturb you?" he asked.

"Nothing worthy of mention." She stepped closer and lowered her voice. "Your father told me before we left that you were planning something with John Parker, though he didn't know what it might be. I assume it's Railroad business?"

"Yes."

"Did you discuss any of it with Frederick?"

"Mother. Of course not. If I haven't told Father, I certainly wouldn't tell another student."

"Very well." She still looked pensive. "Please tell me what it is. It's too worrisome not to know, especially with our responsibility to Miss Winter."

She would not like it, but he didn't wish to cause her

needless anxiety, so he had better confess. "I am going to find Nelly."

She looked at him hard. "Joseph's Nelly?"

"Yes."

"But how do you know she is still alive?"

"John Parker is investigating for me across the river."

"Across the river! So you think you will go into Kentucky and get her?"

"Yes. But it won't be that easy."

She skewered him with a motherly look.

"John tells me," he said, "that the border plantations have been using decoys to offer escape to slaves, then whipping or mutilating those who try to run as examples to the others. So if Nelly is there, I must convince her I'm not a decoy, but a genuine Railroader."

"And how will you do that?"

He reached into his inside lapel pocket and produced the miniature basket. "Remember this?"

She took it from him and opened the little latch. "Nelly's hair."

"And, more importantly, the basket Nelly made for Joseph. She will recognize it and know I am no impostor."

She sighed. "I suppose I don't have to tell you this is ten times as dangerous as conducting fugitives in Ohio." She touched his arm. "I do want you to follow your conscience. At least you have John to help you." She brushed off the front of her bodice. "I'll see you at supper in an hour." She left the room with a soft rustle of skirt followed by the click of the door into its frame.

Something about the Jones family unsettled his mother. But Frederick was a good friend, and Ben had no reason to think anything covert lay behind his presence. The very notion was ludicrous. Frederick had never shown one whit of interest in discussing slavery or abolition.

But on that note, he must remember to go down and speak to the desk clerk before dinner. A letter from John Parker might arrive here at the hotel, and then he and the others would have to part company.

Twelve

THE GASOLIER KATE HAD ADMIRED EARLIER WAS SO bright that it left no kind shadow to shelter her from the gaze of arriving guests. She inched backward toward the wall of the foyer as if she could sink into the frieze of the walnut paneling and become one of its carved wooden figures, still and lovely. But her sea-green gown would not allow such camouflage.

"Miss Winter, come up with us." Mrs. Hanby smiled and gestured upstairs at the retreating satin-clad backs of the women who had alighted from their carriages moments ago.

Kate lifted her silk hem to clear the steps and followed them up.

Once inside the dressing room, the strangers doffed their light hoods. A chamber maid scurried around offering heated irons to repair rebellious locks. A gust rattled the window beside Kate, but the wind's knocking faded in the rising hubbub of female conversation.

Mrs. Lawrence had introduced Kate to all of the women as they entered, but she could not remember a single name.

"Do let me have that iron when you are finished, Mary."

The woman with hard-drawn eyebrows spoke with the flat non-chalance of one who is always obeyed.

The plump woman in carnation pink handed it over without a murmur and turned to Mrs. Lawrence. "We are eager to hear Miss Lawrence play, Ida. And what a pleasure it must be to have her back with you!"

Ida Lawrence gleamed in her full scarlet dress. "Oh yes, Mary." Her countenance grew equally bright. "I have hung on Cornelia's every word and gesture since her return. There's no stopping a mother's fondness after two years' absence."

"It's an elemental force," Madam Eyebrows said, though her air of boredom siphoned all emotion from her words.

Such sophistication seemed designed to intimidate. If so, it was successful. Kate sidled away past another cluster of women and pretended interest in a curio cabinet while they finished repairing their coiffures.

"Don't let anyone frighten you." Mrs. Hanby spoke softly at her elbow. Her dress was not as magnificent as the others, but its brown silk suited her small figure perfectly with its well-tailored bodice. Despite the fine lines on her face, she seemed younger and lighter than the other middle-aged women. It was hard to believe she had eight children. "I will stay by you all evening, if you wish." The small woman's face was gentle.

Kate did not want to hurt Mrs. Hanby by her flight—the thought made her a little sick. But she could not return to the house in Westerville, and she was the only one who could take Leah away from it. Her sister had sustained enough damage to her character already from their situation—she did not deserve to be abused as well.

Mrs. Lawrence summoned them. "I believe the gentlemen

are waiting for us in the parlor. Shall we join them?" Mrs. Hanby took Kate's arm and led her in Mrs. Lawrence's wake.

The resplendent parlor glowed in the light of a gasolier even larger and more crystal-spangled than the one in the foyer. An ebony grand piano stood at one end, while several dozen chairs had been artfully positioned in small groups for the audience. Mr. Jones wore a black evening coat and white tie like the other gentlemen clustered in the back of the room. He lurked in the corner and murmured with a confiding air to two other distinguished men.

Ben leaned over the piano and peered beneath its raised lid with an absorbed expression. His appearance had taken a turn for the better since his rather comical appearance with their luggage at their door earlier. She repressed a smile. He should have let the footman help him, but she liked him for the determination that had filled his face as he stood there damp and out of breath in the hall.

He looked up at her, and she turned away quickly to find a seat. Mrs. Hanby had taken one near the piano, next to Mrs. Lawrence. Kate seated herself, admiring the intricacy of the brocade chair back. Even one chair like this would ornament a family's parlor, but in this grand room there were thirty or more, all equally beautiful.

From the right side of the room, a familiar voice greeted others, and she found it was Frederick Jones in his evening attire, his hair shining. He smiled at her, but she dropped her gaze—it would be improper to communicate across the room. Ben's black-coated figure passed through the edge of her vision as he left the piano and joined Frederick. They greeted one another and stood shoulder-to-shoulder in the way of friends in strange places. Frederick leaned to mutter something to him and Ben laughed, his eyebrows lifting and eyes brightening. But she should not be watching the gentlemen.

Mr. Neil walked to the piano, his hair smooth with pomade and his beard trimmed. He addressed them in a resonant bass. "My friends, I am delighted to present Miss Lawrence, who comes direct from Paris to honor us with a piano recital."

A polite smattering of applause followed and grew louder as Cornelia appeared in the parlor door. Her gown could have been made for European royalty, black with silver threading in the bodice and tiny silver ornaments hanging from each of its three tiers like an exquisite fringe. Its heavy folds trailed behind her as she rounded the piano stool, nodded to the guests, and sat down. Extraordinary that someone Kate's own age could be so self-assured. If Cornelia was nervous, she did not show it, her eyes dreamy as she laid her fingers on the keys, palms arched. One lock of reddish-brown hair curled down over her collarbone.

Then Cornelia lifted her hands and brought them down in a rush of sound, and Kate lost herself in the music.

———◦•◦———

Ben stood against the wall to the side of the ladies' chairs. It was good to have Frederick here—his sense of humor would increase the pleasure of an evening of entertainment.

The music was entrancing. Ben should let it carry him away, just as Kate Winter was allowing herself to be swept up in the melody's spirals and dips. Her eyes were closed in her delicate, pale face, luminous as an artist's Madonna, lifted in a moment of profound peace. She deserved some respite from her cares, and no earthly thing had more power than music to enfold a soul and deliver it from trouble.

But the music was not delivering Ben, despite its rare virtuosity. Cornelia's long fingers sent the notes out effortlessly, her head first lowered and then lifted, her body swaying ever so slightly with the undulating rhythm. An admirable musician, she held the rest of the audience spellbound in her sensitive hands.

Even this fine music could not move him until he knew about the letter and his deeper purpose here.

He should not have left Joseph's Nelly in captivity for so long on the assumption he could do nothing. The scripture would not let him rest. *Inasmuch as ye did it not to one of the least of these, ye did it not to me.* There must have been a greater reason for why Joseph had died at their home—a chance to bring good out of tragedy. He could not bear the thought of anything less.

When Cornelia finished her first selection on a resonant final chord, Ben took advantage of the applause to move to the parlor door. Its bronze knob was warm against his palm as he slipped out into the hallway, where sound from the parlor melted away into red-and-cream carpet and dark wood walls. Cornelia began her next piece: Mozart.

He would go downstairs and inquire again for his mail with the hotel clerk. By the time he returned, she would be finished with the Mozart and he could rejoin the audience.

The staircase was as empty as the hallways as Ben went

down to the front foyer. The clerk, a runty man with mustache waxed to points, sat on a stool and scrawled figures in a ledger.

He looked up and rose at Ben's approach. "Good evening, sir."

"Good evening. Have you any mail for me? I am Benjamin Hanby, guest of Mr. Neil."

Recognition sparked in the clerk's eyes. "Yes, sir. One moment, please." He pushed through the swinging double doors behind the clerk's desk and returned with an envelope in hand.

"My humble apologies, Mr. Hanby." The clerk bowed. "It appears the envelope has been damaged in the post." He placed it in Ben's outstretched hand.

One half of the envelope was mangled, with a jagged tear as if it had caught on the projecting spur of a careless express rider. But that was mere fancy, as the mail had surely come by stagecoach.

Ben maneuvered the letter from the envelope and opened it to inspect the damage. Good. It was all still legible. He folded it again. "No serious harm done. The letter itself is mostly intact."

"Thank you, sir." The clerk was visibly relieved. Perhaps other guests were not so understanding.

Ben shoved the letter in his inside pocket and mounted the stairs again. A few yards down the wide hall, a chair nestled in a secluded alcove. He made his way to the nook and sat down to read the letter in private. The Mozart tune still rippled, muted, through the closed double doors of the parlor. He had a minute or two before it ended.

The paper was crumpled and torn on one side, but he smoothed it back together.

John Parker
Ripley, Ohio
May 23rd, 1855
To Mr. Benjamin Hanby
In care of the Neil House
Columbus, Ohio

Dear Mr. Hanby,

I received your letter yesterday and made inquiries. The errand you wish is possible. The woman in question is still at the plantation across the river. Meet me at The Red Stag in Cincinnati on Friday the first of June, at the noon hour.

Cordially,
John Parker

Ben read it once more to be sure he had the details by heart. He refolded it slowly, then placed it back in his pocket with a rush of exhilaration.

Now, at last, he could go enjoy the music.

Thirteen

TODAY WOULD BE THE DAY KATE ESCAPED TO A NEW future. Her hands moistened inside her light gloves with each twinge of nerves.

She stood on the walk in front of a canvas tent the size of a cathedral, supported by a tall center pole and tethers. Bright square banners announced delights within: Circus and Menagerie, Elephant Show, The Oldest Woman in the World, Lovely Equestriennes.

Whatever had inspired Mrs. Lawrence to suggest a trip to the circus, there could be no more perfect venue for Kate to lose herself in a crowd and simply fail to return. She had given up on the idea of taking her valise, but her one gold necklace lay warmed by her skin under her high collar. Luck or Providence had brought her to Columbus and granted her free lodging. Now she would have to rely on the price of the necklace and her ingenuity to take her to Cincinnati. Her heart thumped under her bodice. She must not think of all this yet. The perfect moment would be after the show, when the crowd streamed out *en masse*. Her companions would assume they had been separated by accident and would not sound the alarm for at least half an hour or more.

"My goodness, a real elephant," Mrs. Hanby said, leaning forward for a better look at the strange creature whose head dominated the center of one banner.

"And Royal Roman Hippodrome with Other Singular Curiosities," Cornelia read from another sign. "Oh, I can hardly wait."

"Endorsed by the clergy, to boot." Mrs. Lawrence pointed to a third, the feather on her hat bouncing as she nodded in satisfaction.

Cornelia took Kate's hand. "Let's go in, shall we?" At her motion toward the entrance, Ben moved ahead to clear the way through the thick crowd gathered. Maybe it was his gentlemanly appearance, but the mob was remarkably polite, as several people stepped to the side to let their small party through.

Ben stood in the cavernous entrance and surveyed the interior. "This side of the ring looks more genteel." He removed his hat. "Perhaps up there?" He indicated an open space high in the steep tower of wooden seats.

When his mother agreed, he led them up the stairs. The stands were rickety, and Kate lifted her skirts to clear each worn plank step without revealing an ankle, ignoring the curious stares of some of the spectators. At the top, she turned and seated herself beside Cornelia on one of the wooden folding chairs. Now she could sit back and enjoy the view, as jugglers performed for the crowd. Her spirits lifted like the pins that flew high in the air, each suspended for a heartbeat above life's cares and even what the future might hold. She had never been to the circus. She wanted to see at least a little of it before her escape.

An organ grinder stood with his cart at the end of the ring and cranked the handle with vigor. His jaunty march played at a breathless pace and occasionally twanged out of tune. Visible behind the others' backs, Ben leaned back in his seat. He winced and squinted his eyes as a jarring flat note pinged at the top of the organ's range. When she flinched in tandem with him, he turned toward her, amusement flaring in his brown eyes. Another sour note sounded and her shoulders hunched in discomfort before she forced them back down. His mouth curved—it was almost a smile—and she wanted to laugh. She would be gone soon—the strangeness of it made her light-headed and almost carefree in his presence.

The organ grinder finished and pulled his cart out the side exit. The seating was filled to capacity, ladies and gentlemen, children and roughnecks elbow to elbow. All around the tent, men shrugged out of their coats as the temperature rose with the body heat of the spectators. Ben kept his coat on, but dampness edged his hairline.

It was better to be seated here at the top edge of the stand, where one could breathe. Ben had chosen their location well.

Cornets blasted a salute. A band in blue, brass-buttoned uniforms strutted into the tent. The audience clapped and whistled with the blare of their music.

Kate peered around in the murky dimness of the spectator area. People still trickled through the entrance below her and to her left. A cooling breeze blew in from that direction.

A big man strode in through the wide door, casually inspected a pocket watch, and then dropped it back in his waistcoat pocket. He did not remove his silk hat and stood off to one side. But she knew that gray hair and stout build. It was Mr. Jones, and

Frederick behind him. They turned into the stands and sat in the lower tier.

It would have been polite to invite them along, Kate supposed, but she was glad the Lawrences had not done so. Frederick's clear courtly interest made her nervous, but with the Hanbys and the Lawrences, conversation was less loaded. She glanced at her companions, but they were rapt in the charge of six white horses across the ring. Women in vivid red costumes stood on their backs as if it were the most natural thing in the world, their slippered feet secure in two small rings over the horses' withers.

The equestriennes vaulted from one horse's back to another, changing places with astonishing precision. A clergyman had endorsed this act, with women in their knee-length tutus and exposed legs in tights? It was no different from the ballet, she supposed. Nonetheless, she sensed Ben's shyness from the determined set of his head, as if he dared not even glance at any of his lady companions while such a display of limbs occurred—not just ankles, but entire calves, practically even knees when the tutus bounced.

Still, something called to her in the boldness of the equestriennes. What would it be like for a woman to stand atop two horses as a Roman rider? Exhilarating, quickening the senses. And they traveled from town to town across the entire country, seeing all the lovely and strange sights of America.

The act ended with a human pyramid of three young girls perched atop the shoulders of the women as the horses raced side-by-side around the perimeter of the ring. The crowd rose to its feet, cheering and stomping on the planks of the stand. Kate's companions stood up to maintain their view over the shoulders of the people in front of them, so she rose as well. The equestriennes took a triumphant lap around the ring.

The vibration from the stomping sent shivers up from the soles of her boots. She sat down with relief when the cheering finished. It was exciting, to be sure, but so loud. Now the music gentled into a waltz.

A huge beast shambled into the ring, its long trunk curled up to its forehead. The crowd fell silent. What a sight—she had never seen an elephant save in pictures. The elephant's keeper raised his arm, and the gray giant reared on its hind legs and trumpeted. Again, the crowd to her right rose to its feet and yelled and stamped on the wood.

A sharp crack echoed like a gunshot through the cheering. Kate jumped and grabbed Cornelia's arm. The noise had issued from directly beneath them.

"What was that?" The whites of Cornelia's eyes showed in the half-light, her nails digging into Kate's hand. Others around them looked down and jabbered in shrill voices. The brass instruments blared on, their sound adding to the din.

Another sharp report. The platform beneath her groaned and then fell away.

Screams sounded in the blur of motion. Cornelia's arms held tight around Kate, who clung to her friend as they fell. A shattering boom like a cannon mingled with the shrieks.

They hit the ground hard, the concussion knocking them apart. Pain shot up Kate's legs and she collapsed on the splintered wood beneath her.

Dazed, she sat motionless, struggling for breath against her corset.

A horde of people sprawled on top of one another, to her

right, in the wreckage of the stand. Screaming continued, along with cries of pain. Kate scrambled backward on her hands, away from the heaving pile.

"Kate, thank the Lord!" Mrs. Hanby ran up and knelt by her, hair disheveled, tiny creases by her eyes smeared with dust. "Are you injured?"

"I don't believe so." Her voice came out faint—it was still hard to catch her breath.

"Let me help you." Mrs. Hanby took her beneath the shoulders and raised her carefully to her feet. "There. Can you walk?"

Kate tested a few steps. "I'm all right." She almost had to shout to be heard in the horrific ongoing clamor. People rushed all around them from the other side of the tent. Most seemed to be running away in panic, though a few stopped to help the groaning victims. She was afraid to look at them too closely, afraid of what horrible sight might print itself on her memory.

"Where are the others?" Kate asked.

"I haven't found them." Mrs. Hanby's reply sheared off. She seemed remarkably level-headed, but her hand trembled as she lifted it to rub her eyes.

Together they edged closer to the mass of wood. Some people were crawling away. At least no one appeared to be buried under the heap.

"Ben!" Mrs. Hanby jumped into the fragmented pile and began to pick her way across. A few yards away, she slipped and her hat fell off.

Kate gasped, then called out, "Mrs. Hanby, be careful!" Ben's mother paused only long enough to cram the hat back on her head. She clambered a few feet farther, then crouched down.

Kate could no longer see her. She could not remain here

while her friends might be injured ahead. A sour taste in the back of her throat made her swallow hard.

She hoisted herself up into the splintered chaos and followed. A man grabbed her skirt, crying for help, blood running down from his scalp and into the furrows of his forehead. She paused. What could she do? She forced down a throb of nausea. "Mary, Mary, stay with me," he said to Kate, his eyes unfocused.

This was no time for weakness. She knelt and rummaged in her pocket. All she had was a handkerchief, but she gave it to him and helped him press it against the wound. Pity rose up in her and she kept her hands still and gentle against the man's brow. But as soon as she lifted her gaze to the confusion around them, her horror returned in force, like a gust of wind pushing her off balance, making her fight for every small motion. She dropped the reddening kerchief and had to shake it off before reapplying it to the man's blood-wet hair.

"Thank you, miss," a middle-aged woman said as she climbed next to them. "Charlie, do you know me?"

"Mary." He stretched a hand toward her. The woman took over his grip on the handkerchief and applied more pressure.

Kate stood again and walked on. She grabbed a jagged spur of wood for balance. A streak of pain lanced through her palm—when she turned it upward, a thick, needle-length splinter stuck out of it. Even the pain did not dispel her sense of walking through a dream. It seemed as if it were not Kate herself but some other young woman who grasped the splinter, jerked it out, and continued.

Mrs. Hanby knelt next to Ben, who was sitting up. He was pale, but not bloodied. A warm flood of relief poured through her, dissolving the strange dissociation of the moment before.

But one of Ben's feet was trapped under the broken planks, from the ankle down. She must get over there to help. Her pulse quickened as she looked for a path across the wreckage.

"Kate!" The call came from behind her. The Lawrences. They stood dusty but apparently unharmed beyond the edge of the collapsed stands while people hurried around them. Thank goodness. Her knees weakened and she blinked back the pin-prick of tears. No time for that, not with Ben still pinned in the mess and perhaps hurt.

"Find a doctor," Kate shouted, hoping they would hear her. "Mr. Hanby is injured." They seemed to understand, for Mrs. Lawrence grabbed Cornelia's hand and led her out of the tent.

Kate picked her way across the buckled wood until she reached the Hanbys.

"I can't get my foot out of the shoe, so that won't help." Ben spoke to his mother with the halting rhythm of pain as he tensed the trapped leg and pulled at it.

"How can we manage this?" Mrs. Hanby inspected the tangled pile of boards. They were woven together like reeds in a basket.

"Perhaps if we move this one?" Kate pointed, then grabbed one end of the board and hoisted it with all her strength. It heaved up, but not enough. Mrs. Hanby sprang to the other end and disengaged it from another piece of the stand. They both pulled, Kate straining her arms as her corset bit into her sides, until her end of the plank slid two feet to the side, and Mrs. Hanby did the rest.

Now just the one board remained on top of his leg. Kate went back to him. It was a larger beam, perhaps a support beam. "I don't think I can lift it," she said to him. A stab of anxiety made her want to sit down next to him and catch her breath. But she must not.

Streaks of perspiration ran down the side of his face. "Will you bring me a piece of wood about the length of my arm, if you can find one?" he asked.

She nodded and cast about, narrowly avoiding a fall into a hole between boards. There. A plank two inches by four inches, and a couple of feet long. She wrenched at it hard until it came free from the one nail that still held it. At least she could do that much—she carried it over with a tiny surge of satisfaction that vanished at the sight of his pain-whitened face.

"Here." She poked it at him awkwardly. He inserted it under the board, in a crevice just beyond the tight vertex that trapped his ankle.

He looked up. "Now place your hands next to mine and we will both push on the count of three."

She did as he said, conscious of the nervous dampness of her hands, hoping they would not slip.

"Wait." Mrs. Hanby positioned herself next to the wedged foot and laid her hands around her son's trouser leg, very gently just above the ankle. "In case you cannot lift it out yourself."

"Good." He held Kate's gaze. "One, two . . . three."

He bore down on the lever and she leaned on it with all her weight.

The beam shifted, only a fraction.

Mrs. Hanby pulled the foot hard. Ben bit his lip and grimaced without sound, but his leg slid out from the trap.

Blood covered the ankle below the fabric of his trousers and smeared his shoe.

Kate's head swam. "You're bleeding."

"Surface cuts, I think." He shifted to his knees and bore down on the good leg to stand up. "You see?" He looked triumphant through his pallor. Then he tried to step on the other foot and staggered. Mrs. Hanby seized him by the coat and helped him regain his balance.

"Lean on my shoulders and we will walk out of here." Mrs. Hanby still had to raise her voice over the shouts and pleas for help.

"You are too small to bear my weight."

"We must leave so we can get you to a doctor."

"I will help." Kate walked to them and stood at Ben's other side. He braced himself on his mother's support, then hesitantly laid his arm across Kate's shoulders. The warmth of his half embrace seeped through her daze. It should not be pleasant, under the circumstances, and yet it was, sending a flutter like birds' wings inside her. He began to limp forward bearing most of his weight on one foot.

Men were heavy. She could tell he was trying not to lean on them, but they strained to support his larger frame. Even after they cleared the wreckage, it was slow going. They were all out of breath by the time they emerged from the tent into the gray daylight. An overcast day had never seemed so friendly and safe—she took a deep breath and felt all the fear of the tent dissipate in a long sigh.

Ben removed his arm from around her. She inched away. She could not look him in the face, and he seemed preoccupied with the dust on his coat.

Mrs. Hanby kept hold of her son, as if afraid to let go. "Ida and Cornelia will come for us with a doctor."

"What happened?" Kate asked Mrs. Hanby. "Why did the stands collapse?"

"I don't know," the older woman said, her brow tightening. "I think the noises were the wood splitting. Perhaps the stomping was too much."

"They must have been rotten," Kate said. "Wouldn't the circus inspect the supports for safety?"

"Whether they did or not, they will claim so," Ben said. "No one will be able to tell, not with everything in a heap in there. Unless the papers somehow discover the cause and report it."

"Those poor people inside. We must pray no one was killed," his mother said.

Ben closed his eyes for a moment. His expression fascinated Kate—so calm, even in pain. What was he saying to God?

"You should sit," Mrs. Hanby said. "Let us help you over there." A cut-out log had been fashioned into a public bench a few yards away.

"I can manage." His skin was drawn and pale as he stood with one foot barely touching the churned-up ground, his shoes crusted with a line of mud above the sole. "Someone else will need the seat more. Too many are injured."

"No one has come for it yet." Mrs. Hanby spoke with the long practice of a mother's persuasion. "You may give it up should another require it."

But even as she said so, a little knot of three men stumbled out of the tent, cradling an older woman in their arms as if she sat in a chair. Her head drooped to the side; her eyes were closed. They shouted to one another in German, a few fragments audible. *"Das ist gud." "Ja, da sind."* One jerked his head toward the log bench and they passed Kate to lay the woman's limp body on it.

More spectators streamed out: Chinese folk in caps, small children with tears on their cheeks, some brunette, fair-skinned women in humble clothing speaking in a musical language.

Ben let his head fall back and made a strangled sound of frustration.

"Is it your foot?" Mrs. Hanby asked.

"No. I'm thinking of my friend, whom I had planned to meet in Cincinnati." He and his mother exchanged a look Kate did not understand.

"I will not give it up," Ben said to Mrs. Hanby. "This may be a mild sprain only."

What did he mean about Cincinnati? It dawned on Kate that she had missed her opportunity to leave. But of course she could not leave the Hanbys here in such a circumstance. But there might be another way. "What was your errand?" she asked Ben. "Perhaps Mrs. Hanby and I can accompany you."

He shook his head. "I'm afraid not."

Mrs. Hanby released her grip on Ben's arm, reached into her handbag, and withdrew a lacy handkerchief. "Turn toward me, Ben."

He did so, and she gently rubbed the grime from his cheek. He flashed a look at Kate, like a chagrined schoolboy.

Mrs. Hanby balled up the handkerchief and said with perfect calm, "Well, I think I shall go with you, as Kate suggests, just in case you need my assistance. She and the Lawrences will travel back to Westerville and I will go on to Cincinnati with you." The set of Mrs. Hanby's chin made her look very like her son for a moment.

"Mother. I hardly think—"

"Someone must go in your place if you have not healed."

"Please—" Kate rushed it out. "Please let me go with you. I might be able to help in some way." And what an additional wonder it would be, if she could get all the way to Cincinnati with their help before setting off on her own. Her shoulders tightened—she must not show her agitation, or the guilt winding her up inside like a spring clock.

"My dear, I'm afraid that's out of the question," Mrs. Hanby said. "We don't even have your mother's permission to take you to Cincinnati. You must go back with the Lawrences."

Ben spoke up behind Mrs. Hanby. "I don't think either of you should go, Mother. I don't think it a safe errand for a woman."

"I've been on such errands since long before you were born, son." Mrs. Hanby's tone was dry.

It was all very mysterious. Would Ben have to venture into some unsavory part of town as part of this errand?

The cab drew nearer, the rings on the harnesses jingling.

Mrs. Hanby placed a hand on Kate's sleeve. "Miss Winter, I do understand. When I was a young woman, I also wanted to see more of the world. But what would I tell your mother?"

"The truth." If Kate did not hurry, the coach would pull up before she could make her case. "Tell her young Mr. Hanby has been injured and we must go on an errand with him."

Ben lowered his voice so only Kate could hear. "You don't know what you're asking." He held her gaze.

She flushed and looked down. Her conflicting emotions

blurred into a single wild spin like the shapes and colors on a child's toy top.

"Ben!" a familiar male voice called. Frederick strode out of the tent doorway, apparently unharmed, his father a few steps behind. In half a minute, they crossed the yard.

"Are you hurt?" Frederick peered at Ben's foot. "You are!"

"It's nothing," Ben said.

"What a fright," Mr. Jones said. "Have you ever seen the like? Thank heaven we've all been spared. Or, mostly." He looked at Ben with regret.

If Kate did not seize this chance, she would lose any opportunity to escape. She must hazard everything, now, while the situation was dreamlike and confused. "Mr. Jones, we have a dilemma." Her words were halting, but she forced herself to go on. "Mr. Hanby is temporarily unable to walk." She took a quick breath. "Mrs. Hanby and I have offered to assist him to travel to Cincinnati, where he has business. But he is reluctant to accept our offer." A pulse pounded in her temples as if it might burst out like a river through a weak dam.

Mrs. Hanby darted a shocked glance at Kate before assuming a polite mask.

The expression of the elder Mr. Jones sparked to interest. "But why not, Mr. Hanby? Do you not wish the company of such charming ladies on your journey?"

"Of course," Ben said. "But Miss Winter doesn't have her mother's permission."

Frederick grinned. "Mrs. Winter will have nothing to fear if her daughter is with you paragons of respectability."

"Frederick," said Mr. Jones. "Perhaps we should all go with

Ben and make a party of it. We have nothing pressing at home, and Mrs. Winter would be quite sanguine if she learned half of Westerville was accompanying her daughter."

"But we have no way to inform Mrs. Winter in time," Mrs. Hanby said, her tone final, her posture stiff.

"Oh, but we do," Kate said. "Mrs. Lawrence can tell her about it when she and Cornelia return, so my mother will not worry."

Ben paused for a long moment. "I would be glad of your company," he said to the Joneses, to Kate's surprise. "My errand is a drab business affair and you may entertain the ladies while I accomplish it."

His mother turned away toward the street.

Victory! Kate did not like to distress Mrs. Hanby, but it would all be perfect now. The Joneses' company would ensure the Hanbys would not take all the blame should Kate disappear. Relief made her weak in the knees, but there was nowhere to sit.

"That may be the Lawrences," Mrs. Hanby said in a tight voice. She pointed to a cab that turned the corner at the end of the street and headed toward them. The team of horses moved at a swift trot as the driver urged them on with a wave of his whip.

The cab halted and the horses stamped next to them.

Mr. Jones grinned. "Then it's settled."

"Thank you, Mr. Jones, for your kind offer." Kate let a hint of her hidden elation creep into her tone. "I have always wanted to see Cincinnati."

Fourteen

BEN'S MOTHER HAD BEEN SILENT AND CONTAINED EVER since their departure from Columbus, and even the impressive courtyard of Cincinnati's Red Stag Inn did not seem to break through her mute contemplation. The hired hackney cab had pulled in, everyone had stepped out of the coach, and servants in livery ran this way and that carrying luggage. Still, his mother remained rooted to the ground in the middle of the yard.

"Mother," he called. "Come out of the way or you will be run down." Several coaches and a delivery wagon vied for wheel room, and a few horses champed their bits or dozed at hitching posts studded around the yard. Mr. Jones and Frederick had already gone inside to see about the rooms and dining. Miss Winter lingered by the hired cab, her blue eyes filled with uncertainty as she glanced first at the veranda of the hotel, then at his mother.

His mother did not move, but beckoned to him, so he limped out into the open space with the help of the temporary crutch the doctor in Columbus had given him.

"What is it? We need to go inside. This is not safe—there is too much traffic."

"I could not be sure of having another moment alone with

you, not while I am boarding with Miss Winter and you are with the Joneses."

"What is it?"

"Your father and I have never discussed Mr. Jones with you because of your friendship with his son. We did not want to prejudice you should our suspicions prove unfounded."

"What suspicions?" A buggy drove past them, too close, at speed, so he felt the wind of its passing. He flinched away on his good foot. "Mother, this is not the place for a protracted conversation. Let's go on the veranda before we are run down."

"Just one minute more. If we go up there, Miss Winter will follow, and she must not hear either." His mother's straw hat shielded her worried face from the young lady's view. "Be careful not to reveal anything about your errand to either of the Joneses. Remember when they lived near us back in Rushville?"

"Yes." He had played with Frederick at frog catching and raft building. After the Hanbys moved away, Ben had not seen Frederick for ten years. But the Joneses moved to Westerville two years ago to give Frederick proximity to Otterbein for his studies, and their remembered boyhood adventures had drawn the two young men together in camaraderie.

His mother whispered, "Did you notice that we never dined with the Joneses, nor they with us?"

"No."

"You were too young to observe such things. But your father always suspected Mr. Jones was responsible for the failure of one of our Railroad missions. Two fugitives who had just left our home were recaptured because someone told the slave-hunters where to find them. Your father thought Mr. Jones might be watching us."

It couldn't be true. "That's all speculative." Other arguments flashed in his mind but vanished, like a lit twist of gunpowder in paper. His parents did not mean to insult Frederick's family—Railroaders did need to show caution.

"That's why we never told you," his mother said. "But I don't like it at all that they came here with us."

"Frederick and I are good friends. And they are wealthy, and his father does indulge him. They probably wished to have a lark with all of us in the city. I don't think we should rush to judgment."

"Perhaps not. But be especially careful, please." Her gaze held his. "You know Mr. Jones is very friendly with the U.S. Marshal in Columbus. The marshal has even come to Westerville before—he went to Sunday services with Mr. Jones. Mr. Lawrence saw him."

That was worth knowing. "I will be discreet." A needle pricked his conscience, as if agreeing to keep his own counsel was an admission of doubt in his friend's honor.

"Thank you. Now, if you don't mind, you can go escort Miss Winter into the inn, and I will tell that porter where to put our bags."

Ben used his crutch to hitch his way over to the young lady, while his mother walked to the back of the coach on the street side, where the luggage had been piled.

"Is everything all right?" Miss Winter asked, only just meeting his gaze before looking away, twisting her gloved hands together. Maybe she regretted her request to join them, though it had been a pleasure to see her ardor for travel give her a moment's boldness. And now that Frederick was here, Ben did not have to worry about the ladies at all while he went on his errand.

He smiled at her. "I am to help you into the inn, my mother says, though I won't be of much use with this." He waved the crutch a few inches off the ground.

Supper was far above the average roadside inn fare: roast squab, soft rolls still warm and buttery, and a strawberry-rhubarb pie with just enough crumbly topping to balance the jellied fruit. Miss Winter wielded her fork with grace. Mr. Jones shoveled in pie without ceremony, between jovial comments to Frederick and compliments to Miss Winter that made her blush. Ben's mother was still uncommonly quiet, which troubled him.

"Ben, you must come out with us this evening to my friend's club," Mr. Jones said. "Mrs. Hanby and Miss Winter will no doubt wish to retire early, after their travel. But we can take a hack to the club and introduce you to our friends."

Ben glanced at his mother. "Do you wish me to stay with you tonight?"

"No," she said. "You should go. We will occupy ourselves for the next day or so with shopping and sightseeing. Is that agreeable to you, Miss Winter?"

The young lady nodded, her expression more alive than he had ever seen it before. The change of scenery suited her.

"Very well, Mr. Jones," he said. "I'll go with you." He didn't have to meet John Parker until noon tomorrow, and he was curious about these gentlemen's clubs. He had only read of them in the papers, and they seemed to be places where much business was done amidst cigar smoking and card playing, but without vulgar drunkenness or immorality. Gambling seemed to be the worst vice of the upper-class clubs, and Ben did not have to play cards if he did not wish.

"Capital!" Frederick grinned and sipped his ale, then blotted his mouth with a napkin. "Let's meet in an hour at the front steps." He got to his feet. "Shall we dress, Father?" Mr. Jones also rose and they made their farewells to the ladies, Frederick bending low over Miss Winter's hand and smiling at her. She probably liked his look, though she was too shy to return his open admiration. Well, what if she did? She was an exceptional young woman, and Frederick was a good man who would make any girl a fine husband. No reason to be disconcerted by any of that, or to be bothered by Frederick's courting of her. Ben should not feel any jealousy—he was merely concerned for a young woman away from her home. So why did he feel disgruntled as Frederick and his father whisked around the end of the dining room and up the stairs?

He went to meet them downstairs after a few minutes, bowing over Kate's hand as Frederick had. He liked to see her soft smile when she felt at ease. She was a mystery, but a very enjoyable one. And Ben had at least one advantage over Frederick—Ben understood her passion for music. Frederick liked all pursuits equally, because his open nature ran calm and smooth. To him all things were agreeable but none sublime. Miss Winter had a more closed nature, like Ben's own, and Ben knew all too well that such private natures channeled their passions more fiercely.

Kate watched Mrs. Hanby as the older woman finished her pie and laid down her fork. She took her time with her meals—but Kate did not want to be impatient after all Mrs. Hanby's kindness.

A stout maid came in to clear away their dishes, her red hair bound under a clean white cap. "Are you Mrs. Hanby, ma'am?" she said.

"Yes."

"I have a message for you and Mr. Hanby from the Negro man."

"Who?" Mrs. Hanby laid her napkin on the table.

"He said his name is Mr. Parker." The maid's sideways flick of her eyes suggested she did not think a black man's name of much import. "He wants you to meet him by the stable."

"Now?"

"He said as soon as you can, ma'am." She piled the last dish on her arm and waddled away.

"Oh dear," Mrs. Hanby said. "And Ben is already gone."

"Shall I come with you?" Kate asked.

"I think Mr. Parker may wish to speak in private—yet I cannot go without another person, or it will be . . . awkward."

She knew that what Mrs. Hanby meant was not "awkward" but "scandalous." A woman could not go meet a man alone.

"I do not mind. I can stand outside of earshot, if he wishes to speak in private," Kate said.

"Thank you. Then let us go down."

———— ·•· ————

When they arrived in the stable, with its earthy smell of leather and horses, Kate stood at the entrance. Mrs. Hanby walked to the end of the barn, where a tall black man waited by the end stalls. Ben's mother looked even smaller in her trim dress and straw hat next to this stranger's giant frame and muscular build.

He and Mrs. Hanby stood a good four feet from one another, for propriety's sake, talking in low voices. From the motion of her hands, Mrs. Hanby seemed to be concerned.

When she turned and crossed the swept stone floor to Kate, her pretty features were set, her eyebrows drawn in resolution Kate had never seen before.

"What is it?" Kate asked.

"We must bring our bags downstairs."

"We are leaving?"

"Mr. Parker needs my help this evening, right away. And I cannot leave you here alone, without a chaperone, nor can I go with him without a companion. You must come with us, and we will just catch the steamboat on its last run for the evening. When we get to his house, you may stay with his wife, which will be safe."

"What about Ben—Mr. Hanby?"

"I will try to send a message after Ben, if I can determine which club the Joneses may attend. I pray Ben will be in time to join us on the boat to Ripley."

Ripley? Kate closed her mouth on the questions that swarmed her mind. Mrs. Hanby clearly did not want to be quizzed. But they were going to a different town—what would this do to her perfect plan to disappear in Cincinnati?

They had to cross the courtyard again to return to the inn building. It was even more crowded than before, filled with travelers coming off the steamboat that had brought Mr. Parker. Every hitching post was occupied by a horse, some thoroughbreds finely bred with thin skin and long legs, others cart horses built for strength. A messenger boy in a red cap crossed the yard with a rapid stride for his short legs, his satchel advertising his profession.

"Excuse me," Mrs. Hanby called to him and stepped into the yard to get his attention.

"Ma'am?" He stopped and turned his face to her.

A carriage careened around the corner from the street, loose cloth flapping from its top. The black horse hitched at the corner took fright, leapt on its hind legs, and reared back against its tie-line, head straining up, eyes rolling in fear. It plunged down and up again, and the tie-line snapped, sending it reeling left—directly toward Mrs. Hanby and the boy. She looked up and froze, her hat tilted back, only a few feet from the flailing legs and their heavy hooves.

Kate ran toward the horse, making the loud hissing sound of an experienced groom, waving her arms like a windmill. The horse dropped back to earth and scuttled back on all fours, more startled by this apparition in its swinging dress than by the flapping cloth.

A man behind it seized the snapped end of the reins and soothed the animal until it stood quivering by the curb.

Mrs. Hanby's brown eyes were large in her white face. "Thank you. I lost my presence of mind for a moment."

"That was uncommonly brave, miss," the boy said. "And you can run faster than any woman I ever saw."

"I'm sure I looked very foolish," Kate said in a low voice. "But I am not afraid of horses. They are all the same when frightened."

The offending coach had pulled up to the other side of the yard. "Sorry, folks," the driver yelled out of the side of his mouth. "Don't know what got into the creature." It was another hired driver and hackney cab, judging from the luggage on top.

Mrs. Hanby began a hurried conversation with the messenger

boy about the local clubs where gentlemen met and where her son might have gone with the Joneses.

Back by the stable, the tall black man was standing by the open double doors. He was watching Kate with a look of mild surprise. She hadn't meant to draw attention to herself—especially not by capering like a scarecrow in front of the yard. He would think her a total fool. At least Mrs. Hanby had not noticed that Mr. Parker was a witness. The less said, the better.

Mrs. Hanby gave the messenger boy a few coins and turned to Kate. "I must go retrieve something from Ben's room. If you will ask a porter to get our bags from the room, I will rejoin you down here." She headed up the staircase.

Kate looked around the yard, still filled with pedestrians, and at Mr. Parker, watching her from the stable doors. This would be her last chance for several days—Kate could try to slip away now, or she could go along with Mrs. Hanby. If she ran or even walked away, Mr. Parker would see her go.

Besides that, if Kate did not go along as a companion, Mrs. Hanby would not be able to travel with Mr. Parker. And it must be very urgent, if Mrs. Hanby would leave without her son.

Kate owed Ben's mother too much to refuse to help her now. They would come back to Cincinnati after this mysterious errand, and then Kate could continue as she had planned.

Now she must get her bag and go to Ripley. By steamboat, into the night.

Fifteen

CIGAR SMOKE DRIFTED THROUGH THE AIR, AN AROMATIC relic of the conversations that snaked through every aisle and chamber of the Metropolitan Club.

"Ben, come and meet my friend," Mr. Jones called from where he stood with a dark-haired man with a serious, distinguished look.

When Ben joined them, Mr. Jones put a hand on his shoulder. "Mr. Hayes, this is my friend's son, Ben Hanby. Ben, Mr. Rutherford Hayes."

"Very pleased to meet you, sir." Ben shook the man's hand.

"Mr. Hayes is a solicitor in town and does much work for the benefit of the public," Mr. Jones said.

"I'm usually at the Literary Club, but business called me here instead," the man said. "If you will excuse me, Mr. Jones?" He looked around the room before finding his target and heading off, elegant in his black coattails.

There were more faces and names, more handshakes and introductions. Many of them appeared to be lawyers. Frederick's easy conversation and interest in the law gained the approval of all the older men. This club would be where Frederick found a mentor in his chosen profession, no doubt. Politicians were often lawyers first, and Frederick aspired to be both. But the lawyers were also congenial to Ben, asking him about his studies and his interests. Several appeared to enjoy his wit, and shared a few quips of their own.

Mr. Jones moved through the club like a bulbous pond insect, skating here and there around the clusters of gentlemen in chairs, but always returning to his son. His face glowed with paternal pride. Several times Ben heard him mention his son's merits to the other gentlemen—not so as to alienate, but with tact, so the lawyers asked more about Frederick's abilities and his education.

It must be pleasant for Frederick to have a father so invested in his life and future—a father who went everywhere with his son and offered companionship and friendly guidance.

But Ben wouldn't think less of his own father, who worked without rest to help those who needed it. Between seven other siblings and his father's commitment to the oppressed, however, Ben had to treasure their saddle and harness work together as the only man-to-man conversation they might find in a whole week.

Mr. Jones clapped Frederick on the back and laughed at some witticism.

Ben would like to see his own father so amused and light-hearted too—but the nature of his work often gave him the same preoccupations as Ben. They did not live in such a merry world as the Joneses, who had chosen not to see many things. He imagined what it would be like not to see, not to remember Joseph's death, not to think of the fugitives he'd seen, and not to feel the constant urge to help. It would be an easy existence, to live within the boundaries of one's own life. Many of the men here had the same bonhomie as the Joneses: the broad smiles, the expensive clothing, the air of untrammeled luxury.

But Mr. Rutherford Hayes had not possessed that look. He had the preoccupied expression of Ben's father.

"Mr. Jones," Ben said, at a pause in the stream of introductions. "What kind of law does Mr. Hayes practice?"

"He takes the cases that fall under the Fugitive Slave Law," Mr. Jones said. "Argues mostly for slaves trying to hoodwink the courts by running from Kentucky. He loves a challenge, but it's pointless work, for the most part. Legal papers are legal papers."

"I see." Ben discovered a new liking for Mr. Hayes.

"But he's a brilliant man, and mark my words, he'll go far someday, if he can turn his talent to more significant matters. He might even be mayor of Cincinnati."

"Yes, sir."

"Now let's go take some refreshment, shall we? Everything we could wish is here at the club—meat, drink, debate, or cards, newspapers for the reading, magazines. We have hours of diversion ahead of us."

Hours? Ben wouldn't like to be gone for too long. His mother and Kate were not frail or dull. They'd amuse themselves or perhaps go shopping as they'd said. Still, he wouldn't want to leave them for more than two hours. He would go back then, even if Mr. Jones wished to stay all evening.

He took some interest in the cards, but only from a statistical standpoint. Watching the men lose money and laugh amazed him—he did not understand the appeal of gambling, throwing away one's hard-earned living as entertainment. The debates tempted him to join in, but he suppressed the responses that rose to his lips and instead listened to the often witty rejoinders from club members. He was a guest here and should not draw attention to himself.

He looked at his pocket watch. Only an hour and a half had passed. He would go observe the new card game Mr. Jones was playing at the corner table, then make his farewell.

The cards flashed white on the green baize, and trails of smoke quivered up from cigar ends and disappeared.

"Mr. Hanby?" A club valet in black tie spoke deferentially behind him.

"Yes?"

"A message." He held a small envelope on a silver tray. When Ben took it, he bowed and retreated out the door toward the front receiving hall.

Dear Ben,

John was early. We have gone to catch the last boat to Ripley—he says tonight is the safest opportunity to perform your errand.

If you do not make it in time, I will help John. I have taken the little basket with me.

Do not worry. God will watch over us.

Your loving mother

He shoved the note in his pocket and rushed out the door, almost colliding with Frederick. "I must go—the women need my help and have gone on a brief visit to the countryside nearby."

"That was sudden," Frederick said. "Everything all right?"

"Fine." Ben relaxed his face with an effort. "They had a

womanly burst of impulse, and I will ensure they are escorted. Good night." He hurried out past the front desk.

He had to make it to the steamboat packet office before the last boat departed.

Sixteen

RIPLEY SAT ON THE HIGH BANKS OF THE OHIO RIVER, and twilight revealed points of light flickering in the windows of many homes.

"Why are there so many candles?" Kate asked Mrs. Hanby.

The older woman hesitated before picking up her cup of tea from the side table. "They are a guide to fugitives from across the river." She took a sip, watching Kate.

Mrs. Hanby had told her about the mission to rescue the slave woman. It did not seem quite real, watching these lights appear that would show John and Ben—or Mrs. Hanby—the way back to Ripley from a dangerous errand. And it was illegal. The thought made Kate twitch, even though she agreed in principle with the abolition of slavery. Aiding fugitives was one thing as a topic for Otterbein oratory, but quite another matter when John Parker was cleaning his pistols on the kitchen table of his home while his wife wiped off the dinner plates.

John came back into the parlor, where Kate stood looking out over the water.

"I'm afraid we can wait no longer for Ben," John said.

"It may be for the best. His ankle has not completely healed." Mrs. Hanby set her tea aside and stood up. "I am quite willing to go in his place. I have done such things before, to a lesser degree, perhaps, but still hazardous."

John's wife, Miranda, came in, her arms full of cloth. "You may need these, Mrs. Hanby," Miranda said, and held up a pair of men's breeches.

Kate stared at them in shock.

"Wait a moment," John Parker said. The new note in his voice turned their heads toward him.

"I think," he said to Mrs. Hanby, "that in order to have the highest chance of success, I will have to take her." He pointed to Kate.

Air huffed out of her lungs and Kate sat down abruptly in the parlor chair.

"No insult intended to you, Mrs. Hanby," he said. "We will need you to stand guard on the Ripley side. But Miss Winter can run like few other women. I saw her back in Cincinnati. And we may need to run very fast back from the plantation buildings to the river."

John Parker wished her to go instead of Ben's mother? This required a moment of reflection, to say the least. She could be captured. Her temples throbbed.

"I see your point, John," Mrs. Hanby said. "But I can't allow it. This is not my child."

"She is not a child," John said. "She is a young woman who must make her own choice about whether to save another from captivity."

Make her own choice. How odd to hear those words from a male stranger who had no way of knowing the turmoil in her home or her plans for this journey. She pressed her damp palms against her skirt.

"Mrs. Hanby, I would like to make my own decision." Kate stood and went to the window again, where the guide lights had brightened in the gloom. She must be honest—she could not risk lives. "I don't know if I am capable. I fear my courage might fail at the sticking point."

"Then do not go," Mrs. Hanby said.

John Parker gave Kate a level stare. "Do you think of yourself as a coward, Miss Winter?"

From anyone else, the rudeness would have shocked her, but there was no malice in him. "I suppose not," she said.

"And have you ever taken a great risk?"

She paused. "Yes." If she had not taken it yet, she would have in a week.

"And your courage did not wither."

"No."

"And why not?"

"Because the alternative was unacceptable." She paused. "I see your meaning."

He contemplated her. "When you see this woman, I do not think your courage will fail."

"Miss Winter, if you are caught, you will most certainly be arrested," Mrs. Hanby said.

Kate stared at the carpet, then looked up at the two of them. "I think I must go." A little chill rippled across her shoulders.

"Very good," John said.

Mrs. Hanby looked between them and then sighed. "John, you don't think you can go alone?"

"If I'm alone, the woman will think it is a trick, a ruse of her master's. But if there is a white woman with me, and she carries that lock of hair you mentioned, Nelly will know our help is genuine. No white woman would go with a black man at night as a decoy for the master. Do you have the lock?"

Mrs. Hanby opened her little handbag and brought out a tiny basket. "Here."

"Give it to Miss Winter, and she will come with me to the plantation's outbuildings. You will wait on this side of the river to be sure there are no marshal's men or bounty hunters waiting for us."

"Will we encounter any?" Kate asked.

"The marshal's men usually patrol the banks, but as I told Mrs. Hanby, they've been called away to keep order at an abolition meeting this evening. It's very rare, and we must make the most of this one night."

"It's better that Ben isn't here," Mrs. Hanby said. "He would have insisted on going himself. Though he would be horrified to know you're taking Miss Winter."

Miranda held up a pair of trousers again. "Young lady, it sounds like you'll be needing a pair of these too." Miranda handed them over, rough against Kate's hands. She would not show any hesitation to don them—she must prove she was strong enough.

A woman who broke the law could not be afraid to wear trousers.

* * *

All was quiet and dark. The boat bobbed like a cradle soothing a baby to sleep.

It didn't calm Kate, who sat immobile in the prow. She laced her hands together in her lap where John Parker could not see them and dug her fingers into the back of her knuckles. She couldn't stop the faint tremble that had started inside her and traveled to her hands. He mustn't see her shaking or he would think her unfit for the errand.

The chirp of crickets set a rhythm for little splashes from the oars as John rowed them toward the Kentucky side. They were quite close now.

She must shake off this dreamlike state. She peered at the riverbank as far as she could see to the left and right. At least there was no sign of a lantern.

They bumped up against the reeds. John jumped out, heedless of the mud and several inches of water. He lashed the tow rope of the fishing boat to a birch tree.

She must move now. She clambered over the side and into the dark water.

The unfamiliar feeling of the breeches increased her sense of having traveled to some different life, some strange body. It could not be she, traipsing around the wild in men's trousers. Someone else entirely had come on this errand—someone braver and stronger who just happened to resemble her on the outside.

A few waterlogged steps brought her to where John stood on the riverbank, like the shadow of a tree in the moonlight.

"This way." He walked ahead of her, straight toward the thickest tangle of thorny bush, slipping sideways into an almost-imperceptible space. Kate followed, though the twigs scratched like cat claws through her cotton shirt. They crossed a small rivulet of water on their way through the woods and pushed through the undergrowth for about ten minutes before the land began to clear out. Kate smelled the dampness of freshly turned earth and made out the furrows of a plowed field in the faint moonlight. Eerie quiet reigned—even the crickets had halted their song. John walked into the field, making a clear track across its neat earthen lines. They didn't have to hide their footprints. Any fugitive who lived next to the Ohio River would go across it—it wouldn't be a mystery to any pursuer.

Kate followed John across several fields. He finally slowed as they approached a tiny shotgun cabin, whitewashed and raised off the ground.

John beckoned Kate to crouch with him under the window frame. The shutter was open. He peered over the sill, then ducked down again and motioned for Kate to go inside.

Too late to change her mind now. She rose to spy over the window ledge. Inside, two people slept on straw mattresses. John clasped his hands into a foothold for her, waiting. She stepped into his grasp and he lifted her up and over the sill.

She crept between the man and woman and knelt to touch the shoulder of the sleeping woman. "Nelly," she whispered, as John had told her.

The woman's eyes flew open, and she took in one terrified breath.

"We are friends," Kate said. *Please let this woman not sound the alarm.* "We are here to take you with us, across the river." Kate pulled the basket from her pocket to say what Mrs. Hanby had told her. "In memory of Joseph Selby, whom we knew. Are you Nelly?"

The woman's face went slack. She touched the basket with her fingertips, then cradled it in her hands.

The sleeping man opened his eyes. He rolled to his knees and then to a crouch, fists clenched.

Nelly looked up. "No." She went and muttered something in his ear. He said something back to her.

The woman approached Kate and leaned close. "I am Nelly. This is my husband, Frank. He must come with me."

Kate walked to the window. John looked up at her from outside with a silent question in the lift of his brows. She nodded to him, and he pulled himself over the ledge into the cabin. Once inside, John towered over both of the others, who were about Kate's height.

"This is her husband. Can we bring him as well?" Kate asked John.

"Yes." John looked at Nelly. "Are you ready?"

Despair filled her face. "No, indeed, sir, I'm not."

John paused for a moment. "We are here now, and freedom is only a short run away," he said.

"We can't leave," Nelly said. "We have a baby girl. The master took our baby to sleep at the big house with Mammy. He knows we won't leave her."

John rubbed his hand over his face. "Follow me."

Nelly and her husband padded barefoot after him across the wooden floor.

The big house was about a hundred yards from the slave cabin. John led them across the grass, edging his way past the barn. Kate heard at least one animal rustling and stomping inside. If there were dogs in there, they would all be caught. This hundred yards seemed wider than the entire expanse of wood and tilled field that she and John had crossed on their way from the river.

They made it to the shadow of the house and crept into the few feet of space under the wraparound veranda. John pantomimed a question to Nelly.

Where is the baby?

Nelly pointed to a window on the ground floor. John would have to go up on the veranda and through that window. Thank goodness for the heat of early June. The master had left his windows open to catch any breeze.

This was too dangerous. They would certainly be captured. What would her mother think?

John reached down and pulled off his shoes, handing them to Nelly's husband. He vaulted up to the veranda, landing with less noise than a cat. Kate held her breath.

John bent down, stepped through the open window, and disappeared inside the house. Kate's fingernails bit into her palms. Deathly silence descended.

A shout of surprise and rage broke on the air as John flew out the window with a small bundle in his arms. He leapt off the veranda past them.

"I have the baby!" he yelled to them. "If you want to see her again, run like the devil!" He shot toward the fields, long legs scissoring, baby in one arm.

A white man in his nightshirt struggled out of the window, yelling. Kate turned and ran as fast as she could after John, as Nelly and Frank followed.

As they raced through the furrowed field, a hue and cry went up at the house. A quick glance over her shoulder showed several men pursuing them from the house. The edge of the woods shook in her vision as she hurtled onward. She tried to find John ahead.

"Wait," the fugitive man called. Kate turned. Nelly had tripped—her husband hauled her to her feet. She limped a few steps—a turned ankle to be sure. But the woman set her face like stone and staggered forward into a limping run. They all reached the edge of the woods.

Someone had unleashed the dogs at the big house. Faster than any human being, they bayed like hellhounds as they bounded across the fields.

Kate led the fugitives down the wooded slope and into the brook. Still no sign of John. They splashed downstream through the water. The terrible noise of the dog pack grew louder. There— the little opening in the brush that would take them to the riverbank. Kate tore through it.

Stinging cuts streaked her arms and legs as she burst through the thicket to open water. John sat in the boat, ten feet out from the shore, the baby wailing but tucked safely between his knees. He had the oars in his hands. In a storm of flying droplets, the three runners splashed through knee-deep water to the boat. Frank hauled himself over the side and grabbed the baby, freeing John to row.

Kate tumbled into the boat and turned to help Nelly.

The first dog emerged from the underbrush and jumped out into the water after them. A pack of six or seven more plunged after the first, barking and snapping.

Nelly dangled halfway over the side of the boat, the thin material of her dress sopping wet in Kate's clenched hands. John thrust the oars in the water and launched away from the shore with a heave of his shoulders. Nelly lurched backward, but Kate seized her under one arm and kept her from falling in the water.

The hounds paddled furiously, but the boat began to pull away from them. With Frank's help, Kate hauled Nelly over the side and into the boat, where she collapsed in a heap.

One of their pursuers ran out on the shore, a dim shape in the moonlight, thirty feet away now. A loud crack echoed above Kate's head—a pistol. More men began to gather around the gunman, and Kate heard the reports of several pistols. With an oath, John rowed harder and snapped at Nelly's husband, "Get the gun from its holster. Under my arm."

More bullets whistled over their heads in the darkness. Frank reached under John's shirt as he continued to pull on the oars like a longshoreman. Retrieving a black, long-barreled pistol, Frank turned to the receding shore. With a steady hand, he aimed at the men with guns and fired. They yelled and dove for cover.

"Hold this." Frank handed Kate the gun. She took it, unaccustomed to its lethal weight against her palm.

The other pair of oars lay in the bottom of the boat. Frank grabbed them and took a seat. He and John began to pull together, sending the boat scudding through the water at top speed. In a few more seconds, they were eighty feet from shore, out of range of the pistols of the furious men.

It was almost a mile to the northern shore—a goodly distance even for two strong men. Another boat launched out behind them as John and Frank rowed. Chilled by river water, Kate held the pistol across her lap, her gaze riveted across the water at their pursuers. Nelly sat beside her and soothed the baby, all the while watching the other boat intently as if willing it to founder.

The muddy flats of the Ohio side eased around their vessel and the boat ground against the bottom. John dropped the oars and scrambled out into the shin-deep water. He sloshed toward the wooden stairs that led up the riverbank. Frank jumped out and took the baby to help Nelly get over the side. Kate's tired muscles had stiffened, but she followed.

Mrs. Hanby slipped out of the shadows by the stairs. Even the moonlight revealed the worry on her face as she approached, very small in her baggy men's trousers.

"Are you all right?" she asked Kate.

"Yes." They both turned without words and ran up the stairs after the others.

Kate's lungs pained her by the time they topped the long stairs to Front Street. They had only a few minutes to make it to their hiding place elsewhere in Ripley. She had broken a sweat as they ran up to a neat house perched on a hillside. At the door, they were met by a stout man in his late fifties who wore a light overcoat over his sleeping attire.

"Mr. Collingworth, we are pursued," John said.

"I saw you coming across the river." He called back into the house, "Dora!"

His wife appeared behind him. She was as plump as her husband, with cheerful pink cheeks and hair twisted up under a rag. She looked at the baby whimpering and squirming in Nelly's arms.

"I'll need to take the baby, my dear," she said.

Nelly went ashen-gray, her grasp tightening on her little wriggling daughter. Then she handed the baby to the mistress of the house.

"We will give her something to make her sleep, and no one will notice her if we put her in our own family cradle," Dora said.

Her husband hustled past them into the yard. "Come with me. You must hide—they will come after you." Nelly took one pained glance at her baby then hurried after him. Kate followed and John and Frank came behind them.

Their host took them to the building behind the house, a wooden stable with three stall doors. A gray horse was tied outside. Mr. Collingworth rushed inside the stable and called, "John, come help me with this!"

"This" was a heavy wooden water barrel in the front corner of the empty stall. John put his shoulder to the barrel and pushed it a few feet to the side.

Stepping to the bare space where the barrel had stood, the stout man inserted his hand in a crack in the wooden floor. He heaved up a small section of the plank floor, revealing a dark hole.

John dropped down in the hole first, his broad shoulders squeezing through the tiny opening. Nelly and her husband went in after him and disappeared into the hiding place. Spiders. Kate shuddered. But there was no help for it. If they could bear it, she could.

She lowered her feet through the hole after them. The stout man extended his hand to brace her, and she dropped into the pitch-black space. Her feet touched the bottom. She let go of his hand and crouched on the floor. Ragged breathing filled the blackness.

The small square of light above them vanished with a thump and the barrel scraped back over the trapdoor. Their host's heavy tread on the floorboards departed the stable. But his boots sounded again on the wood, along with the rapping of four shod hooves. The hoof-sounds moved into the stall above them.

The horse from outside now stood over their hiding place. Brilliant! No one would think to look here.

Minutes passed. No one spoke. Outside, they heard the voices of men, telling their host that report had it the slaves had run to his house. Sounding convincingly weary and put-upon, Mr. Collingworth said they were free to search his property. The men came into the stable, their boots scraping the wood above Kate's head. A pinprick shaft of light fell through the floorboards from their lantern to touch John's face. But when the men saw only drowsy beasts before them in the stalls, they departed.

When all was once again quiet, their host returned, bringing them a lantern, food, and blankets. The lantern light showed Kate their hiding place. It was not as bad as she had feared. This secret cellar was at least ten feet by twelve feet, framed entirely in heavy wooden beams and planks, and though it smelled earthy and damp, the floor was smooth and clean, and piles of straw cushioned the corners. Nelly and Frank huddled in one blanket, and Kate and Mrs. Hanby shared another. It was warmer next to another human body, reassuring. Only John sat alone against the far wall of the little cellar. His feet were bare and scratched, covered with mud and traces of dried blood.

"Mr. Parker—your shoes!" Kate said.

He had left them below the porch of the plantation master's house, across the river.

"It's nothing," he said. "They cannot identify me. I purchased them in Westerville, from Armentor."

The angry master could hardly go to every shoemaker in the state to ask who might have purchased this pair. It was a long journey to Westerville from here, even by stagecoach.

John's face sagged into fatigue. "Let's eat and try to get some sleep. We need rest to make it to the next station."

They washed down the dried beef and bread with some

water, and Mrs. Hanby extinguished the lamp. Kate was so tired she stretched out on the straw without hesitation, rolled to face the wall, and pillowed her head on her arm. Mrs. Hanby spread the blanket over them and set her back to Kate's, comforting in their strange surroundings.

God, if you are there, please help us . . . But exhaustion turned her thoughts murky, and dreams slipped in among them.

Seventeen

BEN POUNDED ON THE DOOR OF THE HOUSE.

A plump woman in a nightcap answered. "Yes?" She looked none too friendly, but then neither would he if someone awakened him at the crack of dawn, when even the pigs were still slow and drowsy in the yard.

"I'm here for John Parker."

"He isn't here."

"I'm his friend Ben Hanby. Miranda sent me."

"And how do I know that?"

"She said to save her some strawberry pie."

The woman smiled and opened the door, beckoning him in. "I'm Dora Collingworth. They're in the parlor."

He limped in, his wrapped ankle still sore. The steamboat had at least given him a few hours to rest, but there would be no rest from here, not if he knew John.

The hallway was short and led to a closed door. Dora knocked three times. A locked door inside a house. The Collingworths had harbored fugitives before.

A bolt slid with a *thunk* and a stout man with a red, full face opened the door. "And who is this?"

"Mr. Ben Hanby, a friend of Mr. Parker's, sent by Miranda."

"Welcome." He shook Ben's hand, still serious. "You wish to see your friends, I assume."

"Yes, sir." Ben waited as the door swung wider.

Two women sat before the unlit hearth. His mother struggled to her feet. "Ben!" She ran a few steps and embraced him. He held her tightly, without care for dignity. *Thank you, Lord.* He blinked and stepped back. Miss Winter stood a few feet away. He smiled at her, tentative.

She seemed unharmed, though there were dark shadows under her eyes and her hair was coming down in a charming, disheveled way.

"I'm glad to see you, Mr. Hanby," she said.

His heart warmed in an odd way considering the danger they still faced. "And I'm sorry to be so late. I've made you do all the hard work for me."

"I didn't mind."

"Where is Nelly?" He couldn't believe he was about to meet her.

"Upstairs, with her husband and John," Mr. Collingworth said. "It's still too soon to have them on the ground level, where they would have no chance of escape. So John went to keep them company."

"You're well prepared, sir." Ben offered his hand. "Thank you."

"We could have lived anywhere, Mr. Hanby, but like many others in Ripley, we live here for this reason."

"God bless you." Ben tried to convey his gratitude in the heartiness of his handshake. For all the bounty hunters and depraved masters in the country, there were also people like the Collingworths.

"I'll take you up to John," Jonas said. His mother nodded and sat down, and Miss Winter did the same. They seemed to have a unity of spirit now, an understanding. He liked to see it—Miss Winter had bloomed so since their departure from Westerville. She was still quiet, but alert and bright, interested in her surroundings, not attempting to shrink from all notice.

On the landing of the staircase, Jonas stopped and turned to the wall. The paneling moved at his touch—a door half the height of a man opened inward. "Watch your head," he said as he ducked and went in.

When Ben straightened up, he found himself in a small room, long and narrow. At the end of the closet-like space, John sat with his back to the wall, his knees drawn up. Facing him were a man and a woman with skin a few shades lighter than John's.

They all got to their feet. "Tardy, my friend," John said with a faint smile. He indicated the woman. "Ben, this is Nelly and her husband, Frank."

Ben couldn't take his eyes from her. The woman stared at him, a long look of question. She was still striking, with heavy black hair and high cheekbones, though her sorrow had left its mark in the droop of her eyelids. "Mr. Parker says you knew Joe," she said at last.

"I did, ma'am."

"You were with him when he died."

"Yes, ma'am. He spoke of you. He wasn't afraid to go, but he was sorry to leave you without a farewell."

Her eyes clouded. Her husband took her hand.

Ben's throat hurt, and he cleared it. He turned to John. "What next, Mr. Parker?"

"We wait for the coach our host has arranged, and then we move."

"What if we're stopped on the road?" Ben asked.

"Don't worry. The coach is equipped for our needs."

——◆——

Kate shifted in the coach seat and pulled her skirt to a more comfortable position. Miranda had sent their clothes to the Collingworths' home, and so Kate was back in crinoline and corset. It seemed more cumbersome after the freedom of the trousers, but she would not want to wear trousers in front of Ben. And John had said they would be safer from discovery in the coach if they were dressed as ladies should be.

Twice in the last few hours, Nelly and Frank had gone into the empty compartments under the seats. Whatever the disadvantages of a bell-shaped skirt, it did make an admirable coach filler and seat cover to distract any nosy townspeople. Between her skirt and Mrs. Hanby's, there wasn't an inch to spare.

Ben was driving, up top, with John riding horseback some way behind. Too many bounty hunters knew John, and he could not draw suspicion by riding with Ben. But it reassured her that he rode behind with his pistol while Ben was armed with another. Especially now that the light was fading and the trees crowded thicker against the road, stretching tall like a German forest where witches might wander.

She must control her imagination. She needed all her wits about her, now that they would not be returning to Cincinnati. The starch went out of her at the missed opportunity, leaving her limp against the back of the seat. No, she would not give up—something else would present itself before they made it to Westerville. It did not seem right to be overly concerned with her own plans just now. The memory of the dogs at the river was fresh. If Nelly and Frank failed, what waited for them was far worse than an implacable mother and drunken father.

The coach stopped. Nelly and Frank exchanged an anxious glance over the baby's head. Kate and Mrs. Hanby jumped up, ready to open the seats.

"It's all right." Ben's voice sounded muffled through the coach roof. They all settled back into place.

Mrs. Hanby reached for the door handle and opened it to call out. "What is it, Ben?"

"We must stop for the night. John told me to stop here." His voice grew closer as he climbed down to the ground, then fainter as he moved to the horses' heads.

Mrs. Hanby climbed out, so Kate followed, impatient with her skirt as it stuck in the narrow door frame. One always had to drag at the crinoline to make it fit through.

She stared around them at the darkening forest. How had Ben known to stop in this nameless place, no different from any other mile of trees on the road?

He was looking at her. With a slight lift of his eyebrows, he pointed to a tree. Carved into the gray bark was the shape of a cross, two feet long, unmistakable even in the gloom. She smiled, self-conscious. Impudent of him.

Nelly climbed out of the coach, much more graceful than Kate in her simple dress without heavy petticoat. Frank handed her their sleepy baby, who whined with half-closed eyes before settling back against her mother's shoulder. As Nelly circled her with a gentle arm, an expression of yearning crossed the fugitive woman's face, clearing for a moment its burden of sadness before it rolled back like a wave that can never depart from the shore. Kate's throat tightened to a hard lump. What did she know of sorrow?

"John gave me directions to a shelter back here through the woods," Ben said. "Mother, Miss Winter, you may stay with the coach. You will sleep in it tonight, but Nelly and Frank must be hidden off the road. They cannot sleep in compartments all doubled up like jackknives."

Frank's lips twitched into almost a smile.

"I wish to walk a little," Kate said. Her legs were stiff from the run of the previous day, compounded by hours of immobility. "Mrs. Hanby, do you mind if I go with them?"

"Not at all, dear." Mrs. Hanby went to her son and took the reins from him.

"Take this," Ben said. "John will be along in only a few minutes, or I would not leave you alone." Ben reached inside his coat and pulled out his pistol, offering it handle-first. His petite mother took it without hesitation. She probably had held a gun more than once if she was familiar with this kind of errand.

The path under the trees was clear where only moss and ferns could grow. The earth was damp, its loamy smell fresh and light here where no one ever tilled and no cattle grazed. Ben led the way, Nelly and Kate followed, and Frank brought up the rear. Kate's legs pained her as bruised muscles knotted and stretched. She visualized the drawings in anatomy class—the musculature charts the ladies were permitted to see. Sinew and muscle were acceptable to study as long as the ladies were not in mixed company, though some other human systems were forbidden completely.

A sound like a whisper or soft laughter grew louder as they walked on, until a small brook trickled ahead of them over fist-sized stones, clear and ankle deep in the channel carved by its passage. Ben slung the canteen from his shoulder and knelt by the water to dip it below the surface. They all went down to the edge, Kate pushing back her skirt to lean down and trail her fingers in the water. If she were still in trousers, she would wade into it, cold and beautiful in the twilight.

When Frank had dipped water into his palms and slaked his thirst, Ben handed Kate the canteen, then offered it to Nelly. They went on over a rise in the land that then fell away down a long incline. Not far down the slope, the dark shape of a lean-to girdled the base of a large tree.

Nelly's baby lifted her head and looked around the clearing, eyes bright. While Ben showed Frank the site and gave him the food he had brought in his satchel, Nelly carried her daughter to the tree and let her touch the bark. "Most of the trees got cut down on the master's place," she said to Kate.

Nelly sat down and let her girl play with the ferns, which made her laugh in her high baby squeal. She grabbed a fistful and pulled with hands too gentle to break the stems. Her little head turned to watch a bird hop into the ferns, where it eyed her, then poked its beak into the ground covering. It was a plain bird, brown, with a spotted breast.

"A thrush bird," Nelly said. "Joe used to show them to me." Her eyes went distant and soft. "Do you hear? Up in the trees."

The birdsong above them resolved from a blanket of sound into separate notes as Kate listened. It was a song of astonishing intricacy, phrases of music whistled from the air, each phrase different, a variety of notes and patterns floating though the leaves.

"I'll tell you what Joe always said." Nelly kept her eyes on the thrush. "See how dull and quiet that bird looks, so no one would see him?"

Kate nodded.

"But it don't matter how he looks. Up there where no one can catch him, he sings that freedom song."

Kate could not speak, her mind a mélange of memories and emotions as the little baby clapped her hands on the ferns.

Nelly stretched out her fingers and let her daughter curl her tiny hands around them. "That's how my baby girl gonna sing someday, Lord willing." A faint smile graced her lips.

Kate turned and walked away through the carpet of ferns, heading blindly in the direction of the coach. She was so small and petty. Her misery in Westerville, her fear of performance, even the recent incident with her father—all so negligible, compared to this woman's suffering and her simple hope for her baby. Would she really run away to Cincinnati and forget she had ever seen them? Pretend that Kate Winter's unfortunate family life was the most important problem in the world, and worth all her effort and attention?

"Miss Winter," Ben said. She started and looked over her shoulder to find him only a few yards behind, hurrying to catch her. She stopped, the hem of her skirt brushing the greenery.

"I will escort you back to the coach," he said. "It's getting dark—you might lose your way. And Frank knows what to do here for his family." His dark eyes held hers, and he paused, then moved a step closer, sidelong, and raised his arm to invite her to take it.

It was not proper—they would not have a chaperone for the walk. Ben's expressive face said all without words, his hesitance, a touch of mutiny against the rules, his desire to help and perhaps to be close to her. And above all, he did not want her to refuse.

She looked away, a shiver moving up her back, and slipped her arm through his. As they walked on, the song of the hermit thrush broke out again in its wild, unpredictable melody. It was the only sound other than the rustling of her skirt through the ferns. She was stirred by the warmth of his arm, but also a consciousness of his whole presence, the support of his physical being only inches from hers, and most of all, his thoughts resting on her and hers on him, more intimate in the walk than any words.

She did not want to leave the private, dusk-softened world under the trees, or let go of his arm. Ahead was the dim outline of the coach, and the figures of Mrs. Hanby and John Parker beside it as they tended to the horses.

Ben gently unlaced her arm and held her hand for the last few steps to be sure she did not stumble at the edge of the road. He released it just before they rounded the coach, and they greeted Mrs. Hanby and John as if nothing unusual had occurred. But it seemed to Kate their thoughts had not disentangled as easily as their hands.

Eighteen

THE TRIPLE-BEAT DRUMMING OF CANTERING HOOVES rose above the crunch of the coach wheels. Ben snapped a glance over his shoulder as the reins vibrated in his hands from the bounce of the horses' backs.

Good, it was only John cantering up from his post behind. But he was waving for Ben to stop. Ben tugged the reins and slowed the horses from a trot to a walk. "What is it?"

"We're being followed." John's mount was in a full lather, its nostrils flaring with every breath.

"By whom?" Ben drew the coach horses to a full stop.

"A group of men on horses, perhaps three miles back. I caught a glimpse of them at the top of a hill and hid myself by the roadside to wait and see what I could discover."

"How do you know they're following us?"

"I heard them. They're bounty hunters. Someone tipped them to the possibility of a prize. They're looking for a coach, but they haven't spotted you yet. But they're making good time."

"I can't run the horses, not with four passengers inside. They would only last a mile or two."

"I know. You're going to have to give me the coach. I'll lead the bounty hunters on a merry chase, and you must take the others onward by foot."

"How far?"

"Washington is only five more miles, and if you cut through the trees it might only be three. Just keep heading northeast and you'll find the road again when it swings back to meet you before the town. When you get there, look for the two-story house at the crossroads. They'll be expecting you. And I must get back to Miranda now, but you'll have help along the way to Westerville."

The sun was dropping to the west in the late afternoon, so it would not be hard to keep direction by it.

"Very well," Ben said. "We must hurry. Tell the ladies and Frank to come out." He climbed down from the driver's seat.

John turned his horse and rapped on the window of the coach. Ben's mother opened the door. "Yes?"

Ben leaned around the coach lamp. "We must go by foot and John will take the coach. Quickly."

Nelly, Frank, and the baby came out first, then his mother shut the coach door again. What was she doing? In three minutes, she and Miss Winter emerged, but changed. They had divested themselves of their cumbersome underskirts, it seemed, and his mother handed Miss Winter one of the tie-backs from the coach curtains. They knotted the makeshift belts around their waists and pulled the excess material of their dresses away from the ground.

Ingenious, and necessary, for who could walk miles through the forest in a dress like a balloon? Miss Winter looked trim and strong in the graceful Grecian drape of her altered attire. But he shouldn't gawk at her like a rude farm boy.

"Let's go," he said, and led the little party off the road,

checking the position of the sun. Behind them, John clucked to the horses and the coach rolled up the road.

"I wonder what they will think," his mother said, stepping over some twigs, "if they stop John and find two discarded crinolines in his coach."

"That he has some unusual tastes in his wardrobe," Ben said.

Kate laughed softly behind him. He grinned without looking around. They had a long and dangerous journey still ahead, but better to face it with a strong heart and good humor.

* * *

The light was fading again by the time they saw the road ahead. Kate's calves were tight and her shoes had rubbed blisters on her little toes. She limped on without complaint. Between her blisters, Ben's still-wrapped foot, and Nelly's turned ankle from the escape, Mrs. Hanby and Frank were the only members of the party with an even gait.

A hedge of bushes stood near the road.

"Wait here," Ben said.

They all crouched down to rest for a moment while Ben peered ahead toward a crossroads. A handful of buildings stood at the four corners, some brown-planked, some whitewashed. "That's Washington," he said. "There's a railroad track there too, but it goes east-west," Ben said. "No use to us."

The baby girl babbled, and the innocent sound set Kate's stomach to fluttering. They had nothing with them to quiet the babe.

"We would never be able to hide on a train anyway," Mrs. Hanby said to Ben.

"You might be surprised." His brief abstracted gaze spoke of previous such hidings, perhaps on work with his father. "But it does us no good to go sideways on an east-west line. We need to go north. And we'll start by going to that house." He pointed to the only two-story building directly ahead of them and beyond the crossing. "After you, Mother." His eyes glinted, though he seemed serious.

"You want me to go first?" Mrs. Hanby asked. In the dusk, her surprise made her look like a girl Kate's age.

"You and Miss Winter. You're least likely to be suspected. If all is well, wave to us so we can come to you," he said.

Of course. That made sense. White women could walk together at dusk without exciting undue notice. Not so for those of darker complexion.

Mrs. Hanby rose, straightened her shoulders, and stepped out from behind the bush onto the road. Her skirt was dirty at the hem and bedraggled, but no one would notice that with the approach of nightfall. Kate scrambled after her, almost tripping on her own hem before she hitched it back up into her sash.

Heart racing, Kate walked beside Mrs. Hanby a few feet up the road and out into the crossing. Noises rose from the houses around them. Two voices wrangled in argument, something metal clinked. The shutters of the house on her right were closed, but the one on the left had its windows open to the crossing. She held her breath as a shadow flitted inside the house, outlined by the glow of light from the room. But no one came to watch.

They reached the door of the house that Ben had indicated. The paint flaked on the door and the doorknob hung askew in a hole too large for it. As long as the people inside were friendly to their cause, that was all that mattered. Kate turned back toward the place where Ben, Nelly, and Frank must be waiting for their signal. Should she and Mrs. Hanby wait for total darkness?

The door opened behind her. Kate flinched and tripped over some tools leaning against the wall of the house. Spades and rakes clattered to the ground, but Kate stayed on her feet.

A brown-skinned, stooped man with white hair and beard gestured to them. He carried no light. "Come in!" he whispered. "Bring them in!"

Turning back, Mrs. Hanby waved three times. Kate hoped Ben could still see her white-clad arm through the gloom.

After a few long minutes, Ben and Frank appeared, then Nelly with the baby on her shoulder. Thank goodness the little girl seemed to have fallen asleep. The three walked steadily through the crossing to the house. Mrs. Hanby stepped inside the door after the old man as Kate and the others crowded her. Ben was the last in and barred the door with a muted wooden thump.

The old man led them through the front room toward a flight of stairs. On the bare floor sat a little girl not older than five or six holding her finger to her lips. Mrs. Hanby smiled at her with a wistful expression. Perhaps she wanted to see her own little ones again.

Kate set her foot on the first step, which shifted under her weight. This household was in need of maintenance. But Mrs. Hanby had made it to the top of the stairs, so it must be safe enough.

Kate was halfway up when a loud knock came at the door. Kate glanced at Ben behind her; he pointed up with a firm hand. Mrs. Hanby flew across the upstairs hallway and into one of the open rooms. Kate followed as the old man pushed past the rest of them to get down the stairs to the door.

Kate heard him call, "Who is it?" but she had no time to listen to any more of his words. Frank and Ben were right on her heels and rushed into the small bedroom after her. But behind them, Nelly turned right and carried the baby into the second bedroom. Frank tried to get out and go with her, but Ben shoved him back and closed the bedroom door with care, in total silence.

A voice spoke from outside. Even through the walls, the words were all too clear.

"Federal officer! Open in the name of the law! Horace Abraham, open your door!"

Horace—for that must be the old man's name—began to argue with them through the door. At the same time, Ben crossed the room and eased open the window's shutters. He stuck his head out the window, looking up. The pounding on the front door increased; it sounded as if it would bring the house down. Ben pulled his head back inside and nodded at Frank. Ignoring the racket below, Ben boosted Frank up and out of sight through the window. Ben beckoned to Mrs. Hanby, who stepped in his laced fingers, grabbed the lip of the roof, and vanished upward as if an angel had flown by and plucked her away. Ben pointed to Kate.

They were about to be caught if she did not hide. There was no time for hesitation. She ran to Ben as she heard the officer and others coming in the front door. She placed her foot in his hands, grasped the upper edge of the window, and pivoted up and out with blind trust. Strong hands caught her, then Frank dragged her over the rough shingles of the steeply sloped roof.

She did not know how they managed to stay up there. Even

a medium wind would blow them off. *God, help us.* If she had neglected prayer before, the sight of the ground far below and the shouting from the house were strong incentive. *God, save us from here, please. Don't let us fall.*

She clung desperately to the shingles beneath her with white, cold fingers. Footsteps pounded up the stairs below, vibrating even through the roof.

Ben was still in the bedroom—had he gone to Nelly?

Just then he appeared, hauling himself over the slight lip of the roof. He slid across the shingles to where another window opened below him, into the room where Nelly was hiding. Ben reached down to the shutter and tapped on it quietly. Frank crouched just behind him, sweat beading on his forehead, his eyes haunted.

Kate heard the door of one bedroom bang open underneath them. With frustrated curses, the voices moved to what must be the bedroom where Nelly was hiding with the baby.

"Not here!" said one.

Kate held her breath. They had hidden well.

"Blast it!" another said. "Carter swore they would be here!"

Who was this Carter who had known that they would come through Washington?

She could hear them still cursing Horace.

"Well, old man," one of them said. "I guess we'll have to do the next best thing." After a pause, he said, "Because your name isn't really Horace Abraham at all, is it? It's Horace Campbell."

Kate did not understand his meaning, but she saw the sickened expression on Ben's face as he pressed flat against the roof. Something was going very wrong.

"That's not my name!" the old man protested, but his objections were lost in the sounds of a struggle. The little girl screamed,

"No! Grandpa!" and the old man shushed her. Then his voice rang out, "You can't take her! She was born free!"

"How you gonna prove it?" the stranger's voice said. "You're a runaway these twenty years, and it's back to Massa for both of you! I'm sure he'll greet you with open arms," he said. "Unless, of course, you want to tell us where the others went. We know they came here."

"They wasn't here." Horace's voice was firm and defiant.

The slap of a hand against a face made Kate wince. But the old man continued to speak to his abuser. "You ain't a federal officer any more than I am. You don't got no right—"

The man broke in, "But you let us in your house, and that's what counts! You're a runaway! *You're* the one who don't got no rights!"

The little girl asked again, "Grandpa?"

A faint wail went up from the bedroom below. Kate's breath caught. *The baby . . .*

Frank crawled toward that window. In a flash, Ben pulled the pistol from his underarm holster. He pointed it at Frank and cocked it. *"No,"* Ben mouthed, though his eyes were anguished.

Running feet thudded back to the bedroom. The slave-catchers yelled in victory as they found Nelly under the bed. The baby wailed in earnest.

"Hey, mama!" one of the men crowed. "And a little baby too. Well, ain't that sweet."

Frank's fists balled up against the shingles. Ben's brow was creased and sweat cast a sheen on his tortured face, but he kept the pistol trained on Frank.

After more taunts, the slave-catchers went down the stairs. The cries of the baby grew fainter as they left the house. Mrs.

Hanby's head bowed toward the shingles, her eyes closed and her lips moving in silent prayer. Frank dropped his head into his hands. Kate was afraid he might throw himself off the roof rather than go on without his wife.

"Frank," Ben whispered. "There are too many of them. They will kill you, right in front of her. We must wait—we'll have to buy her freedom, and the baby's, when they go to auction."

"They'll sell her down the river." The muscles in Frank's face worked.

"That's how you'll be able to buy her free," Ben said, hushed and intense. "John has friends who watch the markets. And the abolitionists will help you find money. Trust me. It's the only way."

Frank stared at Ben with hatred for a moment. Slowly, the rage ebbed from his eyes. It left an agony terrible to behold, as if someone had torn his face in half and pieced it back together with jagged edges. Kate had to look away. It could not be happening. Mrs. Hanby had her hand over her mouth.

The lantern of the slave-catchers bobbed down the dark road and their voices faded away. Ben holstered the pistol and motioned for Frank to go down the roof to the window. The other man complied, swinging himself over the edge and dropping out of sight. Ben helped Mrs. Hanby back down, and then handed Kate over the edge to Frank's waiting grasp at the window below. In her daze, she hardly cared that she was dangling in the air, and went limp when Frank pulled her inside.

The old man and his daughter stood in the bedroom, awaiting their descent. Horace held the little girl in the circle of his arm, where she clung to him with a tear-stained face, her eyes huge as she watched Ben lower himself from the window ledge.

When they had all made their way downstairs, Horace tried to reassure them. "Ain't none of the slavers coming back soon. They have to take the woman and baby across the river first." He glanced at Frank. The bereft man sat by the fire and turned his face toward it, his hand shading his eyes. Horace sighed and shuffled to the stove. He puttered around it for a few minutes, heating a kettle. The little girl maintained a tight grasp on one of his hands, but he did not chide her or even ask her to let go.

"Come here, sweet girl," Mrs. Hanby said from where she sat on a crude bench against one wall, her face haggard. "What's your name?"

The little girl's pretty dark eyes were reddened from weeping. "Rondie." She took a hesitant step toward her.

"Do you want me to fix your hair, Rondie?" Mrs. Hanby asked. "I've done it before for other little girls who visited my house."

Rondie's eyes brightened. "My mama used to do that, before she went to heaven." She scurried over and sat down, and Mrs. Hanby unfastened her hair from the knot on top of her head.

Kate addressed Ben in a low voice. "What about Horace and Rondie? Those men might come back for them."

She should have kept those thoughts for later, as Rondie looked terrified. Mrs. Hanby patted the girl on the back and started braiding. "Don't you worry, Rondie. We aren't going to let that happen." She gave Ben a worried look.

"We'll have to take them with us," Ben said. "They can't stay here now. If the slave-hunters threatened to take them, it's only a matter of time. Horace and Rondie must go with Frank to Canada." Ben was mustering his composure from sheer force of will, from what Kate could see. "And when John finds Nelly, we will bring her too."

The little girl settled back against Mrs. Hanby's knees as the older woman bowed her head, her fingers still holding the braids. After a pause she looked up and continued her work.

Horace shuffled over and handed Kate a worn mug, fragrant with the sharp smell of wild raspberries. The tea rolled bitter on her tongue.

Mrs. Hanby had told her that once they made it to Westerville, another conductor would take over and bring the fugitives farther north. But now it would not be Frank and his family—only Frank, Horace, and Rondie.

A chill passed over her, even with the warm mug in her hands. It did not seem possible that John could find Nelly and her baby. She did not have the luxury anymore to wonder if God could hear. She had to believe it. *Help them, help them. God, please. Protect them, help John find them.* She thought about the bird and its song, and tears slipped down her cheeks.

Nineteen

EVERY BUMP AND JAR OF THE WAGON BROUGHT THEM closer to Westerville. Ben guided the mules with his long driving reins from the box seat, restraining the mule on the right as he eyed the flowering greenery at the side of the road—white hemlock. A few bites of that, and the mule would lose its taste for weeds for good.

Ben's spirits sank lower with each mile. He had not saved Nelly—instead, he might have sent her to a worse fate without her family. He could hardly breathe when he thought of it. Fresh guilt stabbed in his chest. His father would be so downcast. And to compound the situation, all the Otterbein students would now expect to resume rehearsals for the musicale. Ben had never felt less like making music. But he had to go on and hold fast to the hope that John would find Nelly and the baby.

Around them, the houses of Blendon Corners lay scattered like jumbled wooden dice. Blendon was the oldest settlement around, and still roughened at the edges from its former frontier life. The tavern rang with rowdy shouts and laughter, even in the afternoon.

The mules tossed their heads and one shied away from the

noisy saloon. Only a little more than a mile now to go. Thank the Lord for Horace's wagon, which had saved them days of travel. Ben drove on, his mother quiet next to him, as she had been ever since Washington, while Kate sat in the back with Rondie. The little girl was garbed in bonnet and cheap dress like any house servant. There was no reason for anyone to stop and question them, but perspiration dampened his brow. He didn't want to lose Frank or the others. If the marshal or bounty hunters caught Frank, chances were that he and Nelly would never see one another again. Just like Joseph and Nelly.

The tavern receded behind them, though the road stayed wide and the trees did not loom close as they had in the deeper woods.

Ben stopped the wagon and twisted in his seat to address the little girl. "Rondie, remember how I told you there was a time you'd have to get down underneath the floor with your grandpa and Frank?"

Wide-eyed, the girl nodded her small face framed by her new braids.

"Now's the time. It won't be too long. Miss Winter, will you help?" He handed her the iron file from the floorboard under his feet.

They had barely spoken since Washington. He sensed the same weight pressing down on both of them—the absence of Nelly and the baby girl, Frank's slumped posture, his unseeing eyes. It was both horrible and sacred to see grief tearing through a man and exposing his every nerve. He had seen Kate wiping her eyes more than once. Ben had prayed until he ran out of words, and could only say to himself, *The Spirit intercedes for us with groanings that cannot be uttered.*

Kate pushed piles of hay off the wagon bed, clearing a bare space close to the back. She inserted the file into the crack at the edge of the floor and pried until a two-foot-square section of floor shifted upward. She grabbed the edge and heaved it aside.

Ben climbed over the seat, walked back, and beckoned to Rondie, who traipsed down the wagon to the opening. The square framed the faces of Horace and Frank. They took deep breaths of the fresh burst of air.

"Can we get out?" Horace asked. Inky bruises splotched even the small visible area of his chest and arm from the constant rattling of flesh against wood. Frank wore the same bruises the last time the men climbed out of the wagon, in the deep woods.

"Not yet," Ben said. "But we're almost there. Now Rondie has to get down there too. People in town will know she's not a servant in our household." He hauled himself up into the wagon to help.

"Come on, girl," Frank said. He shifted sideways and disappeared. Horace held out his arms to receive his granddaughter and Ben laid her inside, careful not to bump her. He had to force himself to lower the board back over her trusting, solemn eyes. He thrust the image of a coffin lid out of his head and pushed a light covering of hay back over the hiding place.

He turned back and met Kate's bright blue gaze. She had seated herself, her brown skirt pooling around her in the hay. Her eyes remained steady on his as if she knew his thoughts. Then a flicker of self-consciousness crossed her pale countenance and she looked down. He could not imagine how they would ever again speak to one another in small Otterbein pleasantries.

The wagon jostled on as the mules' harnesses jingled. State Street was not crowded, sleepy in the rising heat. Good, the fewer eyes to see, the better, particularly with their road-worn appearance. And his mother and Miss Winter were not in their usual attire, with their deflated skirts, but it would not be noticeable from a distance.

Ben opened the left rein out and laid the right one across the mules' backs to round the corner onto the college avenue. They were passing the recitation hall, white and familiar.

"Ben," a voice called. Frederick waved from the top of the steps and ran down them. "You've returned! I hope your journey hasn't proven too difficult. You gave us quite a turn with your mysterious disappearance."

"We took a tour through the country, as you can see." Ben tried to sound jovial, like a young man out for a lark in a borrowed farmer's wagon.

"It has been quite pleasant," his mother said, but he felt her stiffen on the seat beside him.

Frederick's eyes fastened on their garb and widened before he turned back to Ben, flustered. "A very unusual form of entertainment, I daresay."

"Not so, my friend. Just a pastoral interlude after the delights of the city." He must distract Frederick. "Are you ready for our musicale? Have you been rehearsing diligently in my absence?"

Frederick chuckled with a note of unease. "I am ready."

"Then I will see you tomorrow, here at the building at noon. You should tell any others you see." He strove to keep his tone even. And Frank, Horace, and Rondie must make no sound or all would be discovered. "And now we must be going, as the ladies have had enough of the country."

"A delight to have you back, Mrs. Hanby, Miss Winter." Frederick tipped his hat and stepped back, and Ben clucked to the mules. Their feet clicked in a quick four-count past Frederick. Ben's pulse pounded to the same rhythm and would not settle. It was only Frederick, his good friend, but his mother was so nervous next to him that it wreaked havoc with Ben's own state of mind.

Grove Street and the Hanby home came into view. Next to him, his mother exhaled the smallest of sighs. Ben neither slackened nor hastened the walk of the mules, but drove straight for the barn.

The barn doors were open and a man's shape stood shadowy in the back. Ben chirruped to the mules, who walked all the way into the dimness beneath the rafters. The man moved forward to catch their reins, and Ben's eyes adjusted to the welcome sight of his father.

"Thank the Lord," his father said. "Where on earth have you been?" He reached up and laid a hand on Ben's shoulder as if to reassure himself that his family was indeed returned. His eyes rested on his wife.

"Will you please close the barn doors?" Ben said.

His father's strong face lit with comprehension and he walked back to swing the doors closed and bar them with the long wooden rail.

They had made it, with their ragtag and incomplete company of fugitives. At least now there would still be a chance for Nelly.

———⋅◦⋅———

Kate would have to face her mother in only half an hour.

Mr. Hanby walked up beside the wagon along the wall of the barn, holding up his hands to lift his wife down. Their gazes met with such mutual love as he set her in front of him, his hands on her waist, that Kate looked away so as not to intrude. She had never seen such a look between married persons. Perhaps it was only the Hanbys who loved one another so. More marriages must be like her own parents', she was sure. One could not hope for such a rare bond as the Hanbys shared. A pain lanced her throat.

Ben secured the reins. Kate climbed around the wagon seat and began the process of opening the compartment. Mr. and Mrs. Hanby spoke to one another in low voices. From the corner of her eye, she saw their two forms meld into a tight embrace, Mrs. Hanby's head resting on her husband's chest, his bowed over hers as if in gratitude. Kate's cheeks warmed and she worked harder to remove the panel.

Rondie scrambled out of the hole, while Frank and Horace repressed groans as they dragged their longer limbs out.

"This is Frank," Mrs. Hanby said, leading her husband to meet the fugitives. "And this is Mr. Horace Abraham and his granddaughter. This is my husband, Mr. William Hanby."

"Good afternoon, sir," Horace said.

"Delighted." When Mr. Hanby said it, he looked as if he meant it. He did not ask any questions, but shook the men's hands. "If you would like to come into the harness room in back, we will arrange it for as much comfort as possible, and I will bring food and blankets. Our daughter Amanda is cooking tonight. I'm only sorry we can't have you at our table and offer you our beds, but we must be cautious."

"Of course, sir," Horace said.

As Mr. Hanby took the small party to the back, Frank's step was slow and heavy, unlike the lighter pace of the old man and his granddaughter. The burden descended on Kate like a pile of logs. How terrible it must be for Frank to see freedom, but without his family.

"Kate," Mrs. Hanby said. "We must take you home. But first you'll need to borrow a crinoline from Amanda, and I'll repair you to perfect gentility for your mother's inspection."

———————————

When Kate was washed, her hair pulled up in a neater chignon, her borrowed crinoline in place, and the dust sponged from her dress, Mrs. Hanby walked with her all the way home to Northwest Street. The iron gate was the same as ever, but something in Kate's world had shifted. It made her want to retire to her room undisturbed and rearrange the underpinnings of her mind.

She had promised Mrs. Hanby she would tell her mother the truth about their mission. That would not be a happy conversation. She should probably wait until Ben's mother was gone.

It would not do to walk in unannounced, considering Mrs. Hanby was with her. She rapped with the doorknocker.

Tessie came to the door in her white apron and gray dress. Her mouth opened, then she smiled. "Miss Winter, you're a sight for sore eyes. Welcome." She curtsied and held the door wide.

"Mrs. Hanby, do come in," Kate said.

"Thank you, I will for just a moment."

It was as if they spoke a completely different language under the set script of formal exchange.

Don't leave me.

I am here.

They sat together in the parlor, skirts perfectly arranged as if they had not been wading through mud and brambles last week. Thank goodness the light in her father's study was out. He might be carousing in Columbus, or even in the tavern at Blendon if he were shameless.

A light tread on the stairs and a whisper of fine fabric announced the arrival that was turning her stomach inside out. Her mother descended with measured steps, coming into view bell-shaped skirt first, then belted waist, unbending midnight-blue bodice, and finally that eerily youthful face with its elaborate coiffure.

As she swiveled toward them, blank-faced, an awful hush descended. Mrs. Hanby and Kate stood to greet her. The bruising on her mother's face was gone. At least her father had not repeated his assault.

Kate's mother broke into a social smile. "Mrs. Hanby! Such a delight to see you again. And thank you for bringing my daughter home safely." She seated herself across from them. "We have missed her, of course, but Mrs. Lawrence assured us it was a good cause. And if Ida vouches for it, I have full confidence. She has been a dear to keep me company in your absence, Kate. And Miss Lawrence is a jewel as well."

So this was the way of it. Mrs. Lawrence had placated Kate's mother with visits at teatime, the status and approval she craved.

Mrs. Hanby folded her hands in her lap. "Mrs. Winter, your daughter has shown rare compassion and fortitude in our travels. I have been blessed with her assistance and with the opportunity to get to know her better."

"That is so kind of you."

The conversation bounced back and forth, Mrs. Hanby sincere but formal, Kate's mother smiling so broadly her face might crack.

"Well, I have many duties to resume at home, Mrs. Winter, so I will take my leave." Mrs. Hanby stood.

Kate's mother rose also. "I hope to see you again soon, perhaps at tea with Ida?"

"As soon as I'm able. Good night, then," Mrs. Hanby said. Tessie opened the front door.

"Good night," Kate said.

Her mother echoed it, and the door closed behind Ben's mother.

She turned. "I'm glad you managed to bring some credit to yourself, Kate." The familiar coldness returned to her mother's tone, but at least she seemed to have been jollied into approval of the journey. "What was it, exactly, that took you so far, and for so long?"

Kate steeled herself. "We had to bring some very poor people to a place where they could receive aid. Food, blankets, shelter."

"And were they deserving poor?"

"Yes, they were." Now she must tell her mother that they were also fugitives. She hesitated.

"Good," her mother said. "Charity should be given only to those who will lead lives of virtue. And of course, I would hardly expect that friends of Ida would associate with any inappropriate persons. So very well. Good night." Her mother gathered her skirts and stalked back up the stairs, gaze not quite focused, as if the glorious spectacle of Ida Lawrence in her parlor still entranced her.

Kate stood still. Her mother's indifference was a stunning relief.

I have broken my word. I did not tell her everything. Well, I must do so tomorrow.

But deep down, she knew she would not.

Twenty

"PERHAPS YOU SHOULD CANCEL THE MUSICALE." CYRUS'S familiar voice needled him from the doorway of the recital hall. "We don't have much time, and it may not be up to your standard."

"Kindly leave the directing to me." Ben lifted his fingers from the piano keys and looked up.

Cyrus shifted his cello case in his grip and flipped his curly hair back as if to cast off gruff words like chaff. He sallied in. "Where are all the others?" he asked.

"The rehearsal is not scheduled to begin for another five minutes."

Amanda came in after Cyrus, giving Ben a sympathetic glance over their brother's shoulder. When Ben said nothing, Cyrus headed for a chair and unpacked the cello, while Amanda played arpeggios and tuned up.

"The Handel, please." They turned through their music and he cued them into the opening measures.

"Cyrus, will you please slow down?" Ben tapped his baton on the music rack with metronomic regularity.

Cyrus screeched his cello's bow across the strings. "Any slower and we will all fall asleep."

Amanda stopped and lowered her violin, waiting with sisterly forbearance.

Cyrus pointed his bow at Ben like a long, accusing finger. "Besides, why are we playing this piece? Miss Winter hasn't been here for the two rehearsals since your return. I don't think she is going to sing at all. We should remove this song."

"I'll make that decision tomorrow."

Kate hadn't wished to sing even before they left for what would become such a fateful mission. Her absence was understandable. "Perhaps I'll use it as an instrumental piece only."

"That would make no sense," Cyrus said. "The children are pretending to be trees. No one will understand why they are holding out greenery."

Ben let his head fall back against the chair, gazing at the plaster ceiling and trying to summon patience.

"Why don't you remove the Handel piece, settle the issue, and stop this needless rehearsing so we may move on?" Cyrus's voice grated like a fishmonger's call.

Ben sat up straight and clenched the baton to keep from hurling it across the room. "Will you please attend to your own business and play it? Without that song, the performance won't have a proper end."

"It won't have it anyway, without the lyrics." Cyrus thrust his head forward like an angry young goat.

"Cyrus, let it alone. It's only an extra ten minutes," Amanda said.

"But aren't the others coming at any moment? And we haven't marked the dynamics for the Schumann pieces yet." Cyrus's eyes glinted through his dangling mop of brown hair.

"Just do as Ben asks. He has much to do and we should

make his task easier." Amanda raised her violin again, and Cyrus grimaced but brought his bow to the cello's strings.

"One, two . . ." Ben gritted it out and set the beat.

The door of the recital room swung open. Frederick Jones took in the rehearsal in progress and swung across the floor with easy strides to take a seat and observe. Ben kept the count silently and listened for any variation in tempo. That was better. Sometimes he thought Cyrus wavered in his rhythm just to annoy him.

His peripheral vision registered the entry of the other students. Mrs. Gourney led the young ladies in, and the other young men followed. By the time the Handel wound to its close, they were all assembled.

He should try to be gracious to his company of volunteers, no matter how low he himself felt or how much he might wish to cancel the performance. Kate's number would have unified the whole artistic effect by bringing the children together with the lovely music in an act of blessing pointed up by the lyrics. Ben would never admit it aloud, but Cyrus was correct when he suggested cutting the number rather than doing it without a soloist. The music alone would be confusing without the words. But Ben didn't need Cyrus to tell him his efforts were meaningless without Miss Winter. He could see it quite plainly himself, thank you.

No one else had the correct sound or range for the song, and Kate hadn't responded to Jenny's summons to rehearsal for the last week. And the bleakness of Nelly's loss smothered his soul and made him want to do nothing at all. He went forward on sheer stubbornness to finish what had turned into a disappointing ordeal.

"Thank you for your promptness." He addressed the performers in their separate male and female rows.

Was it his imagination, or did they look as dispirited and

uninspired as he? If so, it was not their fault. The responsibility lay with him, as leader.

He summoned what little cheer would come. "Let's begin by performing it as we will tomorrow evening, straight through without interruption. A dress rehearsal, except for the children. We will add them tomorrow afternoon."

The players nodded and took their places. The read-through progressed. Ho-hum. No one wished to be here, apparently. He wouldn't even speculate on why: it would lower his spirits even further.

Cyrus reached the end of his reading, which preceded the final number, the Handel. "And thus," his brother said, "we close with the greatest and most lovely mystery of childhood, a mother's love, the blessing that never ends." Cyrus's gaze threw off sparks when he looked at Ben. "Oh august director, are you quite certain you wish us to play the concluding piece now?"

"Yes." If Ben said more, he might regret it.

"Even though Miss Winter does not appear to be singing for us?" Cyrus needled.

"Play it."

"It makes no sense." Cyrus threw his hands up in a shrug.

How dare he make a scene in front of the others? Ben's temper flared.

The door opened again.

Miss Winter stepped in, her blue eyes flicking across the faces that turned to her. With her mass of black hair, delicate wrists, and full, light skirt, she was like an ivory-skinned nymph who might flee to the protection of the woods.

He stared, their private walk recurring to him like a dream, the feel of her hand on his arm.

"I apologize for my absence this week, Mr. Hanby," she said. Something in her intonation was changed. And he could hear her from ten feet away, though she was still not loud by anyone's definition.

"Do you wish me to sing?" she asked.

"Very much." Warmth suffused his neck. He must watch his tone in front of the others. "Are you willing, with only a day's rehearsal?"

"I have some familiarity with the song now."

Their last meeting and rehearsal seemed an eon ago. "Ah yes. Then please come in and let's rehearse." He would be all business. "You remember your entrance for the piece? Four measures in."

She nodded. Cyrus went to his chair with a mollified expression and leaned the cello against his knee.

Ben handed Kate the music. She was a better sight singer than she had admitted, and did well even when they moved past the opening of the piece. Her voice was just as lovely as before. When she finished, wonder lingered on every listener's countenance. And when they ran through the complete musicale again after her number, all the readers and Frederick seemed to acquire new vigor and perform with spirit.

He did not know what had changed Kate's mind. Stage fright still drained her cheeks of color and made her hair look even blacker by contrast. But for some reason he could not fathom, she had decided to sing despite the fear.

Though this musicale was nothing but a light entertainment, her determination cheered him. Nelly and her baby had not yet been found, and everything else dimmed in the shadow of that fact. But his musicale might at least help this one young woman whom he admired. Should she overcome her fear in this one public moment, she might find herself less paralyzed with shyness in the future.

The performers finished and gathered their belongings. He praised them with sincere pleasure, his soul still uplifted by the sublime Handel song in Kate's soprano.

She herself had turned to go.

"Miss Winter," he said.

She paused, her sea-green dress trailing the floor behind her as she looked over her shoulder.

He crossed to stand beside her. "I want to thank you for what you are doing."

Pink tinged her cheeks and she kept her gaze down, eyelashes dark against her fair skin. "You are welcome, Mr. Hanby. Music makes others glad, if just for an hour. That may be the only moment of joy or freedom some ever find." She raised her eyes to his. "Such gifts matter. You told me they are from God and should be shared. I am free, and I should sing." She turned away and hurried after Cornelia's sable-clad figure to the exit.

He sat down on the piano bench in the now-empty room. The resolve on her face amazed him—what an unusual creation God had made in Kate Winter. He wanted to call back her presence here and breathe in the faint aroma of flowers that drifted from her dark hair.

He looked at his score, running through the sequence of chord changes and ornamentations for the first song. Tomorrow night was full of new promise. He would make it perfect for her.

Twenty-One

IF SHE TOLD HERSELF ONCE MORE THAT THERE WAS NO way around it, perhaps the fear would give up and slink away. The odor of polished wood from the stage platform brought back the day of the oration, but she wrenched her mind away from the past. The audience had not even arrived—she must not panic.

The babble of children rose in jolly chaos around her. They gathered clean-faced by the walls in a fair semblance of order, but little boys kept darting out of line only to be pulled back by the practiced hand of Amanda Hanby. The seven-year-old girls whispered, while the five-year-olds stood in a bleary-eyed daze, overwhelmed by the lights and colors.

Flowers clustered in large baskets around the stage, and boughs of greenery rested on the mantel behind it. In the final rehearsal earlier that day, Ben had directed the children in how to use the tree branches during Kate's solo.

Her solo. Bitterness at the back of her throat threatened sickness. She refused to be ill. Ben caught her gaze and her heart eased for a minute, before flying off into nauseating spirals. If she disgraced herself, she would ruin his work as well.

She must keep her word to Ben and sing. Only once. She could bear it once, to honor Nelly and her baby. Their encounter had changed her. If she wished to oppose the suffering she had witnessed, she would need to graduate from Otterbein. Only as a qualified teacher could a woman influence others outside her immediate sphere—there were few other occupations that allowed females to have any effect on intellectual and moral opinions. Kate certainly could not choose to be a milliner and ignore the cruelty of the rest of the world.

But all her reasoning did not stop the slow churning in the pit of her stomach.

Frederick Jones, splendid in a high white collar and black coat, towered next to the Parrish girls and Cornelia. He bowed in Kate's direction and took a step toward her.

Ben Hanby reached her side first. "Good evening, Miss Winter."

She wanted to take his arm as she had in the woods and draw comfort from his faith. But that was out of the question, as they were no longer babes in the woods but a young lady and gentleman under the decorous rule of Otterbein.

He gave her a quick, reassuring smile and turned to address the little ones. "Children, you will sing first, and then at the end of the program, you will perform the tree pageant." He spoke loudly over their giggling and chatter until they quieted and stopped fidgeting. Their light and dark heads bobbed in the soft glow of lamplight.

"First is 'Little Boy Blue,' then 'Mary Had a Little Lamb,' then you children will all sit down in the front." Ben pointed to the space. "Then the younger Mr. Hanby"—he indicated Cyrus—"will read his farewell piece. He will introduce Miss

Winter's song and call you up again to perform, just as we did this afternoon. Does everyone understand?"

"Ye—s-s, Mr. Hanby!" they chorused.

"Who is going to call you up?" he quizzed them.

"Cyrus!" called his little brother and sister, echoed by "Mr. Hanby" from several others.

"Very good."

They began to chatter to one another again.

Ben turned to Cornelia. "Miss Lawrence, will you take the children into the library for a few minutes?"

"Certainly." She herded them out of the room.

"I'll send for you when it's your turn," Ben assured her as she passed him.

Townspersons began to stream in. Mr. and Mrs. Hanby and the other Hanby children were first to arrive, followed by the Lawrences. And there was Professor Hayworth. Kate avoided looking in his direction—it would only make her more self-conscious.

A steady stream of families poured in: the Westerfields, the Boglers, the Stoddards, the Griffins.

Kate's mother entered the hall, both wary and proud in her elegant hat. She settled herself stiffly in the back row and motioned Leah to sit beside her. Kate's father was not with them—thank goodness.

In came Mr. Jones and his small, blond wife. The Joneses wove their way through the crowd. Mr. Jones boomed pleasantries to all as he passed.

A noisy buzz of activity and talk filled the room as more and more townspeople came in, standing in the back when no more seats remained.

It was time for the performance to begin.

She could feel the delight of the audience, their enraptured attention to each moment, from Frederick's rollicking songs to the readings, which were full of whimsy. But every song and every reading made the inevitable moment draw nearer.

The children sang, ending with "Mary Had a Little Lamb," their chubby cheeks drawing rib-elbowing and pointing from the doting adults in the chairs.

Cyrus stood and read his piece about motherhood and God's love, finishing with a dramatic pause. "And now—" He ducked his head as if gathering steam for his introduction, a look of pure mischief on his face. "We have been treated to 'Mary Had a Little Lamb' by our youngest singers, but we move to something more stirring for our finale. I introduce to you Miss Mary Kate Winter, our own 'Mary,' and at the piano, her devoted lamb."

She stood pinned under the regard of the audience, as mouths across the room fell open like so many dead fish. What had Cyrus just said? It could not have been what she thought. But it was, for he had shocked the audience.

He was still speaking. "But shall our musical Mary be won by her musical lamb? That answer must wait for another day."

What? He had just implied an understanding—or something—between Ben Hanby and herself. In public. Before her mother. In the hearing of the whole town.

She would be sick. She could not sing.

Cyrus gestured to her with a flourish. "For now, let us give Miss Winter our rapt attention as she gives her unparalleled rendition of Handel's 'Where E'er You Walk.'" He stepped away from the podium and toward his seat, where his cello awaited.

She stood for one frozen moment, feeling the gaze of the whole room on her. She would not run away and increase the scandal. She would walk up onstage. There, she was doing it. The room was spinning, but she could place one foot in front of the other. She would not ruin Ben's performance. If she could make it to her place, she might be able to sing.

Cyrus picked up his bow and grinned at her as if nothing were amiss.

Her ears roared. She looked at the faces—so many faces—were they all thinking of what he had said? Blood rushed to her face, making her dizzy. Her bodice felt too tight; she could not get enough air. The room seesawed around her and went dim. She barely felt the thud of her head against the wood. Arms lifted and carried her as her vision faded.

Twenty-Two

BEN CAME IN THROUGH THE KITCHEN DOOR, clos-
ing it quietly behind him. It was barely dawn, but there had
been business to attend to.

He smelled bacon and fresh bread. "Do you need help with
breakfast?" he asked his mother, who was putting a pot of coffee
on the stove.

"No, thank you." She looked up at him and cocked her head.
"Why are you dirty?"

He looked down at his clothing. He was smudged with
grime, and a few pieces of dried grass ornamented his clothing,
leaving green stains on his white shirt.

"Nothing I may discuss." He brushed off his shoulder and
trousers.

"Did our friends go with Mr. Lawrence?" he asked his mother.

Frank Foster and the Abrahams had still been in the barn
when he left this morning, but when he returned, the three flowers in the window vase were gone. The flowers were the Hanbys'
signal to one another that there were railroad "passengers" hidden in the barn. If the flowers were gone, that meant the three
fugitives were on their way.

"Safely off to Sinai."

"I wish I had known. I would have gone to wish them Godspeed."

His mother removed the bacon warming in the stove and brought it to the table. "They must all go to Canada now. The risk of staying is too great. Mr. Lawrence will report back to us when he returns."

The table was set and breakfast was ready.

"I'll call the others," Ben said.

His father's voice drifted in from the parlor. "It's all right, Ben, I'll wake them up." His father crossed into view, turned on the landing, and headed up the stairs with a spring in his step.

One by one, the children wandered downstairs and assembled in the kitchen. Samuel sat on Ann's lap. Lizzie and Willie perched on opposite ends of the bench, where they would not be tempted to get into mischief. Amanda and Jenny positioned themselves between the smaller ones and helped serve food from hot plates. Anna sat at the foot of the table, distracted and grumpy looking. She was not an early riser.

"Where's Cyrus?" Ben's father asked.

His mother wiped her hands and went to her seat. "He went out to do the stalls an hour ago, but he should have been back by now," she said.

"Well, I suppose we must eat without him." His father pulled up a chair. He folded his hands to pray. "Shall we say the blessing?"

The kitchen door opened and Cyrus came in.

His mother froze in the act of folding Sam's hands, staring at her son. Cyrus was covered in dust and grime. A large bruise darkened the side of his face, which also bore several scratches. His lip was swollen and streaked with red.

He refused to meet anyone's eyes and limped up the stairs in sulky silence.

Lizzie asked curiously, "Why is Cyrus—"

"Shush!" their mother said. She glanced at Ben with reproof.

He did not care what she thought. "Will you pass the biscuits?" he said to Amanda. He took one and began to butter it, trying not to look too satisfied. Out of the corner of his eye, he saw his father watching him.

"We haven't prayed yet, son," he said.

Ben put the biscuit down.

The family bowed their heads, and his father began, "Loving Father, forgive us our trespasses. Help us to remember each day that a gentle word turns away wrath, and that he who lives by the sword shall die by the sword."

Ben opened his eyes. His father was watching him over the bowed heads of the others.

He returned his father's gaze without blinking and waited for the rest of the prayer.

"Lord, soften our hard hearts, and help us forgive one another," his father said.

Small chance of that. He savored again the satisfaction of telling Cyrus with controlled fury that they had a matter to settle behind the barn. Once hidden from view, Ben had said to his brother, "You've exposed an innocent and admirable woman to public ridicule. As you can't seem to behave like a gentleman, I'll give you a lesson in manners. Defend yourself."

With resentment and fear filling his face, Cyrus had thrown a wild punch, and the fight was on. The result had led to his inglorious entrance two minutes ago.

His father closed the prayer. "Amen," the rest of the family echoed.

After breakfast, Ben's father laid a hand on his shoulder. "Will you take a walk with me, son?" It was not really a question.

They left the house together without speaking. As his father strolled down the road toward the creek, Ben followed a step or two behind. He did not want to have this discussion. They passed Northwest Street.

His father dropped back to walk beside Ben and shoved his hands in his pockets. In the protracted silence, the sounds around them seemed louder—their footfalls, some chirps from sparrows, and the rustle of a squirrel overhead in the branches.

"You seem to care for the young woman who sang last night—Miss Winter, I believe?" his father said.

"What of it? I care for many of my friends," Ben said. It sounded transparent and juvenile.

"You know what I'm asking you, Benjamin."

He searched for an answer that was truthful and yet comfortably vague. Nothing sufficed.

His father rephrased. "Do you care for her only as a young friend, or as a grown man cares for a woman?"

He did not want to answer, but it was his father, and he could not refuse. "As a man cares for a woman." Ben fiddled with the button of his sleeve. It was as awkward as the day years ago when his father explained to him the physical side of love between a man and a woman.

"Then it must have been all the more difficult to hear what your brother so foolishly said last night."

Ben could not respond, swamped by the return of raw

emotion. Would Kate ever speak to him again? Her mother would certainly loathe him now.

His father spoke with compassion. "We can't always control our feelings, whether they spring from love or wrath. But we mustn't allow our darker passions to vent themselves on others. I did that once, Ben—when I hated my master above all else. It almost destroyed me."

They were entering a denser part of the forest where the road turned into a path and sloped down to the creek.

The gravel crunched under their feet. "I know you love your brother," his father said. "He has wounded you, yes. But he's your brother."

Ben didn't wish to reply.

"I also need to ask you something," his father said. "You've told me before that you plan to go into ministry and teaching. Is this still true?"

"Yes."

"And we both know those professions will not make you rich."

Where was this leading? "No, sir."

"The most you can hope for is modest comfort, as we have in our own home right now. And we've been blessed with prosperity far beyond that of most ministers' families."

"Yes." Ben waited for his father's point.

"It's most likely that you will be less than comfortable in your material life," his father continued. "And that will affect a wife, and any children you may have. They will make the same sacrifices as you."

"I know Mother has had to make do," Ben said. "But it hasn't been so bad for her, has it?"

"My travel made your mother's life very challenging at times.

I know it caused her worry and sorrow that many wives never know. And it was very tiring, and took a toll on her health."

"But she's healthy and strong."

"Yes, praise God, she is. And it was that strong constitution that saved her in our leaner years. But I chastised myself many times for putting the woman I loved through such hardship." He stopped in the middle of the path and turned to face Ben. "Your mother grew up on a farm and was accustomed to hard physical labor. A minister's wife must be an unusually strong woman, physically and spiritually."

"It's not easy to judge a woman's spiritual strength," Ben said. "Some might say almost impossible, without marrying her. Are we finished with our walk?"

"Almost." His father turned back toward the house, and Ben followed. It was harder going this way, as it was uphill now.

"There can be other obstacles when a man cares for a woman." His father's walk slowed. "If her parents don't approve, then there's no use in pining for what one can't have."

Ben stared at the ground. "How do you know her parents wouldn't approve?"

"You forget, son, that I hear many things in my work as a minister, many things I don't even care to hear. The Winters don't attend our chapel, but they are friendly with some who do. Mrs. Winter is ambitious for her daughter. I doubt she will look with favor on a future minister."

"Well, Father, after what Cyrus has done, I doubt that Kate Winter herself will look with favor on me, or anyone else in our family," Ben said, unable to keep the bitterness from his tone. "So while I appreciate your words, I think they are unnecessary." He glanced sidelong at his father and saw pity on his face.

Ben could not bear it. "I'll see you at home," he tossed over his shoulder, and strode ahead, heedless of his aches and stiffness. His father stayed back and let him go on alone.

⸺•⸺

Kate had kept to her room for two days.

Tessie knocked and opened the door a crack. "Miss, would you like a cup of tea?"

"No thank you, Tessie." Kate sat in a chair turned toward the wall, a lap board balanced on her knees with a Greek reader atop it. Study had been her only respite from what had happened. She was struggling through a difficult Greek passage, but her mind kept wandering as the characters blurred before her tired eyes.

She sighed and let her head droop back against the high velvet back of the chair. The only small consolation was that her father had been away for much of the time since her return, though no one knew where. At least she did not have to fear for their safety in addition to everything else. And he would not learn what had happened at the musicale, with all its searing humiliation.

"Kate, I wish to speak with you." Her mother's dry voice cut the air of the room, and Tessie hurried out. Kate did not blame her.

"Yes, Mother." She turned in her chair and raised her head.

"I need to address the comments made by that Hanby boy," her mother said, her mouth tense and white. She gripped an embroidery frame as if unconscious of it in her hand.

It seemed irrelevant to inform her of Cyrus's name.

"He seemed to imply that you and his elder brother were courting."

Kate closed her eyes but then forced them open. She must not look guilty. She had done nothing wrong—but then, she had hidden the truth about aiding fugitives.

"I hope you haven't been conducting yourself shamelessly without my knowledge." Her mother twisted the embroidery work in her fingers.

Kate bit her lip. "No, Mother, I have no suitors other than the one you know of, Frederick Jones."

"Then why did that idiotic young man seem to think you did?"

"I do not know."

"Don't lie to me." Her mother's hands were so rigid they threatened to snap her embroidery frame in two.

Kate had not intended to lie, but it was a lie to pretend not to know. She did in fact know why Cyrus had said it. She must tell the truth, painful though it might be.

"I believe Cyrus Hanby thinks his brother is—attached—to me." Kate's hand shook at the top of her lap board. She laid the board aside on the small table next to her chair.

"Ben Hanby? Have you encouraged him in some way?" Her mother fired out the words like bullets.

"I don't believe I've done anything improper. I've exchanged no intimate words or promises with Ben Hanby. And I assure you that at this moment, I have not the slightest desire to see him ever again."

"Don't take that tone with me." Her mother's voice lowered the temperature of the room. "I'm delighted to hear you do not wish to keep company with Ben Hanby. He is not fit to court you. He will have no solid living. I forbid you to spend any more time in his company." Her mother stalked out of the room, stiff-backed.

A rush of nausea made Kate sink back against the chair and close her eyes. If she had not joined Ben Hanby's mission and sung in his musicale, none of this would have happened.

Could anyone see her admiration for him in her eyes? Did she show it? Would people believe that what Cyrus said was true? Any romantic attraction to Ben Hanby was foolish, schoolgirl thinking. Look where it had led her. Her most private feelings would become a subject of public discussion. She would have to walk through the town and endure speculations and whispered jokes.

Running away was no longer an option, now that she wished to finish at Otterbein and equip herself for helping others like Nelly. But she had more than enough reason to keep away from Ben Hanby, even without her mother's order.

Twenty-Three

"I WANT YOU TO TELL ME ABOUT KATE WINTER."
Frederick leaned over the counter on the saddle and harness side
of the Haynie & Hanby store.

Ben stopped in the act of hanging a harness on the display
rack. "What do you mean?" Frederick must mean the musicale.
That was rude of him. A flush rose up Ben's neck—he pulled at
his collar with an impatient movement.

"Oh, don't get yourself in a knot." Frederick grinned. "Of
course I'm not referring to what your brother said. I know you.
After all, I had first claim to Miss Winter, and I'm certain you
would never horn in on another man's affairs of the heart." He
sat down on the high stool, still elegant in his light linen summer coat.

"I don't think we should discuss the young lady," Ben said.

"Don't be such an old woman. You're my closest friend, and
I need a confidant." Light spilled into the store window, casting
a heroic light over Frederick, with his bronzed good looks and
his expensive clothing. "I plan to marry Miss Winter."

Ben looked at him for a long moment, then opened the
saddlery account ledger and ran his finger over the numbers. He

must not react in a way that would foment any talk about Miss Winter or make her the object of an open rivalry. "And will she agree with your plan?" he asked Frederick.

"I don't know. That's why I wish you to tell me about her state of mind. You spent time in her company on your return from Cincinnati, did you not?"

"Yes."

"Did she mention me?"

"No." He closed the ledger and took a breath.

"Oh." Frederick's face fell but then brightened again. "Did she mention anyone else who might hold a place in her heart?"

"No." The image of Nelly and her baby in the ferns rose up in his mind. Frederick had no idea who had a place in Kate's heart. Ben took a saddle from the wall rack and pretended to check the stitching in its gullet.

"I don't think I've ever seen you so glum," Frederick said. "You mustn't take what happened too hard. Yes, people will talk for a few weeks, but it will die down. And if she is seen with me a great deal, no one will remember it at all. Though I may have to do some convincing with Mother." He made a wry grimace. "But Miss Winter will make a perfect wife for a politician. She'll never say an inappropriate word in public."

At Ben's sharp look, Frederick added in a rush, "And, of course, she's beautiful and accomplished and I'd find it easy to be swept away by her."

The door to the street opened and the bell jingled.

"Hello, Ben!" Mr. Jones was all cheer and well-fed satisfaction. "Have you recovered from your expedition?" He strode in like a colossus, filling half the small store with his body and the rest with his voice.

"Yes, sir," Ben said. At least Mr. Jones had not asked about the musicale.

"Frederick told me you all looked mighty strange when you came back." Mr. Jones stopped smiling and his eyebrows quirked. "You weren't up to any shenanigans, were you?"

"No, sir." That was odd. He did not like to be questioned on the subject of the journey, and it seemed so long ago. Why had Mr. Jones brought it up?

"Good!" Mr. Jones clapped Ben on the shoulder, grinning again. "Has Frederick told you about our plan?"

Ben turned to his friend, who shook his sleek head a fraction. Not the same plan, apparently.

"No, sir," Ben said.

"It's a capital one. As a result of our visit to the club, Frederick has been invited to clerk in a lawyer's office and learn the profession to be certain it suits him."

"And I know it will," Frederick said.

"Yes, but you must finish at Otterbein before you turn lawyer," his father said. "At any rate, we've decided that Frederick must stay at school for at least the next academic year before taking a clerkship. But his place is assured."

"Very good, sir. My congratulations." He couldn't mourn his friend's departure too much, in light of what Frederick had just confided.

"But we have even better news," Frederick said, and looked at his father with an expectant glow.

"Indeed we do." Mr. Jones lowered his voice. "You may go this fall in Frederick's place, if you wish."

Ben laid the hole-punching tool down on the counter. "Sir?"

"The lawyer from the club was impressed by you as well.

And he works in a very large office. There will be more than one clerkship available in the future. I'll even help you with any necessary expenses. What a boon for you, eh?" He looked back and forth between them.

"Think of it, Ben," Frederick said. "You always take the fall semester off anyway, for your teaching. But now you could study for the law. The two of us might even work in the same office as partners one day. Magnificent."

"That is a very generous offer, Mr. Jones, from both you and the lawyer," Ben said.

The gray-haired man smiled. "You're a worthy young man. Besides which, you may find that study of the law changes your opinions for the better."

"I don't catch your meaning, sir."

"Oh, never mind all that. What do you think—will you go to the clerkship?"

Ben did not know where to begin. Perhaps with the practical considerations. "Mr. Jones, it's true that I usually take the fall term off—"

"Yes, it's perfect, you see." He beamed at Ben.

"But I do so in order to earn my tuition at Otterbein. By teaching schoolchildren in Rushville."

Mr. Jones waved a beefy hand. "Yes, yes, I know all that. But with my support and a clerk's stipend, you would save just as much to put toward your tuition."

"Yes, sir. I must consider it." He cast a staggered glance at the saddles, the leather, everything he and his father labored over to provide their family income. Mr. Jones could offer him entry into a professional living at ten times the earnings of a saddler, with a single wave of his hand.

"You must agree, Ben." Frederick jumped to his feet. "Shh." He raised a finger to forestall objection. "Think on it. There's a month until you need to give an answer."

A month would give Ben the time he needed.

"Opportunity knocks, Ben," Mr. Jones said, quiet for once, and kind. "Choose with care."

"I will, sir. And thank you," Ben said.

Think of all the abolition cases he might defend, like the man he had met, what was his name? Rutherford Hayes. All the good he could do. And he had always done well in oratory.

It was like being struck with a mallet on the head. He had never considered this other way—he had never needed to do so, being set on the ministry. And were it not for Kate Winter, he would still refuse to consider it.

Were it not for Kate Winter.

The bell jingled again and Amanda came in, neat in her summer hat and flowered dress. "Good afternoon." She gave them a friendly smile. "Ben, the mail." She put several envelopes on the counter. The top one jarred him with its familiar writing. It had to be from John Parker. He must read it—he could not wait. "Can you watch the store for me for a little while?" he asked his sister.

"Yes." She came around the counter.

"If you will excuse me, gentlemen," he said, and picked up the envelope. "I must attend to some correspondence."

Mr. Jones flicked his eyes to the envelope, but Ben covered it as he stepped toward the exit.

Mr. Jones stopped him with a raised hand. "We were just going—we won't keep you." He laid his hand on the door handle.

"And thank you again, Mr. Jones."

"My pleasure, son." He left and held the door for Frederick, who walked out with a good-bye to Ben and Amanda.

Ben let Amanda have the stool and stood at the counter. He slid a finger under the seal and opened the flap. He hesitated a moment before unfolding it and breathed a prayer for good news.

Ben,

We have missed Nelly and her baby on the northern end of the slave market. My informant was ill and unable to watch the Kentucky auctions for a few days. He will redouble his efforts to find where they may have been sold, and report back to us. But it will take time, and there is no guarantee of success. I have sent a letter to our contact in Canada to inform Frank of the news.

Yours sincerely,
John Parker

His heart plummeted and he lowered the letter with unsee-ing eyes.

"What is it?" Amanda asked, looking over his shoulder.

"Mr. Parker sends bad news about the woman we tried to help. The scout has lost the trail." Amanda was a young woman now, old enough to be party to everything their family did for the Railroad.

"I am sorry."

"We must find her—it can't happen again."

"What?"

"All of it." The loss of another fugitive—the separation of a husband and wife—the sale of a human soul for profit. He rubbed his forehead and turned away.

He must devise a way to get the word to Kate. Even if she were angry with Ben after the musicale, she would want to hear this. But he was certain that her mother would not receive him in their parlor. And with school out of session, he could not plan to encounter Kate between classes.

But wait—Cornelia had mentioned the other day that Kate was now taking piano lessons from her.

Cornelia would make a perfect go-between. He would ask her to give Kate the news in a discreet way.

Twenty-Four

"YOU HAVE IMPROVED." CORNELIA SMILED AT KATE as they sat together on the piano bench, their skirts spilling off the sides in rich folds.

"I feel like a child plunking away at the keys," Kate said. "But at least it will help me in our music class in the fall."

"Let me hear the gypsy scale one more time," Cornelia said.

Kate ran her fingers up and through the strange, Eastern accidentals. The minor key was a reflection of her mood, trapped as she was day after day in the Winter house with nothing to fill the dreary hours of summer recess. More than once, her resolve had wavered, and she had been tempted again by thoughts of running away, only to be stopped by her vow to finish at Otterbein.

It was worse than before—she was no longer permitted to ride out alone, but must go with Leah, which meant no secret gallops or jumping. And Leah did not even like to ride, so Kate had seldom been on Garnet's back in the last few weeks. She had only two respites from the prison of her home: her piano

211

lessons and buggy rides with Frederick on Sunday afternoons. And the latter, of course, were not comfortable, and less so anytime Frederick grew very complimentary and courtly.

"Excellent," Cornelia said. "We're finished. Would you like to stay for tea?"

"No thank you." Actually, Kate would like it more than anything, but her mother had stipulated that she return immediately after her lessons. Her mother didn't like the proximity of the Lawrences' home to the Hanbys' residence. All in all, it was probably best, for encountering Ben or his mother would be painful. Every day of July had been a lonely struggle between her wish to forget what had happened and her drive to know about Nelly and her baby girl, especially after the brief, bad tidings Ben had sent through her friend.

"Have you heard any more news?" she asked.

"About what Ben Hanby told me?" Cornelia took on a confiding air. "No, I'm afraid not. But he told me that he would communicate anything new as soon as he heard. I believe he was concerned for your peace of mind."

"He must have confidence in you to trust you as a messenger." She yearned to talk about what had happened to Nelly, but dared not confide in Cornelia completely. Ben might have told Cornelia only the two sentences she conveyed to Kate, and that was hardly the whole story.

"His father and mine have been friends in abolition for some time," Cornelia said. "Does this mean you are ready to forgive the Hanbys? Perhaps speak to Ben again?"

Kate rose in haste from the piano bench and walked away to get her straw hat.

"I'm sorry," Cornelia said. "I shouldn't have mentioned it."

No, she shouldn't have. Kate's worry for Nelly and desperation for better news had nothing to do with her feelings toward Ben—no one, not even Cornelia, would be privy to the humiliation that was still so raw and painful. And little did Cornelia know that Kate was forbidden to speak to Ben even if she wished it.

Kate tied the ribbon of her hat and wished her friend a short good-bye, unable to respond to the hurt in Cornelia's eyes.

———◦◦◦———

The milliner's window on State Street was not a place Kate wished to linger. "Leah, let's go, please."

Her sister fumbled with the ribbon around the hatbox that held her new hat. "I want to wear it."

"Don't be silly. You're already wearing a hat."

"I could change them. My straw one will fit in this box."

"It's not seemly to change hats in the street." Being near the milliner's shop haunted Kate. All the pretty curves, flowers, and ribbons of the hats made her think of her former self-centered plans, but also of Nelly.

Leah gave up tugging at the ribbon and grasped it in her hand instead to carry the box as she followed Kate. "I'm glad Father hasn't been home much," she said. "It's quieter."

"Have you wondered where he is?" Kate had, many times.

"In some drinking establishment or other." Leah's tone was hard, and Kate could not blame her.

It might be true—it probably was. But it was still sad to think of her father wandering Columbus, perhaps risking his health and his life with total inebriation. What would their lives be like if he stopped drinking? Imagining such a thing was difficult now. But when she was younger, he had not always smelled of liquor. He had given her a riding lesson when she was four or five, walking her around on a horse so large she sat on its back like a table. A year later, he bought her a pony. A huge smile spread across his bearded face as she flung her arms around its dappled gray neck. He lifted her in the air and embraced her with a laugh. But his drinking worsened and the riding lessons stopped. Leah did not have the benefit of such memories to counter the terrible ones.

"Oh dear," Leah said.

"What is it?"

"I can't find my coin purse." Leah twisted around as if it would materialize on the ground beneath her.

"You must have left it at the shop." Kate sighed. "We'll have to go back."

"Look," Leah said. She pulled out the lining of the concealed pocket of her skirt. It was torn.

"Leah!" What would she do next, show her petticoat?

Her sister ignored her. "It may have fallen out on our way. We should retrace our steps."

"Very well." They turned and scanned the road as they walked back. The little green coin purse was nowhere in sight. They had almost reached State Street.

"You must have left it on the counter," Kate said.

"We shall see." Leah flounced around the corner onto the main thoroughfare and stopped.

Ben Hanby stood on the street in front of the milliner's shop. He leaned down to pick up a small green object from the street and held it up, turning to look in the store window.

Kate could not move—he appeared so conscientious and good, standing there in his light coat and hat with the coin purse, considering what to do. He turned toward them and halted, the coin purse still upraised. He said nothing.

The feeling of his arm under her fingertips, his lean, strong artist's hand, came back to her with a rush. No—she should not want to go to him, speak with him. That way lay nothing but pain. And her mother had forbidden any association whatsoever.

"Were you looking for this?" He held it out in their general direction.

"It's mine," Leah said quickly, stepping forward to take it from him. But he was not looking at her, instead giving his full attention to Kate.

His dark eyes held some question she could not fathom. Without a word, she wrenched herself away and hurried in the opposite direction, leaving Leah to catch up as best she could. When she took one surreptitious glance over her shoulder, he was still standing there, looking after her.

Twenty-Five

AUGUST

BEN WOULD HAVE TO MAKE HIS DECISION THIS week—it hovered in his thoughts every hour, filled every quiet moment in the cellar while he was embossing and stitching leather. If he went to Cincinnati, would his choice encourage Kate to speak to him again? Was it her will or her mother's that had led her to cut him cold in the street? The sting of her silence had not faded even a month later.

"Bring me that small needle, will you?" Ben's father stood at the tallest saddle tree, threads pulled taut in his hands from the horn of a sidesaddle. "This one is too large for the holes."

They had been working on the sidesaddle for the first half of August, as its complex outlines and three horns required a great deal of measuring and stitching.

Ben brought the needle over and removed the larger one, then threaded the replacement for his father, whose left hand was still engaged in the second row of stitches.

His father took the new needle back in his right hand. "Thank you." He continued the double stitch, without rushing, checking to see that each lay flat and smooth.

"I'm considering an offer from Mr. Jones," Ben said. He walked back to the bench, seated himself, and picked up the awl and hammer.

"Indeed?"

"Frederick can't take a clerkship until next summer, so Mr. Jones has suggested I go clerk in his place, in a law office in Cincinnati."

"I see." His father paused and looked at him. "And would this alter your choice of profession?"

"Yes, should I choose to accept."

His father looked back at the saddle and continued stitching.

"What do you think?" Ben asked.

"I am surprised."

"Why?"

"You've indicated to me more than once that you wish to go into the ministry. Your choice is your own, but I hope it will be made with wisdom."

"I met a man in Cincinnati who defends fugitives from the Fugitive Slave Act. He attempts to win their freedom."

"One case at a time."

"Yes."

His father tied off the row of stitches with a practiced twist and knot. He reached for his pocketknife and trimmed the end. "Do you remember the friend I once told you about, the doctor who lived next door to my master in Pittsburgh?"

"Dr. Loftin?" The old stories had made a permanent impression.

"Yes. He came to visit us in Rushville from time to time, after we left Pittsburgh. He once asked us how we felt about making saddles with this third horn." His father touched the leaping horn. "You know it has increased the stability of the ladies' seats for jumping during hunts."

"Yes."

"The doctor didn't like it. In his practice, he saw many women injured or killed on the hunt when they fell with their horses. The horn ensured they were seated so firmly they could not get out of their saddles."

"I've read of such things," Ben said.

"But the doctor never tried to persuade us against putting the leaping horns on our saddles."

"Why not?"

"He knew the customers wanted it, and he knew they would not agree to adopt a style that seemed less secure. It was a problem that could only be addressed by a change of heart—to be truly safe, ladies must ride astride as men do, and the doctor knew that would take many years—that it might not happen in his lifetime. But he continued to work for the cause, to speak to medical students, to spread the word."

"I take your point—you're drawing a comparison to abolition. But it's a false analogy, Father. Human beings are not saddles."

"That's true. And I don't mean to imply that. But I'm concerned that you're losing sight of your larger calling, in your desire for an easy road to worldly happiness."

"What do you mean?" Ben wasn't sure he wanted to hear the answer.

"You wish to see the end of slavery?"

"Of course, more than anything."

"And do you think that with your gifts, the best you can do is defend one fugitive at a time, often losing your cases to a biased court system?"

"They say I'm a good speaker."

"And you are. But is your calling to the law?"

Ben fell silent and began to strike holes in the stirrup leather on the bench.

"Your calling is to the ministry, son. I know it, and I believe you know it, for you have told me so. You mustn't give that up for what you believe is a chance at earthly happiness. Giving up your calling will never lead to happiness, no matter what you may gain as a result."

"But the work will be similar, in many ways. Both require the use of rhetoric and careful study of human nature." Ben struck holes faster, harder.

"It will not be similar. How would you use your musical gifts as a lawyer? There's no possible way. But as a minister, there are innumerable ways you might use it. The Lord suits a man's calling to his gifts. I believe there's a purpose for your ability as a composer."

"What possible purpose could it serve?" His voice rose. If he lost this debate, he would forfeit his one chance with Kate.

"I don't know yet. But I believe your gifts are called to a larger battle than simply one legal case after another, or one fugitive after another."

"You are a fond father and you overestimate my powers." Ben aimed and struck, aimed and struck. He would finish the whole stirrup leather in a few minutes at this rate. "I couldn't even save one woman and her baby—John still hasn't found them."

"Ben." His father walked toward him and stopped a few steps away, his deep-set eyes darker in the lamplight of the cellar. "I believe we will see the end of slavery in our lifetimes. And you have a role to play in that struggle that does not involve legal briefs and evenings at the gentlemen's club."

Ben positioned the awl and struck very hard, taking his frustration into the blow. Now he had spoiled it—the hole was off center. With a muffled imprecation, he jumped up and threw the leather in the corner. "Why must I be called to this? Why a gift in music, of all things, that will not bring me a living to support a wife! Why a talent for teaching? I am heartily sick of my gifts if they keep me from the thing that is dearest to me!" He kept his voice down with great effort, to a hoarse whispered shout. The girls upstairs must not hear.

"It isn't your gifts that stand between you and what you think most dear. It's your passion and your calling. And painful as it is, I must tell you the truth," his father said with equal conviction, his shoulders tense. "I do not say you'll never win the woman you love—no matter who she may be. But you must not abandon your mission to do it. If you do, both of you will always regret such a life, only half lived."

Ben threw the tools after the leather strap, where they clanged into one another and the wall. "I can't speak of this any further." He whirled around and strode up the stairs, out through the kitchen past the girls, and down the stoop into the light rain. The spatter of drops against his face could not soothe the pain of having the truth dragged from his own spirit into the light of day.

He could not accept the offer. And by giving it up, he might lose any chance with Kate.

If she wished to learn to speak in public, she had to begin somewhere. Kate stood on the feed box and turned to face her listener.

"On the Purpose of True Friendship," she said. "An Argument Drawn from Aristotle and Cicero."

Garnet blinked her moist brown eyes and leaned her neck on the stall door, watching Kate with the peculiar calm of the equine race. The rain pattered on the roof of the barn.

"Can a true friendship spring from self-interest?" Kate asked. Garnet flicked her ears forward and nickered softly.

What came next? Oh yes. She cleared her throat. "Aristotle says self-interest cannot create the highest friendship. The only perfect friendship is between two persons of equally good character who are drawn together by admiration."

Garnet tossed her head as if agreeing. This wasn't so difficult. Kate stepped off the feed box and onto the packed earth, to pace before Garnet. "The vast majority of friendships are based on pleasure, not virtue." She turned to look at the mare. "Oh yes, for you cannot convince me that your equine eye fell upon me without knowledge of the apple in my pocket. And I know your affection for me is predicated in part upon the hope of future such apples." Kate smiled.

Garnet was losing interest, eyes wandering, ears sideways. Kate flourished her hand in the air to attract her horse's gaze again. "It is true that certain types of friendship exist between persons who are not equal." She layered her voice with pedantry, amusing herself. "Parents and children, teachers and pupils. Yea, verily, even between a mistress and her mare." She waved her finger at Garnet's muzzle. The mare took a tentative nip toward the carrot-like offering, and Kate snatched it back.

"But the true aim of friendship should be to nurture the same good character which first drew friends together." Now she was back to the real text of her speech. She should try to imagine Garnet as a human listener. She would envision Garnet as—whom? Professor Hayworth. Garnet's whiskers were not nearly full enough.

Kate held up both hands in rhetorical emphasis, as she had seen the young men do in their orations. If she could bring some exaggerated expression to her speech now, traces of it might linger when she faced a more frightening audience. "Cicero reminds us"—she raised her arms even higher, as if she spoke to a whole amphitheater—"that solitary virtue cannot rise to the same height as virtue acting in conjunction with an affectionate and pleasing companion."

"Hear, hear," a masculine voice said from the barn doorway.

She dropped her hands and spun around. Frederick stood watching her, grinning, handsome in a navy pin-striped linen coat and cream-colored trousers.

"Oh," she said.

"You spoke very well." He walked toward her and took off his hat to cradle it in his arm. The sunlight behind him outlined his hair.

"I must look very silly."

"Not at all—you look charming, as usual."

The waves of heat across her face could ignite the hay in the loft.

"I know what you're up to," he said, smiling. "You're teaching yourself to speak, aren't you?"

"Yes."

"I think it's a capital idea to practice to your horse."

She could not respond, rooted there to the straw-littered floor.

"Maybe I can assist you. You were quite at ease before. Now what if I sit here with your horse and you try again?" He went to the plain bench by the wooden wall and seated himself, long legs stretched out and crossed at the ankle, a picture of perfect gentlemanly repose for a lazy summer's day.

"I don't know." Her heart pattered in her chest, faster and faster.

"Come." His hazel eyes were kind. "I'd be glad to think I had helped. Look at your horse and pretend I'm not here."

"All right." She took a breath and gathered her thoughts, staring at Garnet's forelock. "On the Purpose of True Friendship: An Argument Drawn from Aristotle and Cicero." She turned to Frederick. "It's really such a simple topic—I'm ashamed to give it."

"Nonsense. It's true and accurate, and that's enough. Please continue."

His face was distracting—she could not recall the next thought and stood fiddling with her skirt.

He didn't seem taken aback. "Maybe you should begin again and avoid stopping. It's harder to remember if you stop."

"Or maybe this is foolhardy."

"No backing down now," he said. "Your secret practice out here tells me it's important to you to speak, and that is a fine aim. You have exceptional thoughts, and you should share them."

"I care little whether I express my own opinions," she said. "But I would like to speak on behalf of others."

"Even better. An admirably feminine sentiment. After all, who will intercede for your future children, if not you?"

The intimacy of it made her blush hotter, but he presumed too much. She did not have such feminine goals in mind—in fact, speaking up about people like Nelly would be quite the opposite of what Frederick implied.

Now her mind was focused. "On the Purpose of True Friendship . . ." She launched into the speech and hurried through, not looking at him. Before she knew it, she had finished.

"Brava!" he said. He stood and bowed to her. "You see, you can be quite eloquent. And no need to ever attempt a topic that might be too much for you. All you must do is satisfy the professor's requirements, and then you never need speak in public again." He smiled. "Only to servants or tutors, or perhaps a husband."

She forced herself to smile.

"Are you ready to ride? Your habit is quite smart." He admired her from hat to boots. "And Garnet is ready, I see."

"Yes."

"I'll lead her out for you." He slid the bolt and took the reins over the mare's head. "After you."

She preceded him out. Strange how in Frederick's company, she never felt fully present. His attention was flattering and his admiration clear, but he never looked at her as Ben Hanby did, with that close attention that made her feel more solid and real and alive. Instead, Frederick himself seemed larger than life, which made it more difficult to talk to him.

But he had been gracious to try to help her. And now she would get to ride for an hour. He would entertain her with constant talk, and he wouldn't notice if her thoughts should wander. Her mother approved of him, so she would be mollified for the day. And her father's opinion would not matter—he was hardly at home. Though he was no longer absent for days on end, he had settled into a regular pattern of returning late at night after the women had retired. She suspected he was sleeping in his study. On the few occasions she had seen him, he was unable to meet her eyes. But if he was ashamed of what he had done, one thing had not changed—he still smelled of bourbon.

Frederick assisted her to mount from the block, then stepped up into his own saddle with strength and agility. As the horses walked out through the yard, a hermit thrush whistled in the trees.

Twenty-Six

IT WAS TOO COLD TO GET OUT OF BED. BUT BEN must get to the schoolhouse well before his students arrived. Rolling out of his blanket to his feet, he grabbed his folded clothing from the plank shelf that graced the cabin wall. He donned his trousers, shucked off his nightshirt, and yanked on his shirt, vest, and coat as quickly as possible. He pulled on low boots over his woolen socks and blew on his hands. It was only the end of September. Imagine how cold it would be next month. He would need to keep a fire banked through the night. A dilapidated iron stove stood in the tiny cabin, but last night he had not wanted to waste the wood to light it.

The town council had told him he would instruct forty students. That was rather a lot, but he would have to make do. They were paying him seventy-five dollars for eleven weeks, which was better wages than most towns offered. At least the hard work would keep his mind off Kate Winter, or so he hoped.

He must not dwell on her—as his father had said, if he wanted to see the end of slavery, he had to change hearts. But Rushville seemed a lonely and unlikely place to find God's plan for his work, especially while Frederick was taking Kate for buggy rides in Westerville.

He picked up his knapsack and checked to be sure his teaching materials were in it, then added his Bible to the heavy load of paper and pencils. With a heave, he balanced the knapsack on his shoulders and pulled the rickety door of the cabin closed behind him.

Frost whitened the short grass as he walked through the trees toward the building. There it was. The one-room school had been a place of fear for Ben as a six-year-old. Mr. Morgan, the schoolmaster, was demanding and hot-tempered. Early in the term, he had given all the students the task of learning the multiplication tables in one weekend. When they returned on Monday, he stood behind each of them holding a long switch as they recited the tables. Whenever a trembling boy or girl made an error, he lashed their legs mercilessly with his switch. Then he mocked them and told them to resume their seats. Ben had memorized with all his might, but twelve multiplication tables in two days was too much for a six-year-old. His legs were covered in red welts by the time he finished. He hid the stripes from his parents, ashamed of his performance.

Ben wouldn't be bringing a switch to class, that much was certain. Whipping was a barbaric way to educate children. Instead, he would run a calm and orderly classroom, just as he had in Blendon Township—a classroom in which learning was not driven by fear.

The stoop of the schoolhouse sagged to one side, the wood

rotted. The door hung from one hinge and dragged on the ground. Once-whitewashed boards had turned grayish brown.

Inside were similar signs of neglect. Four long tables were rough and scarred. At least two of the benches sported broken or missing legs, and cracks webbed the blackboard. What a shame, as it couldn't be more than a few years old—blackboards were only now spreading through country schools.

The walls were covered with writing and drawings. As he moved closer to peer at them, it slowly dawned on him that many of the scribbles were obscene.

He could not educate children in this building. And yet they had been regarding this filth every day for the past year, and the tabletops were similarly defiled. Who had permitted this? He scanned the room in vain for something to cover the obscenities.

Voices rose outside—the children were coming. Setting his knapsack on the small pine desk at the front of the classroom, he arranged his supply of papers and pencils to look neat, despite the apparent uselessness of such a gesture in this room. He positioned the tall stool beside the desk and sat on it just as the first students walked through the sagging door.

At least ten of them came in at once, scattering to take seats all around the room. They were unkempt and dirty, from the smallest girl to the hulking big boy who had immediately seized the spot in the farthest corner of the classroom.

"Good morning," Ben said. "I'm Mr. Hanby."

They gave him curious stares but no response. More students began to come in, some clean and neatly dressed, others as dirty and ragged as the first group. Holes showed in some of the shoes now ranged under the benches. Forty children had assembled, and a steady, loud buzz of chatter filled the air. It was time to begin. He prepared to call them to attention, waiting for the last group to sit.

Even as he paused, the procession of children continued. He started counting silently. Forty-six, forty-seven, forty-eight . . . they would never fit! And how would he teach so many? He struggled to keep his expression impassive. Fifty-three, fifty-four, fifty-five, fifty-six. At last, the parade reached an end. Children lined up along the walls, poking each other and laughing. Some of the boys were almost as tall as Ben, though he knew they could not be above sixteen.

Gradually the noise quieted. Almost sixty children regarded their new instructor, some with devilish glee, others with worry. Ben only had a few minutes before the rebellion started. Some of the smallest ones goggled at the drawings on the tables and walls.

He stood up and walked slowly to the space in front of the blackboard.

"My name is Mr. Hanby." *Lord, give me the words.* "This is not a fit place for you to learn." Surprise stole over many faces. "We need to make it better. Let us begin in prayer." The younger students folded their hands along with him, curiosity more evident on their faces than reverence. Some of the older boys looked at each other with derision, but Ben ignored them.

"Father in heaven . . ." He kept his eyes open—the Lord did not need him to close his eyes and risk pranks. "These are your children. Many of them have hard lives at home, and this school may be their only avenue out of hardship." Silence blanketed the room. "Help us make the school a safe, clean refuge from our troubles. In the name of our Savior, I ask these things and trust that you will provide. Amen."

"Amen," echoed the children.

A rough-looking boy with blond hair and buckteeth called from the back, "God ain't gonna do nothing for you or for us! He ain't never done nothing so far, so why would he start now?"

"What's your name? You may sit, children," he added to the rest, who did as they were told, some sitting on the floor with their backs to the wall.

The boy glared at Ben. "Jimmy."

"Well, Jimmy, you are entitled to your own beliefs. But you must raise your hand before speaking in class."

Jimmy and the other children regarded him with amazement. A little dark-haired girl slowly raised her hand.

"You have a question, young lady?"

"Ain't you gonna whip him, mister?"

"No, I'm not. I leave that decision to your parents. This is a schoolhouse, not a prison."

"Then I'm leaving!" Jimmy blurted. He walked to the door. "None of us big ones are gonna come back anyhow. We just come to see the new teacher."

"Yeah," a couple of the older boys echoed. A herd of them went out the door, including all but one of the big boys and a couple of the medium-sized ones to boot.

Ben's class was reduced to fifty, at most. The parents would complain against him.

He disguised his sense of failure by turning to the remaining students. "Line up at the door, please."

With much rustling and chatter, the children bunched together, the room being too small to allow an organized line. Ben moved to the front of the little mob. "Follow me, and be careful on the stoop." He led them out.

The school stood adjacent to the village marketplace. As Ben rounded the corner of the school building, women in the market set out their produce and jellies for sale. Now that the harvest was over and the weather so cold, most of the fruits and vegetables were dried or in jars.

Everyone in the marketplace watched the schoolmaster and his many charges. Ben led the throng past the curious women and onto Main Street, which would take them to the shops in the heart of Rushville.

He felt a tug on his coat.

"Mister . . . mister . . ." A little girl skipped to keep up with him.

He slowed down for her. "It's Mr. Hanby." He smiled. "What is it?"

"Where are we going?"

"You'll see in a moment." This girl was one of the smallest, probably six or seven. Her brown hair was plaited in two long braids that fell over her shoulders, and she had a cherubic face with upturned nose and huge blue eyes. "What's your name?" he asked her.

"Jane."

"Jane, do you have a last name?" he asked, teasing.

"Yes, sir, it's Lefort." She rambled on in the single-minded way of young children. "My daddy says you're not a good man. But I like you." Her eyes were bright with hero worship.

The Leforts must be one of the families his father had mentioned. Naturally, the pro-slavery families would remember the Hanbys less than fondly. And with a surname like Lefort, he guessed that this family had Louisiana roots.

"I like you too, Jane," he said. He looked over his shoulder and saw an older girl following a few steps behind. She had the same chestnut-colored hair and blue eyes, though she looked somber. "Are you Jane's sister?"

"Yes, sir."

"And what's your name?" He projected as much goodwill as he could.

"Sally Lefort." She quickened her step and came forward to take her little sister's hand. She looked as if she would like to drag the little girl away from Ben, but daren't be so rude. She put a little more space between them as they walked.

"Well, Miss Sally, I will need your help in a moment. I hope you have strong arms."

"Yes, sir."

They walked within view of the town center.

The Sumners still ran the general store in Rushville. As the large posse of children approached it, a boy ran up to the front of the group and addressed Ben.

"That's my father's store," he said. "Are we going in?"

"Your father is Ted Sumner?" he asked the boy.

"Yes. I'm Stuart." The young boy was as well groomed as the Lefort girls, but mischievous looking, with white-blond hair sticking up in a cowlick above his forehead.

"I've known your family since I was a boy," Ben said. He climbed one step to the store porch and paused to speak to the children. "Stay outside and behave yourselves like ladies and gentlemen, if you please. Stuart and Sally, come with me."

In the musty dimness of the store, Ted Sumner perched on a stool behind the counter, scratching figures in a ledger. At the sound of customers, he looked up.

"Ben! What brings you here?" He saw the children come in

behind Ben and understanding dawned in his eyes. "Ah. How may I help you, *Mr. Hanby*?" He winked. Like his son, he was blond, but his hair had thinned at the temples.

"Good morning, Mr. Sumner," Ben said with equal formality. "We need some whitewash and brushes. About five gallons, and—let's see," he said, taking out his wallet, "how much are the brushes?"

"One dollar each," Ted replied. "And seventy-five cents a gallon for the whitewash."

Ben disguised a wince. He only had ten dollars to last two weeks, until he received the first installment of his teaching wages. "Will you consider a discount for a good cause, Mr. Sumner?"

"Let me hazard a guess," Ted said. "You're whitewashing the schoolhouse?"

Ben nodded.

"Then I'll let you have them at cost. Fifty cents per gallon and the same per brush."

"Thank you." He calculated rapidly in his head. "I'll take six brushes with the whitewash."

"That'll be five-fifty. And thank you, Mr. Hanby, for taking on the task. That building is a disgrace." He added, "I'd have done the job myself, but there was no point as long as your predecessor was here. As you can see for yourself, there wasn't any order in the classroom. Plenty of thrashing, but no order."

Ben paid for his purchases and divided the load between Sally and Stuart. He said his good-byes to Ted and ushered the children back out on the porch. In the street, the boys chased the girls. It took five minutes to restore order and get the children on the road.

But back at the schoolhouse, the children cooperated, excited about their unusual school day. He sent half of them home, with special instructions. They returned bearing a few decorative odds and ends they had wheedled from their parents: some old but decent green curtains, several samplers cross-stitched with Bible verses, and even an amateur landscape painting. In the meantime, the other children scrubbed the filth from the walls and tables with old rags and buckets full of water. What would not come clean was covered with whitewash by a group of little painters, who followed after the cleaners once the surfaces had dried.

Day was almost over by the time the work was finished. The children left, tired but thrilled by the results of their labor—a sparkling white building and classroom, still with a crooked front stoop and sagging door, but transformed in the rest of its appearance. Tomorrow, when the whitewash dried completely, they would tack the curtains neatly over the window and hang the painting proudly with the samplers. As the sun went down, Ben surveyed his building with satisfaction. Tomorrow, he could teach here. A pale reddish light glowed through the window, making the classroom seem homey despite the smell of whitewash. Ben looked out the window at the sun setting through the trees. What was Kate doing? The fall term was in progress at Otterbein. Was she studying?

He gathered his things and headed for his solitary cabin. The last time he saw Kate, on the street in Westerville, her face had gone blank and still. He couldn't expect her to recover from such a public scene and treat him as if nothing had ever happened. But she had walked away as if he were a complete stranger. He couldn't stand it. There must be something he could do to help her forgive him. Because if he couldn't be near her, he certainly couldn't expect . . . but he would think on it no further. It was bad enough as it was, without dwelling on the complicated mess of desires that lurked inside him.

He could apply one remedy immediately. When he walked into the cabin, he retrieved a pen, inkhorn, and paper from his small stock of supplies, and sat down to write Kate a letter.

Dear Miss Winter, he wrote, then stopped.

How would he send it to her? Her mother would refuse to give it to her, after what had happened. Well, he would send it through Cornelia, as he had passed the message about Nelly.

Perhaps there was some hope. He began to set words on the page, writing the best apology he knew how to make.

Twenty-Seven

October

My dear Miss Winter,

    I am tardy in sending this letter only because my great respect for you convinced me that words were inadequate to express my regret for what happened at the musicale. But I find myself compelled to write to you nonetheless because your happiness is of great import to me. I cannot bear to think of you suffering due to the actions of a member of my family. If my sincere apology can help in any way, I offer it to you wholeheartedly. My admiration for your character increased during the time in which I was privileged to observe your compassion and courage. I hope you will one day find it in your heart to forgive, so we may resume the friendship that began through our mutual love of music.

                              Yours,

                              Ben Hanby

She could not expunge the words from her mind—she shouldn't have read the letter more than once. In fact, she should not have read it at all. Now she was even more distracted than usual, even though she had hidden the letter back at her home.

"Miss Winter?" Frederick stood with hand uplifted to help her step down from his buggy. The Joneses' footman stood in uniform at the bottom of the steps to the mansion. Leaves tumbled across the drive in the rising fall breeze.

She murmured an apology and took his hand to make her descent.

Frederick escorted her through the broad front doorway, making no attempt to hide his proud pleasure in doing so. The butler took Kate's light cape and Frederick's hat.

Mrs. Sapphia Jones waited in the parlor as if her greatest pleasure was to greet her son's college friends. Of course, her presence as chaperone was necessary for the party of college students that would arrive soon. She took Kate's hand and then seated herself in a delicate carved chair. Her silver skirt gleamed like mercury where the lamplight touched it. It pooled around her chair like the base of a statue, an effect enhanced by her blond, symmetrical countenance. "I am enjoying the cooler weather. And you, Miss Winter?" Her gentle voice reminded Kate of Ann Hanby, though it was like comparing a magnolia and a rose. Mrs. Jones was sweeter and more lavish compared to the simple sincerity of Mrs. Hanby.

"Yes, thank you, Mrs. Jones," Kate replied.

"Frederick," Mrs. Jones said. "I believe your father wishes to speak to you."

A flicker of chagrin touched his eyes before he stood, the dutiful son. "Yes, Mother. And where is he?"

"In the study. Perhaps you will accompany us in that direction and I will show Miss Winter the library?" Again, the white, soft, perfumed voice. It would be the same in all settings, Kate thought, from parlor to church to funeral home. Perfectly pitched, unchangeable.

"Certainly." He inclined his head, a little stiff, and offered Kate his arm again. His mother followed them as they proceeded down the hallway. Through the glass double doors to their left, Kate saw the white bulk of Mr. Jones sitting behind a desk, like a great caterpillar ensconced in the woody heart of a tree.

"I will rejoin you soon," Frederick said in a low voice, and with a bow, withdrew through the doors and closed them.

"Come, Miss Winter. The library is much more congenial than that gloomy study my husband frequents." Mrs. Jones led her to the next door on the left, which opened into a warm room lit by a wavering fire behind a black iron screen. Red wallpaper accented the dark walnut shelves full of books that stretched from the fringes of area rugs to the crown molding that edged the ceiling. Kate's spirits lifted at the sight. "What a lovely room."

"Thank you."

The faint echo of the front doorbell came down the hall.

"If you don't mind," Mrs. Jones said, "I'll leave you to browse our reading selections. More guests are arriving."

"Yes, ma'am." Nothing would delight Kate more.

Mrs. Jones went out and the sound of her skirt and heels receded. Kate walked to the nearest shelf and gazed upward. So many books, hundreds. Her own family library only contained fifty volumes, and she did not use it often because it was situated in her father's study. Here were Homer, Caesar, Josephus, Aristotle, Plutarch, Ovid—all covered in deep-dyed leathers of blue, green, and brown. Tomes of natural history and American records. A *Webster's Dictionary*. She ran her fingers along the spines, tingling with the pleasure of the masses of titles, the pristine condition of the bindings with their gilt lettering.

A murmur of voices emanated from somewhere behind the books. It grew louder as she walked toward the far corner of the room and a closed door that must lead to the adjacent study. Now she recognized Frederick's voice. ". . . shouldn't interfere."

She should go stand on the other side of the library. Eavesdropping was wrong.

". . . but Ben won't refrain. You know he won't," came Mr. Jones's voice in reply

She halted in midstep.

"Father, is that really our concern? He's in Rushville."

They were speaking of Ben Hanby. An intuition held her in place. She moved a step toward the closed door, where the sound of their voices trickled around the door frame.

"We still have many friends in Rushville, Frederick. And Ben is teaching the children of the town—I fear he'll teach them abolition. He is his father's son. What else does Hanby preach but divisive politics?"

"Ben is my closest friend. He is honorable, and you have said so yourself."

A thump of his fist on the desk made her start. "Son, don't contradict me—this is hard enough as it is! Why do you think Ben refused our offer of the clerkship? Perhaps he didn't want to stop his illegal activities—there's no other reason a man would refuse such an opportunity. His refusal lends credence to the rumor that the Hanbys run fugitive slaves across the state, though I don't want to believe it. I can forgive Ben, who is a good boy led astray by his father. But I can't let him go teach there without warning my friends, just in case. They must keep watch on him. These are children he's teaching, and early impressions sink deep."

"Yes, sir."

"I need you to send a letter to Ben tomorrow, advising him subtly to be wise in his conduct. And I'll send a letter of my own to Mr. Lefort."

"I don't think Ben will teach the children anything he shouldn't, sir, but I'll do as you wish."

"Do you believe in the Union, son?"

"Yes, sir."

"Good lad. Then humor your old man in this. And go enjoy your party."

"Thank you, sir."

She heard the door of the study open and hurried to peruse the opposite wall of the library. Her dismay made the book titles dim and irrelevant to her. What would happen to Ben?

"Miss Winter." Frederick stood at the library threshold. "Do you like our collection?" He came in.

At that moment, his mother appeared in the doorway behind him and dazzled both of them with her all-occasions smile. "Miss Lawrence and the other young ladies are here, and some young gentlemen are arriving, I believe."

"Then we will join them." Frederick shrugged off the shadow on his face and his good nature reemerged like a cork popping to the surface of a pond. "Miss Winter, if I may?"

All of the Philomatheans and Philalethians would attend tonight except for the two Hanbys. Ben was out of town, of course, and Frederick had made it clear that he wouldn't invite Cyrus, out of consideration for her feelings.

Not all of them would be Kate's ideal choices for company, but at least Cornelia was here. She took Frederick's arm and followed Mr. Jones to the parlor.

A noisy buzz announced that all the young people were present, though they had arranged themselves decorously into male and female groups. After a few minutes by the great tapestry in the parlor, Mrs. Jones called them to dinner.

Frederick sat across from Kate, and his eyes lit up every time he looked at her. She couldn't cast off the lingering worry of his strange conversation with his father. Still, at least no one seemed to be thinking of the musicale.

After a delicious custard dessert, Frederick pushed back his chair and regarded his guests with anticipation. "Let's adjourn to the parlor and play a game."

The others agreed to the plan. In a few minutes, they were all arranged in velvet chairs and settees in the large parlor.

"Charades," one of the young men proposed, his thin face eager for fun.

Kate didn't want to act things out. But when she softly declined to play, the others promised her she could just be part of the guessing game without having to pantomime.

"Well, we must have five on each side," Frederick said. "I appoint myself a team captain, and, Rebecca, you can be the other," he said to Rebecca Bogler, who preened at the attention. "But I will claim the first team member," he said. "Kate, of course. Come sit next to me." He patted the empty space on the chaise longue he occupied. Too close for Kate's comfort, and it wouldn't have passed at Otterbein, but she did enjoy the feeling of company, as long as she didn't have to speak too much. It eased the isolation of her own home.

Rebecca winked beneath her blond curls. "Then I must choose a man." She pointed at the thin-faced one. He crossed the parlor and made a point of sitting at Rebecca's feet.

"Where we men should always be, eh, Rebecca?" he said.

Frederick chose Cornelia as their next teammate and soon they were all divided into teams.

The first round went well. They laughed as Rebecca pantomimed working at something that seemed to be a bellows, then dramatically raised her hand to shield her eyes and peered across the room.

"A blacksmith!" someone said.

"No!" she said, redoubling her peering actions.

"A train engineer!" the thin young man said.

"No!" Rebecca pumped her imaginary bellows with fury as sand ran through the little hourglass.

"Time's up!" Cornelia said.

"It was a balloonist!" Rebecca said with mock annoyance.

They all laughed.

"You'll have to do much better than that, I'm afraid," Frederick said with glee.

He was next to act out. He assumed a look of comical terror, and Rebecca shrieked with giggles. Kate had to chuckle too, as he pretended to hide behind a chair, shaking violently and chattering his teeth together with a snapping noise.

"A snapping turtle!" Rebecca guessed.

"He's not on your team," the thin young man said, laughing.

"A frightened skeleton!" Cornelia said, in the teasing spirit.

The sand ran out.

"No!" Frederick said, grinning at them. "It's a runaway slave!"

Carried away by the moment, Rebecca and the others guffawed. Cornelia stayed quiet, and Kate looked away.

She should object. But it would be so rude. Here she had hardly said a word, and she thought to criticize her host?

But she was ashamed of her silence nonetheless. Mrs. Hanby would not have placed politeness above principle.

As the laughter faded, Frederick looked uncertain. "Miss Winter, will you help me retrieve something from the library? We will return immediately."

Her cheeks burned. Mrs. Gourney would not approve. But she stood. He was a gentleman, and she would not embarrass him by noting the impropriety of it.

He did not offer his arm, as if conscious of his transgression against manners.

Once they were down the hall and out of earshot of the others, he turned to her as they walked. "Please accept my apology for my part in the charades."

She summoned her courage. "I must tell you," she said in a low voice, "that I do not think fugitive slaves are a subject for humor."

"I know, I know. I chose the first thing that came to mind. It was in poor taste."

"I don't mean to be rude. I appreciate your hospitality tonight."

"It's always a pleasure for me to entertain guests, but especially you." He spoke softly as well, and more intimately than he had before. She gazed ahead, mute as usual.

They were doing nothing wrong. Frederick had always been respectful to her, and she had no reason not to trust him.

He led her back into the small library, where she stood uncertain in the center while he stepped toward the fire, then turned to face her.

"Kate," he said. His clean-cut, golden face was serious, his eyes catching the flickering firelight. "You know that I care very much for you," he said.

Her heart jumped and she crossed her arms over her bodice. He must not do this—was this why he had wanted privacy?

"Frederick." Sapphia Jones stood in the door of the library. "I believe your guests are calling for you in the parlor."

Thank goodness. Oh, thank heaven for interfering mothers, just this once.

He looked like a schoolboy whipping his hand out of the cookie jar and jumping back. "Yes, Mother. I was simply—"

"I know Miss Winter is an admirer of books. In fact, I did not have a chance to show her some of the best. I will stay with her a moment and then we will join you."

He nodded again, discomfort tightening his features as he turned. "Pardon me, Miss Winter." He inclined his head and walked out into the darker hall.

What a horrible situation, humiliating and strange. Perhaps his mother also thought Frederick had been about to propose. She might even have been watching from some alcove as they walked down the hall. But her interruption would mean she objected to Kate. And was that a result of what had happened at the musicale? Kate's face burned.

"May I join you for a moment?" Mrs. Jones walked in.

"Yes, ma'am."

"We have the loveliest books here. I thought I would show you these in particular. So well made, so helpful."

Kate crossed to Mrs. Jones, who ran her finger down a shelf close to the fireplace. The older woman took a volume down, sliding it out with a gracefully angled wrist.

"You see?" She handed it to Kate.

A Young Lady's Book of Manners.

If Kate had not been so shocked, she might have cried.

"You are welcome to borrow it if you wish." The same magnolia floweriness marked her voice, but it was sharp and unpleasant, like perfume tasted instead of smelled.

"I believe I have a copy at home, but thank you." Kate forced it out in a mumble.

"Indeed?" Mrs. Jones's voice did not rise, but her eyebrows did.

"Excuse me." Kate hurried to the door and out into the hallway.

There was no reason for Mrs. Jones to dislike her, save for the musicale and Cyrus Hanby's insinuation. The young people might think nothing of what had been said, but Kate was not to be forgiven so easily by the town gossips.

She kept her head down, and she did not speak for the rest of the evening. She left with Cornelia and did not look at Frederick as she made her good-byes.

Twenty-Eight

DECEMBER

HOW LONG WOULD IT BE BEFORE JOHN PARKER SENT news? Ben sighed and knelt in front of the schoolhouse stove to throw in a piece of wood. The children would arrive soon. He returned to his desk and finished scratching a line or two onto the paper. He would finish the song about Nelly, since he could do nothing else for her until John found her.

The children stomped on the porch, and Ben put down the pen and went to the blackboard. He always began the school day by writing a new song on the blackboard for the children. Today they were singing "Oh Dear, What Can the Matter Be?" so he scrawled the lyrics with quick jabs of the chalk.

He liked to see the joy in their faces when they sang. Even Jimmy joined in with zeal. Ben was sure that music had everything to do with Jimmy's choice to return to the classroom. Once the ringleader decided to attend, his older friends had come back with him. They all had come in now and seated themselves, half of them talking, the others staring at the lyrics or mouthing them silently.

He tapped his ruler on the desk and, in the hush, started the song. Their light voices lifted in the jolly chorus, "Oh dear, what can the matter be?" The song ended and they looked at him expectantly.

"We can sing one more, then we'll begin our reading," Ben said. "Would anyone like to suggest a song?"

A clamor rose from the children. Ben smiled. The littlest ones were always the loudest in wanting to suggest songs, but had difficulty actually naming a song when called upon. "Jenny, do you have a suggestion?" He pointed to seven-year-old Jenny Green to distinguish her from the three other Jennys in the room.

She leaned up against her big sister Selma. Her little face went still in concentration, then she said something Ben couldn't hear. Selma saw that he didn't hear her sister's words. "She said she wants one of your songs, Mr. Hanby."

"Oh," he said, pleased. That was the first time a student had asked for one of his own songs, though he had taught them two before. "Would you like to learn a new one?" he asked the class as a whole.

"Ye-e-s-s!" half of them shouted.

"No!" the usual contrarians objected, enjoying the argument.

"The Yeses outweigh the Nos," Ben said.

His gaze fell on the lyrics written on the page below him. Should he? It might be risky—but then, he wished to change hearts. "This one isn't complete yet, but I think you will like the chorus," he said. He began to write on the blackboard, the chalk squeaking across the dark surface. "Let's sing this. I'll sing it once, then you sing after me."

He raised his voice to sing what he had written. He pitched it lower than he had written it, and he sang it with a jaunty rhythm to increase its appeal.

> *Oh my poor Nelly Gray, they have taken you away,*
> *And I'll never see my darling any more;*
> *I am sitting by the river and I'm weeping all the day,*
> *For you've gone from that old Kentucky shore.*

They sang it after him, line by line. One or two couldn't carry a tune, but some were natural singers who led the group and held the melody. Jimmy had an excellent tenor for a boy his age, which explained why he loved to sing. Music knew no social distinctions. Jimmy came from a family with nothing, but the mayor's children would never sing as well as Jimmy did, despite all of their advantages.

"Excellent!" Ben said. "Now let's sing the whole thing. Jimmy, would you like to lead it?"

"I s'pose," the boy said, but the way he jumped to his feet belied the nonchalance of his answer.

"Come to the front, then," Ben said.

Jimmy picked his way through the throng of sitting children, stood at the front, and launched into the song. The children were merry and loud.

They had learned it without effort: a good sign. And it wasn't like Ben's lighter songs for parlor entertainment. It was a keen song that struck to the heart of slavery's cruelty. He hadn't been able to save Nelly—yet—but he could honor her through his music and keep up hope. Perhaps it would comfort others like Frank, who for now must live without his wife and their baby, with no way to know what might be happening to them.

They finished.

"Thank you, Jimmy. You may be seated."

As Jimmy went back to his seat in the rear, Sally Lefort raised her hand.

"Yes, Sally?"

"Who is Nelly Gray, sir?" Sally asked, her blue eyes thoughtful, her chestnut hair braided away from her face and waving down her back.

"Who do you think she might be?"

"Well, she lived on the Kentucky shore," Sally said, ruminating.

"What else do we know about her?" Ben directed his question toward the class at large.

"I know, sir," said Bobby Green from where he was sitting with his back against the wall. "They took her away."

"Yes, good, Bobby. They took Nelly away. So who are 'they'?"

That was a stumper. No one answered.

"I'll let you consider it for a while," Ben said. "Let's begin today's copywork."

The younger ones opened their primers, while the older ones copied a stanza from Milton that Ben had written on the other half of the board before class began.

After half an hour, Ben stopped them. "Hand in your papers, please. Ten minutes for recess."

The students were already halfway out the door, struggling into coats and rewrapping their scarves. Such a sunny day was rare for December, but still cold with the bite of winter. The bare trees looked forlorn outside the window, and the hard ground sported only a few wisps of withered grass, like an old man's hair. The children poured across the yard, undeterred in their games and shouting.

As Ben straightened a few desks and prepared to follow the students outside, Sally met him at the door. "Nelly's a slave, isn't she, Mr. Hanby?"

"That's right, Sally," he said. "When I write the verses, the song will be clearer."

"That's a very sad song," Sally said. "Why did they take her away?"

Better tread softly here. "That happens quite frequently." He strove for neutrality and a factual description. "Slave-owners decide they need to sell some of their slaves, for whatever reason. Perhaps the crop isn't as good that year, or it's too expensive to support all their slave families. So they sell some of them to other owners, and the other owners take them away somewhere else."

"They sell families away from each other?" Sally asked.

"Yes," Ben replied. What else could he say? It was the simple truth.

"Oh," Sally said, her clear blue eyes troubled. She turned and went out the door without another word.

The town council sat in conference on the other side of those white doors. Ben waited in the front foyer of the church, forcing himself to stand still. No telling when someone might come out to call him. He crossed his arms and braced his palms against the scratchy wool of his coat. He could stand like this as long as they made him wait. They wouldn't see his jangled nerves if he could help it.

The mayor of a town as small as Rushville was unpaid, of course. There was no city hall, and town meetings took place in the Methodist church. These informalities did not prevent Mayor Bob Banning from assuming every iota of pomp and circumstance that he could squeeze from the position, as he was probably doing at this very moment.

One of the doors swung open and the mouselike face of Robby Reardon poked into view.

"We're ready for you, Hanby," the Rushville postmaster said, his white mustache bristling out from his narrow face like whiskers. He disappeared back the way he had come and let the door close in Ben's face. Ben had to shove it open again to follow Reardon into the main hall of the church.

The past few weeks had made it clear that Reardon was not disposed to be friendly to Ben. Every time Ben went to retrieve his mail, the little old man shoved his letters across the counter and retired to the back room without a civil word. It was not auspicious that Reardon was part of the group that would pass judgment on Ben's work at the school. At least Mayor Banning had been friendly enough, in a political way. But Ben didn't know who else sat on the town council.

The sky was overcast this afternoon, and the gloomy light in the brick church showed five men seated in the front pew, their backs to Ben. He recognized Banning even from the back—the man was well over six feet tall and loomed almost a full head above the others. As Ben approached, Banning pivoted in the pew to regard him.

"Hanby. Come round here in front where we can see you."

When he walked up to stand by the altar rail, he saw that the mayor and postmaster shared the pew with the new town physician and two men Ben had never seen before. One was a middle-aged, prosperous-looking gentleman. The other man was also in middle age, but was dark-haired, mustached, and fine-boned. He was dressed as well as the other men, but his heavy work boots protruded from under his trousers and gave him away as a farmer. A wealthy farmer, then.

Mayor Banning's iron-gray hair and beard coupled with his height made him an imposing figure. He used it to full advantage, rising now to tower four inches above Ben's own six-foot frame. He shook Ben's hand. "Welcome. We will be brief here today, as our business is simple." Banning seated himself again. His lanky legs stretched out well in front of the pew.

Ben remained standing in front of the council.

"These are my fellow town councilmen," Banning continued. "Reardon, Dr. Samuels, Gabriel Lightman"—he indicated the nondescript middle-aged man—"and finally Arthur Lefort."

Lefort. That explained the slight build and Creole face of the fifth man. It also explained why Ben might have been called before these men in the first place.

"So, Mr. Hanby." Banning cleared his throat and shifted on the pew. "We have received some complaints about some of the subjects you have included in your instruction since your arrival here."

Perfect. Not a word of praise, even, to sweeten the gall of the complaint. Not even a comment on the physical improvements to the building.

"Yes, sir." Ben waited for the rest.

"I understand," Banning said heavily, "that you taught an abolitionist song."

The hollowing in his gut must not show on his face. "It depends what you mean, sir."

Lefort's face broke into a scowl as he sat bolt upright in the pew. "Is that all you have to say?" he asked. "You think it acceptable to teach a song full of lies?"

"The song describes the separation of loved ones by slavery, sir. That is an established fact."

"That statement proves further why he should be removed from his position," Lefort said to the mayor before facing Ben again. "You are turning the young against their own parents."

Should he defend himself or remain silent?

Lefort seized the advantage of the pause and addressed the other men, vibrating with indignation. "Do you think someone with such poor judgment should be entrusted with the education of our children?"

So his position was at stake. He had to defend his actions. "I disagree with you, Mr. Lefort. The song is simply the portrait of a very common situation in the South. It contains no falsehoods, nor should it cause any student to disrespect his parents."

"Nonetheless," the mayor interjected, as Lefort fumed next to him, "a schoolmaster must avoid even the slightest appearance of political partiality, especially in times such as these."

"It is a sentimental song from a slave to his vanished love."

Lefort glowered at Ben. "But my daughter came home asking about things she should not be learning in school. Reading, writing, and arithmetic. Not slaves and abolitionists." He turned to the other men, his complexion darkened with repressed fury. "He should be dismissed. May we call a vote?"

"Please remove yourself to the foyer once again, Mr. Hanby," Banning said.

Ben walked back down the aisle with as much dignity as possible, though the heat of shame coursed over his face. Just before the double doors swung shut behind him, he heard a low hum of discussion among the men.

What would his parents think if he were dismissed? Besides the humiliation, the consequent gossip might impede their work with fugitives. He paced back and forth as five minutes went by, then ten.

The doors burst open and Lefort stormed out. "Do not think I have forgotten your family from when your father lived here," he said as he passed by. "You will not succeed in what you are trying to do." Lefort hurled himself out the front door of the church in a blast of cold air.

The others followed, but with no word to Ben. Mayor Banning emerged last. He paused, drawing himself up to his full height. "Mr. Hanby, you have offended some in our community."

"Yes, sir." Ben kept his arms folded and his eyes fixed on the floor, clamping down his anger like the hatch of a storm cellar.

"The doctor and I vouched for your otherwise positive effect on the school, but we were unable to change the decision of the council. You must pack your bags and leave at the end of the day tomorrow. We are only two days from the end of the term, and you will not return to teach here again. Good afternoon." He left in another gale of wintry wind.

Ben sat down alone in the foyer and dropped his head in his hands.

Twenty-Nine

THE STAGECOACH RATTLED ALONG TOWARD WESTERVILLE. Ben didn't relish the idea of telling his parents what had happened. But a peculiar peace stayed with him, as if something deeply right had happened even in the injustice of his dismissal. He did not feel he had made a mistake.

Last night, as he stopped in Cincinnati to wait for the stagecoach, it had begun to snow—beautiful large flakes falling through the lamplight as he looked out the window of the tavern. That snowfall blanketed the ground here in central Ohio. He couldn't wait to smell the cider in his family's home, to embrace his little sisters and brothers, and sit and talk with his parents beside the fire.

Cyrus might not welcome him. They had hardly spoken since their fistfight.

The stage rolled to a stop on State Street, and Ben got out, wishing a safe journey to his fellow passengers who were continuing on to Cleveland. They waved a cheery good-bye as the coachman removed Ben's bag from the top of the stage and tossed it down to him.

"A merry Christmas to you, young man," the driver said, his cheeks reddened even under his black scarf and hat.

"And to you, sir!" Ben picked up his bag to head toward Grove Street. It was the Saturday before Christmas, and the stores teemed with friends and neighbors finding last-minute gifts. Ben had always loved Christmas in Westerville. The Hanbys would invite their friends for the evening, read Christmas stories and poems, and join the carolers. His family could practically form a caroling party all by itself.

His boots crunched through several inches of snow as he passed the Lawrence home. Through their closed windows, he heard the merry tune of "I Saw Three Ships," played with beautiful ornamentation. Only one person in town could play in that style. Through the lace curtain he saw Cornelia sitting at her piano, but her back was to him. Time enough to say hello later. He wanted to see his family first.

When he came in the door, his mother was at the stove stirring something that smelled of cinnamon. Willie and Lizzie hovered at her elbows. At the sound of the door, Lizzie turned and gave a cry of delight. "Ben!"

She threw her small body into his arms. Willie tried to embrace him across Lizzie, so Ben grabbed both of them and lifted them off the ground in a bear hug. He and his mother laughed as he put them down and they jumped around the kitchen.

"That's enough," his mother said gently to them. "You'll injure yourselves if you keep cavorting around like wild animals. Go tell your brothers and sisters that Ben is home."

They stampeded upstairs.

His mother's face glowed as she embraced him. He was still unaccustomed to towering over her petite frame.

She squeezed his arms. "You're home early. Is all well?"

"I'll tell you this evening."

She searched him with a look.

"It's a long tale, best saved for later." He was unwilling to mar his homecoming with any unpleasant talk.

She raised one eyebrow, but turned back to the stove and picked up her spoon.

Amanda and Anna came down the stairs, with baby Sam in Amanda's arms and Jenny trailing behind them. "Ben's home! Ben!" They rushed at him. After many embraces and exclamations, he passed around white candy canes he had hidden in his bag.

As he gave out the last one, Cyrus approached, but remained in the doorway behind the others. His brother's frame looked more solid than when Ben saw him last. Cyrus finally seemed more like a young man than an overgrown boy. He lingered on the threshold with an uncertain look.

No matter what disaster Cyrus had caused, he was still his brother. Ben stepped around the others and crossed to greet him, hand extended. "Merry Christmas, Cyrus. I'm glad to see you."

Cyrus took his hand and pulled him close to clasp him around the shoulders with one arm. "Me too, Ben," he said quietly.

Their mother distracted the young ones by opening the oven and setting the cinnamon twists out to cool. "Oh, Ben, before I forget," she said, shooing Willie away from the hot pan. "Cornelia told me she would like to speak to you tomorrow, if you wouldn't mind stopping by after worship. It sounded pressing."

"Probably just about Christmas music," he said, "but I'll go."

Kate walked down State Street. It was Sunday, and the shops were closed. Still, people strolled the streets, enjoying the holiday feel of the crisp, cold air after church. It had snowed again last night—the snow lay thick and even. *Deep and crisp and even*, as in the words of the new carol that everyone was singing this year, "Good King Wenceslas." She liked it very much herself. She started humming it as she passed Main and turned on Grove.

What had Cornelia meant by promising a surprise? Her friend had given her a small smile and said, "I believe I can do you good, Kate, and I will not be dissuaded."

So Kate had agreed, and now she was headed to Cornelia's home to see what this surprise might be.

She shoved her hands deep into the fur muff that covered them. Her mother had given it to her when the freeze set in. The muff's soft whiteness matched the furry collar of the warm woolen coat that came with it. It was a rare moment of kindness when her mother said, "This collar will look nice with your dark hair, dear." Kate suspected the coat was simply another tool of matrimonial scheming, but she liked it anyway.

As she picked her way through the deeper snow on Grove Street, she looked up at Cornelia's home, its windows brightly lit and adorned with green wreaths. The Hanbys' home just down the road was also warm and festive, with red bows on the porch pillars and pine garlands hanging from the eaves. What a welcoming, happy-looking home. She had not responded to Ben Hanby's heartfelt letter of apology. Surely he knew that she could not write to a man without her parents' consent, and least of all to him. In the imaginary letter she had written several times in her head, she had told him she could not remain angry with someone who was so concerned and good-hearted. But she would not be able to tell him so, as her mother had forbidden her to socialize with the Hanbys.

She mounted the steps of the Lawrence home and knocked with the brass-knobbed handle. Cornelia opened the door, in a festive red day dress that flowed to her feet almost as elegantly as her evening attire. "I've sent the maid off to do her Christmas shopping. Come in," she said, easing the door back to allow room for Kate's skirt.

The parlor was gorgeous in reds and greens, and a six-foot tree stood in the corner as if it were growing inside the house. Popcorn garlands festooned its branches, along with little orange baskets and red ribbons.

"What a lovely Christmas tree," Kate said.

"Have you noticed how many there are in town this year? It's so fashionable now in England, since the Prince did it. And once England starts a fashion, then of course we all must follow! But it's a nice fashion, don't you think?"

"Yes." Kate inhaled the piney smell. "As if we're outside, but without the cold."

"May I get you some cider?" Cornelia asked.

"Yes, please."

Cornelia disappeared into the kitchen, and Kate moved closer to admire the tree. Deeper in its branches, gilt walnuts gleamed where they dangled from satin loops.

A knock came at the door and Cornelia hurried back into the parlor and ran to answer it. Kate could not see her greeting whoever it was in the foyer, but she heard the low murmur of a male voice. Booted feet shuffled on the stoop in the familiar sound of scraping off snow.

Cornelia rounded the corner into the parlor. "Please come

in," she said in a bright tone to someone behind her, but she looked very nervous.

And Ben Hanby walked in after her.

He was still as intense and handsome, with his dark hair and deep brown eyes, as Kate had remembered. More so. Their eyes met and everything else grew indistinct to her. She could not look away from him—he was the only tangible thing in the room. He carried an overcoat folded on his arm and wore a dark blue frock coat that accentuated his broad shoulders.

He appeared as transfixed as she. The silence lengthened. Cornelia said something about cider and whisked herself away to the kitchen.

Kate's face warmed under his gaze. Only one topic came to mind. "I accept your very gracious apology, Mr. Hanby."

"I'm glad to hear it." He paused as if he too struggled for words.

"Won't you sit down?" Formal manners would give her a script for the unscriptable.

He looked around for a place to put his coat. The coat closet was just behind her, in the nook between the parlor and the kitchen. "I'll take that for you," she said, as her mother had taught her she should in the absence of a servant. She shyly approached and reached for the coat.

As he tendered it to her, their hands touched beneath the folded material. She grasped the coat and stepped back quickly. That light touch from his hand rippled through her with such force that she wavered in her path to the coat closet.

When she returned, he stood waiting for her to seat herself. She should not be here—what would her mother do, if she knew? But her entire person would resist going out that door, and the fascination of the present moment overwhelmed any dire future.

She sat down and arranged her skirts on the red chaise longue. He took the nearest available chair, which was several feet away from her.

"Your teaching was enjoyable?" she asked.

"The children, yes. The parents, not always." He smiled. "Teaching is not a vocation for the weak."

It stung, though she knew he had not meant to refer to her. "I am too aware of that. I would like to teach someday. But thus far, at least, I have not shown myself to be strong enough."

"I apologize—I did not mean to offend you. And you are not weak." The concern in his eyes drew out the hurt from inside her, like a poultice on a snakebite.

"You are not to blame if I do not prove to be capable of teaching." Her fingers knit together in her lap.

"You wish to teach? But why shouldn't you?" His furrowed brow softened as interest sparked in his eyes. "You are brilliant in academics. And you have shown exemplary compassion for others, which is a teacher's most necessary gift."

"But I have not successfully spoken to a group in public. And you witnessed the lamentable results of my attempt to sing."

He stood up and walked to the window. "I shouldn't have coerced you to sing." The fabric of his waistcoat tightened over his shoulders.

"You didn't coerce me. I wanted to try, but I wasn't able to do it."

"You would have succeeded, had it not been for Cyrus." He gazed out the window as if he did not want her to see his emotion, but it was clear even in profile.

Her face burned. She must change the direction of the conversation. "I've been attempting to steady my nerves with practice, and perhaps I will be able to speak someday. I sometimes think that's what heaven wants of me. But if that were so, speaking would not be so difficult. I wish I knew." Her words ended like a question, though she had intended to sound confident. But if she could speak of spiritual matters to anyone, it would be Ben Hanby.

He turned with a look of surprise, then crossed the polished floor to return to her. He pulled his chair closer with an impatient flourish, as if to throw off the constraints of the rules. He seated himself and his dark eyes searched hers. She felt an odd sensation almost like the lightness of being airborne on Garnet.

"I am learning to be slower to speculate on what God wants," he said. "Only time can show us his plan. Some trials are meant to temper us, not to turn us away from our paths."

"But how do we even know which path to begin?"

"I don't know if I have that answer." His knees were a foot from her skirt. The breathing reality of his skin, his eyes, his lashes when he looked down, was overwhelming her senses.

"In my own life," he said, "I've chosen what appeared right and good, after prayer. And I will pursue it with all my heart." Something in his tone changed, as if he spoke on more than one level, and it stirred her.

She thought of what they had shared on their journey. "I would like to help others, as you and your family do."

He went completely still. The air was charged with what had been spoken and what remained unsaid.

"You will bring me to my knees." He said it almost in a whisper.

What did he mean? The riot of her feelings coalesced into a more familiar panic that drove her to her feet and around the back of her chair so it stood between them as a makeshift wall.

What about her mother's instruction? She had never spoken so freely to a man in her life. She did not seem to be in command of herself. And yet he was a gentleman to his core, and would not press her when she was so flustered.

But she was not as honorable as he, to stay so long in contradiction of her mother's will. She could not respect herself if she became deceitful, and neither was it fair to him.

"I'm sorry, Mr. Hanby." She clutched the back of the chair for support. "I must take my leave." She kept her tone as even as she could to hide her dismay. "This will sound terribly rude, but my mother has asked me not to associate with you." Her voice shook on the last words and betrayed her.

Hurt sprang into his eyes. He got to his feet. With only a hint of diffidence, he approached and extended his hand in a courtly way to her. She could not be rude to him again. She complied and placed her ungloved hand in his, the pressure and warmth of his palm against hers making her weak in the knees.

"I am determined," he said, gazing into her eyes and moving closer, "that this will not be our last conversation this winter. One way or another. I promise you that." And he bowed slightly over her hand, and for an awful and blissful moment, he seemed about to violate every possible rule of propriety by kissing the hand of a woman he was not even courting. But, with visible effort, he loosened his gentle hold and straightened up.

"Please don't leave on my account," he said. "I live next door to Miss Lawrence. But you have a longer walk, and it's snowy. Stay with her." He walked to the closet, took down his coat again, and headed out of the parlor. He glanced back at her only once without a word. She heard the front door open and close.

Something had been mended and strengthened, and would not easily be torn apart again.

Thirty

December 25th, 1855   50 Grove Street

My dear Miss Winter,

    In the absence of another acceptable means of communicating with you, I have chosen to write. Miss Lawrence has promised to convey this letter to you at your next piano lesson.

    It has been a happy Christmas Day here at the Hanby home. My little sisters and brothers make it very merry for all of us with their squeals of delight at the gifts. It is a simple celebration for us, but deeply felt, as we remember the joyous miracle that took place in the stable at Bethlehem. But our prayers are with Nelly and her baby, for there is still no word from John Parker. Do not give up hope. Mr. Parker is a determined and resourceful man.

    It is late now, very late, and I am alone in the parlor, with only the sound of the wood popping in the fire. I wonder whether you may have thought of me at all, as I have thought of you so often since our most recent conversation.

I do not expect you will respond to this letter. I realize you have considerations that are beyond your control. But I hope you will accept this, and read it, and know that I am humbly

Yours,
Ben Hanby

December 27th, 1855   50 Grove Street

My dear Miss Winter,

For propriety's sake, I have delayed as long as possible in writing to you again—that is, all of two days. But even as I write the word "propriety," I scoff at myself. Propriety has nothing to do with this letter. Instead, I am motivated only by my hope that you may continue to think of me. I was overjoyed to hear that you had accepted my first letter. Miss Lawrence tells me you were reluctant, but I am grateful that you showed compassion for my desire to write to you.

A new year approaches. Who knows what it may bring for each of us? I have been composing two songs. One of them is dedicated to Nelly and relates the story of her life—I have been attempting to write it for years, but at last it seems to be taking shape. The other song is inspired by you, though the melody cannot hold a candle to the real presence it attempts to suggest.

Writing makes bearable my longing to speak with you, but I am still pursued at every turn by the vision of you as I last saw you, radiant with gentleness and beauty. There were many things I wished to say to you. But I presume too much.

The moments are bleak indeed when I think we may never be permitted to resume our friendship. But I refuse to accept that future, for it would be as dismal to me as a life behind bars. This temporary prohibition from your company is trial enough.

Through that trial or any other, I remain faithfully

Yours,

Ben Hanby

December 28th, 1855   71 Northwest Street

Mr. Hanby,

I cannot deny that I was pleased to read your letters, but I am conscience-stricken by my decision to accept them from Cornelia. As you know, my mother has forbidden me to associate with you, and though an exchange of letters does not violate that instruction, it certainly violates the spirit in which her command was intended.

Regretfully,

Kate Winter

December 30th, 1855   50 Grove Street

My dear Miss Winter,

I do not blame you if you are angry with me for writing to you in direct disobedience to your express wish.

Nonetheless, I must risk your anger, for I fear if I do not, I will risk much worse.

To say I was downcast after receiving your letter would be insufficient. I was in the darkest of moods, avoiding all conversation and keeping only my own company to hide my desolate state from any prying eyes or ears.

I know you may be tempted to throw down this letter at any moment, if you read it at all, so I will be very direct. I think there is great harmony between our temperaments. When I am with you, I see you are affected deeply by the suffering of the innocent and you wish to alleviate it, as I do. Even you may not realize that the source of your compassion for others is your own passionate nature. (I expect you may have just cast this paper away from you, but I will continue in the hope that curiosity will drive you to take it up again)

I will not attempt to persuade you to any course of action, but simply plead that you follow the true inclination of your heart. If that inclination leads you away from me, I must accept that decision. But if there is any atom of you that wonders if I may be correct in the presumptuous things I have written to you, then I beg you not to do what is easy and expected. Instead give me at least some time to find a way to remain

Truly yours,
Ben Hanby

Thirty-One

KATE URGED GARNET A FEW STEPS TO THE RIGHT TO clear the path for Mr. Jones's horse, a huge gray that must have Percheron in its blood. It had hooves the size of dinner plates and muscular shoulders and haunches that could easily support Mr. Jones's considerable bulk. He was not a bad rider for a man of his size: one could tell when a rider knew how to sit with balance, even when he was carrying extra weight.

The dogs milled around their handlers, whining and waving their tails. One horse stood in the yard while its gentleman rider mounted its polished saddle. Another horse danced away from a second young man, who had one foot already in the stirrup. He hopped after his horse and jumped up as quickly as he could with an embarrassed glance at the others. The ladies had already seated themselves on their horses, one by one, around the corner, with the aid of the mounting block and a groom.

Mrs. Jones rode up to Kate on a delicate bay horse taller than Garnet. She wore a black hat and riding habit that made her blond coloring more striking. "Good morning, Miss Winter." She appraised Kate with a glance up to her neat riding hat and all the way down to the hem of her green habit without changing her expression in the least.

"Good morning, Mrs. Jones." It was not a pleasure to see Frederick's mother—or at least, not a pleasure to be inspected like a horse at auction. Perhaps Kate should open her mouth and let the other woman count her teeth. But, of course, she did not.

"Have you seen my son?"

"No, ma'am." She had forced herself to come this morning, precisely because she dreaded this moment when she had feared Frederick's mother might treat her as a conniving flirt.

"Well, he will be riding with the men, I believe, so he will not have the opportunity for much conversation."

Kate's cheeks burned, even in the crisp air. She was not even interested in Frederick's attentions. But her protest of innocence spoke only through the blood that rushed to her face, which would no doubt be read as guilt. She must look like a Christmas ornament, with red cheeks and green dress.

A blast from a bugle drew all eyes to Mr. Westerfield, the town founder, in his neat scarlet hunting blazer and black hat. "Ladies and Gentlemen, welcome to our inaugural Westerville Fox Hunt," he said. "As your Master of Hounds, I would like to thank you for the pleasure of your company."

Cornelia pulled her dapple gray horse up next to Kate. "Don't forget you are riding with the ladies," she whispered, and smiled. Kate had confided to her about the jumping.

Cornelia's habit and hat were the proper black for the hunt, like Mrs. Jones's, but Kate had only one habit and so she had to make do with green. There had not been time to acquire a complete new habit in the two weeks since Mr. Westerfield had announced the hunt. Her mother had asked if she shouldn't have a new one rushed by a tailor in Columbus, but Kate did not want such effort or expense for a onetime luxury. Especially when she would not even be able to jump like the gentlemen. Much of the joy of the chase would vanish when she, Cornelia, and the other ladies had to ride sedately through gates and wait for them to be opened by whichever gentleman was unlucky enough to earn that task.

"Mr. Brewer, will you accompany the ladies?" Mr. Westerfield asked a young man across the yard. His thin face fell, making him look like Ichabod Crane on his bony horse.

Frederick called out, "I will be delighted to accompany them, sir. No greater honor or pleasure." He tipped his hat at Kate from where he sat on his horse by the hounds.

Oh, Mrs. Jones would certainly not be pleased. Kate did not look in her direction. Frederick was being gallant, but far better for him to have ridden with the gentlemen and paid no attention to Kate.

Mr. Jones gave his son a knowing look, but not a disapproving one. So. It was only Frederick's mother who thought ill of Kate, and not both parents.

Frederick reined his own black horse toward Kate and the other ladies. His mount was much like his father's, though not as large. Still, it towered a whole hand above Garnet, and given Frederick's own height, they made an imposing pair.

"Ladies," Frederick said, "good morning, and a beautiful morning because you ride with the hunt." He touched his hat and smiled.

He certainly was charming. Kate could only imagine his effect on hearts less distracted than hers. Under the circumstances, however, she would rather he stayed away or at least refrained from speaking to her on the hunt.

Mr. Westerfield rallied the whippers-in, who took the pack ahead down the lane. The tan and white hounds ran from side to side with noses sweeping the ground. A cheerful hubbub of voices mixed with hoofbeats and the jingle of bridles as the party followed in pairs, gentlemen first, then the ladies and Frederick.

Frederick trotted up beside Kate and let his horse fall into a tandem walk with Kate's mare.

"You are an accomplished rider, Miss Winter, on the flat as well as over fences." He grinned.

"I have ridden a great deal, Mr. Jones."

"A gentle hand at the reins is a telltale sign."

She had no reply. She must avoid the thought of his mother glaring at their backs if she wished to be able to converse at all.

"I would like to ride with you one afternoon, instead of always taking the buggy."

She nodded.

"Excellent. If you'll excuse me, I must go speak to my father for a moment. I'll return."

The haunches of his horse rippled as he trotted past the line of gentlemen to the front, where his father rode behind the dogs.

One of the hounds bayed, then they all joined in the discordant call and ran straight ahead. The bugle blasted, and the horses jumped and skittered on the road as the gentlemen gathered their reins. At a signal from Mr. Jones, the gentlemen's horses took off at a swift gallop, down the road toward the woods ahead.

They were thirty yards away when Garnet lurched forward and galloped in their wake, her head thrust forward and up as she seized the bit in her mouth. Kate pulled hard at the reins, but the mare's muscular neck was set against her. The thoroughbred blood was up, and the horse was no longer under Kate's control. Instead of following the hunt, she ran uphill toward the woods.

The trees ahead rushed closer and closer, and the mare's speed jarred Kate's thought into fragments. *Cannot dismount . . . trees may be low . . . Garnet may fall . . .*

All she could do was stay in the saddle and try to survive uninjured. Garnet bolted onto the wide path between the trees, which quickly narrowed. Garnet veered too close to the trees, and the branches reached toward Kate. She flung herself down and clung to Garnet's neck as twigs scraped her back.

The path twisted and rose uphill, and none of the other horses were in sight. Finally, the uphill gallop took its toll, and Garnet dropped back to a canter. When Kate twitched the reins, the mare trotted and finally slowed to a halt, blowing hard, head lowered, the mania gone.

Kate took a shuddering breath. She was as firm in the saddle as ever. She had escaped harm, though she was now a sack of jelly on Garnet's back. But she had two choices. She could try to find the hunt party or wait where she was and hope they passed her again in the woods as they gave chase. The ladies would know what had happened, but she had not seen any of the men look back when Garnet bolted.

She waited a few minutes, allowing her breathing to slow. Then she gathered the reins and asked Garnet to walk. The mare obeyed, her instinct to run played out.

Kate guided her through the trees for a few minutes. Which way had she turned in her wild ride? Thank goodness she had missed that particular branch over there while riding too fast to see. The distant cry of the hounds came to her. She must ride in their direction and hope it brought her out of the woods.

More riding through the trees brought the sound closer, until it stopped abruptly. The fox had gone to ground. Good. The riding was exhilarating—or would be, if she were allowed to jump—but the hunting part did not appeal to her.

Garnet walked on until the path ended at the smooth, opaque whiteness of the frozen creek. Now where? She must turn around.

"Miss Winter," a voice called through the trees.

Frederick rode toward her on his ebony horse, ducking and pushing aside branches that poked at his face. "Are you hurt?"

"No, I am quite well. Garnet has not had enough exercise of late—she lost her head for a moment. But now she is calm."

"Stop here and we'll listen for the rest of the hunt," Frederick said.

"It sounded as if they went to ground over that way." She pointed.

"Good. Let's ride there and hope for the best."

"Thank you for coming after me."

"Of course." His glance lingered on her. "I was concerned for you. Your welfare is of great importance to me."

She must change the subject, now. Something controversial and completely distracting. "Mr. Jones, the game of charades the other evening . . ."

"Yes?" He flushed.

"Are you and your father supporters of slavery? I am sorry to be so direct, but I feel I must know." An inflammatory question indeed, and thus the perfect diversion.

Frederick sighed. "We support our country, Miss Winter.

And the abolitionist movement will lead to secession. My father believes it, and I believe it too. So we must oppose it, and all of its illegal activities."

"I see." She looked away, straight ahead between her horse's ears.

"That displeases you."

"Yes."

"If only you knew some of the things I have been told," Frederick said, almost pleading. "Women have been attacked and property destroyed everywhere that slavery has been cast aside. Even the Negro fugitives on their way to Canada commit crimes, outrages against women and children . . ." He stopped, flushing.

"I do not believe you," she said. She must keep her temper.

"It is true! I will tell you something in confidence, to help you understand. My father just heard that the marshal's men in Columbus caught a slave, a fugitive, breaking into someone's home, to do who knows what evil. Under duress, this slave confessed that the Hanby family had helped him escape from Kentucky to Canada only six months ago. The parents of my closest friend! It grieves me to no end."

"Pardon me? That does not seem likely." Thank goodness he could not hear the hammering of her heart. She breathed slowly—she must not show her distress. "Why would the slave come back, if he had escaped?"

"He claimed he came back to find his relations. But I'm sure he simply wanted to come back to a populous place where living as a drifter or criminal is easier."

"I don't think we should believe ill of the Hanbys unless there is some proof."

"And I do not wish to," Frederick said. "My father is going

into Columbus tonight to interrogate this slave at the old armory before they take him back across the state line tomorrow. Father assures me he will do everything possible to bring the truth to light, and thus, we hope, clear the Hanbys of suspicion."

Kate's heart sank. It must be Frank. Nelly's Frank. He had grown desperate from the waiting.

Mr. Jones was about to head for Columbus, and if the authorities transported Frank south, it might be impossible for the Hanbys to help him. Someone had to warn them immediately.

"Kate!"

She turned to see Cornelia riding through the brittle filigree of the bare birch branches.

"Mr. Jones, you found her," Cornelia said. "Thank goodness." She was pale in her black coat.

"I am perfectly safe," Kate said.

"But we've lost our way," Frederick added.

"Never mind that. I followed you in, and I can find our way out." Cornelia's gray horse neared and she cued it to halt. "The gentlemen are farther downstream trying to pick up the scent of a new fox, as the other one is gone." She beckoned with a leather-gloved hand. "Come along! Is Garnet settled enough to ride?"

"Oh yes," Kate said. "She ran off her oats and now she is much calmer."

"You gave everyone a fright." Cornelia urged her mount forward on the path.

"I apologize, but I'm really quite all right." Kate legged Garnet into a brisk walk to catch up, and Frederick pulled Bayard into line at the rear. In a few minutes, they were out of the trees and in the open field next to the creek, as her friend had promised. A hundred yards away, men clustered together and shouted to one another through the frosty air. The hounds circled in wide arcs between the horses. One lifted its head to the sky and bayed, and they were off again. The men gathered their reins and galloped after them across the field toward the town.

Now was her chance. She must pretend to be carried away as before. Kate applied a strong leg aid and let out the reins. Garnet bolted after the men's horses. But when the hunting party turned east, Kate guided Garnet on straight ahead, back toward Westerville and the Hanbys. The fence loomed ahead, and Cornelia called out in fear behind her, but Kate rose in the air with Garnet and cleared the high obstacle with a foot to spare. Some of the men had slowed and pointed toward her. Frederick broke free of the pack and followed as if to lend her aid, but Bayard refused to jump the tallest of the fence hedges, and when Frederick turned to ride through the gate, Kate left him far behind. Only open fields and high jumps lay between her and the Hanbys. Cold wind numbed her face, but she urged Garnet even faster. Frank was in prison. Without immediate aid, he would be doomed to return to his master and perhaps to his death, without his wife and child.

Let them all think the mare had run away again. As long as she had a chance to warn the Hanbys about Frank, let them all think what they liked. She might never be allowed to ride the hunt again—or even to ride at all, if her mother found out—but what was that when weighed in the balance with a man's life?

The terrain passed in a blur, one fence after another, until she made it to Africa Road. She cantered down the road until it turned into Northwest Street. Garnet labored to continue—she was unaccustomed to so much running. Kate pulled her back to a trot. She could not break her horse's health, not even for the Hanbys or Frank Foster. At a more controlled pace, they rounded the corner onto the college avenue.

As she approached the Hanbys' home, two men came out the front door—Ben and his father. They turned toward State Street, but stopped in the road as Garnet trotted toward them. Kate reined her to a halt. She could barely speak from the exertion of the ride. Ben and his father looked worried. Ben approached and took Garnet's reins to steady her.

"What is it, Miss Winter? Are you in distress?"

She shook her head, taking several deep breaths. At last she had enough air. "Frank is in prison in the Columbus armory. They are going to take him back to Kentucky."

Ben shot an alarmed glance at his father, whose eyes had also widened.

"I'll go tell your mother," Mr. Hanby said to Ben. "We must leave straightaway. We can still catch the afternoon stagecoach, and it will be our swiftest choice."

"Yes, sir." As his father ran into the house, his black coat swirling behind him, Ben kept his hold on Garnet's reins. "Miss Winter, we are in your debt. You are a brave young lady."

"Mr. Hanby, I'll always be grateful to your family. You don't know what you've meant to me." Oh, that might be read in several ways. She must clarify. "Because of your family's faith, and your example. I've not had such an example in my life before." She dropped her eyes to Garnet's mane.

He reached up one gloved hand to touch hers, drawing her gaze back to him. She did not want to look away from his face, which was tender and full of respect.

But every moment she stayed here was further defiance of her mother. "I must go."

He removed his hands from Garnet and the reins and stepped back. "Thank you. We'll do our best for Frank. Pray for us tonight, if you will, Miss Winter."

"I will." It did not feel awkward anymore to speak to him of faith. But she must not forget her last warning for him. "You must know this—Mr. Jones is going to question Frank this evening."

"Indeed?" Ben looked dismayed. "We will be cautious."

She nodded and turned Garnet back toward Northwest Street.

Thirty-Two

By the time Ben stepped out of the stagecoach at the station on High Street, it was dark. Ben and his father stood under a gas streetlamp. A hackney cab could take them across the bridge toward Scioto Street. It should not be difficult to find one. Ever since the railroad came through four years ago, Columbus had boomed, and the business and leisure pursuits of the city went on well after dusk. A number of men and errand boys walked down High Street with preoccupied expressions and rapid strides. A young boy hawked newspapers only yards from where they stood.

His father spoke in a low voice. "The armory was once the state prison. It doesn't have as many guards as it did back then, but I expect there will still be at least two or three watching the armaments."

"Two, I hope."

"The number of guards won't make much difference if we don't have a strategy to get in. Unfortunately, I've never been inside the building, so we won't know our situation until we arrive."

"We're not going to drive right up to the door, are we?"

"No. I want to investigate the building first before we decide what to do. So we'll ask the hack to drop us off farther down Scioto, next to the warehouses there."

"And here comes one now," Ben said. But the cab that approached already carried other passengers, and it was another five minutes before they were aboard a hack and headed across the river.

The single horse pulled the cab at a moderate trot over the plank bridge at the end of Main Street. Like the rest of the streets, it had been cleared of the worst of the snow. The cabbie was a grizzled older man who sported a battered, wide-brimmed hat. "I just took another man across not even an hour ago," he said. "Partner of yours, maybe?"

Ben's father remained silent.

"No," Ben said. "We're a father-son partnership only."

Bad news for them, if that had been Jones ahead of them. Ben took a deep breath.

"Eh, that's right—the other one was headed for the armory, but you're going to the warehouses. A great thing, family business."

"Wasn't the armory once the state prison?" Ben's father asked.

"Yep. It still looks like a prison, but it's full of muskets and munitions, as far as I know. They kept a few cells, though, usually for prisoners being taken through town to somewhere else."

"I see." Ben's father sat back as if he had no worries in the world.

The gray waters moved only a few feet beneath them. Moonlight shone on ice floes and snowdrifts bordering the river. The driver continued to chatter, but Ben's thoughts wandered to Kate. If he ended up in jail, he wouldn't be in any position to win her heart. But Frank needed their help. Ben wouldn't allow any more deaths if he could help it.

The familiar memory returned—back in the Rushville house, so many years ago. Sorrow filled Joseph's eyes as death forced him to abandon Nelly, who would remain enslaved. Ben blinked to dispel the image. No more slavery-spawned partings. The partings ordained by God were trial enough for humankind.

If Ben lost everything, even his freedom, he would still be able to see his family, for no one would bar family visits to a jail. That was more than many slaves would ever have. And if no one made sacrifices, their suffering would never end. He held to the thought to settle his racing heart.

They pulled up to a gargantuan building that loomed in silhouette against the pale Scioto River.

"This the place?" the driver asked.

"Yes, thank you." His father jumped out with the agility of a much younger man and Ben followed. His father paid the fare and the hack drove away, back toward the bridge.

Ben stopped to wait for his father. "Which way?" Ben asked as the hoofbeats faded in the distance.

"We'll go around behind the warehouses," his father said. "From there, we can see the back of the armory."

They walked with caution around the perimeter of the building. From the deepest shadow, Ben peered down the row.

"There's no one around," he whispered to his father.

"Just be cautious."

They slipped from one building to the next, picking through the snow to avoid drifts and holes, until they reached the fourth warehouse. The windowless, two-story brick of the armory squatted thirty feet ahead. Only one small door relieved the featureless wall.

"Stay here," his father murmured.

Ben turned his head to protest, but his father's black-clad figure was already halfway across the open space, stark against the snow. In another moment, he was swallowed by the gloom cast by the armory. Ben listened hard but there was no sound—surely a good sign. Three or four minutes passed, then his father slipped back across the yard.

He spoke close to Ben's ear. "God is providing. There's one sentry. I almost stumbled into his view. He has wandered away from the door to smoke a pipe and left the door open. I'm sure he would be discharged for smoking in the armory, with the munitions in there."

"Could you see inside?"

"No. But we'll have to creep in unnoticed and take our chances."

"I have another idea," Ben said. "Is your pipe in your pocket?"

His father nodded.

"Why don't you stroll by and smoke your pipe with that sentry, while I try to get in the door?"

He frowned.

"Come, Father, you know it's the best way. We need a distraction, and I can't be the one to smoke with him—I'll cough and look ridiculous."

"There could be other sentries inside."

"I know, but we must take that risk."

"You mustn't be caught. You'll be arrested just for trespassing on state property."

"Understood," Ben said. He hurried across the snowy ground to the back of the armory, the slight crunch of his father's footsteps following. When they reached the relative safety of the wall, his father signaled that they should go in opposite directions around the building. Ben crept around to the front, hugging the rough brick wall. He must not make the slightest mistake. They could not afford it.

Ben crouched at the corner and peered around it. The lantern beside the front door cast a pool of light across the snow. The sentry lounged against the building, pipe clenched between his teeth. He struck a match, lit the bowl, and exhaled a cloud of gray into the frozen air.

"Halloo, my man!" came his father's cheery greeting.

"Who's there?" The sentry stood up and stared into the night.

"I'm on business from Westerville," his father replied, and then moved into the light. "There's not a match to be had in the warehouse here, and I'm in need of a bowl of tobacco myself. I see you might have a light?"

"I sure do." The sentry turned toward Ben's father and rummaged in his coat with one hand.

"Let me hold that for you," his father said, and took the man's pipe.

Now.

Ben stole toward the door behind the sentry's back. He heard his father comment on the fineness of the man's pipe, and then Ben was inside the building, in a long, narrow hallway. A candle lantern glowed ten feet ahead in a niche in the wall.

Two corridors crossed the hall up ahead. Every sense heightened, Ben inched up to the first crossing. No sign of anyone yet. Should he turn here or continue on? A few barred cells lined the side passage, and another candle lantern glowed down at the end of the hall, but still no sign of life. Behind the bars of the cells lay dim piles of objects—guns, perhaps.

Lord, guide my steps. He crossed the corridor and moved down the main hall to the next intersection.

Another lantern glimmered in a wall niche down the left-hand corridor. A rustle and a groan rose from the cells there. Stealing past several empty, barred rooms, Ben found the source of the noise. A brown-skinned man sprawled on a straw pallet in the far corner of a cell. His arm covered his face, and black bruises circled his forearm.

He had no doubt of the captive's identity. "Frank," he whispered.

Frank lowered his arm and looked at Ben. His eyes widened. Ben held his finger to his lips. Frank nodded, then got to his feet slowly, as if he had the weight and pain of the world on his shoulders. He made a motion as if turning a key with his hand, looking at Ben with a question in his raised eyebrows. Ben shook his head.

Frank approached the bars and motioned for Ben to come close until he was only an inch away through the iron bars. "There's a man here," he said, barely audible. "Not the guard, another. Look out for him. They keep the keys down there." He pointed to the opposite end of the corridor.

Ben nodded and set off in that direction. At the juncture with the main hall, he paused, ensured there was no one in sight, then crossed. The barred cells on this side were full of weapons—muskets, kegs of black powder, even a cannon carriage and barrel lying disassembled on the floor. At the far end of the hall was a table and, atop it, a plate with a few crusts. That must be the guard post. He walked to it without sound. A rack of hooks, with a key suspended on it. Excellent.

Frank's battered face lit when Ben returned and held up the

key. It scraped in the lock and the hinges of the door grated. Ben looked down the hall but no one appeared. Frank limped out of the cell.

Now, the real challenge—how to get out. He must try the back.

He led Frank down the main hallway until it jagged sharply right and ended at the back door. But the back door was chained shut and padlocked with a huge rusted lock. Ben had not seen any other keys on the rack. There was no way out but the front door.

He headed back that way, Frank following him. As they neared the front entrance, a voice rose from outside.

"Well, I'll be getting back inside," the guard said. "Business to do there."

"Where did you get the tobacco? It's rich." His father's voice rose with good cheer.

"Tobacconist on High, at Town. Good night." The sentry's voice grew louder and closer.

A small recess beside the door would make a good hiding place—but only one man would fit there. He gestured for Frank to go into it. The fugitive ran over and flattened his body into the niche.

Ben ran down to the first intersection of the corridor and hid himself behind the corner. The sentry came in the front door, kicking snow from his boots. As soon as the guard cleared the sill, Frank slipped out behind him and into the night. Ben's father would find him. Ben would meet them closer to the bridge—if he could elude the sentry.

"Hey there, mister!" the sentry said.

"What?" a harsh voice said from the other end of the hall Ben occupied.

Ben moved to the nearest set of bars and melted himself against them, hoping the jut of the wall would protect him from discovery.

A tall figure walked down the shadowy hallway, then turned toward the main entrance.

"Have you questioned the slave any further? Maybe he's ready to talk." The Southern drawl sounded familiar.

"I tried," the sentry said. "No answers yet."

"Well, try again. And don't be so friendly this time. I'm finishing my correspondence, but I'm running out of time."

The sentry sighed. "Sir, why don't you just take him to his massa tomorrow? They're more convincing in Kentucky."

"That may be." The voice belonged to Daniel Jones, he was sure of it. Ben's hands went cold. Bad enough if the sentry caught him, but disastrous if Mr. Jones did.

Now the sentry walked toward the cell where Frank had been, but Jones paused in the intersection of the two corridors, cutting off Ben's avenue of escape.

"He's gone!" the sentry yelled.

"Search the whole building!" Mr. Jones said. He rushed back toward the empty cell and turned the corner, leaving an open path for Ben to the front door.

Ben sprinted for freedom. As he turned into the main hall, Mr. Jones looked toward him down the dim hall. "Stop!" the big man shouted, and ran after Ben.

Ben made it to the front door, but the sentry had closed it and barred it with a heavy beam. Ben strained to budge it. It came loose, but Jones was only steps away from him. "Ben!" the gray-haired man said, his face blank with surprise. Ben wrenched the door open and threw himself out into the night.

Mr. Jones followed. "Bar the door after me and guard it!" he shouted over his shoulder to the sentry. "The slave may still be inside!"

Deep snowdrifts had piled on this side of the building. Ben stumbled through them. This was no good—he could not run any faster than Mr. Jones through the snow, though he would have easily outdistanced him on flat ground. His breath came fast, the cold aching in his chest. He pushed his legs harder, faster, pulling one foot after another from the white trap and shoving it forward. The dim shape of the bridge loomed about half a mile away, dark at the end of the snow-covered plain. A broken line across the whiteness made a path to the bridge—those must be the marks left by his father and Frank. The snow seemed to be growing even deeper. He could not slow down, though his shoes were catching on the tumbling clumps of snow. His breath heaved in gasps, his legs grew numb. He pulled his right foot out of the snow hole, but it stuck and he tumbled on his side. His feet found no purchase and he floundered for a moment.

A hand seized his coat and held firm. He heaved himself away, but Mr. Jones flung his entire weight on Ben's back, knocking the wind out of him, grabbing one of his arms and twisting it painfully behind his back. Ben could not move—he was no match for the sheer size of Mr. Jones.

They both lay there, struggling for breath, for a long, tense moment.

"What are you doing?" Mr. Jones gasped out. "What do you think you're doing, Ben?" His tone was angry, but also aggrieved. "Where is the slave?"

There could be no answer. Ben stared at the snow, inches from his face.

"Why?" Mr. Jones pushed on his arm, overcome by passion.

Ben winced as pain stabbed through his shoulder. "Because it's not right."

"I'll take you back inside there and lock you up to wait for the marshal. This is illegal. You're acting like a criminal." The freezing air gave Mr. Jones's words a cloud of vapor that drifted past Ben's face.

"It's slavery that's criminal." The weight of Mr. Jones crushed the air from his lungs so it was hard to speak.

"You cannot determine that yourself. You are bound by the law."

"I answer to God's law first." Ben ignored the wrench in his shoulder and gritted it out. "Go ahead, lock me up. I'm not afraid."

"Why, Ben? You have so much to offer! You're my son's friend. Why do you make me do this?" The older man sounded truly pained and his grip on Ben's arm eased a fraction. "You're taking the side of those who will ruin this country."

Ben twisted over his shoulder to meet Mr. Jones's eyes. "You're wrong. This country won't survive unless ordinary people stand up for what is right."

The gray-haired man was red in the face, his eyes moist. "How can someone so intelligent be so misled?" He squeezed Ben's arm tight for a moment, then pulled his hands away as if he had touched a hot stove. "I can't do it. It will break Frederick's heart." The weight lifted off Ben's back and Mr. Jones sat back on his heels in the snow. "Get out of my sight."

Ben sat up, stunned.

"And know this. If I ever hear word of this again—or catch your father or mother breaking the law—there will be no more reprieves." Mr. Jones launched himself to his feet, shaking his head. "Go!" he snapped without looking at Ben. "Before the guard comes out here." The big man turned and began to plow his way back to the armory.

Ben jumped up and stumbled onward, following the tracks his father had left. He had to get to the bridge. The other two were waiting.

In the small attic, the roof beams were so low they had to crawl across the boards that had been nailed to the rafters. Ben held up the lantern so Frank could see his way over to the small pile of blankets and provisions.

"Thank you, Mr. Kinser," Ben's father said through the trapdoor to the man below them, who stood waiting to close it after them. This balding, wealthy banker had sheltered more fugitives than his respectable neighbors would ever imagine.

"I'll be up to get Frank in the morning," Mr. Kinser replied. "We must simply be sure that you two"—he nodded at the Hanbys—"are not seen leaving my house."

"We will wait until you and Frank are gone," Ben's father said.

"Very good." The banker closed the door, leaving only the lamplight glowing off the wood of the attic. Ben prepared a makeshift bed from two blankets. Frank did not move, just sat on the rough boards with a faraway look on his face, the sunken parts in shadow from the partial light of the lantern.

Ben touched the man's arm. "Frank, we must sleep. All of us will travel tomorrow, but you will travel farthest."

"I'm not going back to Canada." Frank seemed thinner than before, the wrinkles around his eyes more pronounced.

"Where else would you go?" Ben's father asked as he crawled up next to them and grabbed his own blankets. "You have seen already—it is too dangerous for a man without papers to stay here. You know they claimed you had broken into a home."

"A lie. Someone asked me for papers and I ran into the first place I could. I didn't break nothing."

"But you see," Ben said, "they will invent reasons to capture you, even if you are doing nothing wrong. They all want the bounties for fugitives. No black man escapes without someone demanding his papers on the street."

"I won't go without Nelly." Frank's voice was hollow and weary. "Or without our little girl. It's been too long. Who will ever find them unless I go looking?"

"If anyone will find them, it will be John Parker and his friends," Ben's father said.

"They had seven months! The Lord knows they had enough time, and they ain't gonna do it."

"Don't lose heart," Ben said. "John is the most determined man I know. He has been methodically checking every slave market in the region—even having men go through courthouse records."

Frank pulled his knees to his chest and rested his arms on them. He dropped his head onto his arms, facedown, only the close-cut top of his head showing. "I just can't go back without them." His voice was muffled in his sleeve. "That ain't no life."

"If you don't go back to Canada to wait, you'll risk recapture every day," Ben's father said.

"I don't care." He still would not look up.

"If you stay in Ohio," Ben said, "you must at least go northward. Father, could he go wait in Cleveland, do you think, and work toward her freedom money there?"

"I'm not sanguine about it, son. Even northern Ohio has its watching eyes."

"I won't go back to Canada without her. I want to be close if Mr. Parker finds them."

Ben's father sighed. "Then I suppose Cleveland is our answer. Mr. Kinser can help you on your way, regardless."

"And, Frank," Ben said, placing a hand on his shoulder. "We will be able to reach you there, if you send us word of where you are staying. They will show you to a safe house first. Ask your host there to send us a letter. Then we will know how to find you as soon as there is word."

Frank did not answer. After a long moment, Ben felt the shoulder under his hand quaking and heard a single ragged sob. "What's happened to them?" Frank forced out on shuddering breaths, then wept as Ben had never heard a man weep, as if every cry were torn out of his flesh.

The sound pierced him through, and his own eyes grew damp. He put his arm around Frank's shoulders and prayed with all his heart for the Comforter to meet them there.

Thirty-Three

THE SILVER TEAPOT STOOD NEXT TO A TRAY WHERE
ladyfingers lay in a perfect circle. Her mother and sister perched
in their usual spots, backs straight and skirts pillowed around
the legs of the parlor chairs. Kate took her own seat. Silence
reigned, with the subtle clink of a cup here, a spoon there.

Their father had gone to Columbus again. He could drink
all he wished there, away from prying eyes. And any small worry
she had about him was eclipsed by her anxious thoughts for Ben
and his father. She had not seen them in the two days since the
hunt. Cornelia had heard nothing of their whereabouts either,
though, of course, Kate did not tell her why she had gone tearing away from the hunt or where the Hanbys had gone.

Her mother watched as Leah poured the tea. Leah's hands
were placed just so on the teapot, the way Ruth had taught her,
but the tight lines around her mother's mouth did not ease.

"I stopped at the postal office as I was passing by," her mother
said. Two letters lay next to her on the Oriental side table. "There
is a letter from Philadelphia."

Kate set her teacup back in the saucer, trying to conceal her
surprise. Her mother never spoke about her family in Philadelphia.

The city itself she had mentioned, and the cultured life she had led there as a girl. But never her family. The one time Kate had asked, her mother had snapped that there was nothing to be said on that subject.

Kate could not remember any other time when a letter had come from the city.

From her chair, she could see that the letter was addressed in a crabbed hand in black ink. It was sealed with wax. Her mother looked at the dark seal for a long moment, then broke it with a careless air.

She read whatever was written inside, her face showing only a phantom of indecipherable emotion that was gone almost as soon as it appeared. "It's from my sister," she said in a level tone.

"What does she say?" Leah asked, sitting on the edge of her chair. Her big eyes looked as if they were about to pop out of her face.

"My mother is ill." She spoke again as if she were stating the price of eggs.

Kate did not dare ask any questions. Her conversations of late with her mother had been strained enough.

Leah did not contain herself. "Our grandmother?" She reached up to twist a dark curl with a hesitant finger.

"Who else?" their mother asked curtly.

She stood, the letter in her hand. As she turned to leave, the silver tray carrying the teapot and sugar caught on the edge of her skirt and tumbled to the floor, spilling hot liquid and white powder across the dark floor. Kate regarded Leah with total shock, and saw the same expression staring back at her from her sister's face. Ruth Winter had never spilled anything in her daughters' presence. Never. And certainly not at tea.

But their mother was already halfway up the stairs, her neck as stiff as a soldier's, not a hair out of place in her elaborate upswept coiffure. Her purple skirt trailed behind her. "Have Tessie clean that up," she said to the girls without looking back, and then she was off down the hall and out of sight.

Leah sat silent, her eyes wide. "Will you pass me a ladyfinger?" she finally said, pointing to the plateful on Kate's side of the table.

Disregarding manners, Kate picked one directly off the tray and handed it over. Leah gave her a tiny smirk, then shoved it in her mouth. For five minutes, they ate with an occasional furtively whispered question or speculation. Kate kept glancing at the stairs, afraid her mother would return and hear them. But she did not reappear.

The letter from Philadelphia did not leave her thoughts for the rest of the day. By late afternoon, it had given her an idea. If she could do nothing else in her silent uproar over the lack of word from Ben, she might at least write to him. She sat at her desk, pen in hand. Cornelia was gone to Worthington for another concert and would not return until tomorrow. Kate's only choice was to take a letter for Ben to Cornelia's house and leave it there for her friend's return.

She wrote a few short lines, asking Ben to assure her that all was well and give any tidings of "the man of our acquaintance." She folded up the note into a small rectangle, wrote "Benjamin Hanby" on the outside, and sealed it. While waiting for the wax to cool, she wrote another brief note to Cornelia. She folded the letter to Ben inside the other letter, wrote "Cornelia Lawrence" on the outside of the thick little packet, and held it in her hand for a moment.

She was being too impetuous. She did not need to take it this evening, for it could wait for Cornelia's return. She would put it with the rest of her letters from Ben.

She pushed back her chair and stood, chilled by the draft through her day gown and shawl. A fire smoldered in the bedroom hearth, but it needed more wood. She would get some in a moment. She didn't like to call Tessie for every little thing.

The house was silent. She crossed to her bed and knelt beside it. Inserting her hand between the mattress and its rope support, she felt the lump of papers and pulled it out.

A scrape came from the door behind her. She jumped up and whirled around, hiding her papers in one hand behind her skirt.

Her mother stood at the door with a suspicious look on her face.

"What are you doing, Kate?" She sounded like a Grand Inquisitor, and even looked a little Spanish in her dark red gown, with the comb in her hair.

"Just preparing something for Leah's birthday." Kate could not look her mother in the eye. She was not accustomed to telling untruths. It made her squirm, but if she did not, she would fail to protect Ben, not just herself. Still, a lie was a lie.

Her mother paced toward her with measured steps. "I hope that all continues to be well between you and Frederick Jones," she said with superficial concern, and sat on the bed next to Kate.

"Yes, Mother." Kate turned her head away. She must hope the letters were completely concealed under her dressing gown.

"I suggest you sort out your feelings promptly," her mother said. "You don't have any better suitor, and you won't have any means to live if you don't marry well. You can't expect me to support you if you are so irresponsible as to refuse to marry an eligible and upstanding young man."

Kate stared at the bedpost. The mattress shifted as her mother stood and walked around to place herself in Kate's line of sight. Her pencil-thin, arched eyebrows creased into a line. "Do you hear what I say, Kate?"

"Yes, Mother," Kate said again. Her mother began to turn away, then stopped, her glance moving to the bed and Kate's gown.

Before Kate could move, her mother leaned over and seized a piece of paper that protruded from under Kate's skirt.

"So this is what you are preparing for Leah?" she asked as she scanned the lines. Her face slowly went blank, then filled with fury.

She continued to read in silence for a few moments. "Stand up," she gritted.

Kate could not stand, or her mother would see the rest of the letters beneath her skirt. When she did not move, Ruth grabbed her arm and hauled her up from the bed as she snatched up the letters in a clenched fist. "These are all from Ben Hanby? And all equally—passionate?"

Kate stood paralyzed.

"This is how you repay all I've done for you, all I've given you?" Her mother's voice rose. "You throw yourself away on some pious musical dreamer who will set you up in a wooden shack and hum tunes while you starve?"

"I have not made any promises to anyone." Kate's voice shook.

"I should hope not. I had forbidden you even to speak to him."

"And I didn't. Only once, by accident."

"So you can look me in the face and tell me you have not violated my instruction?" Ruth asked.

Kate avoided her eyes. Her mother gathered the papers together, strode to the fireplace, and tossed them in.

Kate watched Ben's words shriveling and burning, thin lines of orange crawling across them and blackening into noth-ingness. Those might be the last words she ever had from him. She hoped her mother could not see her distress. Heat rushed to her face.

"I hope you are blushing for your own sins, and for the wrong you have done to a good man who is courting you," her mother said.

"I have not deceived Frederick. He has not even proposed to me."

"If he does propose, he is a better man than you deserve. If he knew about this—correspondence—he would leave such a deceitful young woman to boil in her own dishonesty."

It wasn't true. Kate did not think she was deceitful. And yet she had accepted the letters when she knew she should not.

"Let me be very plain, so that you will have no further opportunity for manipulation of my words," her mother said. "You are to have no further contact of any sort with Ben Hanby, nor with anyone in his family. If you receive a letter from him, you are to deliver it to me immediately. Do I make myself clear?"

Kate nodded.

"Answer me!" her mother snapped.

"Yes, Mother," she said faintly.

"I will tell Frederick you are indisposed this afternoon, as you are clearly in no condition to go out." Her mother glided out into the hallway. She pulled the door closed behind her with a thud. That wooden sound echoed in Kate's head until it sounded more like a heavy iron door clanging shut.

Thirty-Four

IMPATIENCE JABBED AT BEN, DEPRIVING HIM OF appetite even though the smell of his mother's cherry pie rising from the plate should have made him ravenous. All he could think about was getting word to Kate about Frank. She must be so worried—they had arrived only an hour ago on the stage. He needed to get away from the dinner table and speak to Cornelia.

But first, he did want to hear what John Parker had to say.

John had come to town on his way north, so of course Ben's mother had asked him to stay for dinner. Over potatoes and ham, he talked with Ben's father about abolitionist orators. The subject was not one to fascinate Lizzie and Willie, but John was such an imposing figure that even the littlest Hanbys stayed quiet for a while when he was around, content to watch him and listen to his rich, low voice. He sat at the head of the table in a chair, as it was completely out of the question for his long limbs to fit on one of the benches. Ben's father sat to his right, and his mother on his left. Ben sat at the foot of the table. His attention to the conversation was impeded by little voices piping at him. Lizzie and Willie could only restrain themselves for so long.

Twilight was falling. Ben's mother rose and lit two lamps

to brighten the kitchen. Now Amanda cut the cherry pie made from the winter preserves in the cellar, and Jenny handed plates around the table. The tart but sweet dessert kept Lizzie and Willie busy a few minutes longer, though they squirmed on the bench as they ate. Anna had already taken Samuel to play upstairs. No toddler could be still for half an hour, no matter how impressive the guest.

John Parker finished his pie.

"Excellent, as always," he said.

Ben's mother murmured her thanks.

The big man pushed his chair a few inches back from the end of the table, making a scraping noise. "I have some news," he said. His face took on a pronounced stillness that drew every gaze to him.

"Perhaps the children wish to go play," he said.

"Of course." Ben's mother nodded toward the steps in the way that told Amanda and Jenny it was time to take Lizzie and William upstairs.

As soon as the little ones were gone, John continued in a low voice. "I told you I am on my way north. I'm going to see Frank. The news I have for him must be delivered in person."

It could not be happy news, not with the somber way he spoke. Ben's mother turned pale.

"I met recently with a friend from New Orleans who had come up to meet with Mr. Garrison," John Parker said. "This friend of mine is a wealthy planter who had a change of heart on the slavery issue after he fell in love with a quadroon years ago. He has been watching the New Orleans slave auctions for me ever since Nelly and her baby were sold down south. I had heard from another informer that they had been sold to one man for several months, but he passed away and his estate and slaves were sold, which sent them back to the auctions. My informant told me they were headed down New Orleans way."

John paused, but no one moved or spoke.

"By going down to the saloons and buying drinks for the slave-running crews, my planter friend found Nelly. He got her slave-master to point her out in the crowd at the slave market. She was together with her baby, but they were dying."

His mother took a sharp breath.

"Cholera had struck the market, which was packed and filthy," John said. "They were quarantined with scores of others. She was too weak to stand, and my friend was not permitted to approach her, nor could he have done so without attracting notoriety. But later, he obtained these from the slave-trader on some pretext." He reached in his breast pocket and retrieved folded papers. He opened them up and handed them to Ben's mother. "I'm sorry. There can be no mistake."

She put them down on the table.

Certificate of Death. Ben could read it from across the table in the black ink of the heading. Nelly's name was written beneath.

His mother's ashy face acquired a green tinge. She jumped up and ran out the kitchen door, which banged behind her. His father strode after her, caught the door as it rebounded, and followed her out.

Ben, Cyrus, and John sat in silence.

After a minute or two, Ben heard his mother sobbing outside, though he couldn't make out the words his father murmured to her.

Ben bowed his head. Frank's face filled his imagination, torn with the agony of his missing wife and baby. Then the dark house of Ben's boyhood rose to his memory, with the lamplight flickering on the dying man's face and the scrape of his hoarse voice, saying, "I'll see my Nelly again." A tide of regret and sorrow swept Ben back to the table and the reality of her death. She had gone to Joseph, at least, but at what cost to Frank? And she ended her days in filth, with her little girl sick beside her.

"Why?" Ben spoke the harsh word aloud, surprising himself.

John regarded him with understanding, but said nothing. It seemed as if they sat forever listening to his mother's quieter sobbing, then his father talking to her.

Why did these innocent people die? Why couldn't he help them? What good could he do, when he and others tried and tried, but the darkness kept rolling in?

His father finally returned, opening the door and entering before his mother, as if to protect her from their view. Her face was blotchy and her eyes were still wet. She walked over to the stove and puttered with some irons. Although she was no longer sobbing, tears rolled down her face, falling and disappearing into the fabric of her dress. She brought a handkerchief to her nose, pressing it to her face as if it could stop the tears.

Ben had never seen her so distraught. But she had wept many times because of the Railroad. Sometimes she wept at the awful things that fugitives told them, sometimes because they left so many behind. Or because they were sick and might die, like Joseph. Or sometimes, when his father didn't come home, she wept while she waited to hear news.

His father walked to the shelves and took down a can of coffee. He held it out to his mother, asking with a lift of his brows if she wanted it. She took it from his hands and started the routine of putting on the kettle.

While his mother went through the motions of taking down cups and saucers, his father came back to sit with them.

"I think it would be fitting," he said, "for us to spend some time this evening remembering Nelly and her daughter, and praying for Frank."

At the mention of the baby, his mother sniffled again.

His father paused but didn't draw attention to it. "We'll pray not only for Frank but for all others who loved someone who died in that market. And we must pray for the eternal souls of the slavers who cost them the life and freedom that only God should give and take away." His voice was rough with sorrow. "We will pray in a few minutes. The little ones will be in bed, and Amanda can join us. Let's go into the parlor." He stood. They all shuffled after him, leaving Ben's mother to the privacy of the kitchen.

In the parlor, silence still reigned. The men sat down. His father handed John a newspaper and took up a Bible himself. Cyrus followed their lead, picking up his book for Latin class.

Ben was too wracked to read. He crossed to the piano, as glossy as it had been the day it arrived a year ago. Seating himself on the bench, he let his fingers pick out the opening notes of a melancholy sonata.

The music eased into the air. The pain in the room lost some of its terrible edge—not much, but the ache became as much as he could bear, instead of more.

He hoped the music might comfort his mother in the kitchen. Could he ask Kate to take on the same kind of burden that his mother had borne for years? Some might think it utterly selfish of him to even consider bringing Kate into this way of life where she would suffer the sorrows his mother had known. The thought hung heavily on him, lingering in the last notes of the sonata as he let it fade.

He shifted into a different melody, a simpler one. He did not sing the song aloud, unwilling to disturb the others at such a solemn moment, but the words ran through his mind. *"Oh my poor Nelly Gray, they have taken you away . . ."*

The time had come. Tomorrow he would finish the song, and he would send it to the big music publishing company in Chicago.

He doubted they would publish it, but he had to try. For Nelly, the baby girl, and Joseph, and all the others lost and beyond his help. The song must tell the story of what was happening to them.

He played the melody slowly, pausing after each phrase, as if his passion alone could propel the song into print.

Perhaps music could succeed where words had failed.

Thirty-Five

IN ALL OF RECORDED HISTORY, A PIANO LESSON HAD never caused such a moral crisis. What if Kate went to her lesson with Cornelia, only to find that her friend had once again arranged a surreptitious visit from Ben?

Her solitary walk out of the house was slow. It would have been better if she had forgotten the lesson.

If she went, she could see Cornelia and hear from her friend more of what had happened to the Hanbys, if Cornelia was privy to any details. Then again, she was wary of Cornelia's scheming. Kate longed to see Ben, but she could not live with herself if she became a habitual breaker of her word. She passed under the graceful boughs of the trees in the quadrangle.

There was not a living soul she could ask for advice. But she knew Ben would ask God.

She closed her eyes. *God, please help me. I don't know what's right. I don't even know whether or not to go to my lesson. Tell me what to do.*

No words answered in her head. But neither was there silence. Instead came a feeling of—someone waiting.

How was that any help? Was he listening? And if so, why wouldn't he give her some sign of what to do?

And then words ran through her mind—like her own thoughts, but at the same time, unlike them—*Love and honor should not conflict with one another.*

That was not an answer!

But the idea refused to dissipate, floating in the back of her mind.

Was it wrong to go if Cornelia might arrange for Ben to be there? Her mother's violent objection to Ben did not seem reasonable or fair. Kate should not reject a man who might not be wealthy, simply because he devoted himself to serving God. Surely there could be worse qualities in a husband. Did that mean her mother was wrong for forbidding her to see Ben? And if so, was that any excuse to defy her?

Kate walked faster. She didn't know. She could only do the best she could. She would go to the lesson, but if he was there, then she would leave.

She cut across the lawn toward Cornelia's home. Cornelia answered the door with a warm smile. Her light blue dress perfectly complemented Kate's green one. Her auburn hair framed her face, drawn into a neat, shining twist at the nape of the neck.

"I love your dress," Kate said. "It's another French one, isn't it? They're so beautifully made."

"Thank you. Won't you come in?"

The house was too quiet. Usually when Mrs. Lawrence was home, she came out of the kitchen or down the stairs to greet visitors in the parlor. But Kate couldn't hear anyone else in the house.

"Shall we begin? How did you find the new Chopin?" Cornelia asked, crossing to the piano bench.

"I was awful at first, but better now."

The challenge of the lesson took Kate's mind off her worries. She struck the last soft chords of an etude and looked at Cornelia.

"That was very good," her friend said. "You could even give the last two chords a little more time to ring."

Kate played them again.

"Oh yes, that's lovely. I believe that finishes our lesson for the week. Well done." Cornelia leaned back. "And I have something else for you."

Kate took a quick breath and glanced around.

Cornelia looked uncertain. "I know you may be angry with me—"

"If Ben Hanby is here, then I must leave," Kate said.

Cornelia touched her elbow. "It won't do any harm to say hello. He told me he must speak with you today."

Kate's resolve wavered. She forced herself up on legs turned to gummy paste. "No, I'm sorry. I can't." She walked across the parlor to the front door.

"Then you may wish to leave through the kitchen," Cornelia said. "He might be waiting at the front door."

Kate whirled and ran back through the parlor and into the wood-beamed kitchen. She pushed open the door and hurried out the back way, down the kitchen stoop, watching her step to be sure she didn't trip in her rush.

She ran into Ben. They collided so hard that she knocked the breath out of herself and he tripped backward. By instinct, she reached out for him, grabbing his arms. His heavier weight almost pulled her off her feet, but he regained his balance.

They were so close, arms entwined, her skirts brushing his trousers. She was conscious of his breathing. Their gazes locked. All she could see was the dark clarity of his eyes.

She pulled away. "Pardon me." She laced her fingers together, her heart thumping. "That was careless of me." She looked back at the steps as if they were somehow to blame.

"Miss Winter," he said, "I have news for you."

"About Frank?" Let it be good news.

"Frank is farther north again, out of reach of pursuers." His eyes were shadowed, in spite of what should have been good news.

"What is it?"

He hesitated. "Nelly and her daughter will not be coming back to him."

Her heart sank. "Why not? John cannot find them?"

Pain filled his face. "They became ill—they have passed away."

She turned from him, breathless. She must sit. A few staggered steps brought her to the stoop, but her skirt tangled around her feet and she fell to her knees on the wooden stairs.

"Miss Winter." Ben rushed to her side. She clutched at the step—its grain seemed so coarse—she dragged in a shallow breath.

He took her hand and assisted her to turn and sit. She clung to his hand, not caring about propriety at all.

"It's sad. It's sad." She spoke through a numb glaze, as if she observed herself from a distance. But the words released something and water welled in her eyes.

Ben sat down next to her. "I am sorry," he said in a low voice, cradling her hand in both of his.

"Her baby girl too?"

"Yes." He seemed to understand the realization was slow and awful, and had to be spoken from the head into the heart, word by painful word.

Tears slipped down her face.

"I regret having brought you into such circumstances. I never meant to cause you sorrow. If I could undo it, I would," Ben said. He pulled out a folded linen handkerchief and offered it to her.

"I would not undo it." She blotted the tears from her face with her free hand, but her voice was still thick with them. "I cannot wish myself blind. I only wish my eyes had not been opened at the cost of their lives." Somehow it did not matter if he saw her weeping—he looked as if he were on the verge himself.

"But I cannot stand to see you hurt," he said. "I love you." The sweetness of his words stirred into the bitterness of the news like a trail of ink in water. She sat in silence with him, the ache beneath her bodice so great she thought it would split her in two. Time passed, she did not know how long—only that even in the pain, he loved her and she was not alone.

He went to his knees on the step below her and lifted her hand gently in his, bringing the inside of her wrist to his lips. He reached out with his other hand to touch her cheek.

She looked at him, speechless, her soul laid open by sorrow, longing for his comfort.

"I want you to be my wife, Kate. I've thought of little else for months. But I can't bring you more of this—more death, more suffering."

"But with you, I might help," she said. "How many more are there like Nelly? I can't forget her." Her lips trembled and she pressed them together to stop it.

He stood and lifted her to him in one fervent motion, his arms around her as she melted into the strength of his embrace, the reassurance and passion that poured from him and circled her shoulders. She breathed in his warm, clean scent in the hollow of his neck, and did not want to move, ever. She drew strength from him, as if she could face any sorrow, even the loss of the baby girl, if Ben would hold her in his arms and walk with her through it. His goodness fell on her like a fragment of heaven, an imperfect mirror giving evidence of something better beyond either of them.

He stepped back and looked her full in the face with dark, intent eyes. "We will be honest with your mother. We won't hide anything again." His hands remained steady at her sides. "Will you marry me, Kate? Can you trust that God will make a way for us, if he favors what we intend?"

She felt the purity of his intentions, his compassion, like a tide pulling her toward him. "I don't know if it's right to agree, given my mother's opinion."

"It can't be wrong if we are open and conceal nothing from her."

"But she has already stated her opposition," Kate said. "And I confess I would be afraid to tell her."

"You may honor your parents and still plead with them for the righteousness of our cause."

She crossed her arms, torn.

He moved closer and laid a warm hand behind her elbow. "Kate, please say you will marry me. If God makes a way."

He looked as if he was holding his breath. She was holding hers as well.

She let out a sigh. "I will, if God makes a way. Which means changing my mother's mind."

His face lit up, and he trailed his hand from her elbow to her wrist, brought her hand up to his lips, and kissed it with reverence. A tingle ran up her arm.

"I will never give you cause to regret your choice," he said, still holding her hands.

"What do we do now?" she asked, shy.

He was serious. "I suppose we must speak to our parents."

She quailed at the thought. "I will need to talk to my mother alone." God would make a way, as Ben said.

But it was hard to believe even the Lord himself could change her mother's mind.

Thirty-Six

SHE COULD NOT AFFORD TO LOOK WEAK OR CHILDISH. The glass showed Kate that her eyes were puffy from lack of sleep, her cheeks pale. She moved to the washstand and poured some water from the porcelain pitcher into the washbowl. After wrapping a towel around her neck to protect her dress, she cupped the cool water in her hands and bathed her hot face. When she dried off and looked in the mirror, she approved of her altered appearance.

Her mother was in her own bedroom, odd for this time of the afternoon when she would ordinarily go to the homes of other prominent townspeople to visit. But since the arrival of the letter from Philadelphia, she had kept to her room. She had been quiet and withdrawn instead of assuming her usual commanding demeanor. But her mother's lowered brow and snappish tone did not bode well for her general state of mind.

Kate opened her door and walked along the upstairs hallway. Midway on her short journey, she had to pause and steady herself with one hand against the wall. God would make a way. She continued to the closed door of the bedroom and made herself give three sharp, confident knocks on the wood.

Her mother opened the door. She was clad in a rust-colored day dress, her dark hair pulled back, her white face impassive. "What is it?"

"I must discuss something with you." Kate kept her chin up and her gaze steady. "May I come in?"

Her mother's eyes narrowed in irritation, but she moved back to let Kate enter.

Kate seldom went in her parents' bedroom. There was something uncomfortable about it, with its massive mahogany bedposts, dark green bedcoverings, and a heavy rug that suffocated any sound. It was more like a mausoleum than a place where people slept. Kate crossed to one of the two high-backed chairs placed against the walls. "Would you like to sit?" she asked her mother. "This will take some time."

Her mother's eyebrows rose, creating the wrinkles in her forehead that she had managed to stave off for so many years. She glided to the other chair and sat with controlled grace, regarding Kate, daring her to begin.

"You have forbidden me to associate with Ben Hanby." Quite a feat that she had even managed to say his name in this house without stammering. Her mother's lips curled in derision, but she still said nothing, her hands folded atop the tiers of her skirt.

"I have obeyed your wishes, until yesterday, when I inadvertently happened to meet him."

Anger began to tighten her mother's mouth and cheeks.

"I wish to behave with respect and honesty," Kate hurried on, "which is why I am telling you of this meeting." Was there a slight relaxation in her mother's expression? Kate seized the moment. "However, I also have found that I disagree with your choices for my life, and I feel they are based on false assumptions."

Now her mother's hands clenched on her skirt. An explosion was imminent.

Kate hurried on. "I have agreed to marry him, but we will not marry without your permission. We hope and pray you will reconsider your opposition and give us your blessing." Her voice trailed away at the end, despite her best effort to keep it steady.

Her mother remained still for a long moment. "Give you my blessing!" she scoffed, her face hard with disdain. She burst into mocking laughter. "You ask for my blessing on your disobedient action? I have forbidden you to see him and you think now I will agree to a marriage?"

Her mother stood up and began to pace back and forth across the carpet, her face trained implacably on Kate no matter how her body moved. "You think you have your reasons and your foolish arguments for getting your way. I assure you that you know *nothing*. You are a silly girl who has fallen for a—a—handsome face and a—a song!—and you will throw away your future on him."

Kate had never seen her mother so enraged. She was grateful for the arms of the chair; she grasped them to hold herself up under the blast.

"Do you think that you are the first to face such a decision?" Her mother's voice rose. "Do you think that my rules are idle whims, based on ignorance? No! I faced the same decision when I was your age. I made the same foolish choice, and I threw away my life for the brief thrill of what I thought was love."

Her mother's eyes glistened.

"You think this sentimental feeling you have will last forever, that he will always treat you like a precious angel and protect you. Well, he won't! He will forget you, and neglect you. He will not care for your wishes. He may even be a drunk, like your father—so many of them are." Her mother's voice cracked. "You will not have your money to protect you, as I did. Your father has seen to that, with his failure to bring a steady income. There will be nothing left for you."

"Mother, I am sorry for what you have suffered. But I do not think our situations are the same. I believe that I—"

"What do you think I believed?" her mother shouted. "No girl knows what marriage is really like! You don't know how men change when the bloom is off the rose. Why do you think you have never met my mother or my father? Because they tried to warn me. They did everything they could to stop me from marrying this newcomer with a—a *charming* smile," she said with heavy sarcasm. "They told me they would no longer have any contact with me if I went against their wishes. They pleaded with me to marry in our society, where I would be safe. We were related to the Willings and the Binghams—we had all of Philadelphia's comforts. But no, I thought I knew better! I thought they just didn't know the wonderful man I had found!" She paced the room, waving her arms in stiff, jerky motions. "So I eloped with your father, and lost everything. Everything but the money my grandfather had already placed in trust for me," she said. "And that is all I have had to console me for my stupidity, all these years."

"You are trying to protect me," Kate said. "I honor that, Mother." She stood up. Sitting was inadequate for what she had to say. "But Ben is not Father. I have known him for some time. I know that his family is solid, that they are good people. And

I know he is a man of faith. If he were ever tempted to neglect me, he would never turn from vows he had made to God." Her heart filled as she thought of Ben's goodness. Her mother was incapable of seeing it.

"Your father acted like a good churchgoing man too," her mother said with renewed anger. "Until we left Philadelphia. Any man can put on that mask when he wants to, talking about God and doing what is right. Talking is all it ever is. When push comes to shove, Ben Hanby will do exactly what he wants, and claim you drove him to it."

"No, he won't. He's a humble and generous man. He is"— she searched for the word—"godly." It sounded strange coming out of her mouth.

"At what point did you become a religious zealot? You are an idiot!"

Kate took a quick breath. "I won't change my mind. If I can't marry Ben, I won't marry at all."

Her mother regained her self-control one facial muscle at a time. She reverted to her usual cold tone. "If you do not marry, we cannot support you. You will be in abject misery. The romantic feeling you have now will fade, and in its place, what will clothe you or feed you? Only loneliness and endless menial work."

Kate walked past her to the doorway. She turned around to see her mother following close on her heels.

"Apparently there is only one way to ensure that you do not see Ben Hanby while I am gone to Philadelphia. I must take you with me on that journey."

"What? What of Leah? She can't stay here alone."

Her mother hesitated, blinking. Then, "I will send her to the Boglers to stay."

"But I will not be back in time for the beginning of the term. President Lawrence said I had to recite in public then or be dismissed." Not that she wished to recite, even after her practice, but it was the only argument that might sway her mother.

"I am certain your professors will agree to hear your speech as soon as you return. We are faced with an imminent death in the family, after all. Get to your room and pack a valise," her mother said. "And stay out of my sight until it's time to depart." She slammed the bedroom door in Kate's face.

Kate stared at the door. God did not appear to be making a way.

Thirty-Seven

KATE HAD NEVER BEEN SO TIRED IN HER LIFE. THE high-backed wooden bench seats of the Main Line had some padding at least, but the constant rattling of the wheels on the tracks wore on her nerves. Though the train had stopped last night to allow the passengers to sleep at a Harrisburg hotel, they had suffered from the rough vibration for ten hours a day, two days in a row. And that was only since Pittsburgh. Before that, the journey from Columbus to Pittsburgh had kept them on more primitive trains for another two days. She was sure her mother was as exhausted as she, but they had barely spoken in the entire journey. Kate kept her nose buried in the Bible Reverend Meade had given her last year. Her mind, however, drifted away with the rhythm of the wheels on the track.

Was he thinking of her? What was he doing at this moment? She closed her eyes and lost herself in the remembered touch of his hand, his words of love.

Her traveling dress stuck to her skin in the humid afternoon air. The dress might be malodorous in more polite company, but one could not even tell given the offensive smells arising from some of their fellow passengers.

Escaping steam from the mighty engine hissed, the whistle blew, and the train lumbered to a stop. Through the windows, she could see that one car away, the blue-capped conductor had opened the door and stepped to the ground.

"Philadelphia, Market and Thirtieth Street!" he yelled.

Her mother picked up her handbag and stood. She did not wait for the porter to hand their small valise down, but tugged it from under the seat and dragged it to the door. Such unladylike haste was not typical of her, but her face was as guarded as ever and showed nothing of what might be animating her sudden burst of motion. Her hair looked as if a maid had dressed it that morning, perfectly twisted and smooth. Kate's chignon was not as cooperative, from what she had seen in the cloudy metallic surface that served as a looking glass in the washroom.

Her mother had stepped off the train without assistance— she must follow. Grabbing the brass handle on the side of the door frame, Kate lowered herself down the eighteen-inch drop to the stone floor of the platform. One must be careful. It would not do to break an ankle so far from Westerville simply because they refused to wait for the porter. Farther down the platform the station hands unloaded trunks and boxes from the baggage car. Theirs would be among them.

The station was a one-story brick building, surprisingly small for an American metropolis. Once a porter found their trunks and loaded them on a wheeled cart, Kate followed her mother through the archway.

"This is Market Street," her mother said. "I am not famil-iar with this part of the city. There was no railway when I left twenty years ago."

Kate scanned the buildings. They were wooden structures,

stores marked with wooden signs advertising tobacco, dry goods, and, of course, liquor.

"Come along, Kate." Her mother led the way to where hackney buggies waited alongside the station building. The porter followed with the cart.

"Need a cab, missus?" a young man on the driver's seat of one buggy asked.

"Yes," her mother said. "To Walnut, between Fourth and Fifth."

They agreed on a fare, and he jumped down to stow their luggage in back. Her mother tipped the porter, and the cabdriver helped them up to their seats. He hopped back up to his own place, clucked to the ragamuffin brown horse, and they were off down Market at a trot.

As the buggy passed Twentieth Street, two-story stone buildings appeared alongside the wooden stores, and the signs of commerce thickened. The street was full of buggies, carriages, and even a couple of covered wagons on their way through town. Their driver whisked nimbly around the slower vehicles.

"This was nothing but open acreage when last I saw it." Her mother's voice bore a note of wonder.

Pedestrians walked past the storefronts, men in top hats and derbies, working men in caps. Kate spotted a few working women in worn dresses, but no ladies yet.

The hack turned right on Twelfth Street.

"Look there." Her mother pointed down a side street. "Girard Row. I went there often with my mother."

The street boasted splendid facades—white stone, high steps, and columns on the ground floor with three stories of brick above. Dark shutters flanked the windows and set off the white of the lintels. Rows of trees conveyed order and beauty: black cherry, maple, crabapple. Two ladies moved sedately down the walk in their bright silk gowns and graceful hats festooned with feathers.

"What took you there?"

"Tea with friends. The Binghams." Her mother's mouth was tight, as if she held in something more private. Her eyes were misty. It was odd to see her like this, a shifting and reordering of all Kate knew. Her mother had never been at home in Westerville, but here she fit.

The driver guided them around the corner, passing a sign marking Chestnut Street. Kate drew in her breath at the sight. Four- and five-story buildings, squeezed wall to wall without interruption. Luxury businesses proliferated: engravers and stationers, entire establishments devoted to fine gloves and hosiery.

"There's the College Hall," her mother said, gazing at a two-story building with classical lines. "And the Fine Arts Academy. I remember the garden as larger, but perhaps I was smaller then." Her face was open, vulnerable in a way Kate had never seen. "The Chestnut Street Theater is still the same, I see." The building she pointed out was all arches, columns, and placards announcing the latest dramatic offerings. After it came a vast lawn, gorgeous spire, and the white-trimmed windows of what had to be the Statehouse. Kate kept silent—she did not know what to say to this mother she barely knew.

The driver turned a corner onto a road marked Fifth Street. Her mother's face grew white and tense. What must she be feeling, as she waited to see her sister and her mother for the first time in twenty years? Even Kate was nervous. For her mother, it must be a kind of agony.

The brick house where the driver pulled up boasted lintels even more ornate than those of Girard Row, though the front steps were low and dark. The driver helped them down and deposited their trunks on the curb. Kate's mother dug in her stocking purse for his fare and he drove off, the horse's hooves thudding softly on the road.

"Come along, Kate." Her mother marched up to the oak front door, maintaining her perfect posture as she rang the doorbell. Kate stood behind her.

Locks slid and clunked and a middle-aged manservant opened the door, his face blank and neutral. "Madam?"

Her mother cleared her throat, a small nervous sound. "I'm Ruth Morris Winter, a daughter of the house."

"Good afternoon." He stood aside and opened the door. "Mrs. Cadwalader is in the parlor, to your left."

Mrs. Cadwalader. It had to be Aunt Mary, her mother's sister, who had married into a prominent family and was now widowed. Her mother had drilled Kate in family names and relations on the train.

Following her mother's lead, Kate gathered her skirts and stepped over the threshold into the foyer. The floor was a deep black-brown, with the look of wood polished not only by the labor of servants but by the passage of feet over decades.

The manservant went out to get their bags. Head held high, her mother turned and walked into the parlor.

The woman standing there looked very much like her mother, as they faced one another, but with heavier lines around the eyes and mouth. She was still refined and slim in her pewter silk gown, but her once midnight-black hair had gray threads too.

"Ruth," Kate's aunt said, "I'm so glad you're here." The

simple statement held a world of regret. Her aunt crossed the room with the same perfect carriage as Kate's mother, her hand outstretched. The sisters took each other's hands, her mother a bit awkward.

"And this is your beautiful daughter?" Aunt Mary took Kate's hand as well, then released it to gesture to the low mahogany table topped with a tea service. "Would you like tea? Are you hungry?"

"Tea, if you please," her mother replied. She seated herself on a green brocade chair in the style of the previous century. Kate sat on another of the chairs. The parlor was bright and warm, covered in layers of beautiful red and blue rugs. The marble of the fireplace was snowy white, carved into columns that had been popular when the house was built forty years ago. The lamps were tasseled, the glass-fronted cabinets filled with books and curios from foreign lands.

Her mother looked at Aunt Mary. "Mother is . . . ?"

"Not well, of course, but hanging on. I believe she wouldn't let herself go before you came."

Her mother stared into her teacup, her face still, and sipped her tea. "Do you have children?"

A faint smile brought light to the older woman's face.

"Four living. Thomas, Georgia, Geoffrey, and Richard. And five grandchildren already. And you?"

"Two daughters, Kate and Leah. Not married yet, but I expect Kate to marry a young man of great prospects soon."

Kate turned away and stared at a portrait on the wall.

"I'm so glad. I hope our children will all meet one another soon. The family has been too long apart. I am so very sorry for that."

Kate stole a look at her mother. Her face was stony and she set down her teacup. "I would like to see Mother."

"Of course." Aunt Mary set down her own cup and rose.

"Shall I come?" Kate asked.

"If you like."

It seemed uncaring not to go with her mother, though Kate felt like an intruder as she followed. Aunt Mary's skirt trailed behind her as she walked back into the foyer and up the long staircase.

The upstairs hall was wide and airy, soft underfoot with the same thick rugs. The dark door at the end of the hall swung open at Aunt Mary's gentle touch.

Kate walked after her mother tentatively, but her mother stopped a few steps inside the door. In the massive, canopied bed lay a tiny, frail old woman. Kate's mother stared in obvious disbelief. It must be shocking—what had her grandmother looked like twenty years ago? Beneath the deep wrinkles and colorless hair, Kate could make out the planes and hollows of bone that must have made her grandmother a beauty in her youth. Her eyes were open, aware behind their curtain of sagging flesh.

"Ruth," she wheezed, a horrible, rasping sound.

Kate's mother hesitated, then crossed to the bedside and took the sick old woman's hand. "Yes."

Kate's grandmother closed her eyes, the tiniest of smiles pulling at her pursed mouth.

"She can't speak much," Aunt Mary said from behind them. "But she will do better tomorrow morning. She is always better in the mornings."

Kate's mother laid the palsied hand gently back on the bed. "Then we will speak more in the morning, Mother." She turned to Aunt Mary, her face strained. "I am very fatigued."

"I understand. Let me show you to your room. Michael will bring up your bags."

She led them out, back down the hall, and into another bedroom. Old dolls and toys sat on shelves. Kate's mother gazed around her and did not speak. An antique bed and cedar chest spoke of years of residence—her mother might even have shared that large bed with her aunt, as she and Kate would now share it for their stay.

"I will leave you to rest," Aunt Mary said. "Do not hesitate to ring for the maid if you need anything at all."

"Thank you," Kate's mother said.

Aunt Mary retreated and closed the door. Kate walked to the window and looked out. When she turned, she saw that her mother had taken an old wooden horse from the shelf and was cradling it in her arms. Her mother touched its yarn mane, gently pressed it against her heart, and bowed her head.

Thirty-Eight

January 12th, 1856   1-19 Walnut Street, Philadelphia

Dearest Ben,

My mother has adamantly refused to allow our engagement. She has not lifted her ban on any communication between us, but instead has asked me to inform you of her refusal via this one letter. As you may have heard from Cornelia by now, we have left Westerville for a journey of at least a month's time, owing to the fact that my grandmother is on her deathbed. I have never met my mother's mother, so I cannot feel it as an intimate loss. Nevertheless, my mother has my pity.

You and I agreed that we would not defy her will, trusting God to make a way. I plan to honor that agreement, and I will not write to you again. Our last meeting already seems far away and impossible. Did it truly happen?

I cannot write more of my feelings.

Kate

January 15th, 1856   *50 Grove Street*

Darling Kate,

   To say that I am deeply disappointed by your news is inadequate. I do not despair, however. The Lord moves in mysterious ways. I will pray for a change in your mother's heart.

   Our last meeting will not fade in my memory. If I close my eyes and think of you, I can almost feel you in my arms again, and smell the soft sweetness of your hair. That is all I can do to bear the knowledge that I will not see you again for some time—at least a month's time, and from what you have written, I suspect it may be longer.

   I will wait as long as need be. Please do not forget.

                  Ben

He could not send that reply. He crumpled it and held its sharp folds imprisoned in his fist.

Mrs. Winter had not given Kate permission to receive a letter from Ben. Any reply he sent would be read only by Mrs. Winter, which would do nothing but harm to his cause. Though it would seem it was a cause already lost. Kate had been gone for three endless weeks.

He rose and let the ball of paper fall into the wastebasket.

"Ben." His father's voice called from downstairs, rousing him from his brooding.

"Yes, sir." He walked out of his room and stood at the head of the staircase.

His father wore a work shirt and held an awl in one hand. "I need to carry a few pieces to the store. Will you assist me?"

"Of course." Ben descended the stairs and followed his father through the kitchen, sidestepping Lizzie, Willie, and Sam, who circled the kitchen like puppies as his mother stoked the fire. They went through the cellar door and on down.

In the wet cold of the cellar, his father gathered a few bridles, slung a saddle over his arm, and nodded at the two harnesses on the bench. "Will you please get those?"

Ben draped them over his shoulder.

A clatter sounded upstairs and then grew louder as boots thumped down the steps. Cyrus bolted out on the basement floor and skidded to a stop in front of him. "Ben! Look what came in the mail." He waved an envelope in Ben's face.

"What? Slow down," Ben said. "I can't see it if you push it in my face like that."

Cyrus steadied the envelope and moved it a few inches farther from Ben's nose.

Oliver Ditson and Company was the stamped return address.

"It's the music company, isn't it?" Cyrus asked, still breathless from his rapid descent.

His father and brother were watching him.

"Go ahead, open it," his father said.

The envelope was thick. Ben broke the seal and withdrew a folded sheet lined with musical staves. At the top, in spiky, ornate letters, *Darling Nelly Gray*. And beneath it, almost as large as the title itself, *B. R. Hanby.*

He touched the letters that formed the title. "They've published it," he said to himself.

"Clearly!" Cyrus said. "Now you will be rich and famous."

Ben checked each page to be sure the lyrics and notes were correct. They were. "I don't think anyone grows rich by writing songs," Ben said. "You notice there is no payment enclosed."

"They'll pay you," Cyrus said. "They'll have to!"

"They won't pay me much, if it sells modestly and fades away," Ben said. "That's what happens to most songs. Writing songs is not a living—it's a pastime."

"What about Stephen Foster? He must be wealthy with all the songs he's sold."

"He may have made some music publishers wealthy, but I've heard they don't pay well. I didn't send this song to Ditson and Co. with the hope of making my fortune."

Cyrus shook it off like a dog shedding water. "I don't think this song is going to fade away. You just wait and see."

And with a sprightly hop, Cyrus snatched the music and bounded up the stairs. Ben heard his mother exclaim. But he did not feel the joy he expected. Everything was muffled, as if a muted trumpet had turned a celebratory march into flat hooting.

Thirty-Nine

BEN BRUSHED THE DIRT CAKED ON THE GELDING'S hocks and tapped the brush against the bottom of his boot to clean it. Gabriel had a way of dirtying himself even when snow lay on the ground—it was the way of all white horses to find any clump of mud and attach it to themselves.

His father strode into the frosty barn, breath puffing in the morning cold, a bucket of water in one gloved hand. He slid the bolt on the stall and set the bucket in front of Gabriel. Water had to be brought from the house in freezing weather like this.

"A tremendous achievement, son!" He patted Ben on the shoulders, his face alight with joy and paternal pride. He had not ceased to celebrate since the news had come in yesterday about "Darling Nelly Gray."

"I think this calls for a holiday, perhaps some music in front of the fire, popcorn for the family. Benjamin Hanby, published songwriter." He grinned.

"I don't think so, Father." Ben tried not to sound terse. "I should still go mind the store. The week's end is approaching. Someone might come in to shop, and we don't want to miss the business." Ben walked out of the stall, set the brush on its shelf, and picked up the saddle to bring it into the cellar. It needed cleaning and oiling, to protect it in this cold weather.

"Wait."

His father's voice stopped him and he turned to look over his shoulder.

"Are you not happy, Ben?" His father tilted his head. "What is it? Don't let the lack of money disconcert you."

"It's not that, Father. I expected very little money, or none at all, should the song ever be published."

"Regardless of whether you are paid, it is a very fine song and a noble cause. I think you should allow yourself some pleasure." He leaned his arms on the stall door.

"I would like to, but I can't." Ben broke off in frustration. "Shall we go? I'd like to just get on with everyday business."

"Hold on. Set down that saddle."

Ben did, with reluctance. His father came out of the stall and bolted it, then sat down on the bench and tapped it to offer Ben a seat next to him. Ben stayed where he was, on his feet.

"You haven't been yourself of late, son." His father's voice gentled. "Is it the girl, Miss Winter? I know she has left town."

"I asked her to marry me. She presented the matter to her mother and was summarily rejected."

"I see." His father reached out for the hoof pick that lay next to him on the bench and lightly ran it over his palm. Eventually he raised his eyes again. "I can't claim to be an expert in matters of the heart. But I would like to pass on something your grandfather once told me."

Ben made no response. His father meant well, but it was unlikely that any snippet of courting advice could alter Ben's dismal prospects with Kate.

His father scratched the hoof pick on the bench. "When I asked your grandfather if I might propose to your mother, he told me he was very glad I had come to him first before saying anything to her. Apparently some other young buck before me had not extended him that courtesy, and instead tried to use Ann as a go-between to argue his case." His father smiled, memory diffusing the focus of his gaze.

Ben flushed.

His father straightened up. "I don't say this to embarrass you, son, but it appears your esteem for this woman is such that her absence deprives you of joy in the publication of your song. In that case, perhaps you need to take action."

"But I have already made a hash of it." Ben's temper flickered, but he quashed it. His past indiscretion could not be taken back by anger and self-recrimination.

"Nothing is ever too far gone for an apology. Nothing. And certainly not a situation like this one. If your grandfather were here, he would tell you to do everything you can to remedy your mistake, to apologize to any you have offended, and to be humble about your flaws before God and man. Or woman, as he told me." His mouth quirked again, but he wiped it away and returned to his sincerity. "But do not hesitate to also lay out your merits."

"And have you ever done this?"

"Once. Why else would I have received such advice?" His father's brown eyes were calm.

"With Mother?"

"I don't think details are necessary." His father stood. "We are discussing your current predicament, not mine." He was firm, but not angry. "I think you should make amends as quickly as possible for not being straightforward with Mrs. Winter."

"You are right, Father. I see that now. I would not behave so again." It was hard to admit. "But they are in Philadelphia. They may not return for months. You think I should write to Kate's mother?"

"I think you should speak to Mrs. Winter in person."

Ben regarded his father in disbelief. "In Philadelphia?"

"You have time before the new term starts. And I have saved your earnings from your work at the school. They are yours."

His father had such faith in him? To encourage him to go on a week's journey, alone, in pursuit of—what? A dream? "Thank you, Father." He pounded his gloved fists together to bring feeling back to his cold fingers. "But what of her father? I should speak to him as well, and he is here."

"Yes, you should. Whatever his faults, he is her father. Go to him first. I cannot promise you success, just as your grandfather warned me he could not and would not control his daughter's response. But if you feel this is the woman for you, you must do everything you can, so you will not have anything for which to reproach yourself in later years."

"Yes, sir." A renewed vigor began to seep through his veins, his bones, his muscles. His father had faith in the worth of this mission, no matter how foolish or doomed it might appear to others. If his father had faith, how could Ben not?

The Winters' Irish maid let him in. The house was empty, most of it dark and cold. Only a meager fire guttered in the parlor grate—the maid must have just lit it upon his arrival.

The bearded man came in, looking out of place in the

feminine, delicate parlor. Ben stood to shake his hand. To his surprise, Mr. Winter's grip was firm, his eyes clear.

"I am Benjamin Hanby, sir."

"Yes, I remember you . . ." He trailed off as if reluctant to remember the scene at the Joneses' house.

"I am here to ask your permission to court your daughter, and to express my regret for not having done so months ago."

"Yes, my wife had mentioned to me her displeasure with you. Something about that musicale. But then, I told her not to force Kate to do it." His nose was red with the broken veins of the alcoholic, but no odor of whiskey or stale spirits floated around him. "But I do not have any say in the household now."

It was not Ben's place to hear such revelations—he shifted from one foot to another. But the man was so lonely that it would be heartless not to respond. "Sir, your opinion is significant to me. Are you willing to grant me permission to court your daughter?"

The fire threatened to go out, casting deep shadows under Mr. Winter's heavy brows. He looked like a soul in torment. "I am telling you that I do not have the right to speak for either my daughter or my wife. My sins have lowered me in their eyes, and with good reason. My wife must decide on your question."

"Sir . . ." Ben hesitated. "You seem quite well today. Different from when I last saw you."

"You mean because I am not drinking. Yes. I am attempting to reform."

Ben could not tell if it was bitterness or pain that spurred Mr. Winter's dry riposte.

"I am going to see your wife, sir. In Philadelphia."

Mr. Winter stopped as if contemplating something deep in

his soul. "Then I would like you to tell my wife and daughter something."

"Yes, sir." He almost dreaded to hear it.

"Tell them they may return without fear of harm, ever. That if the bottle ever masters me again—and I hope and pray it will not—that I will leave them here and never return."

There was no polite response to such a thing—it was not a sentiment commonly expressed in parlors. And so Ben would not treat it so, with mumbled pleasantries and excuses. He would treat it as a man should. "I will tell them, sir. And I respect your intention." He stood and extended his hand once more. Mr. Winter creaked to his feet and shook Ben's hand in farewell.

The maid let him out and Ben walked down the steps, glad to be out in the crisp, open air on the field of snow that covered Northwest Street.

What could Mr. Winter mean by a return without fear of harm? Had the hand he just shook ever been lifted in violence against Kate or her mother? Ben grimaced and wiped his hand on his trousers before he realized what he was doing. But whatever had gone before, a repentant man should not be shunned if he could keep to his resolve.

He would bring Mrs. Winter the message, along with his own. He would simply have to pray that Kate would not be returning to this house for long, and that if Mrs. Winter and the younger sister did, Mr. Winter would not fail them again.

Forty

KATE ARRIVED IN THE DINING ROOM THE NEXT morning to find the table set with silver, crystal, pastries, and fresh fruit. An Irish maid in crisp black and white curtsied to her.

"Good morning, miss. Mrs. Cadwalader should be down any minute." The maid whisked herself away to the kitchen.

Kate wore her best blue morning dress, but still felt shabby in the formality of her mother's family home. Her mother had said they would go shopping after breakfast. It would have been wonderful to be here in the city, with a thousand shops to explore, had her mother's response to Ben Hanby not rained ash on everything. Columbus was just a rural village compared to the magnificence of Philadelphia, but even such urban splendor was bound to be lost on Kate now.

"Good morning, Kate," Aunt Mary said, rustling gracefully into the room and taking a seat across the table. She wore an exquisite maroon dress embroidered with intricate leaves and flowers. She selected a croissant from the small mound on the crystal platter and offered it to Kate. "Do you care for pastry?"

"Thank you," Kate said, and began to butter it. How would she pass all this time with someone she didn't know?

Fortunately, her mother walked into the dining room at that moment, her hair impeccable. Apparently she did not always need Tessie to arrange it for her.

Aunt Mary offered her some breakfast as well. Kate could not stop sneaking glances at her aunt. She was so like her mother, even in some of the words she chose. But so much softer.

Aunt Mary filled her mother's teacup. "I've been in to see Mother this morning. She's still not able to speak. I'm sorry, Ruth."

"You're not responsible for her illness."

"I know, but I believe she has many things she would like to say to you."

"Such as?" Kate's mother sounded very satirical.

Kate was embarrassed on her behalf. They were guests in this house, no matter what had gone before.

Mary dropped her head. "Those are words she must say herself." She spoke gently and took her time cutting a pear into even slices before speaking again. "I hope you will give us the pleasure of entertaining you until she recovers the power of speech."

"Do you think she will?"

"I am sure of it. She had a spell like this before, and it only lasted a few days."

A loud rap at the door interrupted their conversation. They heard the manservant answering and a woman's voice. Then a young woman walked into the dining room.

She looked like Kate, only a few years older. The same dark, wavy hair, piled artlessly atop her head, the same vivid blue eyes, and the same fair complexion. Kate felt a clutching at her heart. This was her family.

Mary rose, delight radiating from her smiling face.

"Ruth, this is my daughter, Georgia Cadwalader Adams. Georgia, this is your aunt, Ruth Morris Winter."

Kate's mother extended her hand politely, but Georgia drew her into a warm embrace. "Aunt Ruth! I am so glad you could come! How wonderful to meet you."

Kate watched in silent fascination. She did not think she had ever seen her mother embraced. Her mother looked slightly shaken but covered it well. "Thank you."

"You will have to come over and meet your great-niece and -nephew as soon as you have a moment." Georgia's smile broadened in welcome as she turned to Kate. "And you, my twin!" She almost crowed in delight.

Kate could not help but smile despite the heaviness in her heart. "I'm Kate. We must be cousins."

Georgia gave her a warm peck on the cheek. "Kissing cousins!" She laughed, and Kate had to chuckle too, both taken aback and pleased.

"Mother," Georgia said, "I have a surprise for us. Dear Arthur has procured us extra invitations to the charity ball tonight."

Georgia reached out to touch Kate's mother's arm. "Would you like to come with us, Aunt Ruth? Please do! Arthur would love to meet you, and my brother Geoffrey is bringing his wife too."

"I didn't bring an evening gown with me."

"But you are welcome to wear one of mine," Mary said. "We look to be still of a size."

"And you may wear one of mine!" Georgia said to Kate. "I will bring it back with me."

"I suppose we can go," Kate's mother said.

"Wonderful!" Georgia clapped her hands.

"If you'll excuse me," Ruth Winter said, "I plan to go on a shopping expedition today, so I'll need to leave soon."

"Oh, I'll come with you, if you don't mind," said Mary. "I have some things to buy too. And I would enjoy the opportunity to hear more about my nieces."

Kate's mother looked as if she wished that her sister would not come along, but she could not say so. "Very well." She headed for the stairs.

Kate smiled at Georgia. She had a cousin, and she liked her already.

———◦✦◦———

The ballroom of Powel House was in the fashion of the previous century, sculpted white molding over the fireplace all the way to the ceiling. The musicians clustered along the wall, strings, woodwinds, and brass, with a large drum and cymbal.

"May I confess something?" Kate said to Georgia under the cover of the swirling music.

"Of course." Her cousin smiled.

"I have never heard so many instruments play together at once."

"Really? But it's only a chamber orchestra."

"I know. I am a country mouse."

"You do not look like one. You look like a belle of Philadelphia, and you will probably receive dance invitations by the dozen."

"But I do not know how to dance."

"Never fear. You will not have to dance if you do not wish it. This is no great affair, just a run-of-the-mill ball to raise support for a local orphans' home."

"Only in this city could there be such a thing as a *run-of-the-mill* ball." Kate smiled, and her cousin laughed.

"Quite true. But the main thing is that you may do as you wish, even if that should mean sitting against the wall and watching. Though I do hope you'll enjoy the music and the refreshments."

"Oh, I'm sure I will."

The violins shimmered into a rest, and the flutes picked up the melody over the rhythm of the cello and double bass. How Ben would love this glorious music. It might be one of the Lanner waltzes Cornelia had played for Kate on the piano, but it sounded so different with the rich textures of the orchestra. She would be quite content to listen all evening.

"Mrs. Adams, you have a lovely guest, I see." A young man bowed to Georgia and smiled at Kate.

"Mr. Cutler, this is my cousin from Ohio, Miss Winter."

"A delight." His brown hair was short, but swept forward in the current style to wisp near his face. He was handsome, she supposed.

"Would you honor me with a dance this evening, Miss Winter?"

Kate hesitated.

"My cousin is not ready for dancing yet, Mr. Cutler." Georgia rescued her. "She is still fatigued from the journey. But she is a lover of music, so I asked her to come sit with me and enjoy the evening."

"Ah. The orchestra is excellent." He seated himself next to Kate. "I am also a lover of music, Miss Winter."

Her mother eyed her from across the room, where she and Aunt Mary had gone to remember old times with some childhood friends. At least Kate's mother was too far away to even guess at the content of their conversation. That would stifle some of the matrimonial speculating that was undoubtedly beginning in her mother's brain.

"And do you happen to know the composer of this piece?" Only belatedly did she realize she was conversing with a strange young man. The music had distracted her. Her tongue grew clumsier and her head emptied.

"Lanner, I believe."

Kate fumbled for more sentences. To her surprise, it was not difficult to find more. Here in the city, she had numerous questions to ask. "Have you heard other orchestras here?"

"Yes, several good ones. But I prefer my music in the opera, or even in the theater."

He had captured Georgia's attention. "Indeed, Mr. Cutler? I did not know that. I'm surprised we have not crossed one another's paths more often. Arthur and I love the theater. Do you frequent Chestnut Street?"

"Usually. Not of late, however."

"Yes, tickets are scarce for *Uncle Tom's Cabin*. Splendid production, however."

"That's in the eye of the beholder." Mr. Cutler's expression grew dark.

"Oh, look, Arthur is coming now." Georgia rose to her feet, tiny beads sparkling on her gown. "Miss Winter, let us go to him. He had someone he wanted to introduce. If you will excuse us, Mr. Cutler."

He stood as Kate did and bowed. He did not seem in a good humor.

"Why is he so vexed?" Kate murmured to Georgia as her cousin took her arm and headed for her husband.

"My mistake. I should not have mentioned *Uncle Tom's Cabin*. Passions are running too high on slavery and the Union." They reached her husband. "Arthur, you said you would like Miss Winter to meet someone?"

Her husband appeared confused, then regained his poise. "Oh yes. Come with me." He offered an arm to each of them. It seemed like a dream that Kate had joined this glittering train of women and the elegant company of dancers out on the floor. Her mind and body were present, but her heart had sent its regrets and was back in Westerville, of all places.

Nothing stirred her but the music, and as soon as the introductions to various persons were finished, she turned to Georgia. "Please, you must go out and enjoy the dance. I would be just as happy sitting by the wall and enjoying the concert."

"But I cannot leave you alone, nor do I wish to."

"But what will Arthur do?"

"He can manage for himself—he is quite the conversationalist, aren't you, dear?"

Arthur smiled. "I have been known to enjoy a good talk." He bowed a fraction and walked over to the gentlemen.

Kate was glad that Georgia stayed with her all evening, as several gentlemen requested dances. Her cousin fended them off on Kate's behalf with gentle excuses of travel fatigue.

Kate's mother spun around the ballroom, her red dress swinging in a graceful arc, dancing with Mr. Cutler, of all people, as if not a day had passed since her debut. Her face was rosy and she smiled and laughed. She must have been a beauty, indeed, when she danced in these rooms as a young lady. Wistfulness touched Kate's thoughts. If her mother's heart had never been broken, would she still smile and laugh the way she did here? Or even weep, as Kate had seen her eyes shine with unshed tears once or twice since they arrived.

The cymbals crashed and the dance ended in a fanfare of trumpets. Mr. Cutler led her mother off the floor in Kate's direction.

"Miss Winter, I have had the pleasure of meeting and dancing with your mother. She is not as fatigued as you, it seems." He wore a barbed smile, but seemed to be only teasing.

"The musicians are leaving?" Kate asked.

Mr. Cutler laughed. "Only taking an intermission to catch their breath. Perhaps you and your mother will accompany me to the refreshments in the next room."

"We would love refreshments." Her mother smiled again, a natural smile warmed by the color in her cheeks, not the social one Kate had seen all these years.

He escorted them into the antechamber where portraits of George Washington and Samuel Powel hung on the walls. A silver punch bowl of immense proportions stood beaded with moisture in the middle of a table covered with fruit and flowers. Where had they obtained such things in late winter? Servants circled the room with trays, offering hors d'oeuvres such as truffles and tiny deboned quail stuffed with crab.

Mr. Cutler offered her a crystal glass full of punch and sipped his own, dabbing the red stain it left on his lips with a white lace serviette. Kate sipped more carefully to avoid the pomegranate's mark that reddened the lips of punch-drinkers across the room.

"Miss Winter, your cousin mentioned *Uncle Tom's Cabin* earlier," Mr. Cutler said.

She turned to face him. He was going to raise the subject again, and she was not as skilled at slipping away as Georgia.

"Yes," her mother said before Kate could summon an answer. "I am not certain I shall let my daughter go, even though Mrs. Adams is attempting to find tickets."

"That is very wise. A pack of lies dressed up in sentiment. Divisive and destructive." His cheeks were reddening to match his lips. Her mother should end this conversation. Kate fidgeted and looked around for Georgia.

"Have you read the novel, Mrs. Winter?" Mr. Cutler asked.

"I have not. I shun politics. I prefer a gracious life."

"You are an ideal woman." He lifted his glass. "I toast your femininity." When he lowered it, he appeared friendlier and his face returned to its normal color. "But I will tell you this. The slaves that woman depicts in her novel do not exist. She attempts to make what is bestial seem human, and thus garner undeserved sympathy."

This man knew nothing of slavery. He must never have met a slave, or perhaps he had seen them and never spoken to them. Men like him had sent Nelly to her death. Little coals began to light themselves, one by one, in Kate's mind, like fires of remembrance for Nelly and her baby.

"I am well acquainted with plantation owners," Mr. Cutler said with self-satisfaction. "The beatings, the atrocities Stowe portrays—well, if they happen at all, they are isolated occurrences, only the rarest situations. And only to the most savage of the creatures."

Even her mother looked uncomfortable. "As I said, I prefer to avoid politics, Mr. Cutler."

"Very wise, very wise. In that way you will not be deceived. Slave families are not broken apart routinely, as Stowe implies. The young ones grow up and then often ask to be sold away to find new mates. But they are not like us. Their affections are fickle and fleeting. They cannot sustain any bond, not even between parents and children. They forget one another and find new fancies."

The coals burst into a full flame. "Really, Mr. Cutler? I must beg to differ."

Mr. Cutler and her mother stared at her.

"I have known these things to happen, the beatings, the hunting down of innocent people by dogs," Kate said. "And most of all, I have seen slave families torn apart." Her calm was almost eerie, belied only by her quick breath. "So I must refute your points. And I find it utterly objectionable for you to say such things at any time, but especially on an occasion such as this one."

Georgia and Arthur walked up behind her mother and halted in their shining clothing, glasses of punch arrested in midair, eyes wide.

"No matter how rare you say these atrocities are—and I do not believe they are—even a few is too many. It is an evil blot on our nation. It is a shameful foundation for what you call the Union, and a union built on shame will not survive." Fragments of things she had thought since her journey with the Fosters melted and rejoined themselves into articulate speech. "I've looked into the eyes of Negroes and seen human souls. Fathers, mothers, and daughters." Her voice remained steady. "I wonder if I would see the same in your eyes, Mr. Cutler. And if you do not wish to hear the thoughts of others on controversial subjects, then kindly keep yours to yourself."

Georgia laid a hand on her shoulder. "Well said, Miss Winter."

"Hear, hear," Arthur said. They looked stunned but not mortified. Instead, they took positions flanking her and glowered at Mr. Cutler. From the corner of her eye, Kate saw Arthur's lip curl.

"I see the lady knows her own mind." Mr. Cutler was scarlet from his collar to his hairline and seemed about to burst his necktie.

"Yes, I believe I do," Kate said.

"Good evening." He gave the barest sketch of a bow with a curt jerk of the head and turned on his heel. His coattails flapped as he headed toward the main doors of the house.

Kate's mother glanced from Georgia to Arthur. "I must apologize for my daughter—"

"Not at all," Arthur said. "It is we who should apologize for leaving you in the company of that odious person for even one minute. Miss Winter, I hope you are not too shaken. I will take you home if you wish."

"No, thank you, Mr. Adams." She took a deep breath. "I find I am looking forward to the rest of the evening."

The music started again in the other room with a swirl of violins. Georgia smiled at her. "Shall we go in?"

"Yes, please," Kate said.

Her mother wore an unreadable expression, one Kate had never seen before. If she did not know better, she might think her mother had been moved by Kate's outburst. But that was wishful thinking, of course. No telling what her mother would say about her breach of etiquette the next time they were alone. No doubt she would chastise Kate for speaking of politics, and the scene would not be pleasant.

But Kate was not sorry for it. And she knew, beyond a doubt, what would be the subject of her first public oration at Otterbein.

Forty-One

"PITTSBURGH, LADIES AND GENTLEMEN! UNION Station!" The conductor pulled open the heavy door between the cars with no trouble and crossed the link. His bent legs kept his balance as well as any sailor's as he stepped into the next car and vanished from Ben's sight.

The air shimmered with the heat of the woodstove down by the door, but here in the middle of the car, Ben had to pull his muffler closer to his neck against the cold. Woodstoves could not combat the drafts from the windows of a wooden box on wheels, speeding across the landscape at twenty miles per hour.

The train slowed to a crawl past the buildings on either side, but everything was blanketed in white and Ben could not distinguish one from another. The train crept to a halt, with a final jerk to announce its arrival.

He would stop here before switching to the Pennsylvania Railroad, the last leg of the journey to Philadelphia, the city named for love. Appropriate, on this lover's mission—though his was certainly not the brotherly affection the name referred to. The image of Kate drove the discomforts of the journey from his mind. His need to see her was so strong that he had dreamed of her face in his restless sleep.

His traveling case sat beside him on the floor. He hefted it in one hand and headed for the same door the conductor had used. The step down to the platform was steep, but he had taken it several times now on the journey and found sure purchase even in the slush over the bricks.

He had arrived at the far end and must walk down to the station door. The platform was a study in gray and white, the shrouded snowbanks on either end of the station broken by sooty walkways under the roof. Cold moisture hung in the air like mist or a fine drifting rain. A crowd of passengers disembarked at the end of each car, women stepping down with the aid of the conductor or their male traveling companions. Ben passed the smoking car where a middle-aged gentleman with a gray beard emerged with pipe still in hand, even in his greatcoat. After him, a dark-skinned woman moved into the opening between cars and looked down at the treacherous step.

Nelly.

For a moment, it did seem to be her—the same dark hair, heavy-lidded eyes, still face. But when she looked up, her nose was broader and her face rounder than Nelly's. The painful contraction of his chest did not ease.

The woman glanced from side to side and grasped the handle beside her. The porters would not help her down, of course, not with so many white passengers on the train.

Ben quickened his step and made it to her before she took the risk of descending alone.

"May I assist you down, ma'am?" He held out a gloved hand.

"Why, thank you, sir." She accepted his hand, and as she

stepped down, he had to catch her elbow to ensure she kept her balance.

"May I take that bag for you, ma'am?" Her luggage seemed to consist of one threadbare valise she had set on the link behind her to make her descent. He reached in and lifted it down.

"You are very kind." Her voice was not like Nelly's either. It lacked the Southern cadence.

"You are headed into the station?"

"Yes, sir."

"Then I'll accompany you, as I'm headed there myself." He slowed his walk to allow her to keep up in her female attire that made slick walkways more precarious.

Inside the building, the temperature was more comfortable, though the air reeked of stale cigars and wet wool from the overcoats of travelers. "Are you continuing by rail, ma'am?"

"No, sir, I'm meeting my sister here. Coming to live with my family."

"A happy occasion." His smile felt halfhearted. She did look so like Nelly from the side.

Rows of benches sat along the walls of the station. "Would you like to sit to wait for your family?"

"That would be fine." She made her way to the nearest bench and seated herself with care, like a lady. He placed the valise beside her.

"Thank you, sir."

"Of course, ma'am. Are you certain they will come for you?"

"Oh yes." She grinned. "They know what'll happen if they don't."

He smiled in return. "Good afternoon, then."

She focused her attention on the station door to the street.

He turned to go and fought off his unease. It seemed an ill portent for his journey, to meet Nelly's double here. Perhaps God was sending him a message. But he had told Kate he would pursue his path—and her—with all his heart, and so he should, whether his spirits were high or low.

"Paper! Paper!" a boy called from just inside the door, holding one in his hand.

"I'll take one," Ben said.

"Very good, sir, the best news in town!"

He pressed a coin in the boy's hand and took the paper. The *Pittsburgh Gazette*, since 1786, read the banner.

Then this paper had existed long before even his father's days in Pittsburgh. He folded it in one hand and went out through the station door into a wintry blast of wind.

Hackney cabs waited outside. He approached one driver who hunched against the wind, and his poor horses looked half frozen as well, leaning into one another. "I'd like to go to a hotel: one without lice in its beds, if I can."

"I'll get you to a good one, sir." The driver straightened up at the prospect of a fare.

Soon Ben was aboard under the half roof, and the hackney made its slow way through the snow-covered streets. They were not crammed with coaches and wagons as his mother had described to him. The snow had kept all but the most determined of workers and shoppers indoors. But the shops seemed to be open, judging from the lights inside. There was a glover, a seller of spirits, and a grocer. And what was that sign half covered by ice? Palmer and Sons, Music.

The cab stopped. "Right there, sir." The driver pointed the

tip of a gloved finger at a large building across the street. "Liberty Hotel. Nice and clean, but not too hard on the purse. And they even have a piano player some nights."

"Here you are." Ben pressed money into the man's hand and jumped down into the snow, then lifted his traveling case from the luggage rack. As the cab pulled away, he hefted his case in one hand and turned around to head for Palmer's Music. He could not walk past an entire store devoted to music without investigating.

The bell rang and he tapped the snow off his boots on the entry mat. No proprietor came out, so he walked farther in, to the spectacle of entire racks of sheet music. The song titles ranked in alphabetical order, scores of them. A cursory inspection showed at least fifty percent must be Stephen Foster's. The man had genius, no doubt of that. Ben inched down the aisle past "Camptown Races" and toward the Ds.

Just a blank space in the rack where "Darling Nelly Gray" should appear. No sign of his song.

Well, he should not have been so vain as to think his song would be in every store in the land. But he had hoped—he had hoped. It had seemed his one chance to use his gift for a serious purpose. He should not have placed such hope in it, among all the hundreds of songs published each year.

And why couldn't he get Nelly's face out of his mind?

Head down, he left the store. The proprietor never came out.

Across the street, the hotel beckoned. He pushed through the gusts of wind and in through the heavy door.

"Welcome, sir." A stout woman in cap and apron came out of a back room into the large common area set up as a dining room with trestle tables. Two ladies dressed in travel attire sat in the upholstered chairs by the fire, and several men sat apart from one another at the tables, reading papers.

"I am Mrs. Pye, the manager. Will you lodge with us tonight?"

"Yes, ma'am."

She told him the price for room and board. He set his luggage down and paid her.

"Dinner will be served in an hour." She handed him a key. "We usually have music before, but our player did not arrive. Snowbound, I venture." She gave a rueful look to the upright piano in the corner farthest from the fireplace.

One of the middle-aged ladies turned from her contemplation of the fire. "Such a shame, Mrs. Pye. We so enjoyed his playing last evening. My sister is quite crushed. It lifted her spirits so, you see, and she has been melancholy." And it did seem the other lady was quite downcast, her eyelashes lowered to her cheeks, her face strained.

"I do apologize, Mrs. Fereday," said the landlady. "But it can't be helped, I'm sure you understand."

Ben hesitated. "I play a little, ma'am," he said to the woman by the fire. "Would you like me to stand in for the missing musician?"

Both Mrs. Pye and the two women straightened up.

"Oh yes," said the one named Mrs. Fereday. "Mrs. Ellsing, do you hear? There will be music after all."

The other woman regarded Ben with interest, her sagging face not as defeated. "That would be lovely," she said in a faint voice.

"Then I would be glad to oblige." Ben went to the piano. He pulled off his gloves and kneaded his hands together, then lifted the lid over the keys and sat down. "Would you like something cheerful, or a little more stately?"

"Stephen Foster is her favorite," Mrs. Fereday said.

He repressed a wry grin and began the opening bars of "Jeanie with the Light Brown Hair." It was good to see the care fall away from the sad lady's face as the song progressed. The men at the tables had looked up. When he finished with a run up the keyboard, the ladies applauded.

"Camptown Races!" one of the men called out. He looked like a working man, but did not seem rough, just simple.

Ben obliged with the jaunty tune. The man started to sing, and another joined in. Mrs. Pye beamed and walked back into what must be the kitchen

He played for an hour, until he had almost exhausted his popular repertoire. Each new song was greeted with tapping feet and nodding heads. He played every Foster tune he knew, enjoying the camaraderie. The men sang along to several of the Fosters and the other well-known tunes.

Finally, he was out of well-known songs. Without sheet music, he could not go on. And perhaps it was a good time to stop, as the smells rolling out from the kitchen were making his mouth water and it must be near dinnertime.

"Oh, just one more, please," the sad woman said.

All he had left were his own songs. Well, he did not like to disappoint her. "Darling Nelly Gray" was good enough to be published—he would play that one.

The chords rang out, and he embellished them to bring out the plaintive quality of the tune.

The working man called out from his seat, "I've heard this one."

He had? Then maybe the song had been distributed here after all. Or maybe the man was simply mistaken.

"But let's have something happier, shall we?" the man added.

"Hear, hear," said another one of the men, seated at the far end of the table, who looked like a supercilious lawyer. He did not look up from his paper.

"Oh yes, Mr.— What is your name?" asked Mrs. Fereday.

"Hanby," Ben said.

"Mr. Hanby, let's not end with something sad. Would you mind playing another Stephen Foster for my friend, just to end on a good note? So to speak?" And she giggled.

"Not at all." He shoved down his hurt pride. "How about 'Camptown Races' one more time?"

"Oh, perfect."

The men grinned and the other woman pressed her hands together in gratitude.

They were not bad people. They seemed quite decent. It was Ben's song that was not appealing.

He was no Stephen Foster. The song would probably sell a few copies and disappear. He resigned himself to the ache of another failure. But he wished it had not been so. The disappearance of the song seemed doubly heavy, because with the song would die away those faces and voices he had known: Joseph, Nelly, her baby. It was as if he had failed them a second time. His music was not strong enough to support their story. He had let them vanish as if they never lived.

He had lost his appetite.

Forty-Two

"RUTH, COME UPSTAIRS." AUNT MARY STOOD AT THE foot of the stairway in a cream morning dress that frothed over her elbows and slippers. "And you too, Kate. You must go up and see her now."

Her mother crossed the rugs to the stairs. Kate followed, disguising her reluctance. She did not want to see her mother in grief—it was like seeing her unclothed.

Down the dim hallway and into her grandmother's bedroom they went. There she lay, still inert and apparently unconscious. Perhaps she had lapsed back into oblivion in the short time it took them to come to her. The room's now-familiar sense of loss shrouded Kate, the feeling of a past emptied and impoverished, of wasted time and stunted love.

Kate's mother approached the bed and sat in the chair positioned close to the head, so Kate took the chair on the opposite side and waited in silence. Her mother touched the thinning hair, where her grandmother's scalp was showing through. "She always had beautiful, thick hair that I asked to brush when I was a little girl. I always wondered why she didn't wear it long, in all its magnificence, until she told me one day that grown ladies didn't do that."

Kate kept quiet, awash in the memory of begging to brush her mother's hair, when she was only four or five. How she had adored her mother then.

"Mary thinks the end has come." Her mother spoke in a low, unemotional voice. "It won't be long now for Mother. And still no word from her. It would make it so much easier, somehow."

The shiver of pain and pity that assailed Kate so often in this home returned.

Would Kate one day have to sit at her mother's bedside, with so many questions unanswered and so many old hurts? Perhaps her mother also thought this, as they sat there in the loaded silence. Kate could so easily see the estrangement building and dividing her from her mother as history repeated itself.

Her mother lifted her hand and stroked her grandmother's head. She must have suffered too. And inexplicably, a long-forgotten line sprang to Kate's mind: *Though a mother forsake her child, he will not abandon you.* What was it like, to be a child completely forsaken, and without the comfort of a real faith or even a tender marriage? The emptiness in her mother's face was giving way to a living pain that hurt to witness.

Then her grandmother's eyes opened. She appeared more cognizant of her surroundings than she had seemed since their arrival.

"It is Ruth," her mother said. "I am here."

Her grandmother nodded her head just a fraction of an inch.

Her mother took her grandmother's limp hand. "I forgive you, Mother." Her eyes grew wet, and tears ran down her cheeks. Kate wanted to look away but could not. Her love for her mother stirred and awakened like a bear after winter—hungry, angry, pained from long absence. She wanted to comfort her, to tell her she was sorry for that lonely young woman who had been cast out by those who should have rallied around her.

It seemed to Kate that her grandmother's hand moved ever so slightly, as if she had squeezed her mother's hand with fading strength.

"I understand," her mother said. And they sat there until her grandmother closed her eyes again.

Kate wanted only to flee before she wept. She rose without speaking, left the bedside, and went downstairs, walking back into the parlor, finding comfort in its rich warmth. She wandered around, peering into the cabinets. That porcelain statue had come from Thailand, but where had her grandparents acquired the three miniature ivory carvings? Perhaps Aunt Mary would tell her.

A copy of the new *Godey's* lay on the table. Kate picked it up, leafing through it, seeking anything to take her mind off the sadness. *Godey's* was her favorite, for its historical features and the engravings. As she flipped the pages, she saw the usual printed page of sheet music. A song in every issue, the cover always promised.

"With the permission of Oliver Ditson and Company," it said, "and in response to requests from our readers, *Godey's* presents 'Darling Nelly Gray.'"

She read the lyrics. Then she saw the name under the title. *B. R. Hanby.* Surely not. She read the name again in disbelief. But who else could it be?

She went to the piano and sat down, skimming the first line, laying her fingers on the keys, reminding herself of the sharps and flats. She began to play the melody only, which was quite easy after her practices with Cornelia.

> *Oh my poor Nelly Gray, they have taken you away,*
> *And I'll never see my darling any more;*
> *I am sitting by the river and I'm weeping all the day,*
> *For you've gone from that old Kentucky shore.*

It was the song for Nelly, the one he had mentioned in the letter. And it was a beautiful song, haunting, as if she should remember it from some other time and place. He had published it—bittersweet pleasure on his behalf dripped through her with every line she played. The chorus was as good as the verse, the lyrics touching. She played through all four verses, and by the time she finished she was singing the chorus, under her breath, so no one could hear her.

Aunt Mary came down the stairs, her cream skirt ruffling after her like foam against the carpet. "Kate, you know that song? It's lovely. I heard a friend's daughter play it the other night."

"A song from *Godey's*." That must explain it. Nothing spread as fast as a tune in *Godey's*.

"It's called 'Darling Nelly Gray,' isn't it? I've seen mention of it in the papers."

"In the newspapers?"

"Oh, it's all the rage, apparently."

Kate kept quiet, wondering.

"I have good news," her aunt said. "Arthur procured some tickets for *Uncle Tom's Cabin* this evening, as our last outing together. I am sorry you must leave, but at least we may offer you this one big-city entertainment first."

"Thank you." That penetrated even her Ben-induced fog. *Uncle Tom's Cabin*, her one and only chance to see it. How kind of Arthur and Georgia—they had known Kate would love to go.

Her mother spoke from behind, startling her. "Mary, would you mind if I took the carriage to the shops this morning?" She must have come down silent as a ghost on the stairs. She still looked pale.

"Not at all. Would you like me to accompany you?"

"No, thank you. I have some purchases that I must make in private."

"I understand." Aunt Mary lowered her voice to a discreet murmur and stepped closer to Kate's mother. "But please don't feel that you must buy us parting gifts. We are family, and you are welcome here at any time."

Kate's mother nodded, turned, and hurried back up the stairs, saying over her shoulder, "I will be down in ten minutes to leave if your carriage can be ready."

"Of course." Mary crossed to the bell pull on the wall and rang for the servants, though it did not make a sound in the parlor.

"Kate," she said when she returned, and the last footsteps had faded on the stairs. "Will you play the song one more time? I do love it."

Kate began again, and this time dared add the left hand to bring in the harmonies. It was soaking in Ben's presence, calling him back to her mind and heart, remembering joy that overcame the old sorrows of this house.

She did not mind if she played it fifty times. But her aunt might find it strange.

Forty-Three

BEN UNFOLDED KATE'S LETTER AND READ THE ADDRESS again, though he had committed it to memory on the train: 119 Walnut Street.

"119, please," he said to the hackney cab driver.

"Yes, sir." The houses of Walnut Street passed by in restrained elegance as the horse trotted on. The cab stopped. Ben climbed down. "Wait here, please." The driver nodded, accustomed to well-dressed gentlemen who paid at the conclusion of several errands.

He had donned his clean coat, shirt, and tie and taken care to look as gentlemanly as he could. The hotel valet had cleaned his hat so it gleamed. But his neat appearance did not ease the hammering of his heart. He rehearsed his speech in his mind, then stepped up to the door and rang.

A middle-aged man in servant's livery answered. "Good evening, sir."

"I seek Mrs. Isaiah Winter, whom I believe to be a guest here. It is a matter of some importance." He handed his visiting card to the servant.

The card disappeared into his hand and he opened the door. "Please come in."

Ben stepped over the threshold into the foyer. He noted the molded paneling, the rich wood floor under his feet—signs of the wealth Mrs. Winter wanted for her daughter.

"This way, sir." The servant took his hat and ushered him to the left, opening double doors into a high-ceilinged parlor with blue-draped windows, a red medallioned carpet, and elegant mahogany chairs softened by lace doilies. The man closed the doors behind him and left him alone.

The warmth of the fire soothed his cold face—he approached the snowy white marble hearth and the portrait on the wall above it. The lady in the painting was black-haired and blue-eyed, like Kate. His pulse quickened, outracing the tick of the tall clock to his right with its long brass pendulum under etched glass.

The doors opened and Mrs. Winter entered. She wore a green silk dress and walked as if she were born to own such a house—and he supposed she was. She stopped six feet away, as if he were a tradesman.

He would behave as a gentleman nonetheless. Inclining from the waist a few degrees, he bowed to her in the most formal and polite manner possible.

"Mr. Benjamin Hanby," she said, inspecting him from toe to crown.

"Good afternoon, Mrs. Winter." He stood like a private before the general, though he had never imagined a general in dangling diamond earrings and lavender scent.

"It is a surprise to receive you here in Philadelphia, Mr. Hanby." Her tone was chilly.

"I hope you will forgive my unannounced visit."

She stared at him without reply. Was Kate here? He could

not think of it now—it would not matter if he failed to win over her mother.

"And your purpose?" she asked, her eyes a steely, unreadable blue.

He took a breath. "I am here to humbly ask your pardon, ma'am."

She continued her cold silence, a perfect portrait of Old Philadelphia so like the oil painting over the fireplace.

He tried again, ignoring the whispers of failure in his mind. "I have wronged you and your family by pursuing my affection for your daughter in a less than upstanding manner."

One of her eyebrows quirked, as if to put an exclamation point on his confession. "And you traveled for days simply to make this apology to me?"

A twist of nerves brought a rancid taste to his mouth, like an old lemon. Of course he wanted more than just to apologize. He desired to see Kate, craved it so ardently that in a heartbeat's relenting he would rush through those doors and up the stairs like an uncouth barbarian, to throw himself at her feet wherever she might be.

But he had not behaved well, and he must accept Mrs. Winter's verdict, whatever it might be.

"My husband wrote to tell me you had been to speak with him on a similar subject. He told me he would permit me to decide whether to accept your apology." She turned away and paced across the room to stand by a curio cabinet, her face averted from him. "My daughter has not been herself lately, Mr. Hanby."

He did not know whether to nod or apologize.

"We attended a ball with her cousins not long ago. She spoke intemperately to a gentleman there. I have never seen her do such a thing." Her eyes sliced him to ribbons.

"I can only assume she must have had ample reason, ma'am." His temper stirred—he must defend Kate. Mrs. Winter seemed so harsh.

"Do you think it is your influence that has changed her?" she asked.

"I could not presume to claim such an influence, Mrs. Winter. Your daughter is a woman of deep feeling and conviction. I did not make her so, though I admire it."

"But she has not always voiced those strong feelings or opinions you say she possesses, Mr. Hanby. And that is where I am tempted to hold you responsible."

"You must do as you see fit, ma'am." His hopes faded. "Your daughter's opinions are as intelligent as any man's, and I would not wish her to keep silent at all times. I am well enough acquainted with her to know that only ignorance or cruelty could provoke her to what you call intemperate speech." Now his cause was lost. He dropped his gaze to the ornate grid of the carpet and waited to be dismissed. Tendrils of pain and disappointment began to curl around his heart.

"You are correct, Mr. Hanby. The reason for her outburst was an objection to brutality."

He looked up. The middle-aged woman had a preoccupied expression, as if reliving some past scenes in her mind's eye.

"I do not wish my daughter to be a silent ornament unable to defend herself or others against cruelty." Mrs. Winter's voice caught, but she went on as if nothing were amiss. "I approve of the recent change in my daughter. Sit down, please."

An air of unreality made the reds and blues of the room

more vivid as he walked to one of the dark-framed, oval-backed chairs. He waited for Mrs. Winter to sit in another before he seated himself.

"I don't know if I understand you correctly, ma'am." Had she just indicated some positive impression of him, despite the lack of emotion in her face?

She regarded him as if peering at the innards of a mechanical toy to see how it worked. "I don't know why you have affected my daughter in this way. But"—she paused, looking aside— "during our time here, Mr. Hanby, I have had ample time to reflect upon the relations of mothers and daughters. And I find myself—"

The double doors swung open and Kate walked through them, her gaze on several parcels in her arms as she balanced them. "They were all wrapped and ready, Mother," she said, "so I was able to finish more quickly than I—" She looked up and froze.

Ben stood, drinking in her startled beauty, her trim figure and flowing skirt, the dark mass of her hair against the curve of her neck.

Mrs. Winter remained in her chair and addressed Kate. "You see we have a caller."

She remained there, clutching the packages, her bright blue eyes huge.

"Come sit with us," Mrs. Winter said.

Kate edged over to another chair, closer to her mother than to Ben, facing him. She sat down very slowly, the packages still gripped in her white fingers.

"You may give me my purchases." Her mother extended a hand. One by one, Kate passed over three boxes, each decorated with the subtle patterns favored by expensive merchants.

Mrs. Winter scoured each box, looking at the neat, fine printing on top. "This one," she said, and handed it back to Kate.

Kate had not taken her gaze from Ben, nor he from her. She fumbled at the box and half dropped it in her lap with a self-conscious flutter of the eyelids. "What—?" she broke off. He wanted to cross the parlor and embrace her, feel her breathing presence warm in his arms.

"You may open it," her mother said. "I had planned to give it to you privately, but our unexpected visitor has altered my plan."

Kate pulled at the ribbon, which fell away from the box. She grasped the edge with her fingertips and pulled the top off. Inside was a folded rectangle of white.

"Unfold it." Her mother remained inscrutable and solemn.

Kate looked around, then rose to her feet to walk a few steps to the table in the center of the room. She set the box on it, took out the fabric, held it by two corners, and let it fall out to its full length.

It was a large piece of lace, several feet across. The fine gauze in the middle was bordered by a wide swath of delicate floral embroidery. It billowed down from her hands and pooled on the floor.

What was it? A curtain? At least it was reassuring that Kate seemed equally confused.

"It's Irish lace," her mother said.

"It's exquisite, Mother. Thank you." Kate sounded puzzled.

Mrs. Winter regarded her for a long moment with a serious look. Kate darted a glance at Ben and shifted back to the lace.

"It's a wedding veil," Mrs. Winter said.

Kate looked at her, still uncomprehending.

Ben stood, his heart pounding.

Mrs. Winter also rose and walked to her daughter to place

a light hand on the back of her shoulder. Ben had never seen a tender gesture from her—Kate turned her face away as if unsure whether to run or to accept it.

"It's for the day when you marry this young man," her mother said.

Kate dropped the lace. It slipped to the carpet like foam on a wave. She looked at Ben, her eyes glistening. He had to swallow hard.

"You have my consent to marry him. And your father will agree, if I speak to him," Mrs. Winter said. She turned away and walked to the doors of the parlor. "And now I will leave you to discuss my generosity and discernment, which I'm sure is the uppermost subject on your minds." The corner of her mouth turned up, and she glided out. The doors shut with a click.

For a moment, he could not move. When his limbs unlocked, he took a few steps to Kate and took her in his arms. He held her close, then swept one arm under her and lifted her in the air, her skirts piling around his arm and spilling over her feet. A whoop of joy and triumph threatened to leap out of his throat, but instead he spun her around so fast the fabric of her dress swung around them.

She made a startled sound of protest and then laughed softly. He carried her over by the fireplace and gently set her down on her feet. She was giddy and off balance and threw her arms around him to stay upright, her cheeks curving with her smile.

Her soft, light embrace sent his pulse pounding—he went still, and she gazed up at him with firelight flickering in the blue depths of her eyes. Her face was so delicate and perfect—he reached a hand to the satin sleeve of her dress and reveled in the firm warmth of her shoulder before satisfying his overwhelming desire to touch her bare skin, where the dress ended at the hollow of her neck. A visible tremor went through her and she closed her eyes for a moment, mingled longing and trepidation on her face. He moved close and gathered her in his arms as she opened her eyes halfway. Her parted lips drew him and he leaned close and kissed her, his heart pounding as he held her so close he could feel hers beating too. She wound her arms around him and ran her fingers up his neck into his hair. The surprise and delight of her response made him grip her fiercely and cover her face with light kisses. She sighed.

He pulled away and took a steadying breath. There would be time enough for all this, and more.

They stood arm in arm, a little shy, and watched the fire dance in the grate.

Forty-Four

THE THEATER WAS LACQUERED IN RED AND GOLD, THE boxes plush with red velvet. In the dim glow of footlights that barely reached the balcony, Kate reveled in Ben's nearness. His coat sleeve was only inches from her bare right arm, as a couple could sit only after promises had been made. The fact that her mother had given her ticket to Ben and stayed home made it all the more intimate, with only Arthur and Georgia accompanying them in the box.

The pale pink satin of Kate's borrowed gown ran rich and smooth over her chair. Its cap sleeves and scoop neck bared her collarbone in a line of delicate tulle and satin rosebuds—a style that would be daring in Westerville, but the ladies seated in the dark arches of the other box seats wore the same design. She inhaled the unfamiliar but heady aroma of clean, starched linen and masculine skin when Ben leaned toward her. Had it not been for the unusual power of the scenes taking place onstage, she would not have been able to concentrate at all.

The players onstage held the audience rapt, creating the horrible reality of the death of good-hearted Tom, enslaved to a terrible master: Kate knew it from the novel.

"I know you can do terrible things," said Tom to Simon Legree, as the tyrant stood over him with whip in hand. "But after ye've killed the body, there ain't no more you can do." The slave's blood-covered face was resolute. Legree raised his whip once more and lashed Tom until he slumped lifeless onstage, then threw the whip on the ground with a careless flourish and stalked off.

A young man arrived too late to save Tom and stood over his limp form, devastated. "Blessed are they who mourn," the young man said, almost in tears, "for they shall be comforted."

The theater was dead silent. *Blessed are they who mourn* . . . The face of Frank appeared in her mind's eye, the sadness of Nelly's lovely eyes, the laughter of her baby. *They shall be comforted.*

She wiped away tears with her handkerchief. Ben sat with his head bowed. The scene closed and the curtains came down. Loud applause turned into cheering and whistling from the men in the pit. Kate blinked and looked around as if waking from a trance as the thunderous ovation continued. Clusters of people stood up in all the boxes on the balcony, applauding. She joined them and Ben rose with her.

Cheers of "Brava" and "Bravo" went up from the boxes across the way.

The curtain went up again. The audience quieted itself. An actress, dressed in Grecian robes and holding a torch, walked to the edge of the stage. The epilogue, of course.

The actress had a fine voice, and a noble figure she made, like Liberty herself. "A day of grace is yet held out to us," she cried. "Both North and South have been guilty before God; and the Christian church has a heavy account to answer. Not by combining together, to protect injustice and cruelty, and making a common capital of sin, is this Union to be saved, but by repentance . . . justice . . . and mercy!"

It rang to the rafters.

"It's all a lie," a harsh voice yelled from the crowd. "This play is an evil lie, you hypocrites."

Another voice joined in, "The Yankee woman needs to shut her mouth!"

A third cried, "The mouths of them that speak falsehood will be stopped," to a small chorus of "Hear, hear!" and "You said it, brother!"

Something flew in the air and bounced off the actress's chest—she started back and lifted her arms to ward off a few more missiles that began to volley in. It rolled on the ground— an apple core.

Kate wanted to sob, to tell them it was real, that she had known an innocent woman and child who died, herded like cattle in a pen.

"Get off that stage," a man snarled at the cowering actress.

She straightened in her robes and approached the edge of the stage, face intent, fists bunched. "I will not. This tragedy will not end until every voice cries out!" Boos arose from other men, quarreling voices broke out in the pit.

More men shouted her down. "I'll show you a tragedy!" "You're a traitor to our country!" "Take this, lying mouthpiece of Satan!" A lunch bucket flew up and clanged on the side of the actress's head. She staggered and stumbled back, then ran offstage.

This could not be—Kate would not watch it idly. Her face grew so hot and full it felt like she would have a stroke. How dare they torment this woman, assault her for showing the truth and believing it. They were ruining the beauty of the play, staining it, and claiming God was on their side. Kate jumped to her feet and stepped to the edge of the railing.

"Stop!" she shouted, in a voice that echoed to every curtain and every box of the theater.

The voices below ceased, mustached faces peering upward, mouths agape. They had likely never seen a gentlewoman speak from the boxes in their whole lives. A hush fell over pit and gentlefolk alike—she could feel the entire theater listening, the shock of the women, the glee of the scandal-mongers. It simply made her more determined, more angry. Who were they to deny Nelly had ever existed, to say these things were false?

Her agitation emptied her head. Would she have anything to say? This was not some ballroom debate.

She might not have the words to refute them, but she knew something by heart that others would recognize. She grabbed the railing and took a deep breath.

She sang out as loudly as she could, though her voice shook a trace: *"Oh my poor Nelly Gray . . ."*

The theater was so quiet her voice filled it, effortless and clear like a bell vibrating over snow. She would not stop until they heard. *"They have taken you away . . ."*

Several voices joined in. *"And I'll never see . . ."*

Half the theater burst into it from the pit, a chorus of rough men's voices, *"My darling any more . . ."*

She let them take up the chorus and stopped to listen.

Ben clutched the railing next to her and stared down at the pit, his face open with wonder. "What?" he said to her under his breath. "How do they know?" He shook his head a fraction, still gazing at the crowd. He brought one hand to his mouth as if stifling a cough, then closed his eyes and went to his knees as if the railing were all that held him up, his head bowed. She knelt with him, laid a hand on his shoulder, unwilling to leave him, heedless of who saw them or what they thought.

Did he not know what her aunt had told her, that his song was everywhere? That it was the anthem of abolition, and changing hearts by the hundreds and thousands? He looked at her with tears in his eyes and she nodded to tell him yes, it was true, wanting to weep for gladness for him, for what he had done, for what he had only just learned as the notes continued to resound through the building.

"*I am sitting by the river and I'm weeping all the day . . . ,*" the audience sang, even the respectable ones in the boxes. The song overpowered the faint hecklers, who stormed out one by one, waving their arms, yelling inaudible threats.

Ben passed a hand over his eyes. She knew what he was thinking—she could not get them out of her mind either. No more deaths—slavery must end, and by God's grace, it would. Nelly and her baby had not died in vain. Their lives had mattered—their story had been told, and they would never be forgotten.

"*For you've gone from that old Kentucky shore.*"

The melody ended, triumphant, and the applause and cheering redoubled, as if the roof itself would lift at any minute, and the shouting and singing would spread across the whole country. Ben got to his feet, slowly. He held his hand out to her, palm up, as he would on the day he took her to be his bride, and she placed her hand in his. Drawing her up to stand with him, he placed a gentle arm around her and whispered in her ear, "It is beginning." He did not move away, but kept his face to her neck, where his warm breath sent a thrill through her and made her long for that wedding day.

And she knew what he meant, as she leaned into his embrace and felt the warmth of his body next to hers.

The power of the song was in the joining of voices, and she and Ben would sing it together as one, as long as they lived.

Afterword

History and Fiction

"DARLING NELLY GRAY" TOOK THE NATION BY STORM in 1856 and was called the *Uncle Tom's Cabin* of song." Like Harriet Beecher Stowe's novel, Ben Hanby's song was renowned for its power to rouse people against the evils of slavery. Ben earned very little money for the song due to the sharp dealing of his publisher. He wrote other great songs that are still performed today, the most famous being "Up on the Housetop," the classic Christmas song. (I bought an illustrated children's version of "Up on the Housetop" just so I could delight in the name "Benjamin Russel Hanby" on the cover.)

After raising two young children with his beloved wife, Ben Hanby died of illness at thirty-three, and Kate Winter Hanby never remarried. She described Ben thus: "[He had] dark curly hair, and beautiful eyes . . . Fond of jokes, a fine storyteller, and a brilliant conversationalist, he was a kind, helpful husband and fond of his children" (Shoemaker 108). That testimony alone would make Ben Hanby a real-life hero in my book.

I changed some family relationships in my novel, but Ben's parents and siblings are portrayed as in life, all called by their real names. For more on the story of Will Hanby and Ann Miller Hanby, see *Fairer than Morning*, the first novel of this series.

The real Kate Winter (full name Mary Katherine Winter) was extremely shy and soft-spoken, though intellectually gifted and beautiful. She was the first graduate of Otterbein College, which was one of the first colleges in the nation to admit women. Her parents were Elizabeth and Isaac Winter, wealthy and influential people in the village of Westerville. Kate's mother was socially ambitious and opposed Ben Hanby as a suitor for her daughter due to his lack of prospects as a future minister. A young music teacher named Cornelia Walker secretly aided Ben and Kate to meet at her home and eventually become engaged, which is why Ben dedicated his song "Darling Nelly Gray" to "Miss A. C. Walker." In life, however, Cornelia Walker was the daughter of an Otterbein professor, not of the college president as in my story. The college president at the time was Lewis Davis, and like the fictitious President Lawrence of the novel, he was also an Underground Railroader who worked with William Hanby.

There is no historical evidence that Kate Winter worked on the Underground Railroad with Ben Hanby before their marriage, as she does in *Sweeter than Birdsong*, but she could have done so easily once she and Ben lived in the same house. They married in 1858, when he graduated from Otterbein, and lived together as man and wife for several years before the Civil War began.

John Parker is an amazing figure in history who lived in Ripley, Ohio, and aided fugitive slaves. An ex-slave himself, he owned an iron foundry and employed white men, some from across the river. His life story reads like the tale of an action hero, and I wrote his character to reflect his courage and toughness.

There is no evidence that John Parker ever worked with the Hanbys on the Underground Railroad. Nonetheless, I felt that no account of the Railroad could be complete without portraying the contribution of free African Americans who risked their lives so others could find freedom. I decided to write John Parker into the story and included some of his real deeds in my account of the fugitives' escape from Kentucky (*His Promised Land* 111).

Ben did teach in Rushville as a substitute teacher for the winter and found the school in disarray, just as it appears in *Sweeter than Birdsong*. He enlisted his pupils to paint and redecorate, and he taught songs at the opening of each class. In reality, he was not dismissed for teaching abolitionist songs, but instead was very successful and remembered fondly afterward by his students.

The facts behind this series come from *Choose You This Day*, a biography of the Hanbys by Dacia Custer Shoemaker published in 1983 by the Westerville Historical Society. In addition, I consulted Brainerd Hanby's booklet *The Widow*, a biography of his mother, Kate Winter Hanby. *The Widow* is preserved in the Hanby collection at Otterbein College, an institution founded by William Hanby and attended by several Hanby children.

Readers seeking more information about John Parker will find it in *His Promised Land*, an autobiography edited by Stuart Seely Sprague and copyrighted by the John Parker Historical Society (W. W. Norton, 1996).

Acknowledgments

MY HEARTFELT THANKS GO TO MY HUSBAND AND daughter, who shared my time with good grace and didn't laugh when I walked around muttering to myself.

My editors, Ami McConnell and Meredith Efken, are the reason this novel made it into your hands. They guided me through the revision process with great insight, and I count myself blessed to have had the help of two of the best editors in our industry for this project. I'm grateful for their dedication to the highest standards.

Thanks to all the others at Thomas Nelson who create such beautiful work and provide support at key moments: Allen Arnold, Kristen Vasgaard, Becky Monds, and all the other lovely folks on staff there.

Thanks to my agent, Rachelle Gardner, who made it all happen from the beginning.

My critique partners sustained me through several drafts of this novel. In particular, Lorena Hughes and Dave Slade read through the entire final draft with great determination and speed, in order to make my deadline, and I am grateful for their help. Barbara Leachman was a great encourager when it came to spreading the word about my work. And Gwen Stewart stuck with me through the most stressful time in the whole process, the Christmas holidays of 2010. When everybody else was celebrating the season with family, Gwen's staunch friendship and writerly advice consoled and lifted up a lonely and discouraged pre-deadline novelist.

My beta readers Angie Drobnic Holan and Rachel Padilla also gave me valuable insight on this project.

My author friends are a lifeline for me, including Katie Ganshert, Jody Hedlund, Bonnie Leon, Wendy Paine Miller, Keli Gwyn, and Allison Pittman. The Wordserve Literary gang is also a huge source of encouragement, and I thank you all. The list of all those who showed kindness or offered professional assistance is too lengthy to include here, but please know how grateful I am to all of you. I also appreciate my reviewers, both professional and in the blogging community, and all the readers who take time to write to me about my novels. You're an inspiration and your comments keep me going when it gets tough.

Thanks to Bill and Harriet Merriman of the Westerville Historical Society, Pam and Jim Allen of Hanby House, Beth Weinhart of the Westerville Public Library, Mayor Kathy Cocuzzi of Westerville, and President Kathy Krendl of Otterbein College. And a special thanks to Dennis Davenport and his students in the music department of Otterbein for a terrific and moving presentation of Ben Hanby's music.

Much love to Michelle Fuchs and Gena Wooldridge and thanks for your friendship and support.

My sister, Kathryn, and her husband, Josh, were always ready to lend advice and amusing quips at the right time.

Thanks to my small group, the Felziens, Guzmans, and Crowders. And thanks to Donna O'Rear for a conversation at a key moment. I send gratitude and a smile to my friend Lee Thomas, for her friendship and grounding influence throughout the process, as well as for unknowingly lending me the character of her horse Garnet, the chestnut mare.

Thanks to all my friends from LSMSA '88–'90 and all the others who have stuck with me throughout the years—you know who you are.

And, as always, thanks to the original Author, who gives me hope and a future.

Reading Group Guide

1. Why do you think Kate is so fearful about speaking in public? Is it her temperament or her personal history? Have you ever known someone who had this phobia? What effect did it have on that person?

2. Even though Kate suffers from great social anxiety, she is completely comfortable with her horse and willing to perform feats on horseback that others consider physically daring. Most people have similar odd mixes of courage and fearfulness, but we never learn those secrets about them. Is there an area in which you are courageous or fearful that might surprise those who know you?

3. How might Kate's married life look if she married Frederick Jones? What does he seem to expect from her, and how does it differ from Ben's attitude toward her?

4. Why is Ben so driven to find Nelly and liberate her? How does such a strong passion for a good work help a person? How can it cause problems or mistakes?

5. How would you describe Kate's relationship with her sister, Leah? What gets in the way of their closeness?

6. The circus performers include women who vault and do tricks on horseback in knee-length tutus. How did this violate social

custom of the time? Why might it have appealed to Kate even as it shocked her? How might others in the audience have perceived those women in positive or negative ways? How do you think you would have reacted to them if you had lived in the 1850s?

7. John Parker was a real African-American hero who worked on the Underground Railroad in Ripley. What would it have been like for a black man to own a foundry right across the Ohio River from a slave state and even employ white men? What everyday challenges might John face, and what personal qualities would he need?

8. How does the journey with Nelly and her baby change Kate?

9. Why is Ben tempted to take the law clerkship? Is the advice his father gives him correct, and is Will Hanby wise to give his adult son such firm direction and principles? Under those circumstances, would you advise your adult son of the right path or keep silent? Do you think you would listen if you were the adult son or daughter in Ben's position?

10. Why does Ben think "Darling Nelly Gray" has failed when he passes through the music store and the inn in Pittsburgh on his way to Philadelphia? Why does this failure affect him so deeply? How does the end of the novel affect your perspective on this moment in Pittsburgh?

11. In the historical afterword, we learn what happened to the real Ben Hanby and Kate Winter after their marriage. Despite the unexpected events of their life together, do you think the real Kate Winter was glad she married Ben Hanby? If you were Kate, would you think it was all worth the pain and sacrifices?

12. What are some of the reasons this novel is titled *Sweeter than Birdsong*?

Ann dreams of a marriage proposal from her poetic suitor, Eli—until Will Hanby shows her that nobility is more than fine words.

FAIRER
THAN
Morning

— ROSSLYN ELLIOTT —

THE SADDLER'S LEGACY

BOOK ONE IN THE
SADDLER'S LEGACY

{ ALSO AVAILABLE AS AN E-BOOK }

Rushville, Ohio
15th July 1823

Proposals of marriage should not cause panic. That much she knew.

Eli knelt before her on the riverbank. His cheekbones paled into marble above his high collar. Behind him, the water rushed in silver eddies, dashed itself against the bank, and spiraled onward out of sight. If only she could melt into the water and tumble away with it down the narrow valley.

She clutched the folds of her satin skirt, as the answer she wanted to give him slid away in her jumbled thoughts.

Afternoon light burnished his blond hair to gold. "Must I beg for you? Then I shall." He smiled. "You know I have a verse for every occasion. 'Is it thy will thy image should keep open, My heavy eyelids to the weary night? Dost thou desire my slumbers should be broken, While shadows like to thee do mock my sight?'"

The silence lengthened. His smile faded.

"No." The single word was all Ann could muster. It sliced the air between them with its awkward sharpness.

He faltered. "You refuse me?"

"I must."

He released her hand, his eyes wide, his lips parted. After a pause, he closed his mouth and swallowed visibly. "But why?" Hurt flowered in his face.

"We're too young." The words sounded tinny and false even to her.

"You've said that youth is no barrier to true love. And I'm nineteen." He rose to his feet, buttoning his cobalt cutaway coat.

"But I'm only fifteen." Again Ann failed to disguise her hollowness.

She had never imagined a proposal so soon, always assuming it years away, at a safe distance. She should never have told him how she loved the story of Romeo and Juliet. Only a week ago she had called young marriage romantic, as she and Eli sat close to one another on that very riverbank, reading the parts of the lovers in low voices.

"There is some other reason." In his mounting indignation, he resembled a blond avenging angel. "What is it? Is it because I did not ask your father first?"

"You should have asked him, but even so, he would not have consented. Father will not permit me to marry until I am eighteen."

"Eighteen? Three years?" His eyes were the blue at the center of a candle flame. "Then you must change his mind. I cannot wait." He slid his hands behind her elbows and pulled her close. His touch aligned all her senses to him like nails cleaving to a magnet. With an effort, she twisted from his grasp and shook her head.

His brow creased and he looked away as if he could not bear

the sight of her. "I think it very callous of you to refuse me without the slightest attempt to persuade your father."

"I do not think he will change his mind. He has been very clear."

"Then perhaps you should have been—clearer—yourself." His faint sarcasm stung her, as if a bee had crawled beneath the lace of her bodice.

He dropped his gaze. "You would not give up so easily if you cared. You have deceived me, Ann."

He turned and walked up the riverbank, the white lining flashing from the gore of his coat over his boot tops. Before she could even call out, he topped the ridge and disappeared from view.

She stared blankly after him. She was so certain that the Lord had intended Eli to be her husband. But that once-distant future had arrived too early, and now it lay in ruins.

Numb, she collected the history and rhetoric books that she had dropped on the grass. She must change her father's mind, as Eli had said. If she did not, all was lost.

She clutched the books to her like a shield and began the long walk home.

In front of the farmhouse, her two young sisters crouched in the grass in their flowered frocks. Mabel pointed her chubby little finger at an insect on the ground. Susan brushed back wispy strands of light-brown hair and peered at it.

"Have you seen Father?" Ann asked them.

Their soft faces turned toward her.

"He's in the workshop." Mabel's voice was high and pure

and still held a trace of her baby lisp. She turned back to inspect the grass.

"He said he is writing a sermon and please not to disturb him," Susan added with the panache of an eight-year-old giving orders.

Without comment, Ann angled toward the barn, which held the horses and also a workshop for her father's saddle and harness business. Like most circuit riders, he did not earn his living from his ministry, and so he crafted sermons and saddles at the same workbench.

He glanced up when the wooden door slapped against its frame behind her.

"Ann." His clean-shaven face showed the wear of his forty years, though his posture was vigorous and his constitution strong from hours of riding and farmwork. "I asked Susan to let you know I was writing." There was no blame in his voice. He had always been gentle with them, and even more so since their mother had passed away.

"She did. But I must speak with you."

"You seem perturbed." He laid down his quill and turned around in his chair. "Will you sit down?"

"No, thank you." She clasped her hands in front of her and pressed them against her wide sash to steady herself as she took a quick breath. "Eli Bowen proposed to me today."

"Without asking my blessing?" A small line appeared between his brows. "And what did you tell him?"

"That I cannot marry until I am eighteen. That you have forbidden it."

"That is true. I have good reason to ask you to wait." He regarded her steadily.

She summoned restraint with effort. "What reason? I am

young, I know, but he is nineteen. He can make his way in the world. He wishes to go to medical school."

"I don't doubt that Mr. Bowen is a fine young man." Her father's reply was calm. "But I do not think your mother would have let you marry so young."

"Dora Sumner married last year, and she was only sixteen." She paced across the room, casting her eyes on the floor, on the walls, anywhere but on him. He must not refuse, he must not. He did not understand.

"I am not Dora's father." His voice was flat, unyielding. He turned to his table and gently closed his Bible. When he faced her again, his demeanor softened. "Your mother almost married another man when she was your age. She told me it would have been a terrible match. She was glad she waited until she was eighteen." He looked at her mother's tiny portrait in its oval ivory frame on the table. "She said that by the time she met me, she knew her own mind and wasn't quite as silly."

"I am not silly. I know how I feel. And he is not a terrible match." Her voice grew quieter as her throat tightened.

"I am sorry, Ann. I must do what I think is right." He was sober and sad.

Or what is convenient. For who else would care for my sisters, if not me?

But such thoughts wronged her father, for she had never known him to act from self-interest.

"But how can he wait for me? He is older than I am. He will want to marry before three years are out." She did not try to keep the pleading from her voice, though her face tingled.

He paused, then leaned forward, as steady and quiet as when he comforted a bereaved widow. "Then he does not deserve you."

"No, you are simply mistaken. And cruel."

He stood up and walked to the back of the barn.

Clutching her skirt, she whirled around, pushed through the door, and ran for the house.

She would not give way to tears. She must stay calm. She slowed to a walk so her sisters would not be startled and passed them without a word.

Her bedroom beckoned her down the dark hallway.

She did not throw herself on the bed, as she had so often that first year after the loss of her mother.

Instead, she went to her desk, lifted the top, and fished out her diary. Her skirts sent up a puff of air as she flounced into the seat and began writing feverishly. After some time, the even curves of her handwriting mesmerized her, and her quill slowed. She lifted it from the page of the book and gazed ahead at the dark oaken wall.

What if he does not wait for me?

She must not doubt him so. Eli would regain his good humor and understand. He had told her many times that she was his perfect match, that he would never find another girl so admirable and with such uncommon interest in the life of the mind.

Besides, she had been praying to someday find a husband of like interests and kind heart, and God had provided. Eli loved poetry and appreciated fine art, but he was nonetheless a man's man who liked to ride and hunt. And, of course, he was every village girl's dream, with his aristocratic face. No other young man in Rushville could compare.

She doodled on the bottom of the page. First she wrote her own name.

Ann Miller.

Then she wrote his. Then she wrote her name with his.

Ann Bowen.

Ann Bowen.

Ann Bowen.

She smiled, pushed the diary aside, and pillowed her head on her arm to daydream of white bridal gowns and orange blossoms.

ELL
33292012668509
wpa
Elliott, Rosslyn.
Sweeter than birdsong

About the Author

Author photo by Amy Parish Photography,
New Mexico

ROSSLYN ELLIOTT GREW UP IN A MILITARY FAMILY and relocated so often that she attended nine schools before her high school graduation. With the help of excellent teachers, she qualified to attend Yale University, where she earned a BA in English and Theater. She worked in business and as a schoolteacher before returning to study at Emory University, where she earned a PhD in English in 2006. Her study of American literature and history inspired her to pursue her lifelong dream of writing fiction. Her debut novel, *Fairer than Morning*, was the 2011 winner of the Laurel Award. She lives in the Southwest, where she home-schools her daughter and teaches in children's ministry.

Praise for BETWEEN A WOLF AND A DOG

'Blain just gets better and better. The clarity, warmth, and precision of *Between a Wolf and a Dog* brings to mind the formal beauty of an exquisitely cut gemstone. Blain looks at the big questions — mortality, grief, forgiveness — through the lens of one family's everyday struggle to love each other. This portrait of marriage and work, of sisterhood, mothers, and daughters is resolute and clear-eyed; so commanding and beautifully written it made me cry.'
Charlotte Wood, author of *The Natural Way of Things*

'Heartfelt, wise, and emotionally intelligent, *Between a Wolf and a Dog* is a beautifully tender exploration of the complications of family love, self-knowledge, and the struggle for forgiveness.'
Gail Jones, author of *A Guide to Berlin*

'What a marvellously clear eye Georgia Blain has for the ways in which we love and harm one another. Whether she is observing a "coconut-ice" grevillea or meditating on everyday consolations and sorrows, Blain is a quietly profound writer and this is a remarkable book.'
Michelle De Kretser, author of *Questions of Travel*

'*Between a Wolf and a Dog* is an elegantly told story describing the ambiguities within human relationships. Each evening, when my children slept, I would enter the world of this book — coming to know a flawed, courageous, and creative family of characters, as they struggled to be good, to be whole, and finally, to let go.'
Sofie Laguna, author of *The Eye of the Sheep*

'Picking a favourite Georgia Blain novel is like picking a favourite child ... Blain intelligently asks the big questions — about mortality, grief, forgiveness and how hard it can sometimes be to love those we're supposed to.'
North and South

'[A]n elegant novel, written in lucent and, at times, luminous prose. It is a work of delicately detailed emotion and beautiful balance, and it is so well paced that its narrative is utterly compelling. It is a remarkable portrayal of family relationships, and the complex and often competing desires and sensitivities that drive them, but it is mostly a book about love and forgiveness, and holding on to our good fortune and our loved ones, even and especially in the face of loss. It is heartfelt and resonant, and a remarkable novel that lingers long after its final page.'
Fiona Wright, *Weekend Australian*

'Captures the elusive moment when it's time to forgive, when it's time to stop fighting.'
Australian Women's Weekly

'Blain writes enchantingly about the interstices of life, the places where morality and meaningfulness blur, and characters try to justify their actions or deal with their emotions ... lyrical and lucid.'
Herald Sun

'Blain is a writer of such lucidity and strength that her characters speak, undeniably, for themselves ... What makes it possible to contain tragedy in words, so that the reader enters into the experience and passes through it, cleansed? The Greek playwrights had their own answers to this question; but the question, I suspect, is far older than their version of it. Each generation of authors must find the right words for writing about death. Part of the reason *Between a Wolf and a Dog* succeeds so well is that everything in the novel is heartfelt without being in the least sentimental.'
Dorothy Johnston, *Sydney Morning Herald*

Praise for THE SECRET LIVES OF MEN

'Many adjectives have been used to describe Georgia Blain's work, including evocative, powerful, atmospheric, haunting, rich, thought-provoking, skilful, uncompromising, and finely detailed — all of which apply to this collection of short stories.'
Bookseller + Publisher

'Subtle, beautifully paced stories ... a finely tuned collection, thoughtfully written and arranged, with profound and unsettling things to say about love, loneliness, and risk.'
Denise O'Dea, *Australian Book Review*

'Richly imagined characters ... told with lovely restraint. The authenticity of the writing is such that you feel you are standing in the shoes of these characters whose lives are at a particularly intense point.'
Herald Sun

'[A] skilled, disenchanted reckoning of the way we live now.'
Peter Pierce, *The Saturday Age*

'There's a quiet, understated quality to her prose, an introspection in her narrative that makes her words glow dully with slow-burning intensity ... Relationships in all their combinations and permutations are skilfully dissected by an author with a keen eye and a firm grasp.'
Thuy On, *The Age*

'Blain's achievement with the short story form is to render it a mid point between the overt artifice of fiction and the covert artifice of life-writing ... her stories fill up with ambiguity ... characterised by an irresolution that mimics the resistance of experience to shape and comprehension.'
Stella Clarke, *The Weekend Australian*

'Told with subtlety, tenderness and skill, *The Secret Lives of Men* displays Georgia Blain's superb ability to convey both the joys and struggles of daily life and its impact on each of us. Blain is a gifted writer: through her storytelling we come to know ourselves better.'
Tony Birch

'A haunting, unsentimental exploration of the vexations and joys of modern life, family, love, and desire.'
Kirsten Tranter

'It is the mark of a superior book of short stories when each contribution is able to stand in its own bold outline, yet also go to make something more and whole. This is such a book ... It is a mature work from an author with a special sensibility and a comprehending, humane outlook.'
Judges' comments, NSW Premier's Literary Awards 2014

BETWEEN A WOLF AND A DOG

Georgia Blain published novels for adults and young adults, essays, short stories, and a memoir. Her first novel was the bestselling *Closed for Winter*, which was made into a feature film. Her books have been shortlisted for numerous awards including the NSW, Victorian, Queensland, and SA Premiers' Literary Awards, the Stella Prize, and the Nita B. Kibble Award. Georgia passed away in December 2016.

Also by Georgia Blain

Closed for Winter
Candelo
The Blind Eye
Names for Nothingness
Births Deaths Marriages
Darkwater
Too Close to Home
The Secret Lives of Men
Special

BETWEEN
A WOLF
AND
A DOG

GEORGIA BLAIN

SCRIBE
Melbourne • London

Scribe Publications
18–20 Edward St, Brunswick, Victoria 3056, Australia
2 John St, Clerkenwell, London, WC1N 2ES, United Kingdom

First published by Scribe 2016
Reprinted 2016, 2017 (four times)

Copyright © Georgia Blain 2016

All rights reserved. Without limiting the rights under copyright reserved
above, no part of this publication may be reproduced, stored in or
introduced into a retrieval system, or transmitted, in any form or by any
means (electronic, mechanical, photocopying, recording or otherwise)
without the prior written permission of the publishers of this book.

The moral right of the author has been asserted.

Typeset in Adobe Garamond Pro by the publishers
Printed and bound in the UK by CPI Group (UK) Ltd, Croydon CR0 4YY

Scribe Publications is committed to the sustainable use of natural resources
and the use of paper products made responsibly from those resources.

9781925321111 (Australian edition)
9781925228540 (UK edition)
9781925307481 (e-book)

CiP data records for this title are available from the National Library of
Australia and the British Library.

scribepublications.com.au
scribepublications.co.uk

For Rosie and Anne, Odessa and Andrew

NOW

This is the dream: Lawrence is alone. It is not quite dark, between a wolf and a dog; a mauve light is deepening like a bruise, the cold breath of the wind a low moan in his ear.

He stands on what feels to be the highest point in a landscape that he knows to be desolate and barren, although it is too dark for him to see. Hills roll away, dry grasses beaten low by the weather; pocked boulders, dappled with creeping lichen, appear to tumble, heavy, down a steep slope.

Is it breathing he hears? Or just the night sigh?

Fear tickles the back of his neck, the hairs on his wrists bristle, his eyes widen, and the darkness is thickening.

He should not be here.

There must be somewhere he can go, a light in the distance.

Perhaps if he calls out ... and he opens his mouth, but his throat tightens.

It is like an elastic band pulling in, a peg clip on his vocal cords.

He tries to speak, but his mouth is drying, the palate hard like bone, the trachea clenching, and he cannot utter a sound.

In his dream, he panics, and he tries to wake himself, aware at some level that this is only a dream, but he can't rise from the depths; there is a weight keeping him down, the pressure — like an ocean — above him. He needs to breathe.

Calm, he tells himself. It will be all right. *Calm*. And so the clamp loosens, his mouth opening, his throat a little less clenched as he finally speaks.

'Hello.'

Unable to utter more than that, a single word whispered in all that emptiness, as around him the wind builds, and he feels the cold, sour breath of night, and the rain like sharp pins slashing the clamminess of his skin.

Sitting up in the darkness, Lawrence lets his eyes adjust. He has left the window open, and it is raining, damp and miserable, seeping down from the sill onto his bed. He reaches over to close it, the swollen wood bringing the sash to a standstill, so he has to jiggle the frame, slot it into a new groove before it will slide all the way down.

He hates that dream. It leaves a rusted aftertaste, ferrous flakes in his mouth, and a panic like poison — the hollowness of sadness and despair coursing through him as he lies back down in the bed. He hasn't looked at the clock — years of insomnia have taught him the foolishness of doing so — but the sound of the first suburban trains lets him know that he is at least on the right side of the darkest hour for those who don't sleep. Outside the rain continues, softer now that the window is shut, and he closes his eyes, hoping he at least will find a sense of calm before morning comes, although he knows that this is unlikely. He has had that dream before, and it always leaves him, mind awake, trying to rid himself of the last vestiges of that man: a man alone, exposed, and afraid; a man he knows more intimately than he would like.

ALL THROUGH THE NIGHT it continues to rain; heavy, relentless, 'malevolent' a client had called it yesterday, and Ester had looked at him across the space of her consulting room and smiled. 'That's a strong word to choose,' she'd commented.

She wakes at four to a brief pause in the downpour, a stillness that descends over her house, and she sits up, her feet on the cold, bare boards, reluctant to leave the warmth of her bed, but also disturbed by the quiet. Outside, a car turns off the street, the hiss of its tyres on the wet road soft in the silence. The branches of the she-oak scrape on the roof, a familiar groan of bark on tin, and then the rain begins again, not gently but with full force, torrential sheets of water running down the windows, pouring out of the downpipes and into the streets, rising and falling with each obstacle in their path, gushing up around the wheels of parked cars, bubbling over the rubbish blocking the drains, scooping up the soil and mud and leaves and sticks and plastic, all in a rush, until they are dumped against the next obstacle, the flow continuing, unstoppable, on and on to the lowest point.

Sitting on the edge of her bed, Ester listens.

As a child, rain had made her anxious. She remembers nights by the river, the room where they slept leaking like a sieve. Whenever it rained, Maurie would put all the pots and pans across the floors, rolled towels under windows and doors, the constant drip, drip, drip of water on metal keeping her awake, along with her worry that the pots would fill and overflow, or the towels would fail to stem the leak between sill and frame, and everything would just float away.

Rain still makes her unsettled.

In the darkness of the corridor, the dog lies pressed against her door. He began sleeping there shortly after she moved to this house, disturbed by the change and wanting to be as close to her as possible. She lifts his body with her foot, the warmth of his coat soft against the cold of her skin, and he jumps, nails scratching on the bare boards, only to stand just in front of her so that she walks into him again, blind in the dark.

'Otto.' She doesn't want to wake the girls. Clicking her fingers and pointing towards the kitchen, she tries to direct him to where his mat is, never used, but he ignores her.

'Move.' She knees him again, and he shifts slightly before sighing heavily and slumping to the ground once more, eyes open and glittering white-blue in the darkness, making sure she doesn't leave his sight.

The door to the girls' room always creaks when she opens it. She turns the handle slowly, attuned to the shift, and when that doesn't work, she twists it as quickly as she can. It doesn't really matter. Once they are asleep, they don't wake.

The streetlight shines in through a chink in the blind. Lara hated this when they first moved here. She couldn't go to sleep with any light on, insisting that the room was totally dark.

'I can't fix it,' Ester had told her. 'The light is there and I can't make it go away.'

She remembers. She had sat on the edge of Lara's bed and she had wept. In all the preceding months, she had gone into the bathroom to cry, or into her bedroom, once even hiding in the pantry cupboard, while they ran around the house calling for her, over and over again. But that night, she had just given in.

'You're going to have to live with it,' she'd said.

Lara hadn't uttered a word, not calling out as she usually did, not getting up and rubbing her eyes as she complained she couldn't sleep. She had stayed where she was. And she had never mentioned the light again.

Standing at the entrance to their room, Ester sees the slope and curve of their bodies, the slow rise of their chests, the golden tangle of their hair, the loose abandonment of a limb, the soft pad of Catherine's heel, and the smooth muscle of Lara's calf. They always end up in the same bed, curled into each other; two beautiful bodies, alike to everyone but their family.

They are hers, and they are not hers. They are growing to become unique, distinct beings who will lead lives of their own in places of their own.

She loves them.

And the warmth of that is a blessing in the night, at an hour when no one should be awake. Ester breathes it in, a great draught of it, full and rich, while outside the rain continues unceasing: silver sheets sluicing down, the trees and shrubs soaking and bedraggled, the earth sodden, puddles overflowing, torrents coursing onwards, as the darkness slowly softens with the dawn.

Ester's appointment diary is open.

9.30am: Louisa

11.00am: The Harcourts

1.00pm: Daniel and Sarah

2.15pm: Chris

4.00pm: Hannah

In her head she sees the structure of her day: post-natal depression, school aversion, relationship crisis, death, and loneliness. Lawrence used to call her diary 'The Happiness Book'.

'Ho-ho,' she'd respond. 'What a wit.'

But she hadn't been averse to teasing him about his own work. Lawrence conducted polls and surveys. *He measures dissatisfaction*, she would say when people asked her what he did. A state he was fond of indulging in himself.

She closes the diary. When the girls are with Lawrence, the client hours can continue well into the evening — but not tonight. Tonight, she is finishing early. And this morning, she is up before they are awake, her yoga mat laid out in the lounge room. It is only just light, and the rain is continuing, no longer torrential, just steady, plastering wet leaves against the cold glass — crimson, brown, and green.

Each time she tries to go into dog pose, Otto licks her face. She puts him out in the hall and he whines, scratching against the wood, the noise harsh and insistent.

She hates it when the girls go to Lawrence, but where the girls go, Otto goes, and the break from him is always welcome. Breathing in, she tries once again, the stretch easier this time, the knot in her back unfolding as she lowers her hands to the floor, ignoring the dog as she exhales and inhales, slowly, deeply.

Her phone chimes. The text message on the screen is from her mother: *Cold Men*. She can only assume this means 'Call me', as this is what Hilary usually wants, but as she never wears her glasses, and her phone has an old form of predictive text that she uses in an unpredictable way, the words that she sends usually bear no relation to what she means.

'Why don't you just call me?' Ester asks.

'Because I didn't know if you were up yet,' Hilary replies.

Hilary sleeps badly, although she has always ignored any suggestions Ester gives to try and help, telling her daughter that insomnia gives her more time to work. Ester knows she frequently gets up before dawn and goes to the studio Maurie built for her — a room that leaks a lot less than the river house, his first project all those years ago. She sits at a desk in the corner, computer screens in front of her, the surrounding walls covered in images: cards, letters, scraps from newspapers, old family photographs, a piece of flimsy fabric, shiny wrappings from Easter eggs, ribbons, drawings from Catherine and Lara, and there in the centre of it all, Maurie's horse: beautiful, wild, the charcoal lines black and sure, the strange mixture of panic and pride in its eye enough to stop everyone who entered Hilary's room.

'It's his portrait of me,' Hilary would always say.

She tells Ester her film is ready, and will have its first screening at the Pompidou Centre in a month.

'I want to show you before I send it off,' she says. 'And they've sent the program notes for my approval, but I can't understand a word of them.'

Ester and Lawrence had lived in France until just after the girls turned one, and although her French is rusty, she has enough to get the gist. 'I can't today,' she says. 'Tomorrow?'

Hilary wants to know if tonight is possible.

'I'm going out,' Ester tells her. 'I promise I'll come tomorrow.'

She doesn't want to say anymore, to tell Hilary anything about her plans for the evening. It is too fragile, and she needs to keep it close for the present.

But Hilary rarely gives in. 'It will only take an hour.'

Ester is silent for a moment. She sighs, relenting with reluctance. She will come after work. 'But I can't stay.'

Outside, the streetlights have turned off and the first watery wash of morning colours the sodden sky. The rain continues. Across the road, Ester can see her neighbour getting into his car. He sits with the door open, trying to close his umbrella, the drops soaking into his suit and splashing onto his shoes, and she watches as he shakes the now closed umbrella into the gutter.

Catherine and Lara are awake. Their room is still dark, and

Ester pulls up the blind. The grevillea presses against the window, coconut-ice flowers and fine feathery leaves.

'Up,' she tells them.

Catherine ignores her, continuing to whisper to Lara. She is using the language she and Lara shared for the first four years of their lives, a secret language that neither she nor Lawrence could ever understand. He used to worry about it, to try and get them to use English only; Ester was always less concerned. 'They'll drop it in their own time,' she would say, which they had, although they still occasionally liked to revert.

'We don't want to go to school,' Catherine tells her. 'It's too wet.'

'And we don't want to go to Dad's,' Lara adds.

'We just want to stay here. In bed.' It's Catherine's turn now. She smiles at them, and pulls back the blanket.

'Please,' Lara persists.

Catherine whispers something in her ear, giggling as she does. Lara replies in their language.

'Enough,' Ester tells them. She had made the mistake of succumbing to this request in the early days of the separation, and they still try, prying for the chink.

'I'm being bullied,' Lara tells her.

Ester laughs. 'You are not.'

'We don't like Dad.'

'That's not true either.' She resorts to a bribe. 'Hot chocolate if you're up by the time I count to twenty.'

They like school. This occasional reluctance to go is something new. She wonders whether they do this with Lawrence as well. She knows Lara was recently in trouble for setting off the fire alarm, with Catherine initially taking the blame. It was Lawrence who had dealt with that one, although the school informed her as well. She also knows they don't like their teacher this year. She is one of the old ones; a woman who has been there for years and only shows enthusiasm for the classroom footy-tipping competition and describing re-runs of *Judge Judy* episodes to the wide-eyed seven-year-olds who love the shameless airing of conflict. If the homework they bring back is any indication, the actual schoolwork is boring and repetitive, so much so that she offered to write them both a note to say she didn't want them doing it. Lara leapt at the chance, but Catherine was more nervous. 'She ignores those notes,' she said. 'She still shouts at the kids who don't do the work.'

She imagines asking Lawrence how they are with him, whether he too has noticed a slight shift in their attitude to school, whether he thinks it is a matter that should concern them.

In her sessions with Victoria, she is working on her communication with Lawrence — on her forgiveness, really. Because that's what it all comes down to, always. Can you forgive?

'You *have* to forgive,' Hilary would urge her, too often and too soon. 'We all have to forgive.'

As children, Ester and April rarely fought, but when they did, Maurie would make them apologise to each other. He hated conflict around him, although he was never averse to arguing his own point, loudly and frequently. She remembers the time she ruined April's new shorts, wearing them into the river and tearing them on an overhanging bough that she used to haul herself out. They were flared blue gingham, April's pride and joy, and Ester had been jealous because April looked so pretty in them. Despite being two years older, April was the same size as her, slender and delicate with long legs and thick golden hair. Looking down at the shorts, Ester knew she would be in trouble. She took them off and hid them under the verandah.

Denial was useless. When she was discovered, she didn't want to apologise. They always shared clothes, and what had happened had been an accident. She'd hung them on the bush so that they would dry out, she lied. They'd blown off.

April cut up her favourite T-shirt.

It took Maurie two days to get them to speak to each other without rancour. He refused to talk to them until they each apologised and forgave the other. Hating her father's disapproval, Ester gave in first. She remembers saying she was sorry, she really was, her words calm and clear as she genuinely tried to resolve the issue. And then April cried — she cried with shame at how badly she'd behaved, at how much she'd hated that this had come between them, at how much she loved Ester, she really did. Maurie cried, too. The house was awash with their tears, and if Ester felt that it was ridiculous, over-dramatic, too much — well, she kept this to herself, because this was how it always was with April.

Standing in the kitchen, she wonders how Maurie would deal with them now if he were still alive.

It is eight o'clock, and Lawrence will be here to get the girls in half an hour. Their bags are packed by the front door.

'Don't think I don't know what you're doing,' Ester says, taking the red hair-tie out of Catherine's hair and swapping it for the blue one in Lara's. She does this for the teachers, to help them distinguish between the two of them, but it is probably useless — they are likely to switch as soon as they are out of her sight.

'What are you going to do while we're at Dad's?' Lara asks.

Ester smiles. 'Sit up late, eat pizza, watch bad television.'

'Or go out with Steven?' There is muffled giggling, nervous glances, kicks under the table, and Ester looks from one to the other, momentarily silenced by their audacity.

They have been at her phone, checking the calendar she keeps separate to her work appointment book. She remembers putting his name in, fear making her fingers clumsy, just as her voice had felt unlike her own when he had called her, and she had answered, aware of who he was the moment she heard him speak, lowering her tone so that she didn't sound herself. She became sensible, serious, dull.

She had met him at a family-mediation course. She had been late on the first day, taking the last seat at the table. He had spent most of the morning session surreptitiously sending and receiving texts. When they were paired for a role-playing exercise, he had no idea what they were meant to be doing.

'You're passive and I'm aggressive,' she told him.

'I'm Steven, actually,' and he held out his hand.

A woman called Heather was their mediator. She asked them both to give her a brief précis of why they were here, the nature of their conflict. She was nervous and shy, her voice almost too soft to hear.

'I don't know,' Steven said.

'We're negotiating a financial settlement,' Ester told him.

'Do we have much?'

She smiled. 'Aside from a house and pitiful savings, there's anger, hurt, and pride.'

His eyes were smoke, clouds, and soft winter sky. He looked embarrassed when his phone chimed again. 'It's work,' he explained. 'I'm so sorry. They're sacking someone I've been working with. It's messy.'

He was a counsellor for executives, brought in by companies when they were concerned that their top-level staff were not performing to the best of their abilities. 'It can be a tricky line. The company pays my bill, but the person is my client.'

'Can we get back to the settlement?' Heather asked, sniffing anxiously as she saw the other groups well into the scenario.

In the break, he offered to make her a cup of tea.

'I don't drink it,' she told him.

'Well, there's a first,' he smiled. 'Someone else who doesn't like tea.'

'I try,' she said. 'But it's the tannin. Makes my tongue curl and my teeth feel like chalk.' She grimaced.

'Clearly, no one has ever made you the perfect cup.'

'They've given it a go,' she told him. 'But it's never changed my mind.'

He asked her where she worked.

'At home,' she told him. 'I'm a counsellor. I specialise in family therapy.'

'Do you like it?'

'Sometimes. On the good days.' She smiled.

'Do you have a family of your own?'

She looked straight at him as she answered. 'Everyone does.'

He laughed, and for the first time she witnessed a flicker of nerves. 'That was a clumsy way of trying to find out if you're on your own.'

She was embarrassed. She remembers and blushes even now. *It is so hard to do this*, she thinks. *To laugh, and be light, and take those first steps*. It is a wonder anyone ever does it — that extraordinary, shimmering fragility so delicate and open. There, high above the city, standing next to an urn, a fake teak box filled with teabags, and, next to the box, carefully stacked white china cups, both of them surrounded by counsellors, she had felt it for an instant — the sparkling brightness of the moment — and it had made her look down at the carpet, his shoes, her boots, the stolid ordinariness of them not quite enough to ground her.

After the course, he suggested they have a drink.

'I only have an hour,' she told him.

The girls were with Hilary, and she called and asked her to feed them. She was running late, she said.

They went to a bar, all warm wood and dark corners, and full of people younger than them. He asked her what she would do if she could start again, 'if money and training were no option and you could do anything, anything at all.'

She considered the question for a moment.

'Maybe a gardener.' But she was lying really, and she confessed as much. 'I wouldn't want to do the actual work; I'd just like to plan it, and then look at it once it was done.'

He asked her about her family.

'My mother is a filmmaker,' she told him, 'and my father was a painter.'

'Siblings?'

'A sister. She was a singer. She is a singer.'

She didn't want to talk about April, and she picked up the coaster, damp beneath her fingers, and then put it down again. 'What about you?'

'I like what I do,' he said. 'But if I could start again, maybe a surgeon. I spent six months in hospital. With a virus that went to my lungs and my kidneys. It was awful, but that whole world, the intensity of it, the drama, the fact that what you do matters,' he smiled. 'It was seductive. I could see why there are so many hospital soaps.'

She liked him. A half hour passed, and then she called Hilary. An hour later, she called again. When she finally left, she was slightly drunk, and the softness of his lips on her cheek as they kissed goodbye had lingered, warm.

It has been a year since she moved to this house, she thinks, two years since Lawrence sat in front of her and confessed. And despite being so tired of the taste of it, she has held his betrayal close.

She looks at the girls now; Lara is uncertain as to whether they have gone too far, Catherine is nervous for her sister.

'I *am* going out,' Ester tells them. She smiles at Lara. 'And what an extraordinary guess. I'm actually having dinner with someone called Steven. Clearly, you're both geniuses or clairvoyant.'

Lara giggles anxiously.

'Will it ever stop raining?' Ester asks them.

Opening the front door so that she can hear Lawrence when he arrives, she looks out across her street, the trees bent low in the downpour, the gutters awash with stormwater, the sky low and sullen overhead. She wonders whether clients will cancel. She wonders if Steven will cancel, and she feels the push and pull of both relief and disappointment at the thought.

And then Lawrence pulls up, his navy-blue station wagon idling out the front, the wipers going backwards and forwards, the headlights on, as he sounds the horn and she calls them — 'Quick, your father's here' — asking Catherine to get Otto on the lead, kissing them and telling them she loves them. She buttons up their raincoats, not letting herself look towards the car until they are out the front door and running through the downpour to where he waits, back door just ajar so that they can get in straightaway.

HILARY OFTEN FORGETS that Maurie has gone. When she wakes, she reaches across the bed, searching for his warmth, feeling the cool of the sheet before she shifts towards his side, stretching a little further out, her fingers certain they will touch him soon.

He died in the middle of the night. She had got up, as she often did, finding her way down the stairs and along the corridor, her night vision never good, hands seeking the walls and then the door frames, not wanting to switch on a light because that would kill all possibility of getting back to sleep. In the kitchen, she had poured herself a glass of water, the plumbing groaning as she turned the tap off.

If she *had* heard anything — and she was never sure later whether or not she had — it would have been difficult to discern above the thump of metal pipes, the heavy clunk as the water ran down towards the drains. Sometimes, she is certain he called out. It was her name, she thinks. Other times, she is not so sure. Perhaps the pain, the massive heart attack he suffered, was just too sudden and swift — all life shut down before he even had a chance to register that this was happening to him.

All she really knows is that when she returned to their room, he was no longer present. He was gone. It was not the shape of him. That had given no indication. It may have been the silence, the complete and utter stillness; no breath, no shift or movement, nothing. But she doesn't think it was quite so prosaic. Maurie —

all that he was and had been and could be and wanted to be, all that she had loved and at times loathed, the great space that he had filled — had left the building.

As the realisation had begun to slowly disperse, cold tendrils unfurling, she wanted only to sit by his side until the first film of day washed across the walls, and the sounds of the street below drifted up: car doors opening and closing, a voice calling out, a dog barking.

Her eyes had slowly adjusted to the light and she saw him then, his face contorted with pain, and she had to look away.

Strangely, it had been April she had called — despite the fact that Ester was calmer and better in a crisis.

'Maurie's died,' she had told her, and April had done what Hilary had known she would do. She had cried, a great outpouring of grief, a wailing, interspersed by questions, her voice still husky from sleep as she had asked how and when, only to sob over Hilary's attempts at answering.

'I'll be over,' April had promised.

Hilary had heard the muttering of a male voice from the bed, and then the flare of a match as April lit a cigarette, the intake of nicotine.

'Don't go anywhere,' she had said.

'Where on earth would I go?' Hilary had asked, only to realise her daughter wasn't actually talking to her but to the man lying next to her.

The bedroom she had shared with Maurie was the only under-furnished room in the house. When the girls had left home, Maurie had knocked two upstairs rooms into one, opening the space up to the northern light. They had painted the walls white, and put their bed in the middle. On the floor was a patchwork kelim. Nothing else. All their clothes were in the back bedroom, along with the spare bed.

It had been Maurie's idea. An empty room to help her sleep. And for two people who had always lived in clutter, it was a strange space, one that surprised her whenever she opened the door. It was like stepping into someone else's room, she thought, and she never quite knew how she felt about that.

She also hadn't slept any better; she still didn't sleep any better, but now that he was gone, she didn't even attempt to for long, often turning on the light to read, or getting up well before it was light to go and work in her studio, only to return to her bed when everyone else was eating breakfast.

This morning, as the rain pours down, April is sleeping inside, the door to the spare room still closed when Hilary went into the house for a coffee. There was something ominous about April's presence, like having a grenade or landmine in the house, or harbouring a criminal; it was enough to send Hilary back to the studio, rather than upstairs for her morning nap.

She closes the doors to the deluge — the sound is disturbing — and pulls the heater close. She has one copy of the film in a postbag, a version uploaded onto Vimeo, and one on her computer ready to show the girls. Like all her work, it is made from fragments — old pictures, images from Maurie's notebooks, archive footage, and film she has shot over the years. She works in collage, layering images on top of each other in order to untangle larger ideas about life. Her work is often called autobiographical, and she resists the term, hating how confining it feels. She prefers to see her work as teasing out complexities that affect others as well as herself, sometimes using her own life as a springboard but never staying there.

This one is called *Keepsake*. She struggled to define it in her notes for the festival. Yes, it is about death, but it is also about living — about what we cling to and what we relinquish — about how we remember, she supposes.

The final footage she shot four years ago, shortly after Maurie died, when it rained like it is raining now. She had gone to their shack on the river, wanting a few days there to help her decide whether it should be kept or sold. She had simply filmed, with no particular project in mind. The swollen river was brown, murky, and ugly, the peak right at the top of the banks. Sitting on the step at the bottom of the path, her raincoat pulled over her head, she had filmed the flow, the swirl and eddy, the relentless rush and then, there, under a knot of tree roots, she had seen a fallen branch, heavy enough to create a small dam — a pool where the flow was stopped, and the leaves and twigs swirled helplessly, with nowhere to go.

Maurie had built the shack when Ester was one and April three. He had gone there every weekend, often with several friends, leaving her at home alone with the babies. When she complained, which she did frequently, he would brush her off, telling her to come with them, oblivious to how impossible it would be to sleep under a tarp with the two girls, let alone to keep them away from nails and tools while he built.

When he took them to see the end result of his labour, he made them all wear blindfolds. Ester in one arm, he led her and April down the track, the smell of eucalypt sharp in the air, the crushed leaves of the lemon-scented gums underfoot, the burn of the sun on her skin, and the tickle of an ant as it trailed its way across her ankle, while overhead there were bees, a soft drone that ebbed and flowed with a hypnotic rhythm.

'The family palace,' he announced.

She wasn't sure what she had expected. She never was with Maurie. Perhaps a one-room dwelling, a caravan attached. He called it a shack, they all called it a shack — then and in the years to come — but it was so much more than that. An Indian pavilion, she thought: the play of the roof, pitched and falling, pitched and falling, the graceful sweep of the old windows that he had salvaged from a demolition site, the delicate turns and curves of the wooden columns, and the generosity of the deep, wide verandah looking out on a row of poplars, their crinkled-paper leaves on slender branches shimmering beneath the sky.

Inside there were two rooms: a huge open living room, and, behind that, a place to sleep, a curtain to divide them from the girls. The floors were old planks, some wide, some thin, the walls a mixture of tin and gyprock, and the ceiling was patched together, painted sky-blue.

'The kitchen,' Maurie showed her proudly, waving in the direction of an outdoor oven and a sink, both sheltered by tin walls and a tarp, and then, beyond that, the bathhouse — an old enamel tub, deep green, under the shade of a cottonwood.

It was one of his finest works.

She had looked at him with tears in her eyes and told him it was beautiful beyond imagining, and, holding the warmth of his face in her hands, she had kissed him, there in the entrance to their shack, while a swallow darted in through the open door and wheeled and turned under that crazy roof — the angles leaning seemingly without method, yet creating a kaleidoscope of pattern that had an order so intricate it made her head reel.

When she told Ester and April that she wanted to sell the shack, it was Ester who begged her not to, although Hilary knows she feels differently about it now, that she now wants the place gone, all memory of it having been tainted. But at the time, Ester had been upset with Hilary's decision, and Hilary had been surprised. Ester was the only one of them who regularly threw out clutter, who sorted old clothes and gave them to the charity shops, who admired the children's art and then surreptitiously slipped it in the recycling bin, who put the lidless Tupperware out with the plastics, and who liked just one work of art on a wide expanse of white wall. Ester let things go — or so Hilary had thought.

April, on the other hand, had told Hilary it was a good idea. She was the one who had gone there as an adult, trying to write her last album in the heat of the summer, only to give up after a week with just one song and mosquito bites covering her long golden limbs. Her voice had trembled slightly as she confessed that she had spent most of the time sitting on the verandah, bored and wanting to come home — a fact she soon forgot when she returned there some time later, only to wreak pain and havoc in all their lives.

April was a hoarder. She would open her handbag to search for cigarettes, and the chaos of her life would spill out: bills scribbled on, broken lipsticks, books she had borrowed, a singlet, a restaurant menu, all spread across the table. Her apartment, bought after the success of her first single, looked out over Rose Bay. The top floor of a grand art deco building, the rooms were magnificent in their sweep, seemingly impossible to fill. She had covered the walls with Maurie's art, selling off paintings as she needed the money, and then replacing them with images that she liked: drawings from the twins, pictures from Hilary's films, even sketches she herself had done. The floors were layered in rugs, her clothes were strewn across the furniture, and the windows were draped in badly hemmed curtains she had made. But when you first walked in, when you first saw the dance of colours and textures, it was alluring, the messiness beneath not evident to the new visitor, only the thrill of such complete disregard for order.

Hilary had thought April would be the one to beg her not to sell the river shack. But she hadn't. Feet up on a chair, coffee cup in one hand, she had barely looked up from the paper. 'Sure. It's up to you.'

And so she had put it on the market, travelling up there to see what needed to be fixed, Lawrence offering to go some months later to do the work.

It had failed to get the price she wanted. In retrospect she was foolish not to take the first two offers, but she hadn't, possibly influenced by her own sadness at letting go of the place. She had taken it off the market, telling the agent to only show people who were genuinely interested, but not to worry about advertising it. No further offers were made until the most recent one — which was a third less than the figure she had initially rejected, but one she would be foolish to let go of, the agent said. Unlike the city, the country was a buyer's market apparently.

She signed the contract three weeks ago, with settlement in ten days.

Looking out the doors towards the house, she watches the rain running down the glass, the light from her desk lamp revealing her own reflection, the face of a seventy-year-old woman surprising her, because she still thinks of herself as so much younger than she is.

Inside the house, April is up. She sits at the kitchen table, wrapped in Maurie's old robe, her beautiful golden hair knotted at the base of her neck. In a rare moment of stillness, she too is watching the rain, raising a hand in greeting as Hilary opens the studio doors, an old newspaper held above her head to protect herself from the downpour.

April had turned up the previous evening, the sweet smell of wine on her breath, cigarette smoke clinging to her wet clothes, her voice loud as she came in, calling out: 'Hello, are you home?'

She'd met a friend for a drink at the pub around the corner, and thought she'd walk down here and crash, rather than try and get a cab. Opening the fridge and pulling out some scraps — cheese, pickles, cold meat, pasta sauce — she'd begun to pile them on a plate, talking, talking, talking.

'I've been thinking about taking myself off to London. Meet up with people that I recorded with, you know?' Her mouth was full of food, and she grinned that beautiful, wide smile as she realised how she looked. 'Sorry,' she laughed. 'Starving. Josie — you remember her? — she's over there doing back-ups, and Simon, he's producing again — and the timing is right. I'm not working at the moment —'

Hilary had to interrupt: 'At the moment?'

April ignored her. 'I could rent out my place, and just go — there's no reason why not. And you're coming to Paris — we could hang out, mother-daughter time, it'd be fun.' She kicked her wet boots off, and ran her finger around the edge of the plate, then licked it, her eyes alive with the energy of a new idea. 'It's what I need,' she said, and then as her phone chimed, she looked down at it, and pushed it away. Moments later, it chimed again.

'Someone wants you,' Hilary said.

April shook her head, eventually picking the phone up and texting back. 'So, what do you think?'

'If it's what you want to do.'

April looked at her. 'But do you think it's a good idea?'

'It doesn't matter what I think,' Hilary told her. 'You're a grown-up, and you seem to be very good at doing whatever you want to do.'

'What does that mean?' April's pale-green eyes were glittering now, glass and razor.

'Nothing,' Hilary told her. 'No hidden agenda.'

April's phone went off again, this time it was a call. She pressed silent. 'If you're referring to Ester —'

'I'm not.' Hilary cut over her, exhausted at the prospect of another argument. 'I've said all I can say. I don't want to say anymore.' And then, wanting calm, she sat down opposite her daughter and took her hand. 'I love you. You're both my daughters and I love you.'

'I've tried,' April told her, eyes welling with tears now. 'You know I have. I fucked up. But I've tried to fix it.'

Hilary helped herself to a slice of cheese. 'Do you want to look at my film?' She wanted to change the subject, but she also wanted April to see it.

'Do we have to go out there?' April nodded in the direction of the doors. The rain poured down the glass, pooling in the courtyard and then forming a river that rushed down the side stairs that led to the street.

'I've used a recording of you in the soundtrack.'

'Which one?'

It was a favourite of Hilary's, one of the first songs April had written as a child: a delicate song that was principally voice and guitar, the husky crack in her daughter's voice almost breaking several times. Listening felt like walking a tightrope — dangerous, too vulnerable.

'I'll show you in the morning.'

'Sure.' April had picked up her phone again, wanting to check the previous message, and then she stepped out into the lounge room to return the call.

Now, as Hilary comes in from outside, she sees how tired April looks. She has no make-up on, and the light from the excitement of the previous evening's plans has gone. Her face is thin, the pale honey of her skin looks washed out in the grey morning light, and there is a smudge of mascara under her eyes, a black thumbprint, like a bruise.

'Coffee?' Hilary asks her.

She holds up her cup, rubbing at her temple with her other hand.

'How are the girls?' she asks, not looking at Hilary as she speaks but at the drawings pinned on the wall. 'Are they okay?'

There is a momentary ease in the rain, a silence, and Hilary glances outside. It hasn't stopped; she can see the surface of the pools of water, pocked by the lightness of the fall.

'They're good,' she tells April. 'They both had a haircut and insisted that it be exactly the same.'

'Do they ever ask after me?'

'Probably,' Hilary tells her.

'I miss them, you know.'

There is so much Hilary could say. She looks around the kitchen, April's dinner plate still left in the sink, along with an empty bottle of wine that she'd stayed up to drink after Hilary had gone to bed, her wet boots by the back door and her coat draped over the end of a chair. She colonised every space within moments of arriving.

She remembers the brief period April and Ester had shared a flat. Ester had moved home after two months.

'I can't bear it,' she'd complained. 'She wears all my clothes, she uses my shampoo, my sheets — and if I say anything, she tells me I'm uptight, ungenerous, that she would happily let me use anything of hers. Which she would. But I don't want to. There's no space between us.'

There was never any space with April.

'Do you think …' and then April shakes her head at the foolishness of the thought.

'What?'

She bites on her bottom lip before continuing. 'Maybe when they are over at your house, you could let me know. I could come over. Just quickly. Just to say hello.'

Hilary sighs. She does not want to be pulled into this discussion again. With her back to April, she rinses the plates. When she turns around, she ignores the question.

'The river shack settles soon,' she says. 'I'm going up there tomorrow. Just to have a last look.'

April glances across at her. 'Do you want me to come?'

Hilary shakes her head. 'I'd like to see it for the last time alone.' She runs her hand down the softness of April's cheek. 'Let's go look at the film. There's footage of the house that you'll like, of Maurie, all of us.'

In the studio, April stands next to the image of the horse, while Hilary finds the files. April hums under her breath, the sweetness both honeyed and rough, and when she comes to sit next to Hilary, the musky smell of her is unwashed but good.

My beautiful child, Hilary thinks, leaning over and kissing her. *My messy, beautiful daughter.*

The voiceover is Hilary's own, and the opening image a close-up of her hands holding a camera.

Like all of her works, it demands trust from the audience, that this seemingly random scatter of images will find a narrative order. From cardboard suitcases carried by children sent to the country during the second world war to Maurie's paints; from her own cluttered studio, and memories of their life together, to footage of a local hoarder's house; from the girls when they were young to herself and her work — the film asks questions of what to keep, what to discard, what clings despite all efforts to dispel it, and what slides away.

On the screen now, Maurie sits on the verandah of the shack. He is eating an apple, chewing slowly, while he stares out across the field of poplars, grey eyes focused on the distance, dirt on his cheek (and Hilary can almost feel the warmth of his skin when she looks at him, the roughness of the stubble, and the lean line of his jaw), his arms stretched out along the back of the bench, long legs crossed. At his feet, April and Ester are fighting — just a slow niggle at first that builds and builds, until Ester hits April and April screams, Maurie oblivious, and as for her, well, she was behind the camera, letting the girls fight because she wanted the footage. And then the camera pans down to the dolls they have been playing with, made by Hilary's mother and posted over from London, still kept, finally dissolving into an image of them as they are now, in the trunk in the hallway.

'I miss him,' April says.

Hilary doesn't reply.

She knows the girls sometimes wondered at how she felt, how calm and practical she had appeared after his death. Ester in particular had urged her to talk more about it, recommending counsellors, giving her books about grief.

She didn't want to.

All that he was and all that their life had been together was pulled inside, a great condensed force, dark and roiling, leavened moments later with a purity and joy that was as sweet and restrained as the crisp clarity of an autumn morning. It was hers, to be savoured and brought out when she needed it, to hold and marvel at, not to be flattened with banal words and sentiments.

As the film comes to an end, Hilary turns to April. Her daughter is sitting in front of the screen, absorbed and still. Hilary takes April's hand in her own and asks her if she is all right with the footage.

'Of course I am,' April tells her.

She had liked the later images of her and Ester going out, wearing Hilary's fifties frocks, the cotton stiff, a twirl of flowers as April spun for the camera, so aware and yet so unaware of the fact that her image was being recorded, while behind her Ester stood, self-conscious and trying to hold her stomach in.

'I still have that dress,' April says. 'Somewhere.' She smiles, standing now, her gaze focused on the rain. 'It's beautiful,' she says to her mother. 'You always capture something — the elusive that you try to hold, and can't. You do it.' She tucks Maurie's dressing gown tighter around her body, and tells Hilary she's going to have a shower and head home.

'But you're not taking that with you,' and Hilary tugs at the sleeve because she knows April's tendency to secret what she likes into the cavernous space of her handbag. A pick-pocketer's bag, Hilary has always called it.

'Can you drive me?' April asks, one arm stretched out to the rain.

When Hilary says no, she asks for money for a cab.

'I have no money,' Hilary tells her. 'Get a bus.'

And she watches as her daughter walks down to the house, not even bothering to shield herself from the steady drizzle, letting it soak into Maurie's gown and ruin the old socks that she stole from Hilary last night, letting it fall on her hair, a mist on the tangle of gold, and she knows that April will stay in the warmth of the shower for ages, before rifling through Hilary's cosmetics to find the moisturiser she likes, perhaps slipping it into her bag, as well as the lipstick that has always been her favourite.

Hilary turns back to the computer screen, the image locked on the credits. This is her last film. She hadn't begun it knowing this, nor has she told Ester or April; she hasn't told anyone. She doesn't want their grief or anxiety, or attempts to fix her with surgery or chemotherapy or radiotherapy, or any of the therapies the doctors have suggested. She is seventy years old and she has been loosening herself, trying to unpick the grip of life from her limbs, aware of how quickly time has been pushing her forward, shoving her now, relentless and sure, into this tiny space — the last moments — where she needs more strength than she has ever needed before.

WHEN LAWRENCE GETS to the school, there's nowhere to park. His windscreen wipers sweep backwards and forwards at a furious pace, and still he can't see. He opens his window slightly, and the rain drives in. Last time he double-parked, he was caught by the camera at the crossing and sent a ticket.

'You're going to have to run,' he tells the girls. 'Really fast.'

'Oh bloody hell.' Catherine looks out and shakes her head, her expression so like Ester's that he's momentarily taken aback.

'It's a shit of a day,' Lara adds, always wanting to take it one step further.

He doesn't bite.

'Quick,' he tells them, leaning behind to open the door.

Catherine is out first, her bag tangled in Lara's. He gives Lara a quick push. 'Just go with her.' He sees them, straps caught, having to run right next to each other, across the playground and into the school.

And then it's just him and Otto, who is panting in the back seat.

Neither he nor Ester had wanted Otto when they separated. It was one of the few things they agreed on. He looks at the dog now — wet, smelling like earth and rotting leaves and old meat — and he knows Ester won't have walked him in this weather, and that he really should take him out before he heads into work.

He drives to the park at the end of the street: a miserable

square of weedy grass, frequently covered by rubbish. It's the flocks of scabby ibises that cause the carnage; they pick out food scraps from the bins, spreading the rest of the garbage in their wake. Lawrence hates them.

He lets Otto out, telling him to 'chase the birds', but Otto just stands there, bedraggled in the downpour, and refuses to participate in the charade that this is some kind of walk.

There is a barbecue shelter about 50 metres away and Lawrence makes a run for it, giving the dog brief joy. He huddles under the tin awning, while Otto sniffs out the food scraps and takes the occasional bored piss against the play equipment. He'll give him ten minutes, Lawrence decides, and then bundle him back into the car, smellier than ever.

An email alert flashes across his phone, and he supposes Edmund has sent through the numbers from the latest poll. It's a standard one on the government's approval rating, which he can guess sits only slightly lower than last time. He hates this government — they appal him — and he knows he will try to spin the results to make them appear even more unpopular, phrasing his press releases to emphasise any bad news.

That's what he always does.

But sometimes he goes a little further.

He feels a strange sense of vertigo, almost nausea, at the thought of adjusting down again, just very slightly, and only for one of the questions. Leadership unpopularity. Just the smallest correction to the figures. Not enough to put him noticeably out of line with the others, and always staying within the three per cent margin of error, but perhaps a little more than he's done in the past. The first time was just a matter of rounding percentage points the wrong way, so small as to be insignificant. More the action of a peeved and bored child, who acts because he can. The second time he was a little more daring, going up a percentage point in a couple of questions. Last time, he'd nudged a question about the Prime Minister further than he had in the past, hoping he might spur one or two different kinds of stories, secretly glad when there was an article about whispers of a leadership challenge again.

He mustn't.

He swore he wouldn't again.

But there is something about knowing he can mess with the figures that he finds hard to resist.

Lawrence used to love doing the polls. They were a sideline, fun, work he did to alleviate the boredom of designing endless questionnaires ranking customer's delight (or lack of delight) with their latest car or fridge or holiday experience. Work he hoped might bring in more interesting research briefs. He ran a couple a year for the paper, before the research company transferred him to Paris. On his return, the editors of the paper wanted him back. The junior who had filled in for him was ambitious, and happy to let the polling go. It didn't bring in much revenue and it didn't look good on his performance review. No one factored in the value of the media coverage — coverage that increased with the return of Lawrence, a man who looked good on camera and knew how to frame a quote.

And so when Lawrence received the call from HR shortly before he and Ester separated, he managed to negotiate taking the polls with him when he left. His job no longer existed, he was told. The latest restructuring had left them without a place for him. HR had put together a package for his approval.

As he was packing up his desk (which didn't require much work — it had been reduced to a 700x500 hot-desk space since his unrequested return from Europe), he received a call from the newspaper. Negotiations were quick, a plan made on the run — if he took this one client with him, it might be enough to tide him over while he tested the waters with music again. He was the face of the polls, the client wanted him, and, as he stressed to the company, the revenue they brought in was miniscule, and a lot less than lawyer's fees for the wrongful dismissal action he was tempted to commence.

At first it wasn't enough work, not nearly enough to survive on, but the media coverage soon brought in other clients, bread-and-butter marketing surveys that he'd always hated and could do in his sleep, research that paid the bills. Polls were reserved for elections, or the occasional divisive policy issue.

The change was gradual. An extra one here and there, increasing as leadership in both parties became more and more unstable, and slowly building into a monthly sport, the results eagerly awaited by journalists across the country.

Otto flops at his feet as he scans for the email attachment from Edmund, a collating of the phone responses. He needs his glasses, but it seems that Edmund has forgotten to send it — which is unlike him.

The dog has found an old chicken carcass, and he cracks the bones noisily as he bites into them. Lawrence tries to kick it away, but Otto lunges for it, displaying no reluctance to go back into the downpour if there is rotting meat to be had.

The rain drums on the awning, fat drops gathering in each dip of the colourbond, swelling and falling, a curtain of silver around him, as he puts his phone back in his pocket.

Otto barks, loud enough to startle Lawrence.

It's an ibis — wanting the carcass. It flaps its wings and honks, and, for one moment, Lawrence thinks it may even try and fight the dog for the scraps, but Otto's snarl sends it beating a retreat.

This time he'd wanted to put in a question about leadership popularity. Who did voters like better — the Prime Minister or his Communications Minister? The editors weren't interested.

'No one wants a leadership challenge story at the moment.' But he'd included it anyway. Perhaps he could play a little with the results of that question, drop it into his media release, make sure to mention it in each interview he does.

He looks down at Otto, who has a piece of alfoil stuck to the corner of his mouth, and tells him it's time to get going.

'I have work to do,' he says.

Not that Otto cares.

'Opinions to report.' He whistles once, and Otto stands.

They could make a run for the shelter of a tree and then a dash for the car, or they could not even bother trying and just get wet. He chooses the first option, Otto the second.

LOUISA HAD THOUGHT she was going to have to bring Jasper with her. She tells Ester this as soon as she arrives, her words tumbling out in a rapid, breathless torrent as they often do at the beginning of a session.

Her mother had called that morning saying the rain was too much. She was anxious driving when it was like this; she didn't think she could come over and mind him after all.

'She helps so little,' Louisa says to Ester, and she glances around the room as though there is someone else there with them, listening to her betrayal and judging her.

'So, what happened?' Ester asks.

'I told her that I really needed to go. That I wasn't coping.' Louisa sniffs loudly, and then bites hard on her lip. 'I mean, I'm not, am I?' Her anger is building now.

This is the usual pattern, and Ester doesn't reply, knowing there is more to come.

'Anyway, she came, but she was pissed, said I needed to call the childcare centre again and demand a place. It was ridiculous how long I'd been waiting.' She tucks a strand of hair behind her ear. 'She has no idea. She thinks it's just me, being hopeless.' She looks out the window, the rain drumming down a hard beat behind their conversation.

Ester moves her chair a little closer. 'It's difficult to hear,' she says, smiling.

'I'm sorry,' Louisa apologises. 'Everyone tells me I speak too softly. Probably because I do. But if I let myself speak louder, it'd be a shout before you knew it.'

It takes a moment or two for Louisa to continue; Ester can see her biting back the harshness lurking behind each word. 'When I thought I was going to have to bring Jasper, I thought I'd just cancel.' Her gaze is challenging. 'You know why I come here? It's just to get a couple of hours to myself.' She has to look away at this point. 'If I could just leave him with mum, go to a café somewhere, buy a pack of ciggies and smoke the lot of them …' She shrugs. 'Maybe I'd be fine.'

Ester smiles.

'Sometimes I imagine getting in the car and driving to the airport.' Lousia's voice drops. 'I could move to London, New York. Or even bloody New Zealand.' She grimaces slightly. 'I'd send him mysterious birthday presents each year, and then when he was eighteen I'd fly him over to meet me. My son.'

Ester's clients always sit on the two-seater sofa. The room is clean and light, even on days such as this; the large wooden windows face north, overlooking the front garden and the street. There is a single Persian rug on the floor, a beautiful pattern of weeping willows woven into the thick wool, and only one painting on the wall opposite where she sits.

Ester sits back in the armchair that had belonged to Maurie, the one she'd re-covered in deep-green wool. Louisa remains upright, looking ready to leave, while outside the branches of the trees press against the glass; they shiver and shake with each burst of rain.

'It's a cow of a day,' Louisa says.

Ester nods, acknowledging the comment before returning to the issue.

'Last week we talked a bit about your lack of joy.' Ester pauses for a moment. 'In being a mother.'

Louisa stares at the window, not turning to look directly at Ester who watches her, kind, ready to listen. And then, glancing at her feet, Louisa reaches for one of the tissues.

'I keep hoping that will change.' There is a slight tremor in her voice. She has been biting her nails again, and she tries to hide this evidence of her distress by sitting on them.

'How do you think it will change?'

Louisa has her eyes on the floor, like a naughty kid trying to guess the correct answer. 'Time?'

Ester doesn't respond.

There is silence, space for Louisa to continue, which she eventually does. 'Every day I wake up and I think I made the worst mistake of my life. I shouldn't have had a kid. I was insane. Life was so much better before. I spend every waking moment when I'm not caring for him — and there aren't many of those — trying to figure how I can escape.'

She glances across at Ester, and quickly looks away again.

'But you are continuing to care for him,' Ester says gently.

'I picked up my meds last week.'

'And have you started taking them?' This is what Ester has been trying to nudge Louisa towards. Actually getting the prescription filled is a significant step.

Louisa shakes her head.

She tells Ester she had stood in the chemist, feeling like such a failure as she handed the prescription over to the pharmacist. *Another mother who couldn't cope*, and then she looks across at Ester, suddenly still, her pale gaze steady. 'I bought them and then I don't take them.' She reaches for another tissue. 'I mean, I don't know if I'm depressed. I know I might look it.' She blows her nose.

Ester waits for her to continue.

'But who wouldn't feel like this? I don't get any sleep. I spend all my time looking after someone else's needs. I don't see any grown-ups all day. And when Patrick comes home, I put Jasper in his arms and go to my room just to get away. So we never see each other.'

Louisa looks up at the ceiling. 'So of course I feel like shit. I reckon there'd be something wrong with me if I wasn't feeling like this.' She glances across at Ester, who is smiling, just slightly.

'No one wants to spend great chunks of life feeling terrible, unable to cope,' Ester says. 'We need to identify some strategies to help you feel less overwhelmed. Anti-depressants could help with this. There are also practical things you can do.'

'Did you feel like this when you had your children?'

'I don't think there would be many women who haven't felt like this. But it's not how others feel that matters. It's how you feel.'

Louisa stares at the ceiling. 'I can't be the only one who doesn't ...' and she stops here, not wanting to utter the words.

Ester waits.

'Love her kid.' Louisa breathes in before continuing. 'I know lots of women talk about how difficult it can be, how hard they found it. But no one comes right out and says: "I made a mistake. I don't love him." I mean, why do you have to love your kid?'

Ester waits until she's sure Louisa has finished. 'I understand you mightn't think your response requires treatment, but what is it that makes you come here? Why did you pick up the antidepressants?'

Louisa doesn't reply, and Ester wonders for a moment whether she has taken a wrong step. 'I suppose what I'm trying to say is that even if you aren't "unwell" as such, you may still want some assistance in coping. The pills could help.'

Still staring up at the ceiling, Louisa shakes her head. 'It's not just that,' she says. 'It's how out-of-control anxious everyone else is around me.'

Her voice a pitch higher now, she begins to tell Ester about the previous evening. She had told Patrick she was going to the movies. She had got into the car, the rain hammering on the metal roof, wet leaves sticking to the windscreen, each window misting up as she sat there, the back of her head resting on the upholstery. She had the keys in the ignition, but she didn't turn them any further. She just stayed where she was, letting the heater warm her feet, the radio on softly, the outside world no more than a general blur. She knew she ran the risk of flattening the battery, but she didn't care.

She could see the light on in the lounge room of her house. Patrick would be watching television, sometimes turning to his phone to play a game, or check out a newsfeed. Jasper would be asleep in his bassinette, probably on his back, arms no longer wrapped tightly by his side, peaceful now. She knew she should be in bed herself, trying to snatch some sleep before she was woken just after midnight and then again before dawn.

Patrick had been glad she was going out, wanting to see this as a sign that she was re-entering the world, that she was happier. 'That's great,' he'd told her. 'We'll be fine.'

He was a gentle man. A kind man, who tried to understand what had happened to her but couldn't.

An hour later, she was still in the car, the rain still falling, steady and cold, the street glittering, slick, and dark. She didn't even notice Patrick coming out to put the bins on the street. She didn't see him realising the car was still there, and heading over because something wasn't quite right, peering into the window to find her slumped against the driver's door, and when he opened it, the cold of the rain hit her like a slap, and she jumped up, screaming because she thought he was an intruder, a rapist, who knows what.

'What are you doing?' she shouted at him.

It took a moment before she saw the shock on his face.

'I thought you'd killed yourself,' he'd told her, his skin blue from the light of the dashboard, his lips pale. 'Come inside,' he'd urged her.

She'd wanted to ask him for just a little longer. Another twenty minutes, but she hadn't. The rain soaking through her coat, she'd followed him, the hall light too bright after the dim quiet of the car, the house cold.

'Why did you just stay out there?' he'd asked.

She'd opened her mouth to speak, and then Jasper had started crying, and she'd taken her wet coat off and gone to him, feeding him in the dim light of their bedroom.

Later, as they'd lain side by side, the sound of Jasper breathing next to them, he'd made her promise that she would start taking the antidepressants.

'I don't think the therapy is enough,' he'd told her.

Louisa looks at Ester now. 'He was shit-scared. He made *me* feel scared.'

Ester meets her gaze. 'Are you concerned for yourself?'

Louisa sits back and shrugs as she closes her eyes. There are tears at the corner of her lids. 'I don't want to be like this. I don't know if I'm sick. But I don't want to be like this.'

Ester watches her.

Louisa leans forward. 'You know what I'd like?' she sniffs back the tears. 'I want to fast-forward. That's all I really want — not drugs or therapy. I want to see me loving him.' And looking straight at Ester, there in the consulting room, the rain steady outside, Louisa waits for words of comfort, a promise that she will soon feel the way she wishes she could. 'But I can't, can I?'

So many of Ester's clients want this at one moment or another in their therapy. Often they reach for her, as though she can haul them out of the abyss they have fallen into and pull them up onto a land of joy, a mythical place they believe they should be able to reach. *I want to be happy again*, they say, looking to her to provide this emotional state.

The words she gives them are careful. Often they don't listen, the need glittering in their eyes, the desire blocking out anything she might say. Occasionally, they hear and they are angry — why can't she give them what they want?

And then sometimes they are like Louisa — bleak and far from home, asking her for a shortcut to the place they long for, all the while realising it doesn't exist.

Ester remembers her own despair after the girls were born. It was intermittent, but when it struck, she would lie in bed and — like Louisa — wonder whether she had made a terrible mistake that she couldn't rectify.

The isolation of living in Paris had made it worse. Lawrence had been offered a two-year contract, and they'd decided to go. There'd been no plans of a baby. She thought she might try to get some English-speaking clients, and, if that failed, she would learn French, cook, discover a new city, read the books she'd always wanted to read.

The flat they were given was on the outskirts of the city, and it was ugly and grim. Two weeks after she arrived, she learnt she was pregnant with twins. She remembers ringing Hilary some weeks after they were born and just crying. There had been no words to describe how she'd felt finding herself alone in an apartment with two babies she felt incapable of caring for.

'That's what it's like,' Hilary had told her in her usual blunt way. 'But it does pass.'

'How quickly?' she'd wanted to know.

Hilary didn't remember. 'Everything feels so momentous at

the time. But when you look back, you realise how brief it was. Insignificant, really.'

She would like to have delivered a long-distance slap.

Ester picks up the tissues Louisa left behind and takes them out to the kitchen. She always keeps the bin in her consulting room empty, clearing up after each client before she runs through the session notes, quickly adding in a few details so that she has all the information she needs to write them up later.

What Louisa really needs is sleep, Ester thinks, *and practical help*. It's what most women with new babies need. That, and time to adjust. But the antidepressants could help shift the state she's now stuck in.

When Ester had the girls, she'd had no family or friends nearby. She remembers the relief of finding a student who came each day for a couple of hours. She'd booked herself into French conversation classes, and although her memory had been severely limited by tiredness, simply going out and talking to an adult had been such a respite. She'd also been glad of the Parisian disregard for small children. In Paris, she was encouraged to bottle feed, to leave the babies to cry, and to hand them over to someone else whenever she needed a break. In Australia, mothers were expected to put all their own needs last.

Still, she'd not been happy there. Neither of them had been. Lawrence had disliked his job, and she'd been bored and lonely. That was where the fighting had begun, the first sowing of a grit that became more and more abrasive.

'I've fallen in love,' she'd told April shortly after meeting Lawrence, barely able to do more than whisper the miraculous words, the sheer glow of them dancing lightly on her tongue.

'Who? Who? Who?' April had asked, pouring them each another drink, the burn of whiskey on ice crackling in the glass, the flare of a match as she'd lit up the joint she'd just rolled, taking a long drag before passing it to Ester, lipstick-stained and soggy to the touch.

As soon as Ester uttered his name, she wished she'd held it back.

'Lawrence!' April had thrown her head back and laughed, raucous, loud, slamming her glass on the table as she'd sat up. 'That sly old dog.' She'd reached across the table for the joint, taking it straight out of Ester's fingers, and shaken her head in disbelief.

He'd played in bands — one of which occasionally appeared on the same bill as April. On the night she'd met him, Ester had been standing at the back of the bar, her beer warm in her hands, wondering if she could leave. It was hot and still, the oppressive air in the room making her feel ill, and she'd edged closer to the door, looking out at the shine of the street, headlights, street lights, the silvery freshness of the evening so enticing.

She'd liked him straight away, the spark in his eyes, the warmth of his smile, as he'd looked at her and said he was sure he knew her. 'It's not a line,' he promised, stepping back slightly. And then his grin had widened. 'Pyschology. I was in your tute for a couple of weeks and then I had to shift. I was more of a stats man — different timetable.'

She didn't remember him. But she liked him even more when he said he was happy to give April's performance a miss, and go somewhere a bit cooler and quieter.

They'd ended up sitting on the beach, the sea a great black heaving beast, sighing and rolling under the white light of the moon. They'd sung all their favourite songs, replacing the word 'baby' with 'monster', and then when he'd suggested that she came back to his flat, he'd confessed. 'I've taken a trip. I might be up talking — for quite a long time.'

'He's a drug pig,' April had told her. 'So unlike you. But he is devastatingly handsome. Also charming when he puts his mind to it.'

And he had talked. For 24 hours. Kissing her in between each roll and lilt of thought. Slow kisses that were like breathing in air. When they both woke, a day and a half later, he'd looked straight at her in the soft light of the room. 'If you survived that, we could survive years together.'

'Everyone thinks they are in love with Lawrence,' April had said.

And Ester had just poured herself another drink, and said he was coming to pick her up soon. She had to get ready.

She had finished her undergraduate studies by then, and was hovering between either really trying to paint as a career, or accepting that she didn't have the fortitude, and continuing her studies to become a practising counsellor. She still had a studio space in Maurie's warehouse, and she would go there in the mornings, sleep-deprived and hungover but languorously happy, her whole body warm and still wrapped in the memory of Lawrence's skin.

Ester has a client who has recently fallen in love. She'd talked about it during her last session, the glow of it suffusing each word and gesture. It's rare that she hears about love in her consulting room. Most of her clients talk of anger, failure, boredom, depression, conflict: the flipside to love. That session had been like opening each of the windows to her room, heaving them up, sashes groaning, and letting in the freshness of an early spring day.

Lawrence, too, had been teetering between a career in music or a full-time job as a researcher. Music was what he wanted, but as April once pointed out, he had the looks but not the talent. He was a 'serviceable guitarist', she said, but he was never going to make a living from it.

And so they had met, both on the brink of letting go of youth. He became a pollster, and, despite the occasional sardonic joke he made about himself, she knew he liked having a media profile. As for her career, he went from quips about her 'Happiness Book' to downright dismissiveness. She pedalled false hopes to a spoilt middle class. She handed out security blankets to children who should just grow up.

And yet, when everything had blown apart, he had begged her to go to therapy with him, and she had refused.

Ester likes to keep half an hour between appointments. It gives her time to empty her head of one client before she begins work with the next. She sits in her room, reading through the previous week's notes for the Harcourts, while outside the rain stops and starts, the sky still resolutely grey. *It might rain forever*, she thinks, staring out at the bleakness of the day.

Across the road, she can see Jenny and Damon have pulled up, ten minutes early. They are sitting side by side in their car, neither of them talking.

She watches them for a moment and then looks down, aware that they can possibly see her. Closing their notes, she puts them back in the file, and then she checks her phone is on silent.

It is, the screen showing a message from Steven. He's booked a place to eat. Is 7.30 okay? Glancing up, she catches sight of her reflection in the window, her fear and excitement illuminated by the desk lamp.

It's been three years since she and Lawrence separated. After a year she had tried to date again, trawling through the various websites, and wishing she were one of those women who could approach the task with a business-like practicality (which is probably how she would advise her clients to tackle dating, she thinks, ashamed at the thought). *If you want to meet someone, you have to put your mind to it. It's much harder when you're older, when everyone has partners and when you don't go out and meet new people.*

Those were the words she'd once uttered to friends who'd found themselves alone, never realising how difficult it was to enter the world of online dating.

She'd gone through the men in her age group, alarmed at how old they all looked, because she still thought of herself as young. She dismissed all the ones who referred to wanting to find a 'lady', along with the many who nominated *The Shawshank Redemption* as their favourite film. It only left a few. There was one she liked, a man whose profile made her smile. He was looking for a woman who agreed that 'there was never any excuse for vertical blinds — ever'. He was probably gay, she thought, and she sent him a 'Kiss', deeply embarrassed by the whole terminology. He never responded.

A week later, she did go on a date. His name was Angus. She had contacted him, and he had emailed her back arranging to meet for a coffee. As soon as she arrived, she knew it was never going to work, dismissing him for surface reasons while battling with herself about how wrong it was to do this. He was seated near the door, legs stretched out in front of him, socks with sandals in full view. (Later, she would laugh about this, turn it into a story, but then it was only part of the sad loneliness of the experience.)

They talked for about half an hour, telling each other what they did. (He was a telecommunications salesperson who was writing a novel in his spare time. He liked going to the movies, eating out, bushwalking, swimming.) (She was a therapist who painted as a hobby, and also liked movies, eating out, bushwalking, and swimming — but she was different, she thought, clinging on to this. Yet surely if she was so much more than this summation, so might he be?)

At the end of the coffee, he asked her what they should do.

'What do you mean?'

'Shall we take this further?'

She looked down at table, breathing in before she met his eyes again. 'I'm sorry,' she told him. 'I just don't think it's going to work.'

'Why not?' he asked.

And she didn't know how to respond. 'I just don't feel a connection,' she eventually said, hating the banality of the words as she uttered them.

He nodded, standing up as he did so.

She stood also, only wanting to leave. 'Thank you for meeting me,' she offered, and as they said farewell at the door, he took her hand in his.

'Could we have a hug?' he asked.

She stood there, frozen, mute, as he hugged her for what seemed an interminably long time but was probably only seconds, before he broke away and said goodbye, leaving her alone on the footpath.

AFTER HE'S DROPPED Otto at home, Lawrence goes to his usual café. It's around the corner from the single-room office he rents at the back of a warehouse. The café owner is guitar obsessed, usually sitting at the table with Lawrence to show him his latest online find.

'Dave in America sent me this,' and he hands over his phone so that Lawrence can scroll through the pictures. 'He wants two grand, but I'm trying to talk him down a couple of hundred.'

Lawrence shakes his head, smiling as he does so. 'And this would be the sixth this year?'

'Seventh,' Joel admits. 'And each a thing of beauty.'

As far as he knows, Joel barely plays, his repertoire limited to average renditions of 'House of the Rising Sun' and the chorus of 'Stairway to Heaven'. Lawrence used to see him at the bars and pubs all those years ago, when they were both younger and leaner.

Lil, the waitress, brings his short black over, and sits with them as well, oblivious to Joel telling her that she's meant to be working, not chatting up the customers.

'Oh please,' she laughs. She takes the phone from Lawrence, and has a look. 'I don't know how you could buy a guitar without playing it first. You have no idea what the action is like.' She sips the coffee she's made for herself.

She's a singer — slow country and western that verges too close to the somnambulistic to ever really thrill him. Fortunately, she's never asked him what he thinks of her songs, and if she did, he'd lie.

'Got the girls this week?' Joel asks him.

Lawrence nods.

Outside, the trees bend and bow, shivering under the weight of another downpour. The sky is dark, the clouds thick and low. A woman comes in with two small kids, all three of them dripping wet, the children demanding a babycino and a biscuit, and Lil takes their order, smiling sweetly as she tells the kids she didn't quite hear that last word they said, 'was it a please?'

'I don't think it's your job to teach my children manners,' the woman tells her, and her eyes are hard, her tone cold.

'Nor do I,' Lil responds, the sweetness of her smile never diminishing.

Lawrence barely glances in Joel's direction, but he catches the shaking of his head and the muttering under his breath as he tamps the coffee, uncertain whether he should be making the order or not. Lil has a way with the rude customers, and they often leave before anything to eat or drink gets to the table.

'I'm paid to serve. Not to be treated like shit,' she mutters as she takes the flat white from him, fending off any possible disapproval he might dare to express.

Lawrence slept with Lil a couple of times in that terrible first year of separation. There was even a night when he convinced himself he was falling in love with her. He'd gone so wrong; marriage, serious jobs, children — none of it was what he'd wanted. Lil was almost twenty years younger than him, but they had a connection. He split the second ecstasy tablet between them, and told her he felt lighter and freer than he had in years.

'I've come back to myself,' he declared. 'This is who I am.' He'd been aware of how ridiculous he sounded as soon as he uttered the words, but he banished the thought, or tried to, until Lil looked at him and smiled, the ecstasy making her a little more tender than she would otherwise have been.

'This is who you'd like to be at the moment. But don't tell me that all the rest wasn't real.' She shook her head, and then pointed at her chest. 'Wisdom from the young,' she grinned. 'Frequently dismissed.' And then, still smiling broadly, she'd told him she didn't want to hurt him. 'Don't you go falling in love with me.'

Wasn't that what he was meant to say to her?

It had been a bad year. One in which he'd disappeared into the terrifying limitless expanse of freedom, a vast terrain that he'd been incapable of controlling, and so he'd roamed untethered, never still, never wanting to rest on the ramifications of what he'd done.

April had told him to pull himself together. 'It's bad,' she'd said. 'I know it. But there's no need to keep making it worse.'

She, too, had been kind to him, although he had been wary about taking her kindness, unsure of what to do each time she came round to see him when he'd had the girls, until Ester had put an end to it, telling him it was wrong. It was too confusing for Lara and Catherine — her not talking to April, him playing house with her.

'I'm not playing house with her.'

'Whatever it is you're doing, I don't want to know about it. I just want her out of our lives.'

And now, here he is, alone.

When there is a pause in the rain, he walks around the corner to his office, the tin door locked, the corrugations streaked iron-grey and rust-red. All the other studios are occupied by artists, most of them young and dreadlocked, who produce fairly average work from found objects and recycled rubbish. The whole building is run by Joachim, who sleeps in his studio and never washes, but he is always cheerful, and often leaves a loaf of bread, scavenged from the bakery around the corner, for Lawrence.

Lawrence took on the space in the terrible year — it was part of reclaiming his youth — and despite knowing it's not really a place to see clients, he's stayed.

The rain is thunderous on the tin walls and tin roof; from inside, it's like a stampede of wild animals overhead, yet when he looks out of the single window, rubbing a hole in the fogged-up glass, he sees that the downpour isn't as heavy as it seems.

He doesn't mind the noise. There's something elemental about its insistence, and he turns on the heater and switches on his computer, calling up a Bonnie Prince Billy playlist before he begins to read through the poll results. The gothic edge to the sweetness of these songs reminds him of April's music. She released her first album when she was only twenty-two. Sometimes he still listens to it, to the throaty crack in her voice, the soar that never quite touches the peak it yearns for, the delicate pick of her guitar, the brush of the snare drums, and the sadness of the piano; they all make him ache. She used to perform in pubs, always managing to still a crowded bar; she would sit out the front, long-limbed, bathed in gold, her gap-toothed smile giving her a cheeky likeability, and that voice, the crack in it always unsettling, the notes never quite where they should be, and yet there was something so relaxed about her performance that each song lifted you with it.

She'd asked him to go on tour with her shortly after he'd started seeing Ester. A guitarist had dropped out, and she'd needed a replacement quick.

'Why you?' Ester had asked. It was still early enough in their relationship that she wouldn't have been disparaging his lack of talent, but he'd wondered the same thing himself.

'I know you,' April had explained, 'it's just so much easier.'

She'd encouraged Ester to join them.

He had too, not wanting to be separated from her for a month.

But in the end she hadn't come — and it had been his last gig as a musician, one in which he'd known he wasn't up to scratch, frequently playing so poorly that he'd been tempted to just quit halfway through if it hadn't been for the fact that he'd left his day job and needed the pay cheque.

While the rain continues, loud and clattering, harsh and hard, Lawrence trawls through his emails, deleting as he goes; junk, an invitation to dinner, a suggestion of a drink from a woman he'd met a week ago, a client wanting a survey on chocolate-buying habits, another wanting one on leisure activities, and then, last, the email from Edmund with the latest poll results.

When he'd glanced at it in the park, he'd opened the attachment without reading the message at the beginning.

Now, as he scans it, he feels acid rise in his gut.

Edmund wants to talk to him. There seem to have been disparities between the data he has been sending through to Lawrence and the resulting reports in the media.

He hovers, wanting to ignore the request, but then he sees the end of the message. Edmund doesn't want to send through the latest report unless they speak.

Lawrence doesn't know Edmund well. He's only met him a few times, always finding him serious, dogged, dull in his laboured determination — all excellent qualities in someone who produces data. He is also a Christian. He has told Lawrence about the church he belongs to in the north-western suburbs — a new one started by a zealot with a passion for linking faith with material success. At twenty-nine, Edmund already owns three investment properties.

Foolishly, Lawrence had assumed the adjustments he had made to the data were so small, Edmund wouldn't notice. Perhaps if he'd only done it once, this would have been the case — a simple mistake he could explain away, perhaps even putting it on the shoulders of the client. The second time might also have slipped through the net. But the last time ... He'd been drunk. He'd gone too far.

He answers the email with bluster. They have a contract that specifies a delivery date and time. He has results to get through to the client, with a pressing deadline, and no time for talk. This is work that he has paid for, and Edmund's job is simply to deliver the information, and not to question how it's used. If he wants to continue to have Lawrence as a client, he needs to do just that.

He hovers the cursor over 'send', and then lets his hand fall back into his lap.

He knows that charm is his best offensive. It always has been. And so he leaves the email open on his screen and calls Edmund. It only takes two rings before he answers.

His voice smooth and calm, Lawrence quickly deals with the pleasantries — how is he? It's raining cats and dogs down here, he tells him, a deluge of biblical proportions, and he regrets the reference as soon as he utters it.

And then to business. He's just opened Edmund's email and he doesn't understand.

Edmund clears his throat. 'I do read the results,' he tells Lawrence.

There is a brief silence between them.

'The first time, I just looked at the media reports in passing, and it didn't seem quite right. The second time, I was sure a mistake had been made. The third time, I actually went back and checked.'

Edmund's voice is soft, sibilant. Lawrence has always disliked it, particularly now.

He hovers between loud denial and puny excuses, choosing neither. 'I need to deliver the latest numbers this morning,' he tells Edmund. 'We have a contract. And there is nothing in that agreement that gives you any right to question what I choose to do with those results.'

Edmund takes a moment. But this is what he always does. If Lawrence cracks a slightly distasteful joke, Edmund will even take a few seconds before he clears his throat in dismissal, the silence emphasising his disapproval. *He's a sanctimonious prig*, Lawrence thinks, and he feels ill as the full weight of Edmund's response to his actions sinks in a little deeper.

What he has been doing is tantamount to interfering with the political process, with democracy itself, Edmund tells him, the low hiss on each 's' scraping like nails on a blackboard. Edmund may have a contract with him, but as an independent, free human being who sets great store by choosing the moral path, he no longer wants to work with Lawrence.

The rain beats down.

Lawrence looks out the window. 'What we *do* is an interference with the political process,' he eventually says. 'The questions we ask, when we ask them, how we interpret them — they all shape the debate. You know that. I know that.'

Edmund interrupts him. 'This is different.'

But is it any worse? Lawrence wants to ask him if in all honesty he really thinks it is, but he's already said too much. He can hear another call on his mobile, the beep of the phone harsh in his ear. He is happy to terminate the contract, he tells Edmund, but he does need those last results.

'Which will be published without alteration?'

'Of course,' Lawrence promises.

'And I will receive full payout for the year's work?'

Lawrence has no choice.

Edmund is silent again. 'I will need to think.'

It isn't over. Of course it isn't over.

Lawrence leans back in his chair and puts his hands over his eyes. What was he thinking? He breathes in deeply, and stares up at the ceiling.

As a child, April had hated the bath. She couldn't stay in one place, and she would slip and slide and squirm, splashing great waves of soapy water over the edge before leaping out, running through the house naked and dripping half the bathwater along the way, Maurie and Hilary oblivious to the fact that she was still filthy and that the entire exercise had been a waste of time.

But at the river shack it was different. Maurie would run it hot, the steam rising into the open air, disappearing well before it reached the tracings of branches overhead — fine ghostly gums that cut white-limbed across the sky. She and Ester would take an end each, stretching out luxuriously beneath the trees, the smell of eucalypt sharp as leaves and twigs dropped down into the water, and they would make boats, sailing them forth from April-land to Ester-land and back again.

More beautiful still were the night-time baths, the black-velvet, star-glittered sky, frosty in the winter, warm and soft in the summer evenings, the mournful cry of a bird, or the crackle of dried twigs as a wallaby ventured shyly forth, slipping back into the bush at the sight of two naked sisters lying in a canopy of white steam.

April still isn't fond of baths at home, but this morning, in Hilary's house, she runs one, emptying a bottle of expensive salts into the water, and pinning her hair up on her head before stepping in carefully, the heat gripping her with a pain so tight she has to step straight out again.

She runs the cold, trying to course it through the water with her hand, imagining it as a stream of silver twisting and turning through the fire of molten lava, waiting until she can step in again, one foot at a time, careful now.

She'd lied last night when she'd told Hilary she'd just been having a drink around the corner. She'd been drinking in her apartment alone, the windows wide open to the rain, the great shaking deluge of it shimmering across the distant harbour, sparkling on the streets below, and then, as the wind had shifted and the rain had slanted into her lounge, she'd realised that Sam had no intention of showing up, and the faint chill of having possibly made a fool of herself burnt into her skin, slapped by the brisk breeze.

He was too young for her.

She'd known that.

And so she'd sent him a text. *Can't remember if I asked you over tonight?? Sorry if yes — had to go out.*

She'd caught a taxi to Hilary's so that she wouldn't be waiting any longer.

As she lowers herself into the bath, she feels the disarray of her life in every limb, a jangling switchboard, all wires knotted and unplugged. She does not want to cry. She is thirty-six now, alone, unable to write in the way she used to, and she has fucked up. Badly.

She glances across at herself in the mirror, face pink from the heat, and then she rests her head against the cool of the enamel and closes her eyes.

April has never really known loneliness until now; she has had small tastes of its dregs, like cold milky coffee curdled at the bottom of the cup, but she has always had faith in the fact that it would pass. Now, she is not so sure. And this loneliness is entangled with her failure as a musician, another certainty in her life that seems to have gone.

Most days, she tries to write.

She sits by the window with her guitar and picks idly at notes, strumming chords underneath, humming to herself as she does so. But nothing ever sticks, and she feels as if she is just pretending, playing alone outside a room she can no longer enter.

When she wrote her first album, she didn't even see herself as making a record. She just trimmed and cut and shaped the material she had been working with for years, the songs she had played in pubs and clubs, selected and honed with the help of the producer, until she had it: complete and whole. She had neither chased success nor expected it. To have recorded an album was enough.

But success came. Her songs were played around the world. They are still played. The mark of that first album remains — in fact it has recently restamped itself, with a couple of the songs being covered by younger independent artists, their new versions faint replicas of the original. That collection of songs is who she is. The second album has been forgotten; the third has never eventuated.

April lifts one leg out of the bath. The colour of the bruise is spectacular — mauve, crimson, yellow, and grey. She had been dancing at a party above Bondi three nights ago, the salt of the sea breeze stiff and sharp, everyone young and rich, with careers in film or television. She used to come to the same place in her early twenties when the building had been a run-down boarding house. A friend of hers called Dave had got permission from the owners to build a lean-to on the roof, not dissimilar to the kinds of structures Maurie used to build. Now it was a block of apartments, with a penthouse owned by someone who had only recently turned thirty.

April danced and danced under the polar-white moon, occasionally aware of others around her, often not. When she noticed Lawrence drinking by the railing, she stopped. It had been months since he had told her Ester didn't want her visiting when he had the kids, and she hadn't seen him since.

Handsome Lawrence, she used to call him.

He still was handsome, with his short dark hair, olive skin, prominent cheekbones, and those dazzling white teeth. 'Do you put those strips on them,' she used to tease him, 'or paint them each night before you go to bed?'

'And each morning,' he would reply. 'Lunch time too, if I have time.'

But that was so long ago.

They were shy with each other now, careful, and she came up to him, smiling hesitantly. He introduced her to Sam as his sister-in-law, correcting himself immediately to 'ex-sister-in-law, actually.'

'So I'm an ex, too,' she said, and he ignored her.

Sam was a television-ad director with a short film that had gone to Cannes. 'Are you a dancer?' he asked her, and April laughed.

'I don't know what I am,' she told him, shaking her head.

'You're a singer,' Lawrence said. In the white spill of the moon, she could see the kindness in his eyes, and it had surprised and touched her.

April just shrugged, and then, reaching into her bag, she offered them both a joint. 'I'm also very old-fashioned,' she smiled. 'I still like to get out of it.' She lit the match, shielding its flame against the breeze, and then offered it to Lawrence, who shook his head.

'I've gone modern on you,' he told her.

'No drugs?'

He nodded. 'Well, most of the time.'

She smiled sadly. 'Exercise, too? Organic food? AFDs?'

'That's me, I'm afraid.'

She snorted in disbelief.

Sam took the joint, telling her he was happy to go old-fashioned for the night. He wanted to know about her singing, but she didn't want to talk about it. 'Let's dance,' she suggested, and she turned back to the music, Sam leading the way, Lawrence staying where he was.

'I'll just be a moment.' She had stopped, thinking she would tell Lawrence how lovely it was to see him, perhaps kiss him lightly on the cheek because there was no gesture, really, that could express the layers of loss and sorrow, all attempts frail and sad, but she wanted to at least have tried.

He had walked away.

And Sam had reached back for her hand, pulling her into the throng, apologising as he misdirected her into a table edge.

April dries herself slowly, rubbing Hilary's moisturiser into her legs and arms, and then searches through the bathroom cupboards for some make-up. There is a tan-coloured powder, and a lipstick that is too orange. She rubs a little of each on the back of her hand, and then leaves them next to the sink.

She tries on Hilary's pendant, a great round dish of mother of pearl on a heavy chain, and admires it before wrapping herself once more in Maurie's old dressing gown.

She had planned on heading home. Outside, the rain continues, pouring down the rusted gutters in a great rush, and she watches for a moment before checking her phone messages. There are several from the friends she was meant to meet for drinks with Sam, none from him, of course, and then she checks her email — one from her publisher to let her know that there's interest in one of her songs from a film producer.

This is how she survives: small drips of income from sales of that first album, and regular APRA royalties. She used to get asked if she were interested in writing, but after failing to deliver one time too many, those requests have stopped.

She looks out to the studio. She can just see Hilary through the glass doors, her glasses down on the end of her nose; she is running her fingers through her white-grey hair as she talks to someone on the phone. The conversation finishes and she hangs up, staring out at the rain, oblivious to April watching her from the house.

When April goes in to say goodbye, Hilary is still looking out at the rain.

'You're off then?' Hilary wheels her chair out from her desk and over to the saggy corduroy sofa she'd brought back from the river shack. 'Have a seat for a moment,' she tells April.

Sensing a talk, April begins to fidget. 'There's a bus in ten minutes,' she says.

Hilary laughs. 'You've never checked a bus timetable in your life.'

It's true, and she sits reluctantly, tapping her fingers on her knees as she waits for her mother to speak.

'I don't want to talk about Ester,' Hilary says, and she reaches to still April's hand. 'I've told you I can't say anymore about that. I can only hope time will bring some kind of healing, but I don't know.'

April looks down at the ground.

'I want to talk about you.'

Outside, there is a strange silence, a tentative shift in the day; it's too soon, though, to tell whether the change will last for more than a few moments or whether it will be smothered by a new roll of dark clouds, unable to gather any real force just yet.

'I know you are struggling.'

April bites her lip.

'Creativity is unpredictable. Some people have to make sure

they don't waste a drop, while others have it in great armfuls, so many riches that a lifetime isn't enough. Maurie was like that. Most of the time. But he could struggle, too. There were periods when he couldn't paint, and then he would have to turn to other outlets,' and she waves her arm around the studio. 'That was when he built. You know I also painted before you girls were born?'

April can feel Hilary looking at her, and then her mother cups her chin in her hands and lifts her face so that she is forced to look into her eyes. 'I need you to listen to me,' she says.

'I am,' April replies.

'I gave up. I had years and years before I found filmmaking. And they were hard years. I doubted myself so much. When I made my first film, I was like you — I not only managed to create something special, I was lucky. It was the right work in the right place at the right time, and it had so many blessings showered on it.

'And in some ways, I was even more fortunate than you are. I didn't have to deal with fame. Not in the way you did. And I'm a little tougher. A little more bloody-minded. Perhaps through having kids, perhaps not.' Hilary shrugs.

She looks at April, her grey-green eyes deep and kind, focused and sure. 'I don't know if you'll write another album. You may not. You may start again next week, or in fifty years' time. But you have to let all that go. You have to return to a place where you don't even think about that, you just reconnect with the joy you had in music. You have to forget all this current mess, you have to search for other things that feed you. Get out, read, garden, work, help others, be part of the world.'

And she kisses April, who is crying now, not in the way she usually cries, with none of the drama that April usually gives to tears, but with a sadness and shame that makes her wipe her eyes as soon as she feels the sting.

'I have to go,' she tells her mother.

Hilary tucks a strand of hair behind her ear. 'I love you,' she says. 'I don't want you to ever forget that.' Then she smiles, standing close to April, and holds her palm out. 'Pendant,' she tells her.

April touches the silver around her neck. 'Could I borrow it?' she asks.

Hilary looks at her, the look of someone who wants to soak in the other, drink them up and hold them, precious and close.

'Of course,' she tells her, with a tenderness April had never expected.

ESTER HAS LEFT her desk lamp on, as well as the overhead light, but still the room feels dark and gloomy. She sits with her back to the window, Jenny and Damon opposite her on the couch. She can smell the dampness of wet wool, a soupy smell she has always hated. It is resignation and despair, old men in boarding houses, school jumpers, slippers and dressing gowns.

Jenny is agitated, but this isn't unusual. They have had three sessions so far, and each time she sits on the edge of the sofa, her slender legs crossed, neat dark hair short and boyish, dressed for work, ready to race straight into an appointment with a client. Today, she looks particularly tense, pale and drawn, her eyes darting from Damon to Ester and back again.

She is a solicitor, a partner in a large law firm. 'It was never what I wanted to do,' she'd told Ester. 'It just became too hard to leave.' She'd picked at a small sore on the back of her hand. 'I don't have time to think about an alternative. I thought having children might give me that time. I kept having them, but no solution came.' She'd shrugged. 'I seriously considered having a fourth the other day. But I wouldn't, of course, not with the way things are with Marlo.'

And Marlo is why they are here.

'He has school refusal disorder,' Jenny explained at the first session, doing most of the talking, her sentences clipped, always to the point.

She'd found the term on Google. 'I google everything. I hope that one day I'll phrase my question in just the right way to bring up the answer to every worry I have.' She shifted in her seat. 'Computer gaming addiction, disassociation, lack of empathy, hatred — I've googled it all.'

Ester had turned to Damon, asking him to tell her a little about himself.

He brushed his hair out of his eyes. 'I'm a mathematician.' He smiled shyly. 'And I'm a father and a husband, and a person who loves his work and his students. I'm not sure how to contain myself in a simple description, or what you need to know.'

Ester had smiled back at him. 'And your relationship with each other?'

It was like a funnel. This arms-wide gathering of information, the slow sifting through to the grains and grit that remained stuck.

It was Damon who answered, glancing across at Jenny and then back to Ester: 'We love each other.' He squeezed Jenny's hand. 'I'm the luckiest man alive.'

There was something of the child in him, Ester had thought at the time, and it was an impression that had remained. There was an innocence, a wonder at the world, a dust that faintly glittered.

'I don't understand,' he'd said about Marlo, and he genuinely didn't. 'All that time shut up in his room, playing those games in the darkness by himself — I can't fathom it.'

They had taken Marlo to a specialist, Jenny had explained. 'Greg Mahony.'

Ester had heard of him. His work with addiction and adolescents was world-renowned.

'I pulled favours to get that appointment,' she'd said. 'I didn't think he'd come. I was immensely relieved when we got him in the car without protest.' She'd rubbed at a tic in her eye, all the sharp brightness in her face collapsing into pain as she recalled the moment when Greg Mahony had told them there was no point in seeing Marlo unless he actually wanted to be there. And so he'd asked Marlo directly, and Marlo had looked delighted.

'The smile on his face,' Jenny said, 'when he realised it was up to him. He just got up and walked out.'

Sitting now on the couch, Jenny tells Ester that she and Damon are at odds.

'I don't see the point in us being here,' Jenny says. She has a single gold ring, with a pearl setting, on her middle finger. It is curiously old-fashioned for someone who wears, as Jenny does, well-cut suits and little make-up apart from mascara and a deep-red lipstick. She twists the ring, looking directly at Ester as she speaks. 'Everything we try makes no difference. Last week started well. He was helpful, he even talked with us. He went to school on Monday, and then Tuesday came. I discovered he'd run up a $600 bill on my credit card buying new games. I accused him. He locked himself in his room and didn't come out until the weekend.'

She tries to still her hands, one clasping the other in her lap. 'I'm tired of talking about him. I'm tired of thinking about him, and it never improves. I can come here and tell you how terrible he is, how worried I am, but what will it achieve?' She glances at Damon.

His fringe is in his eyes again, and he brushes it back. 'I'm not so sure that you're expecting the right things from this. I don't want to speak out of turn, or for you, but it feels as though we need to find a different way of living with this situation because we are not doing that well.'

Damon has a hole in the elbow of his jumper, and one in the sole of his shoe. He's taken them off to dry his socks, explaining when he arrived that buying clothes isn't something he's very good at. He sits now, resting an ankle on his knee, only to discover that there's also a rip in his sock. 'That's embarrassing,' he says. 'Two poor items of clothing was more than enough.' He puts his foot down, his smile apologetic.

Ester waits for a moment, unsure whether he has finished speaking.

He hasn't: 'We're not here to find out how to change Marlo, or fix him, but just to try and ...'

She looks at him, expecting him to continue. Jenny, too, is waiting. But when he opens his mouth, there is no sound.

'Not ...' The word he utters breaks down into a sound that is animal, guttural. It is a sob of elemental pain and fear, and in the darkness of the room, it is chilling.

Ester opens her mouth to speak, but Jenny holds up her hand. She leans into her husband, all of her focused on comforting him, Ester a silent witness as the rain falls and Damon cries. He cries as Jenny rubs his back, and Ester hands them her box of tissues.

'I'm sorry,' he says when he finally looks up, his cheeks damp with tears, his Adam's apple working nervously in his throat.

Ester tells him that this is one of the reasons why he is here: to let it out.

'What if ...'

Jenny's eyes are wide, her nostrils flared as she looks across at him.

'I'm so scared he'll ...'

Outside, a black cat slinks quickly across the fence, its fur jewelled with raindrops, its dash to shelter so fast and smooth that it's gone almost as soon as it appears.

Damon watches it, breathing slowly, trying to regain his composure before he turns back to Jenny.

Ester leans forward. 'The situation you're in is very difficult. Unfortunately, it's up to Marlo to change his behaviour; I can't, you can't — no one can but him. Which is why Greg didn't want to see him unless he wanted to be there. And he doesn't at the moment. But I can offer you both coping strategies. And information,' she adds, 'about what you're dealing with.' She has already sent them links to various articles about school refusal and different approaches being trialled by different therapists, as well as a useful article for parents of addicts.

'It's up to you as to whether you want to continue — either together or just one of you by yourself, although I think that dealing with this as a couple would be better. But you need to make that decision.'

Jenny nods. She is picking at a fingernail, and then she takes it up to her mouth and snaps at it, small white teeth cutting through it.

'You've never met Marlo,' she eventually says.

Ester shakes her head.

'He's over six foot. And he's big — broad-shouldered, heavy-set. If he wants to play a computer game, I can't stop him. If he doesn't want to go to school, I can't get him out of bed and into the car. If he won't help with clearing the table, I can't make him. I know I can't force change. I know.' Damon has taken her hand, her pale fingers curled up inside his hold. He strokes her arm gently, and she seems to ease a little, uncrossing her legs, her shoulders slumping slightly as she continues to speak: 'Last week, I took all the keyboards and locked them in the car. He smashed the car window to get in.'

She glances across at Damon. 'Sometimes I hate him.'

Damon pulls her close, his arm around her, rocking her. Even as the cracks in the world around him widen, he has love to give. It is wide and deep, sure flowing and constant, there to carry her moments after he himself has plummeted. Ester sees it; the warmth of its certainty fills the room each time they sit together on the couch opposite her, and it is there now as the rain beats steadily on the cold glass of the windows, running down the panes like sheets of silk.

The clock on the desk shows their time is almost up. She looks at them both.

'You're right,' she says. 'You can't force change for him, but you can change your responses. And you have such a good basis from which to work together. I'd like to talk more about this — boundaries that are possible to draw and ways in which you can enforce them without escalating conflict further. We began to touch on this at the end of our last session, and that's the place I'd like to return to. Sometimes when we are in very difficult situations, it's tempting to keep going over our helplessness rather than focusing our attention on areas in which we do have some power.'

Damon nods earnestly. 'That sounds good,' he says with the enthusiasm of a young child for a project. 'I want to do that, we can do that.' His watch is loose on his wrist, and he pushes it back up again as he reaches for his boots.

Jenny is staring at the floor.

Ester turns to face her.

'Why don't you both talk about this at home?'

Jenny nods.

'I'd like to continue working with you together, but obviously that's up to you.'

When she stands, Jenny only just reaches Ester's shoulders. Her cheeks are flushed as she puts her bag on her shoulder and takes out her phone. 'I've got a meeting,' she says. 'A merger that's gone ugly.' She looks out the window, not really talking to either of them as she composes herself, and then turns back to face Ester, all vulnerability masked. 'We'll be in touch.'

This is what her clients do. They breathe in, leave her house, and re-enter the world, heading back to home or to an office where everyone is answering emails, talking on the phone, seeing clients, making tea. All of them with their own pain — divorce, parents dying, illness, trying to have children and not being able to, daily tragedies like shadows, growing, shrinking, growing again.

A world of ghosts, Ester thinks.

She shakes her head. This is the world she lives in. Here, in this room, it is the shadows that talk. *I am the third miscarriage; the fear each time my ex-husband contacts me; my regret at putting my mother in a nursing home — and my unbelievable sorrow about my son.*

She talks to their shadows, but they never talk to hers.

LAWRENCE SITS ALONE in his room, staring at the computer screen.

Normally, he would have delivered the results by now: summarised data, accompanied by a media release that will form the basis of the next day's front page and a double inside spread. He would be on the phone to Paul, the editor, talking through any queries, trying to nudge the story in a particular direction, usually with little success. He also has interviews tentatively booked in with three radio stations, the evening television news, and a couple of blogs. It is likely that there will be more requests coming through today.

Edmund will be enjoying taking his time deliberating. This is what a man of conscience does. Will he let Lawrence off the hook with a sanctimonious lecture and an end to their relationship, or will he go straight to the paper to inform them that Lawrence has been 'adjusting' the data?

Lawrence contemplates the possibility, a cold stone in his stomach as his mind slips into a habitual weighing of outcomes. On a scale from one to ten, how serious would the impact be on his life, with ten being the most serious?

The answer is as it always is: It depends.

Is he talking about the impact on him as a person, on his identity and sense of self, on his reputation? And if so, would the paper keep quiet, wanting to protect its own reputation? Or would others find out? Is he talking about the financial impact? Again, this would depend on whether his other clients got wind of the scandal. He uses Edmund for other jobs. How far would he go?

One question is inevitably capable of opening so many more. Lawrence shakes his head, and checks his email once again. Still nothing.

And so he stands and stretches, the panic in his gut becoming colder.

His office is sparsely furnished. There is a desk under the small window that looks out over the street, and, next to it, a filing cabinet. A large rug, deep-orange wool, covers the floor, and on the other side of the room is a long, low mid-century couch that he bought for an exorbitant sum when he first separated from Ester. He had thought it was stylish, and it is, but it is uncomfortable as well. There is a coffee table next to it, also far more expensive than he had been able to afford, and, around the walls, speakers, one expense that he does not regret.

He turns the music up a little, but it is hopeless with the drumming of the rain. He cannot hear the slow lilt of Bill Callahan, the tired, sardonic drawl drowned out by the steady rhythm on the tin walls and roof.

He needs to think.

No, more importantly, he needs to buy some time. He should call the newspaper and let them know there has been a problem with the data, that there might be a delay. And then he should alert each of the other interviewers.

He looks at his computer screen.

If he doesn't call them, they will call him.

There is one message on his phone — the number unknown, the time earlier in the day. He remembers now. It was when he was talking to Edmund. It's likely to be another request for an interview, although it's unusual for him not to have the number in his phone. He'll check it in a minute. First, the paper.

Paul answers on the second ring. They are friends of sorts. He and Ester went over for dinner a couple of times, and then, after the divorce, Paul took him out for a drunken night, detailing his own misery at home for most of the evening. Sarah was either haranguing him or cold and dismissive. *I don't love her anymore*, and he'd leant across the table as he'd made this admission, his face flushed and ugly from too much red, his breath stale. Lawrence had recoiled, wondering at how repulsive so many men could be, and then when Paul had asked him what had led to Ester booting him out, he'd shaken his head and lied. *We grew apart*, he said, which, while not untrue, wasn't the whole story.

Paul answers now with his usual clipped work response, a 'gidday' that launches straight into the matter at hand. He hasn't had a minute to look through his emails, he's assuming no major surprises in the poll. And then, before Lawrence has a chance to answer, Paul says he's been wanting to chat to him, to talk about the future. The cost cuts are going to mean big changes, and it's going to affect them.

'But I've got an editorial meeting happening five minutes ago, I'll have to call you back —'

He is about to hang up, and so Lawrence speaks over him. 'No results as yet,' he tells him. 'Which is why I'm calling. There's been a hitch with the data.'

'How serious?'

'Not sure yet,' Lawrence says. 'I'm on the case.' He can hear someone laughing loudly in the background, and that, coupled with the incessant drumming of the rain, means it's difficult to catch Paul's response. Something along the lines of 'get it sorted' and 'talk soon'.

At least he knows Edmund hasn't spoken to them yet.

Jesus Christ, he hates Edmund. Always has, he realises.

Although the intensity of his dislike had crystallised when he had told Edmund that he and Ester had divorced. He doesn't know why he told him — it wasn't like they ever talked about anything personal — but he'd been such a mess at the time he'd frequently found himself blabbing without thinking. Edmund had told him that he didn't believe in divorce. *You make a vow and you keep it.*

Perhaps this is a good thing after all. He'll find someone new. And then he shakes his head again. Who's he kidding? This isn't a good thing. It's a mess, and he doesn't know why he did it. He'd begun when the previous government had hit rock bottom in popularity. He supposes he'd just wanted to make some feeble attempt to counter the relentless flow against them, a flow that his work had helped to create.

But was that all it was?

Ester had once accused him of being in love with the power of lying and cheating. There had been previous girlfriends who'd voiced similar sentiments.

He sits down on his over-priced lounge and looks out at the gloom of the day, his phone still in his hand. The sweat on his palms makes his grip slippery, and he drops it between the cushions, only remembering the missed call as he searches for it by feel, the darkness of the room making it impossible for him to see.

When he finds it, he dials his voicemail, but is unable to hear a word.

He needs somewhere quieter.

He lies down on the couch, pressing his ear on the phone and the phone against the cushion in an attempt to muffle the sound of the rain.

It's Hilary. She needs him to call urgently.

And she leaves her number in case he no longer has it.

AFTER APRIL LEAVES, Hilary goes back to the house. Her daughter's coffee cup is still on the table, the imprint of her lipstick like a fossil on the rim. Her plate is next to it, a half-eaten piece of toast sitting in the centre, now cold.

She leaves them where they are, holding onto the traces of April's presence for just a little longer.

In the hall, Maurie's dressing gown is draped over the bannister, and Hilary leaves that too, breathing it in as she walks past, the faint turpentine from Maurie mingled with April's talcum sweetness. It is almost too much, this increasing bombardment of the senses, each instant passing with a slowness that is pure and painful. It is as though her life has been in fast motion until now, racing forward, a great crush of people, places, moments, anger, joy, love, despair all coming to a sudden stop, colliding into each other at the gate, while she slips through, walking onwards, alone in a quiet land.

Upstairs, she takes two painkillers. The headache is there again, at the edge of her temples, like a dense cloud clotting. She can see it in her eyes and in the tightness with which she holds herself, shoulders and back straight, face staring directly ahead. The doctors have told her that initially the pills should help in dealing with the pain, however they will soon not be strong enough. She hopes that moment hasn't yet come.

The first headache struck on the evening she completed the

rough picture cut. She thought she'd been working too hard, that she might have strained her eyes, although the intensity of the pain had alarmed her.

Something wasn't right.

And then a fortnight later, the world collapsed into a throbbing centre, her entire being at the mercy of its force. Lying in her darkened room, she could do nothing but ride it out, let it wash over and through her, until a day later she emerged, shaken and weak, and booked an appointment with her GP.

There are two tasks to complete before she sees Ester this evening. The first is simple. She has to go to Henry and pick up the drugs. The second is meeting Lawrence. Hilary splashes her face with lukewarm water and then puts on the red enamel ring that Maurie gave her when she turned twenty-seven. She wears it when she particularly needs his presence, the warmth of the copper base against her skin and the weight of the round red disc solid enough to ground her.

She remembers that birthday. They had been living in a studio in Paddington, not far from this house now. It was tiny, surrounded by monstera, the green glossy leaves pressing against each window. She used to call it the 'Triffid room', and although she hated the determined growth of that plant, its thick fleshy stems and pods too alien and alive, she did love the softness of the light filtering through, the coolness of that chlorophyll veil.

They had invited everyone they knew, too many for the flat and the slender concrete balcony that ran along the front, too many for the hall and the driveway, and for the small garden off the street. There had been a moment when she had thought they were going to bring down the long outside landing, everyone tumbling into the monstera, caught in the great spread of its leaves, giant green hands waiting to catch them all.

The record player gave up by midnight, the needle so blunt it couldn't follow a single groove. The alcohol also came to an end early, but no one minded — they rolled fat joints and passed them around, damp Tally-Ho paper pink with lipstick, the sweet smell of grass.

Later, when the crowd had thinned, she found Maurie sitting on the low-lying wall that ran along the footpath. He was staring up at the stars, pinpricks of light in the midnight sky, humming softly to himself. It was unlike him to be alone, and she came up behind him, wrapping her arms around the warmth of his body, burying her face in the softness of his hair.

'We should get married,' he said when he turned around, his voice so hushed she wondered whether she had heard him.

He waited for her to speak.

'Not us,' she eventually told him. 'It's a beautiful night. I love you. But I don't want to marry anyone. Ever.'

He had looked at her and smiled, taking her face in his hands, her cheeks cool beneath his skin, and he had kissed her, once on the mouth, and then the forehead. 'I knew you'd say that,' he whispered. He kissed her again. 'Which is why I asked you.'

Across the road, a drunken couple laughed loudly, and somewhere back in the flats a glass shattered, a sharp, staccato bell as it hit the concrete. Next to her, Maurie had continued staring up at the sky, the warmth of his body close, the smell of alcohol and smoke and paint, and, beneath that, a deep richness that she knew so well.

'We're going to have a good life, you and I,' he told her. 'Years and years and years in front of us, and so much love.'

The roughness of his cheek was fresh against the smoothness of her own skin, the coldness of the night air swallowing her in great gulping gasps as she moved closer to him under the darkness of the sky.

'You're my home,' he had told her.

'And you're mine,' she had replied.

She had been so fortunate, carrying the gift of that love within her, along with an awareness of the keenness to its edge: the possibility of loss glinting just in sight. Perhaps this was why she had always held a certain part of herself in reserve. Or perhaps this was simply who she was. But not Maurie. He saw nothing but the joy, and he wanted to scoop it all up, roll around in it, throw it in the air; a fabulous toy that never ceased to surprise and delight.

'Let's have children,' he'd said on the third night she'd slept with him. 'Hundreds of them.'

Hilary had laughed. 'And will they look after themselves?'

'Absolutely,' he'd insisted. 'They'll grow and flourish and burn bright without us ever having to do a thing.'

He hadn't wanted to stop at Ester. He would have kept going, child after child after child, their entire life reduced to milk and nappies and prams and blankets, heaters drying clothes, the cry of babies like kittens mewling.

'That's it,' she'd insisted, refusing to sleep with him until he had a vasectomy.

And there had been war in their house, silent, pacing war — who could hold out the longest? — a war he never had a chance of winning. It was what she had to do, temper his enthusiasm with a strain of harsh reality, a role she'd sometimes hated him for.

But now, here alone on the other side of their life together, she looks back on those flashes of anger as simply that: no more than jagged cuts of lightning in the sky, so brief against all that stretched before and after.

Out on the street, Hilary drives slowly to Henry's house, the wipers clearing a small arc of vision. She can feel the rain on her skin, sweet and cold, slanting through the window, which is open to clear the fog that persists despite the loud drone of the demister.

It is only a couple of kilometres, a walk if the day had been fine, down the twist of streets to the gully, Henry's home a small flat that looks out on a sandstone cliff, where morning glory tumbles through the cracks, its drooping purple flowers and tissue-thin leaves tangled in the rock.

Once, when Maurie was very drunk, he told a reporter at an opening that Henry was the artist he admired most.

'Henry who?' the reporter had asked.

'Henry Goldstein.'

'Do I know his work?'

Maurie had laughed, his great deep belly laugh rolling through the gathering, making heads turn. 'He's probably produced two finished works. And both have disappeared. So I doubt you've even met his work, let alone know it.'

They had gone to art school together, the three of them; Maurie the loud, confident one, she quieter and more serious, a beauty then, with a tumble of blonde hair and long, slender legs, and Henry, tall, thin, dark-eyed beneath a fall of fringe, softly spoken and alive with ideas.

Henry was in the sculpture department, his work a search for purity, minimalist and austere. He once told her that the only logical conclusion to this desire was to create nothing, which was one of the reasons that he never finished his degree. But then, when she first met him, he was working in marble, making perfect eggs that slid apart, another one inside. Smooth Russian dolls. She had noticed his elegant hands first, and had asked him if she could sketch them.

He had smiled shyly (but with a certain amount of pride) as he held them out towards her. 'How would you like me to pose?'

She thought about it for a moment, the palm of his hand in her own, his beautiful flat almond-shaped nails, smooth olive skin, and the delicate shape of his fingers creating lines and planes of perfection.

'In prayer position,' she told him. 'Here.' And she adjusted the direction just slightly so that the light fell right along the arc of his thumb.

She still has the sketch she did. It is pinned on the wall in her studio, a square of thick creamy art paper with the beauty of Henry's hands almost captured, there in the centre.

(She slept with Henry once — long before Maurie claimed her as his own — and she has never told anyone. She remembers it now as soporific, a blur of limbs, soft and undefined, but they had both taken smack, and the haze of the whole day had wrapped everything, including the sex, into the slow passing of time. In truth, Henry was always asexual, surrounded by friends but never in a physical relationship, nor seemingly interested in one, and her memory of their intimacy is without any sense of his corporeality.)

Over the years, she was the one who stayed in touch with him, not Maurie. Sometimes she would spend the afternoon in his apartment, sipping tea and talking about a film she was making, always grateful for his quiet insights and suggestions. His calm was an antidote to Maurie's ebullience. She knew he had other friends, but he kept people separate, giving her the strange sense that he belonged to her alone.

Outside his block of flats, she stays in the car, watching the rain. There is a sad, seeping slowness to the drizzle now, a blank grey sky and a steady dampness. She can see it rising up the sandstone wall, the gold and pink darker where the rain has soaked into the porous stone. The potholes and cracks in the road form tiny ponds, offering blank reflections to the stillness of the sky above. It is only plants that gain any true beauty in this weather, she thinks. A grevillea is jewelled with rain drops, silver pearls clinging to the trembling tips of the flowers and the fine ends of the spiky fronds; a passionfruit vine gathers clusters of rainwater in the open hold of its leaves, shaking them out in a shower with each whisper of breeze.

The world is a place of wonder.

The gallery opposite Henry's is opening up for the day. Hilary watches as the young woman unbolts the heavy glass doors and steps out under the awning for a moment. She is dressed in red: a crimson wool dress, vermillion fishnet stockings, and rose suede boots, her long black hair styled like a seventies rock star. If it weren't so wet, Hilary would cross the street and tell her that she is her own work of art, no doubt more spectacular than the ordinary paintings lining the high white walls of the front and back rooms.

Next door to the gallery is a small travel agent's. A man hovers in the doorway, smoking a cigarette, cup of coffee clutched in his hand. He glances across to the woman in the gallery, and they nod and smile at each other. He is dressed in grey, a dull foil to her brilliance — charcoal sweater, and jeans that sag at the crotch and run tight along his calves down to his black boots. He blows out smoke, a faint wisp that disappears into the milky sky almost as soon as it appears, and then he drops the last of his cigarette onto the pavement, leaving it to smoulder and sizzle in the damp.

The rest of the street is quiet. This is not a day when people go out unless they have to. It is a day for staying inside.

Hilary told Henry she would get to him by eleven. It is half past. Not that it matters. He isn't concerned by time. She has never noticed a clock in his studio, nor does he have a mobile or a computer.

When she buzzes on his doorbell, he lets her in without a word. The hallway is damp, hard lino floors smeared with crushed leaves, mud, and rain, a row of locked letterboxes along the wall, and a pile of suburban newspapers covering the bottom step, never picked up, just replaced by the new issue each week.

Henry's flat is at the back of the block, his door slightly ajar. He stands awkwardly next to the fold-out couch, thinner than ever, his body like a stretched elastic band, hair still falling over his eyes, silver now, dark pupils an ember of intensity cloaked by a shy hesitancy as he looks at her, uncertain whether to step forward and embrace her in greeting or stay where he is.

Looking across at him, she is overwhelmed, the tightness with which she has bound herself momentarily loosened at being in the proximity of the only person who knows of her decision.

He takes her hand, his skin like cool, crisp paper, the shape of his fingers still beautiful, and he kisses her on the cheek. He hasn't asked her if she is sure, if she knows what she is doing, but she nods all the same.

'I don't quite know how to behave in this situation,' he eventually says.

She smiles slightly.

'Do we have a cup of chai, and just talk as we would always talk?'

She nods again, not trusting herself to speak.

The spices are rich, and their aroma fills the single room as he takes the only two cups he owns out of the cupboard. She sits on the couch, staring out the window at the sandstone. At her feet is a copy of Derek Jarman's *Chroma*, opened at the second last chapter 'Iridescence'.

A beautiful word.

Biting hard on her lip, the salty taste of her own flesh there on her tongue, Hilary looks up at the ceiling, and then, as she takes the cup from him, she tells him she has sent her film off. Work. This is what she could always turn to — safe when all the rest of life was too unbearable to hold; calm, contained, manageable.

'And are you pleased?'

'There was no more I could do,' she says with a smile.

He stretches out his long thin legs, crossing one over the other, and takes her hand again. 'That's the place you want to reach.'

He looks at her now, his eyes resting on hers for a moment, and then he turns his gaze down, focusing on his knees, bony beneath his trousers. 'Do you remember when we were at school together?'

She smiles. 'Of course I do.'

'I was in love with you. And I was in love with Maurie. I was in love with both of you.' He brushes his hair out of his eye, and there is the faintest tremble in those fine fingers. 'But then I found the drugs, and I chose to live my life with them, so there was no sadness, loss, or bitterness where either of you were concerned. Just a faint memory of a love I had. A memory that's still there, on certain mornings when I wake and look back.'

She strokes his hand.

'I once told Maurie I loved him, and do you know what he did?'

Hilary shakes her head.

'He squeezed me so tight my bones rattled, and he laughed.'

It is like Maurie is there with them, the recollection of his hold and that laugh filling the small space.

'After you called I had a brief moment of wondering whether I should be brave and go with you. Living as I do is becoming harder. I'm getting too old. But I'm too much of a coward to do anything other than hope that the decision will be made for me by accident.'

Behind them the refrigerator hums, the motor whirring into life and then dying again, the silence afterwards more pronounced.

Taking his face in her hands, Hilary turns him to look at her, because she wants to say: 'I can't talk about this, please stop.' But she doesn't speak, she just leans forward and kisses him, closing her eyes so that she can feel as if they are young again, his mouth cool on hers, a trace of tears that could be hers, just there, and then gone.

She doesn't want him coming with her.

She looks around his flat, the complete containment of his life within these walls. Even this has a pulsating beauty. Henry once told her he had calculated his life, exactly. The cost of heroin with price fluctuations built in, the other bare necessities he needed to survive, and the money he had from an inheritance. An equation that was occasionally tinkered with, but that had ruled his life with an iron grip for so long, never allowing more than the most minor deviation.

He stands now, the deep softness of his corduroy pants like the ocean, and she picks up the book, the pages opening to 'Into the Blue', and she smiles as she reads the first few paragraphs. This was a film she could have made, an exploration of colour. There were so many films she could have made. She looks up at Henry, watching him as he searches behind one of the piles of books, his body bent down low to reach the package.

Snow white.

Ghost white.

Whitewash. White lies.

'Here it is.' He holds the plastic bag out towards her. 'Jerome was flummoxed when I changed my order. He's been delivering the same amount to me for so long without any need for conversation or question. When I asked him for this extra delivery, he questioned me, several times.' Henry smiles. 'I told him there must be very few dealers who refuse to take a larger order. I was very specific with him about the purity so that our calculations are correct. I've tried it, and I am as certain as I can be that he has told me the truth.'

She puts the heroin in her bag, laughing as she looks at it. 'Imagine if I were arrested on the way home.'

'You remember everything I showed you about how to take it?'

She does. He had been surprisingly businesslike when it came to the logistics.

Outside, there is the sound of a door opening and then closing with a heavy thud, followed by footsteps down the stairs and then the ring of a phone. A woman answers, her voice shrill as she tells the caller to fuck off.

'The tone of the neighbourhood seems to be on the slide again.' Henry raises an eyebrow. 'I've seen it go up and down, and I'm sure it will rise and fall again. The other day I realised I have now been living here for forty years. It's a long time. And I spend most days inside this room, only occasionally going out for a walk or seeing people such as yourself. Some would say I've had a limited life.' He shrugs. 'But it's never really felt that way.'

'Sometimes I wish you'd kept sculpting, or creating in some way,' she tells him.

He looks at her, both of them aware that she has never before commented on his life choices.

'Why?'

'I would like to have seen another one of your works.'

He smiles. 'I couldn't now. I probably couldn't have for quite some time. I made the choice before I really knew what choice I was making. It's the danger of youth. And then there was no turning back. The only blessing is that the choice I made has given me a certain insulation against regret.'

The warmth of the gas burner has diminished now, and the room is cold. Hilary shivers. She puts her bag on her shoulder, the weight of the small package inside it amplified in her consciousness. She doesn't want to say goodbye, and she couldn't bear Henry asking her to stay, or telling her he will miss her. She hopes he knows this.

'The chai was beautiful,' she says.

He replies just as she had hoped, with one hand on the door, opening it to the dullness of the hallway as he leans forward to kiss her on the cheek.

'I'm glad you liked it.'

And he brushes his hair out of his eyes as he steps aside to let her pass.

THREE YEARS EARLIER

April had been alone at the shack for ten days when Lawrence arrived.

Each morning, she woke with the first sunlight momentarily soft through the curtain-less windows but soon intensifying, the glare harsh and hard. She hung a blanket, hammering nails into the worn grey corners, but it wasn't enough. There was always a gap at the side, a chink that allowed the daylight, insistent, demanding, to reach across the room and assault her, not as cold as a slap, more a thudding punch in the face.

And so she would lie there, eyes closed, and try to pretend it away. Like when she was a child and she hated Ester, or one of her friends who had come to stay with them for the week and wanted to be with her all the time. She would bend all the force of her will to wiping out their existence, denying every cell of their body with a high-pitched focus like a sonar scream that obliterated all in its path. And so it was now; with eyes tightly closed, fusty bedding pulled over her head, she would grind her teeth and tell herself the day was not yet there, not for her, not at all, trying to summon the denial she had once found so easy to access.

But it was too airless, too unpleasant, to stay there for long. And so she would get up reluctantly, head heavy, and wonder how she was going to fill the slow stretch of daylight until the evening came again, bringing with it the relief of a few hours of unconscious sleep.

She had arrived with a car full of supplies and a heart full of the best intentions. The afternoon had been soft, a pale mauve tinging the gold of the westerly sun when she pulled up outside the shack, the music from the car stereo seeming suddenly loud in the stillness. Here she was. Two bags of clothes, her guitar, a laptop to record herself, and three boxes of food, all healthy, of course: teas and vegetables and fruit, and even brown rice and tofu.

She brought everything inside with a brisk efficiency, play-acting the role of someone else; the creak of her step on the dry boards of the verandah, the thud of the door swinging shut behind her, the rattle of the glass as she opened each of the windows, all too loud, like the sounds an actor in the theatre makes. And that's what she was, April Marcel playing the part of Someone Who Had Come Away To Write.

When she was a child, they had driven here most weekends. She and Ester would sleep in the back seat of the car, surrounded by blankets, pillows, clothes, and food, waking occasionally to the soft glow of the light from the dashboard and the low muttering of Hilary and Maurie talking, sometimes arguing, the radio a hum behind their words.

'Look at the stars,' Maurie would whisper as he carried her in, and she would stare up at the dancing swirl, like a splash of silvery lace under the hem of a twirling skirt, only to close her eyes again straight away, waking hours later, miraculously no longer in the car or his arms, but on one of the divan beds underneath a window.

She had loved that, the transition from one to the other seemingly happening by magic.

She was always the first up, heading down to the river on

her own, oblivious to how damp and dirty her pyjamas became as she sat in the silky sand of the bank and built castles and palaces, singing to herself in the still clarity of the morning light, staying there until Hilary or Maurie's voice rang out from the shack, calling her — breakfast was ready — and she would run up, barefoot, smelling the sugary lemon of the pancakes or the salty fat of the bacon, starving now, the table out on the verandah, Ester setting it as she was told, the birds hopping forward and back, beady eyes alert for any crumbs.

The place had not been used since she was here some months ago. There was the smell of dust, the must of the ash still in the fireplace, and, lingering below it all, smoke from her cigarettes.

As she opened the door to the back bedroom, there was a foulness, the rottenness of death, and she stepped back momentarily, tempted to just close the door and leave it, to sleep in the old divan bed. But once she'd let it out, it was no longer possible to ignore it. It was a bird, only recently dead, ants crawling across the dullness of its once glossy feathers, and she looked, not sure how to deal with it, before regaining some measure of practicality and scooping it up with a plastic bag — the lifeless body a small concentration of weight in her hands — and throwing it some distance away into the bush.

She had nothing to drink.

She had done this on purpose, thinking that purity might help creativity.

How could she have been so stupid?

Outside, the darkness was thickening, soaking into the flat expanse of grass and beyond that the row of poplars, their first spring leaves trembling along the skeletal branches, pale and new.

She would need a drink.

And so, only half an hour after arriving, she got back in the car and headed into town, arriving at the pub just before dark.

The decision was fraught. Should she get one bottle and ration herself to a glass a night until she had to come back for more supplies, or should she be honest with herself and buy half a dozen?

The bottle shop attendant waited.

'Oh God,' April smiled at her. She shifted from foot to foot. 'I have become completely incapable of deciding.' She grimaced, reaching for a bottle and then drawing her hand back.

The woman looked at her, bored.

Shiraz. One.

And then she went back to the shelf.

'You know you can bring them all up at once, love.'

Pathetically, she bought three. Neither here nor there, an each-way bet, a completely useless compromise. Enough to allow herself to slip into the fourth and fifth glass each night, but not enough to save her from having to head back to town sooner than she would like to.

It was completely dark as she drove back, and she was nervous. She remembered Maurie once hitting a kangaroo, the terrible thud of its body, and the shudder of the car as they came to a stop, steam hissing from the radiator. It had been so cold that night, the briskness of the air slapping her cheeks as they walked, each carrying one bag, up the dirt road, abandoning the car to be dealt with in the morning.

'Did the kangaroo die?' she had asked Maurie over and over again. 'Are you sure?'

When he had finally told her that yes, it had died, she had cried and cried, horrified that they had been responsible for its death, and in the end Hilary had stopped, exasperated and exhausted, shaking her as she told her to pull herself together. 'It died. This is what happens. It's terrible. But there is nothing you can do.'

And she had thought her mother was some kind of alien, her

harsh pragmatism so very foreign to all the pain she, April, felt for that poor kangaroo.

She drove slowly now, feeling each pothole and rut, her whole body craned forward as she looked for the dip and bend in the road that she knew so well, but never quite trusted herself to find when it was this dark — and then, there it was, the shack a darker bulk in the distance, one light left on, piercing the night.

She was back. This time with wine. Ready to begin again.

The first few mornings, before she hit upon the idea of putting a blanket over the window, April woke earlier than she had in years.

She slept in an old pair of Maurie's pyjamas, still there, under the pillow. They were flannel, too long and too loose, but they smelt of her father, easing the panic of loneliness and failure that was nipping at her, sharp little bites that threatened to take a chunk of her flesh.

She lay there, listening to the quiet, until she began to discern layers of sound: the call of a bird, the creak of a branch, the slow brush of the breeze, her own breath, rising and falling, and, beneath it all, the pumping of her heart.

She hated sleeping alone, and yet it had been so long since she'd shared a bed with anyone for more than a few weeks. Lex had been the last — ten years younger than her, he'd only just arrived in Sydney from Melbourne. She'd met him at a party, and taken him home for almost three weeks of what she finally had to accept was average sex that rapidly declined to bad.

But there was a sweetness about him, an eagerness, which had at first meant she was happy for him to hang around. He'd just finished a communications course and wanted to work with a film company. He had a hit list, ringing a few producers a day, his voice loud and jocular, his jokes slightly wrong, his laughter too exuberant as he tried to progress the call to a meeting. And then, after those few attempts, he gave up for the day, thumbing through her record collection, putting on his favourites too loud and dancing around her living room, before suggesting they go out to eat. *Like a puppy*, she thought, *clumsy, cute, and irritating.* The same in bed, all over her with a slobbery eagerness that never appealed, and yet when she watched him sleep afterwards, lean and smooth, silky hair ruffled, no hint of a middle-aged snore, she began to see his charms again.

She was happy to let him stay for a while. And then he got work, and she came home to a note and a bunch of daffodils.

She felt no rancour; in fact, she was relieved to have her place back to herself, and even though he promised he'd stay in touch — and they did leave a few messages for each other in a half-hearted attempt at catching up — the wisps that had briefly connected them soon spun away into nothing.

And now she was alone again.

Outside, the days were perfection. Sitting on the verandah, April spoke to the grass, the trees, the flat blue sky, the magpie that watched her, the spider catching flies between the posts and the roof, and the ants that crawled across her toes, tickling the winterwhite of her skin. She told them what she was having for breakfast, the meal she was contemplating for lunch, and then — when she was absolutely convinced they weren't listening — she confessed her fear.

'I am going to leave here having written nothing.'

'Nothing!' She shouted at the magpie, whom she'd come to dislike, frightened it would swoop each time she walked to the stove or bath-house.

It regarded her for an instant and then flew away.

'Do you hear me?' she asked the spider, as it dropped a thread, bouncing, bouncing, bouncing, until finally all was steady enough for it to begin its ascent back to the heart of the matter.

She picked up her guitar and told them she was going to sing them a song, and they'd better be honest when she asked for their opinion. She strummed aimlessly, her voice touching on the possibility of a tune only to dart away immediately.

Inside the house, it was darker. Built to capture the early morning light and then provide shelter from the heat of the summer days, it was always a little gloomy. She made toast with the last of the bread, and yet another cup of insipid herbal tea. She'd buy coffee when she went back into town, and chocolate. This idea of purity was clearly a failure, she told a cockroach as it scurried across the floor.

Sitting on the floor of the bedroom, she opened the old shipping trunk under the window, taking out the clothes that Hilary kept. Heavy cotton summer shifts with huge lurid flowers, caftans, a knitted pantsuit. April used to dress up in them when she was little, and she would have pilfered them years ago if it wasn't for the fact that Hilary was at least six inches shorter than her, and they made her look like she had tried on a doll's outfit rather than her mother's clothes.

At the bottom of the trunk were old notebooks, drawings, and letters. With bright fabric strewn around her, April sat cross-legged on the floor and pulled them all out. She knew the letters between her parents, and she put these aside. Some were in Maurie's dark scrawl, others in her mother's strong slanting pen. She had once started reading them and then felt embarrassed, ashamed, the intimacy too close, and with it the familiarity of both her parents distorted — they became young and in love and passionate, people she did not, and should not, know.

She liked the cards she'd written home when she'd toured Europe. They were tied together with red ribbon, and as she sat and read them, she remembered. It was too simplistic to just say she'd been happy then. She hadn't known how momentous that time was; it had simply happened, and she'd floated along. It was only now that it was gone, she realised how special it had been.

Hilary had also kept drawings they'd done as children, and April took these out as well. Ester's were so much better than hers, which were invariably messy and unfinished. She laid a couple across the floor, remembering the afternoon they'd done them. They'd been on the verandah, and Maurie had given them paper and crayons. 'See that tree?' They'd looked up at it. 'Drink it in,' he'd instructed. 'Now, run inside and draw it.'

She'd scrawled a few branches, and then, bored with the task, had covered them in birds, bright, ridiculous birds with feathery crowns and jewels and fans, and even pipes they were smoking.

It wasn't what they were meant to do, Ester had complained when Maurie had seized April's picture in delight, laughing at the expression on the rooster she'd placed right at the very top.

She looked at Ester's now, and there was a beautiful grace to the lines, an elegance and symmetry. Ester had always drawn well; she was the one destined to become the next artist. And then she'd turned her back on it. Hilary had told her it was a shame. That being a counsellor was dull. Surely she didn't really want to spend day after day listening to dreary people talk about their problems.

Ester had been furious.

At the bottom of the trunk were diaries, the ones they'd kept as little girls. April's rambled from strange fantasy to strange fantasy, tales of animals taking her to live with them, an outpouring of passionate love for a new friend she'd made, a plan to run away and sail around the world (not that she'd ever even been on a boat) — and no mention of Ester.

Her sister's on the other hand, were filled with April's name, anger in every page, as she recounted slights and injustices in fine detail. *How could April have done that? Why hadn't she got into trouble? Surely their parents could see what a liar she was.* April had read it once, completely surprised by the resentment that Ester had carried within her. She hadn't known — and she'd called Ester right then and there, saying they needed to talk. She loved her. She didn't understand how Ester could have misjudged her. It was awful, too awful — and she'd cried into the phone, Ester silent on the other end.

When she finally spoke, her words were dismissive. 'Oh, April. We were children. I don't know why on earth you need to talk about it.'

Like her parents' letters, she didn't read the diaries now. Instead, she took out the drawings that Maurie had done of each of them, rough sketches on scraps of paper that he would have thrown out if Hilary hadn't kept them. April liked these. She'd meant to take them with her last time but had forgotten, instead throwing everything back into the trunk in her clean-up, because she'd faced both Ester and Hilary's anger when she'd left the shack a mess, and it was easier to just put it all back rather than sort through.

But this time, she put the drawings straight into her own bag, and then she wandered back outside to where she'd left her guitar, abandoned on the old daybed.

Under the texta-blue sky decorated with tiny puffy white clouds, she followed a yellow-dirt track. If she drew herself now, she would be a stick figure, she thought, dressed in a red cotton dress, the only person amidst the bold colours of this country. Because it *was* bold today, the sky sharp and bright, the gums stark, the wattle coming out in golden puffs, the green almost iridescent. Nothing but the sound of her boots scrunching on the gravel, and then, as a bird swooped low overhead, the whoosh of its wings.

She should give up and go home.

At the end of the track, there was a truck, engine running, and choking black clouds of diesel rising into the sky. Les, who had an orchard on the river flats, raised his hand in greeting.

'Didn't know you were here.' He squinted into the harshness of the midday sun, closing the gate behind him.

April smiled. 'Been keeping to myself.'

'Hilary still interested in selling?'

April guessed so, although she hadn't spoken to her mother about it recently.

'Nice bit of land your dad bought,' Les told her. 'Just a bad time to be on the market.' He handed April an orange from the front seat, and she held it in her hand, smelling its sweetness for a moment, before she began to break the peel with her thumb, the juice spurting up into her eye.

'Last of the crop,' Les said.

Looking down to the river, April told him she was thinking of going in.

He shook his head. 'You're bloody mad.'

Mouth full of orange, she just grinned.

'Guarantee you'll get no further than your feet.'

She swiped at a fly. 'I'm going to run straight in, fast as fast. Right under.'

Back in the truck, he took his hat off and threw it on top of the oranges next to him. 'Want a lift?'

She smiled. 'Need to walk. Get the heat up.'

And he shook his head again, raising a hand in farewell, as he put his foot on the accelerator, the truck groaning as the engine began to tick over, each panel shuddering as he drove slowly along the corrugated road, leaving a cloud of fumes and dust behind him.

April waited, and then followed in his wake.

The river was still, the banks winding in great curves and loops below the sheer cliffs on the other side and the more gentle incline on this. If she shouted, her voice would hit the grey boulders opposite and bounce back, loud but hollow. Somewhere, a long way upriver, she thought she heard a child, a high-pitched squeal, followed by laughter, and then silence again.

She was alone.

Kicking off her boots and letting her dress drop to her feet, she looked around her once, twice, and then ran naked, straight into the icy chill, the grip of its cold ferocious on her legs, her arms, her chest, until she was completely submerged, all of her encased in ice, expanding, ready to explode.

'I did it,' she shouted at the top of her lungs, perhaps loud enough for Les to hear miles downriver, hopefully loud enough to startle that bitch of a magpie and the cow of a spider. And she shook herself, diamond drops of river water, pure and clean, flying through the air, sparkling in the sunlight, her flesh white and goose-pimpled, before seizing her clothes in her hand and running, as fast as she could, up the bank and across the grass to the bathhouse.

LAWRENCE HAD NEVER found it easy to say no to Hilary. Few people did.

She'd hired the trailer and given him a neatly printed list of everything she wanted brought back.

'I would have asked April to do it, but you know what she's like.'

He didn't really mind. It wasn't as if he were busy at work. And now that the time had come, he was glad to be getting away from home for a few days.

The previous evening, he'd been out until four in the morning. It had been an album launch, a crush of people in a small bar in Redfern. He'd spent the day half-heartedly working on a customer satisfaction survey, followed by discussions around the next poll. He'd intended to just stop by the launch on the way home, or at least that was what he'd told Ester, but he had a restlessness inside, an emptiness at the pit of his stomach, a thirst he knew was dangerous.

The night was chill, and he'd walked to the bar, where everyone had spilled out onto the pavement, the speeches behind them forgotten, the launch itself irrelevant really (he didn't really know any of the band members) and he'd found himself leaning against a brick wall, talking to Jerome and Rebecca, before leaving with them to go to their place.

They lived around the corner, in an apartment above a shop,

the traffic faint below, the rooms spacious and empty. He'd had a brief relationship with Rebecca when they were both young, and when Jerome was out of the room, she said she'd always regretted letting him go.

Which wasn't how he remembered it.

She'd taken too much of something; her whole body was agitated, her eyes darting nervously, her long, fine fingers moving too quickly as she brushed her hair out of her face, scratched at her arm, reached to pour them both another drink and then forgot to complete the action, leaving him to do so.

'I think Jerome might be gay.' She leant close to him as she whispered the words, and then pulled back nervously. 'But I don't know how you tell.'

'Perhaps just ask him.' He raised an eyebrow, bemused by where this was going and how he'd managed to find himself here having this conversation.

'Oh God,' she laughed loudly, unable to meet his eyes. 'As if I could do that.'

He wondered whether she had some kind of mental illness, his memory of her no more than a faint impression; they'd just gone out a lot, drank a lot, taken a lot of drugs, had sex often, and found they had nothing in common on the rare occasions they were together sober.

'You did it all the right way. Stopped all this,' and she picked up the bottle and set it down again, too heavily, on the coffee table between them, 'got a proper job, found a good woman, had a family. Good on you.'

He really should have left then.

But Jerome came back with lines of coke, and, being the drug pig that April had always accused him of being, Lawrence once again failed to say no, the acrid taste cutting through the alcohol fog as he lit another cigarette and grinned.

'Are you gay?' he asked Jerome, who laughed loudly, and then poured himself another drink before looking at Rebecca and telling her she was a stupid fuck. 'Just because I don't love you anymore doesn't mean I'm gay.'

She'd started crying, and then she'd turned to Lawrence and hit him, a rain of angry slaps and punches coming down on him as she'd told him he was spineless, a man with no moral fibre, a fucker, in fact.

He'd tried to stand, the couch so bloody soft it was hard to actually lift himself out of it and get out of there.

He couldn't remember where he'd put his coat, and then he saw it on the other side of the room, but Jerome had stopped him, pulling him back.

'You can't just take my coke and go.'

Unsteady on his feet, Lawrence tried to find a hold on the evening, something to grasp, and he looked directly at Jerome, speaking as though he were talking to the twins when they were naughty, his tone fatherly, sensible — ludicrous in the surreal drift — as he said it no longer seemed appropriate for him to stay, there was clearly something going on between them, and he pointed at Rebecca, who had slumped off to sleep, and then turned back to Jerome, who was laughing.

'There's always something going on,' Jerome replied. 'Oh for fuck's sake. What are you going to do, wander the streets coked up? Or drink with me?'

Neither option was particularly attractive, and Lawrence almost laughed as he weighed the two choices up, wishing he had never got himself to this point in the first place. He'd promised Ester he wouldn't be too late. He should have sent her a text ages ago.

'I've gotta get home,' he told Jerome. 'I really do.' And then he glanced across at Rebecca, who was fast asleep, small body curled up, fists clenched, a slight sweat on the pink of her cheek.

If Jerome didn't love her, he should leave. Or she should leave. One of them should go.

But of course he didn't utter those words out loud. It was no business of his. And she was right — he was a man with no moral fibre, so who was he to pass judgement?

Standing at the door, he didn't look back. He just wanted to be out of there, alone under the crisp coolness of the night air, regaining some sense of sanity in a solitary, and very lengthy, walk home.

The next day, as he drove the trailer through the first of the afternoon peak hour, the seediness of the previous evening still clinging to him, he was glad he'd agreed to go to the shack for Hilary.

He and Ester needed a break.

He'd told her he might stay a couple of nights, and she'd said he could do as he pleased, polite and distant.

She'd been awake when he finally made it home, sitting up in bed and reading, or pretending to read. She'd switched off the light as soon as he opened the door.

'Sorry to wake you,' he'd whispered.

She hadn't replied.

And then, an hour later, when he was finally hovering on the edge of true sleep, her alarm went off.

'I thought you were dead.'

He'd had no idea what she was talking about.

'You said you'd be home early. I sent you texts. An embarrassing number of them. I thought someone had bashed you, or you'd been hit by a car, or fallen over dead drunk somewhere. I should have known.'

They'd had this argument before, but this time it was different. There was just one fierce outburst of anger, her face white and pinched as she'd got up and left, heading off to her consulting room without saying goodbye.

He'd called her at lunch time to say he was leaving for the shack, cowardly in his pretence that the argument was over, even trying to tell her about Jerome and Rebecca but wishing he hadn't as soon as he began. And then he stopped, apologising for failing to look at his phone the previous evening.

'I didn't think you'd worry. You know me. That's what I'm like.'

A sadness had settled into Lawrence's life. It was dank and slow in its creep, damp and stale. He was morose at home, his boredom with work and the stillness of middle age seeping through both of their lives. 'Change it,' Ester used to say when their arguments were still capable of moving into an attempt to understand each other. And do what? They were no longer on the same track, and they both knew it. Hers was the high road, and his — without a doubt — the low.

Outside the car, the city made way for large blocks, huge brick houses with steel roller doors to mark out garage from living, flat dry lawns, and perhaps a sad pony or two. A few miles on, the houses thinned even further and there were turf farms, emerald under the late afternoon sun, great rows of sprinklers tick-tick-ticking over each flat stretch of impossible green. By the roadside, horses slowly chewed grass, ears twitching as a car passed, and then they would bend their long, graceful necks and resume grazing.

He should have brought Catherine and Lara with him. They loved the horses. They loved the river. He imagined pulling over, the gravel crunching beneath the tyres, the chill in the air as the three of them waited still, patient, for one of the mares to slowly lift her head again. They would stroke the warmth of her, her breath grassy and hot as she nuzzled close, the harrumph as she shook herself, one hoof stamping, and the girls wide-eyed in delight.

But the back seat was empty, and he was alone.

When he reached the town, he stopped to have a coffee. The mall was cold and deserted, only one café still open.

'Double shot,' he told the woman behind the counter.

She took a huge mug down from the shelf behind her, and he asked if she had a smaller cup, 'you know, normal coffee size.'

Without a word she reached for another, and he watched with some dismay as the coffee came out of the machine, thin, grey, and disappointing, incapable of lifting the haze of tiredness that had settled upon him.

He was back on the road as soon as he could, following it down to the valley that hugged the river, bitumen slicing through the steep rolling slopes of olive-and-blue scrub, until finally he reached the flats as the sky purpled, great streaks of bruising, slashed with crimson and orange, lurid and beautiful.

When Ester had first taken him here, so many years ago, he had thought it was one of the most special places in the world, a secret valley, so close to the city and yet remote. He had never seen an orange farm before — 'orchard,' she'd laughed, 'not farm,' — or known that water so pure still existed. 'You can drink it,' she'd shown him, scooping up handfuls and gulping them down.

Smiling as he remembered, he drove slowly, aware that this was the time when kangaroos could leap out onto the road. They watched him as he drove past, lifting their heads, their soft eyes unblinking, before bounding away into the dusky dark of the bush.

Pulling over, Lawrence called her, the phone ringing and ringing until Lara picked it up.

'Daddy,' she shrieked across the room. 'It's Daddy.'

Catherine took the phone from her, wanting to tell him that Lara had been in trouble at daycare for hiding her lunch. The story was long and complex, broken by Lara's protests at the untruths of her sister.

'Is Mummy there?' he asked again, his voice thin and hollow in the car, the chill of the night settling around him. He wanted to get to the house before it was too dark to see. 'Can you get her for me?'

Lara called. And then Catherine.

And then Lara told him that Mummy was busy.

'Doing what?' he asked, frustrated.

But Catherine had seized the phone now. When was he coming home? Why hadn't she seen him this morning?

In the background, he could hear Ester saying something.

'In a day or so,' he promised Catherine. 'I'll bring you some oranges.'

The last section of the road petered into a dirt track, the bend down to the shack sharp and sudden. He missed it, driving almost as far as Les' farm before he realised.

Turning back, he slowed right down, stopping at every gap in the trees, until he finally saw what he thought was the gate. He searched for the padlock key, his hangover making him truly hopeless, and then, when he thought he had the right one, he stepped out into the now cold evening, the air tight against his skin, astringent in its briskness, the metal of the lock chill against his fingers, only to discover it was unlocked, the gate ready to swing open as soon as he lifted the latch off the pole.

Of course. April was there.

Lawrence looked down to where the lights were on in the house, glad there would be company, and he drove through, the bumper scraping over the grate, the darkness now surrounding him, all last remnants of the day swallowed by the night.

BACK IN THE CITY, Ester looked at the phone. She had listened to the girls talk to Lawrence, and had waved them away when they had held the phone up, telling her that Daddy wanted to speak to her.

It wasn't because she was still angry about that previous evening. She had reached a point of distance that disturbed her. Seeing him asleep that morning, the rotten smell of alcohol and cigarettes clinging to his skin, his face waxen beneath the darkness of stubble, listening to the low rumble of his breathing, she had seen him as someone she no longer knew.

Their lives had changed. They had children, a house — they were older — and yet, somehow, he was still way back there, dragging his feet, kicking up dust as he trailed behind her, bored, sullen, and then running to catch up, apologising, only to do it all again.

She could have taken the phone and talked to him. He would have told her about the drive, how beautiful it was as the night flooded the valley, still trying to pretend that the argument was behind them and the rift that kept widening didn't exist. She would have heard his words, responding with so little warmth or interest that, in the end, he would have tried for a moment to be angry with her. Shifting the blame, like a dirty piece of laundry. Shoving it back and forth between them.

And so she didn't.

At that point in their lives together, she hadn't liked herself all that much, and no doubt Lawrence had felt the same way about himself.

For the first time since she had arrived, April slept well past dawn.

The light that cut between blanket and window was soft, pearly, and she lay there for a moment, lifting one corner so she could see the sky, smooth and pale, as delicate as cotton wool. Against it, the arc of a scribbly gum traced a sure swoop, graceful and lean, and high up in the branches she thought she saw the magpie. Watching her.

She let the blanket fall.

Next to her the bed was empty, the pillow still slightly dented, the smell of cigarettes and skin (warm, like animal hide) — there was always a distinct smell — and she turned her head not wanting to breathe it in.

She closed her eyes, too.

But she was still there.

He had arrived as night had fallen, the darkness smothering the last of the day, and because there were no clouds until much later, it had been cold. She had lit the fire, using the last of the wood, the tang of eucalyptus as the leaves shot up the chimney in sparks, the twigs catching soon after.

As a child, laying the fire had always been her job. Maurie would take her out into the dusk to gather the right kind of wood. 'Dry, dead — nothing green or rotten.' He would kick aside stumps, soft and crumbly, damp and mouldy, loading her arms up with twigs and leaves, while he brought in the heavier logs.

It was like building, she thought.

'Rip the paper sheets in half,' he would instruct. 'Screw them up into a ball — not too tight, not too loose.'

And she would balance the twigs like a tepee — just the right amount of air — before throwing in the match and squealing in delight at the roar and rush, the shooting flames.

Next the larger logs, and there were lessons in how to put them on — where and when — as well as detailed instructions in how to revive the dying embers. Maurie loved to teach.

Last night, she had made a fire of which he would have been proud.

She had run a hot bath after her swim in the river, soaping herself, and washing her hair, letting out the water and refilling it, steam rising, until it had simply become too cold to stay in any longer. And so she had dried herself by that fire, putting on Maurie's old pyjamas and singing — loudly, happily — without even being aware that this was what she was doing. Because it always took time here, but then, when you weren't looking, the rhythm of the empty days seeped into your blood, and you found yourself living at a pace that was right, and the beauty was that you didn't even know how this had happened.

Her voice was loud and clear, running along the edge of a new melody that had been teasing her all afternoon, still not quite strong enough for her to try and trap it, and she had let herself float around it, oblivious to the door opening behind her until she felt a sudden rush of cold air, and he said her name.

She jumped, shrieking loudly as she turned to face him, brandishing a burning stick without even realising she had seized it from the fireplace, only to find that it was Lawrence. Of course it was Lawrence. She had completely forgotten Hilary mentioning that he might be coming up.

As she lay in bed now, she could hear him, his boots on the verandah, and she kept herself perfectly still. He was bringing in wood. The heavy thud of the logs as he dropped them by the door, and then his footsteps again. She didn't want to move, to get up and have to face it all. And so she kept her eyes closed tightly, the blankets pulled up over her head — *foolish, foolish, foolish girl* — while outside the magpie chirruped and warbled, the throaty pitch of its song cutting through the softness of the morning, broken only by the heavy thud of more logs and the clump of his step as he went to fetch another load.

Last night, he had stood by the doorway with his bag and a couple of bottles of wine, the night descending behind him. Handsome Lawrence, and she had dropped the burning stick into the fire as he had smiled ruefully. He was a little under the weather, he had told her — so much so there'd been a moment when he thought he'd never find the turn-off.

Cocking her head like the magpie, she'd assessed the damage he'd done to himself and told him he had a choice. 'It's either abstinence or the full coat of the dog. Just a hair will do you no good. Trust me, I know.'

If it had been a few days earlier, she would have welcomed his arrival. She'd craved distraction, but, strangely, at that moment she'd only wished him away. The peace she'd found was so fragile and so at odds with the jangling heaviness that cloaked him, a state she'd also been in on arrival.

He'd brought food with him too, and she'd been grateful for that, tending to the fire as he'd heated up soup and bread, his hand shaking slightly as he'd offered her a bowl.

Beautiful Lawrence, with his silvery eyes and coal-soot hair. She remembered how they'd all loved him, every woman and half the men. It was a pity he'd never had the talent. You would have made a fortune from him.

He'd told her about the launch and Jerome and Rebecca, and she'd laughed, snorting slightly as she put the soup bowl down. 'She was mad. But you were always so drug-fucked when you were with her that you never saw it. She set fire to two houses she lived in.'

'Why didn't anyone tell me?'

April had shrugged. 'I guess we just took whatever was dished up as normal. That's what you do when you're young.'

He'd shaken his head, stretching out his legs and staring up at the ceiling. 'Why do some of us grow up more easily than others?' And then he'd corrected himself. 'Or more to the point, why does growing up have to involve letting all that go?'

'Maybe it's just that there are times that shine,' she smiled. 'They have a brightness that's hard to let go of.'

She pointed to the bottle of wine, but he held up his hand. 'I think I'd better take the abstinence approach.'

(And so they hadn't even been drunk, the excuse she'd always had ready should the past have been unearthed.)

She poured herself a glass and then put the bottle away, telling him the river would cure him. 'Tomorrow. At dawn. I'll march you down there myself and throw you in. It's brutal but beautiful.'

'Do you remember the lakes?'

She did. She looked away for a moment.

They had been in England, the first brittle bite of winter in the air, diamond frost across the rolling green fields, crunching beneath the soles of her shoes as they made their way back to the pub after a night in a castle.

He'd been the disinherited son of a Lord.

'Anthony?' she asked Lawrence, who didn't remember.

He'd taken them back there after her show, breaking in through a window, his plan a simple one — he wanted to trash every room before dawn. Because he hated his father. And his mother. And his sisters.

And as he threw the first vase to the floor, April had collapsed in giggles.

'Aren't you glad you didn't fly home?' she'd asked Lawrence. 'When will you ever get another chance to trash a castle?'

They'd slipped out well before he'd finished the first floor, the lake silver in the dawn.

'That was the coldest I have ever been,' April said. 'I remember feeling as though someone had seized my heart and my lungs in an ice grip.' She'd touched her chest. 'And ripped them out. I thought I would never breathe again.'

'Would you do it now?' he asked her.

'Trash a castle? Swim in a freezing lake?'

'Either or.'

She would. 'Which is probably tragic.'

'I don't know if I would,' he confessed. 'Which is even more tragic.' And then he smiled. 'Actually, I would. My tragedy is that I try and pretend I wouldn't, but if the opportunity arose (which is unlikely), I would be in there throwing everything to the ground, or leaping in that lake. And then I would try to lie about it the next day.'

She'd laughed at him then. 'Go on.'

'Point me in the direction of the local castle.'

She'd winked. 'Can't help with that. But I can provide you with a river at the end of winter.'

'Brutal but beautiful, I believe.'

'Precisely. Get your gear off. Run down there. And I guarantee you'll get some of that shimmer back. Or at least shake off whatever it is you're dragging around with you.'

Now as she lay in bed, sheets pulled over her head, she heard him come back inside the house, his footfall tentative. All those years ago, when they were young and at the lakes, he had only been with Ester for a few months; it had been easy to pretend that there'd been no real betrayal, just a drunken loss of direction, a quick career down the wrong path, the mistake never mentioned to anyone or talked about by either of them. It might never have happened.

And then, last night, he had taken them back there.

He had gone out onto the verandah, shedding his clothes in the night air, running across the grass, through the avenue of poplars and down the muddy track that led to the river, while she had sat in front of the fire, clutching her glass of wine, suddenly aware that she was standing at the edge of trouble.

'April,' he called her name softly.

'April,' his voice was a little louder as he put his head around the curtain that separated bedroom from living space, letting the morning light into the room.

She was a coward.

Shifting the sheet slightly, she looked out at him, not knowing what to expect now. Because last night, when he had returned from the river, there had been no shimmer, just a momentary bravado, and then a sadness that had shocked her. Wrapping him in the warmth of a blanket, she had watched as he cried.

'I made a mistake,' he told her.

She hadn't known what he had meant.

'I tried to become someone that I'm not.'

She hadn't said a word.

And then he had shifted, wanting only to brush aside that sadness. 'I don't think the swim was meant to do this,' he smiled. 'I'm just tired, and hungover, and no good at taking drugs anymore.'

But as she stood to leave him, he'd pulled her down again, and they kissed, the softness of his lips, the sweetness of the river water, and it had been so long since she'd had good sex, really good sex, that she didn't care.

Someone had once told her that the beauty of sex was the loss of self.

And perhaps that was all they'd wanted. Perhaps it didn't really matter.

Now, as he came over to the bed, she reached her hand out from under the sheet, her skin pale, a long scratch down her wrist from the walk yesterday, the taste of him still there on her fingers.

He lay down next to her, so close that she could see his pores, each dark lash, the line of his mouth, the curl of his hair still damp from a morning swim, and she kissed him again.

It was only four days. Not long when it's held up, so very contained, against the great rush of life on either side, but long enough for Lawrence to believe — just briefly — that he had fallen in love.

The rain had come, washing over the brilliance of early spring, softening it with a grey mist, shaking out the small buds that had begun to appear and leaving them sodden in the dirt.

That first morning, when he had left April asleep and gone down to the river to swim, he had felt the restorative power she had promised he would find, the shine he had failed to touch the previous evening. Alone, his body heavy from sex and lack of sleep, his heart confused and ashamed, he had stood on the bank and looked across to the steep incline of the other side, the scrub silvery against the deep blue-grey of granite.

At his feet, the river was perfectly still. Dark slate, pocked by small islands of white sand, each fringed by rushes. He swam out, the cold fiercer than the previous evening, and he drank in the water in great gasps and gulps, swallowing it as he stared up at the flat grey sky.

He would pack up and go. Make it work with Ester. He and April would never speak of this. He could trust her silence, he knew that.

But then, as he stood on the bank drying himself, he didn't want to go home. Opening his front door, calling out Ester's name, trying to find equilibrium; he didn't think he could do it anymore. The bracing cold of the river, the softness of the morning; he felt as though his heaviness had been lifted. It was beautiful here. And he was at peace.

Climbing back up the bank, he gathered what dry wood he could find, twigs scratching his arms and legs. He would chop some logs for the evening.

Maurie had once tried to teach him how to use an axe, laughing loudly as splinters of bark flew through the air, Lawrence's fury mounting at what he perceived to be some kind of test that he was failing. Hilary had watched from the verandah, arms folded, a slight smile on her face, until eventually she had spoken, her voice soft but clear: 'You know, you don't have to agree to be his amusement. There's plenty of wood already chopped.'

He had put the axe down, grinning at Maurie, the release so quick and easy he couldn't believe he had failed to see it for himself.

Later that day, as April lit the fire, she asked him whether he was going to go home that evening. Neither of them had touched on what was happening; they had been so careful to not even glance in the direction of what lay before and behind them that her question almost made him jump.

'I wasn't intending to.' He looked at her for affirmation that he was welcome to stay, but she refused to give it.

The twigs and leaves blazed, brightening the dullness of the room, and she stood, stepping back from the heat.

He had to speak.

'I would like to stay for a few days.'

Her eyes widened.

'But it doesn't have to be like it's been,' he hastened to add.

'I just need a bit of time. You can keep trying to write, and I'll do the painting Hilary wanted done, I'll pack up the stuff.' He smiled. 'You can pretend I'm not here.'

'Ha.' Her laugh when it came was loud, and she shook her head, wiping at her eyes, the smoke stinging the corners. 'What's that Oscar Wilde quote about losing your parents?'

He couldn't remember.

'Losing one is misfortune, both is carelessness? Falling for your sister's partner once may be misfortune?' She rolled her eyes. 'I believe we are well and truly in the land of carelessness.'

He watched as she turned her back to him, carefully placing some of the larger logs on the fire before she closed the door, leaving the flue still open. She didn't know where to sit, he could see that, and he shifted over so that there was plenty of space, so she didn't have to be too close.

'Besides,' and she looked out at the soft mist of rain, 'it's hardly painting weather.'

It was unlike April to be direct. In all the years he had known her, she had danced around and at the edge of every matter of substance, a quality that could be both charming and irritating. But she was different now. There was a stillness to her, a calm he had never seen.

'I have a suggestion,' he eventually said.

She reached for her tobacco, the smell of caramel as she began to roll a cigarette, the paper thin and delicate, eyes intent on the task.

'We are so deep in the land of carelessness, let's stay here, just for a few days. There's nothing we can do to make it any worse, so let's allow ourselves to enjoy it. To pretend that nothing else exists, and just be bad, roll around in it, and not even attempt to deal with any of the ramifications. Just be.' Oh god. He looked across at her, still staring at the cigarette paper in her lap, surprising himself with how strong the plea was, the need. Because they were the bad ones. The ones who hadn't grown up. Although he had tried — all that time in Paris, with the job and the twins, and all that time since, pretending that he was a responsible man when, pathetic as it was, he didn't want any of that. Or maybe he just had to turn his back on it briefly, be as bad as he knew how, to be able to willingly become the man he should be. He didn't know. He just wasn't ready to go home. Not yet.

He remembered that night at the lakes, how different it had been. Both of them drunk, all the while knowing that this was not what he wanted. He had woken the next morning and crept out of her bed, his flight leaving from London that afternoon. The note he had left had been curt — a simple 'See you soon, Lx' — and he was gone, every part of him craving the calm of Ester.

But this time, he hadn't been drunk.

This time, he wanted to stay.

After three days, the rain stopped.

They hadn't left the shack. In the morning light, April saw the kicked-back bedsheets, their clothes on the floor, the dishes in the sink, and she covered her eyes with her arm. She smelt of him. His skin, his tongue, the bristles on his chin, the grasp of his palms, his thighs, he was all over her.

She was going for a walk. He should pack up the trailer.

She suddenly felt as though she had been sinking with a drowning man, and she was exhausted.

She took herself upriver, cutting through the scrub to a small bridge to the other side. She wanted to climb out of the valley. The incline was steep and slippery, and she found herself scrambling, hauling herself up with her hands. Above, the sky had cleared, a watery wash of blue, last tufts of clouds speeding south, and the air was rich with mud and mulch and twigs.

Finally, she emerged on the dirt road that looked down over the river that curled below her, silty with days of rain. Beyond that, she could see the shack, the strange pitched roof that Maurie had constructed, a shape that seemed impossible, and yet had a beauty to its rise and fall. She could see the poplars, a delicate line of feathery branches, jewelled with new spring leaves, and, at the end of the grove, Lawrence loading up the trailer.

She looked away.

The shame made her feel ill.

As the day became hotter, she followed the road that led to the valley, a good ten kilometres that would take her downriver from home. There was no sound but the scrunch of her boots on the gravel, a beat that kept time with her breathing, and occasionally, an echo of a call from somewhere far away.

High overhead an eagle followed her, floating on the wind, disappearing and then arcing up into the sky again. She watched its flight, the great breadth of its wingspan a beauty to behold.

Finally, as the sun began to shift further to the south, April reached the end of the road. She was back at Les' orchard.

She could see him in his shed, fixing machinery, and she walked towards him, exhausted now.

'Still here?' he looked up at her, a smear of grease across his chin.

She nodded.

'Hazel made some marmalade she wanted to give your mother. Was going to bring it over this afternoon.'

April looked up to the house. 'Is she there now?'

He nodded.

The house was dim, the wood-fire stove burning, everything quiet. She knocked and called out, until eventually Hazel came around the side. She'd been feeding the chooks.

'Cup of tea?' she offered, and April said that yes, she'd love one.

The walk had been longer than she'd expected. She was buggered.

'You're looking a bit worse for wear,' Hazel agreed, and April felt ashamed. 'Sit yourself down and I'll run you home.'

They talked briefly, mainly about Hilary, and then Hazel asked her how Ester and that handsome husband of hers were.

He was here, April said. Clearing out furniture. She hoped she didn't blush.

'Did he bring the girls?'

April shook her head.

'They're a handful, those two,' Hazel smiled. 'They look the spitting image of you when you were their age. I remember when your dad first bought you here. Hard to believe you were the same age they are now.'

April smiled weakly.

It was darkening on the drive home, the last of the sunlight smeared across the southern ridge. It would be cold tonight, April thought, and she looked out the window, through the fine film of dust, the scrub a soft blur as the ute bounced over the potholes and corrugations in the road.

'I'll jump out here,' April told her, 'no need for you to turn in.'

Hazel reminded her to take the marmalade. 'You need to feed yourself up. You're looking peaky.'

She waved goodbye and walked alone up the track to the house, its lights on, smoke from the chimney, and Lawrence's car with the trailer fully loaded out the front.

'All packed,' he told her. 'I'll leave in the morning.'

That night, as they lay in bed together for the last time, she should have counselled him to keep his silence, to say nothing, to realise this for what it was: a brief escape that they both needed to forget. But she didn't. She thought there was no need.

They didn't have sex.

They just lay side by side, skin on skin, their sleep fitful, the haze between dream and wakefulness thick and smothering, until eventually April got up, the night still heavy outside, the last embers of the fire burnt right down. She opened the flue a little, placing a few of the smaller twigs on top, and watched the flames rise.

She didn't hear Lawrence as he came into the room. He sat next to her, still naked, his skin cold. His face was so familiar and strange, and as she turned to face him, she began to cry, shushing any attempts of his to talk, not wanting soothing words but instead just to let herself cry for what she had done, the terrible mistake of it all, the sheer folly of having laid waste to so much, all of her now out on a limb, miles from safety, alone with her shame.

Lawrence had Hilary's checklist in his hand. The trunk, a cupboard, an easel, a box of crockery, and a crate of books. There wasn't all that much. The rest could just go with the house, she'd told him.

WIWO, April had said.

He'd looked at her quizzically.

'Walk In Walk Out,' she'd explained.

He shook his head.

'I love a real-estate acronym.'

She'd gone for a swim, running down to the river in just a towel, jumping in with a whoop that echoed out across to the cliff and all the way back up to the house. He heard her, the loud throatiness of her scream, and then she was running back across the stretch of lawn and straight under a hot shower in the bathhouse.

He was almost fooled by her spirits, by the way she sassed past him without a stitch of clothing, by the clothes she chose — a short denim pinafore, an old Sherbert T-shirt, and a bright-green cardigan (cute and cheerful to an extreme) — and by the way she told him it was high time he left. She needed to get on with her writing.

'Not that any was happening, but there's plenty of fuel for a tortured love song or two now,' and she'd raised an eyebrow.

He'd kissed her on both cheeks, on the tip of her nose, and on her forehead.

'Well,' she'd said, stepping back from his embrace. 'What can I say? Drive carefully? See you back in town?'

With his hand on her arm, he tried to draw her close, but she pushed him away, shaking her head, and there was something harsh in her smile; it was a little too bright.

Out on the dirt road, the trailer jarred and banged behind him, a loud clanging that accompanied him all the way to where the dirt levelled into flat grey bitumen winding along the river flats, past the first houses in the valley, the horses again, and it was so very strange to be re-entering the world. It had only been four days, but when he caught sight of himself in the rear-vision mirror, still unshaven, eyes hooded from lack of sleep, a nick on his bottom lip from where April had bitten him, it was the face of a man he didn't know. His phone beeped several times, messages coming up on the screen. Two from home, both from the girls, one from Hilary with further instructions just in case she caught him before he was out of range, one from Jim asking him out for a drink, and another from a client wanting research into what women want from a mascara. The crowd of demands depressed him. He pulled over to the side of the road and sent a text to Ester — *On my way, see you soon* — and then turned his phone off.

On the outskirts of town, he considered a coffee, but the memory of his last stop those few days ago made him change his mind. He would just keep driving. He needed to get home.

Home.

The realisation of where he was headed sank in.

He saw other cars, and people shopping, and children and prams, and families squabbling, and he wound the window up, wanting to block it all out. The petrol gauge was low, and he pulled over at a service station.

There, he noticed that his hands were shaking. Trying to still himself, he breathed in deeply, twisting the plain gold ring on his finger before taking the keys out of the ignition.

He and Ester hadn't believed in marriage. Sometimes late at night, in the early days of love, they would propose to each other, elaborate declarations of love and fidelity. He had never lived with anyone before, a fact that made him slightly ashamed. In her, he saw the possibility for stability, calm, maturity — states of being that he felt he should embrace at this stage of life. But it didn't have to entail marriage. Neither of them had ever really wanted that. And then, when he was offered the job in Paris, he was told it would be much easier for her to come if they were husband and wife.

They had made their vows before a marriage celebrant, words they'd chosen from the various options on display in plastic folders, each of them trying to find one that came as close as possible to how they saw themselves and the occasion. Nothing was quite right.

They'd been told they could write their own vows, but in the end they didn't. Nor did they have any photos of the celebration itself. It wasn't that kind of wedding.

Wearing a red wool dress with a plain square neckline, her dark hair tied back in a simple ponytail, Ester had been as she always was — elegant, beautiful, cool, and calm.

'I love you,' he had whispered to her, moments after the ceremony was over.

'I love you, too.'

The few friends who were there hadn't known. It was just a Sunday lunch, or so they'd been told.

'We weren't sure how to do this,' Lawrence had said in his speech. 'Weddings aren't our thing.'

'Well, don't start making them your thing,' someone had called out.

'We could have just left it at the registry, but that seemed strange. And yet we didn't want all the fuss and the presents, and so we decided to just surprise you.'

Their friends had cheered and whooped as they kissed in the clear sweetness of the day, their small garden home to a party that had been better than they'd expected.

Later, as the afternoon became chill, Micky and Louise suggested they all kick on. Micky was drunk and she stood unsteadily, lurching slightly as she clutched at the table before losing her balance. Two months earlier, she'd made a move on Lawrence. He'd been at a party, Ester had gone home, and they'd been dancing. She'd run her hands up and down his sides, leaning in to kiss him. And he had kissed her back, forgetting, as he was so capable of doing, that those days were over. He had almost gone home with her, but then he'd stopped. The music was too loud, her eyes were pinned, and the sweat on her skin had smelt stale.

That afternoon, as she fell, she pulled everything onto the ground. The shattering of glasses and plates and the crash of cutlery rang like bells, and then, on top of it all, a long stained tablecloth, bringing the lunch to a resounding end. Micky looked around dazed, hoisting herself up as everyone began to laugh.

'Well, you sure know how to clear a table,' Lawrence told her. 'Where to next?'

And then, as they began to argue loudly about an array of choices, he suddenly realised he didn't actually want to go anywhere: he wanted to stay home with Ester.

'My wife and I are not going to join you,' he pronounced to the table, and as Micky threw her napkin at him and booed in disgust, declaring that this was what happened to married couples, he folded his arms.

'Everyone!' There was silence. It was Ester shouting now. 'This is a momentous occasion. And I'm not talking marriage.'

Lawrence had shaken his head, grinning as he did so.

'Lawrence is staying home!' She raised the only unbroken glass and gave out a loud wolf whistle to calls of 'shame, shame' from Micky, who was soon shouted down by cheers from others around the table.

'I should've gone,' he told her later. 'We both should've gone.' He looked at her warily, unsure of her response, and she rolled her eyes.

'I don't want to change,' he protested, and then he'd drawn her close and kissed her. 'You knew what you married. Who I am doesn't mean I love you any less.'

But it wasn't the entire truth. Part of him had wanted to change. He had thought that if he wore the clothes, he would become the man. He really had. And yet it was never going to work. The outfit was ill-fitting, the cloth and cut wrong, and he had always known that. Now here he was, the last vestiges of that suit shed with a fierce desperation, leaving him unsure, so very unsure, of the man that remained beneath.

NOW

As the lunch bell buzzes through the silence of the classroom, the teacher looks up. It was only two years ago that they used to send a student out to ring an actual bell, the brassy clang sometimes rhythmic, sometimes jagged and unsure, depending on who was doing the honours. Now it's electric, rung from the admin office, like a loud fire alarm. It still makes her jump, even when she's been watching the clock at the back of the room and longing for its sound.

'Everybody still now,' she calls out, clapping her hands together.

One of the twins is standing, the other pulling her back down to sit.

Outside, it's still raining, wet leaves stuck like scraps of sodden paper to the window, the sky a blank, even grey. The playground is deserted, and pools of muddy water gather in the cracks and dips in the bitumen. C playground is a complete mudbath, and, beyond that, the vegetable garden is bent low from the morning downpour.

Inside, children's raincoats and gumboots are stacked in a riot of bright plastic, tumbling over each other in the corner, and the room smells musty, like wet wool and dirt.

'I don't think anyone's going outside today,' the teacher tells them. Both the twins have their hands up, and are only just managing to stay in their seats.

'Can we get the lunches?' one asks.

Strictly speaking, she hadn't yet given either of them permission to talk, but she relents, knowing she's been tough on them this morning, and not because she doesn't like them, but because they chatter endlessly.

She nods, and it's Catherine, she thinks, who runs to get the washing basket they use to collect the canteen lunches, slowing down as she sees she's being observed.

'Carefully,' the teacher reminds her, the well-worn warning no doubt forgotten as soon as they leave the classroom.

ACROSS TOWN, HILARY sits in her car, hands on the steering wheel.

The key is in the ignition, but she has not yet turned it all the way. Instead, she stares at the pearling drops of rain on the windscreen, each one clinging, poised to slide away, perfectly formed, the entire world held in its translucent beauty. Winding down the window slowly, she reaches out to touch one, chill on the tip of her finger, impossible to hold.

Her head aches. Her vision bends and warps. This is a bad morning.

On the radio, a woman talks about reconciliation and forgiveness, her voice rich and deep, soothing, as she speaks of work she has done with trauma victims, studies with people in countries such as Rwanda.

'But sometimes forgiveness isn't enough.' The announcer speaks in brisk, friendly tones. 'How do you learn to forget?'

'Ah yes,' the woman laughs. 'There is forgetting as well. But the point I am making is that true forgiveness changes even the memory of the event. There is no longer anger attached to the recollection.'

Hilary turns the radio off. Attempts to simplify human behaviour, to rub it smooth, have always irritated her. But she had listened for longer than she normally would have because this is her anxiety, the frayed edge that threatens to unpick her plans. The lack of reconciliation between Ester and April makes her anxious, and it kicks her, hard, on these bad days. It is so easy from the outside, from the edge of a life, to see the mistakes people make and why — to see and understand. But from the midst it is different, and she knows that both her daughters are there, right in the middle, too close still to reflect.

She looks across to the blank face of Henry's apartment building, the bricks washed in the rain, each of the windows the same and yet different: unadorned; grey curtains; crumpled venetians; a torn blind.

She wonders what made Henry turn to heroin — whether it was simply the foolish choice of someone young who wanted to experiment, or whether there was a deeper canker, a grit that had scratched and rubbed and needed to be soothed. She knew very little about him, really. His family were Queensland country people who had no understanding of who he was. 'Maybe I was adopted,' he'd said, a fantasy so many people hold at some stage of their life. 'They probably regret their choice,' he'd added, and then he'd slid away from talking about himself, turning to the music they were listening to, or the shadow of a branch on the window, remaining as private as ever.

Out the front of his building are two frangipani trees. Strange that she has never really noticed them before. The branches are bare; silvery knots streaked with rain arch over the entrance stairway, like a puzzle. Closing her eyes, she tries to recall the fragrant milkiness of a flower, peachy petals in her hands, star-like, scattered over summer pavements, bruised in the shiny sunlight.

LAWRENCE CLOSES HIS EYES. He once did a meditation course with Ester, and, although he made fun of it at every opportunity he got, he still tries to find that moment of absence he had reached. He remembers it. They were all in rows, listening to a young nun in saffron robes. She glowed with happiness. She joked and laughed as she talked to them, and around him, middle-aged women with long blonde hair wrote notes in floral cloth-covered notebooks, their silver bangles jangling as they tried to transcribe each of her words of wisdom. He hated it. But when the time came to meditate, he achieved a total absence of thought that he recalls with longing.

He has never found it since.

He has Hilary to phone back, Edmund to deal with, and then, ultimately, there is Paul, the editor. All three jostle, shove, and lay claim to his mind, a space that refuses to empty, as the rain beats against the tin walls and roof of his room.

And so he gives up, opening his eyes to the gloom as his phone rings again, Paul's number appearing on the screen. He is out of the meeting and needs the polls ASAP.

'This hitch — is it fixed?' he asks.

Lawrence cuts over him, his voice soothing, fast, assured. He is a practiced liar, a man who moulds the world around him into changing shapes to suit his need. The problem doesn't look like it's going to be remedied as soon as he'd like. He realises this throws them out, and he couldn't be more apologetic, but it's out of his control. As Paul would know, nothing like this has ever happened in all their history together, and he'll make sure it doesn't happen again. He's also more than willing to work together in whatever way they can to — and here he is cut off.

'There's been a lot of discussions about the cost of the polls,' Paul tells him. 'I've been behind you as much as I can. I know the value of what you do. But those new robo polls, they're cheap, and the amount of people you can interview is unbelievable. That's the way management wants to go. I was hoping we could hold off for longer but ...' Paul sighs. 'We've got a slip-up like this, and it's going to be tough. I can't stem the tide, mate. Not after this.'

'Jesus.' Lawrence stares at the ceiling. 'You know how inaccurate they are. People don't respond to a recording in the same way as they do to a person.'

Paul is silent.

'Let's at least talk about this face to face.'

'Sure,' Paul replies. 'I'm flat out at the moment, but when I surface —'

Lawrence stops him. 'Is my contract being terminated? Officially?' He can hear the silence on the other end of the line.

'That's the way it's looking,' Paul eventually tells him. 'There was only this and one more to go before we renewed — and with the data slip-up, I don't think they're going to be willing to pay you out. I probably shouldn't be telling you this. Joel's putting it all in a letter.'

His voice is hushed now, difficult to hear above the sound of the rain. Lawrence just stares at the wall. This is his livelihood. But he can't say that. To beg, to be needy — he knows it wouldn't help. Normally, he'd have the wherewithal to try to talk Paul out of the decision, to guarantee him that if he gives the robo polls a try he'll soon find that their inaccuracy will only be an embarrassment. He knows, he's seen them in action: the automated calls that ask a series of questions in a robotic voice, directing respondents (or those that don't hang up, at least) to a very limited range of answers.

He shakes his head. 'I thought our years together would at least have given me the opportunity to come in and make my case.' His words trail off. Does he really have any kind of case to make?

And then, as he opens the email from Edmund that has appeared on his computer screen, he realises it is only going to get worse.

AT HOME, ESTER HAS the radio on, a low hum behind her in the kitchen, and she turns it down as she hears the word therapy mentioned, and then searches through the fridge, taking out dinner leftovers for lunch.

The rain is loud in this part of the house. She glances outside, thinking it must be getting heavier again, but it has settled, monotonous in its constancy.

Sitting at the bench, absentmindedly picking through cold pasta, Ester stares out the window, her stillness at odds with her mounting nerves at the thought of this evening's dinner.

'I am too old to be getting date jitters,' she tells herself, speaking out loud because this is what she does on the days she works at home alone. When Otto is here, he gets the benefit of her conversation; when he isn't, it's the walls and doors that have to listen.

She has booked herself a telephone appointment with her own therapist, and she is due to call in ten minutes. Because she likes to be organised, Ester has written down her fears. She glances at the list now, throwing it in the bin moments later.

Sex. That's all it comes down to really.

It's been so bloody long since she's had sex.

And even longer since she's had sex with anyone other than Lawrence.

Biting her lip, Ester stares up at the ceiling.

Gone are the days when she would get rotten drunk before

taking someone home for the first time, the alcohol giving her enough courage to initiate or respond.

'Oh good God,' she says out loud, pushing her plate away, unable to eat any more.

Standing in front of her own reflection, she tries to draw herself a little taller, to look composed, and then she gives up, shaking her head and letting out a shrill scream to banish the nerves, just as the telephone rings.

It's Victoria.

They never waste any time before they get down to business. Therapist to therapist.

'It's sex,' Ester tells her. 'I'm terrified.'

'Of what?' Victoria asks.

Oh God, Ester thinks. 'Everything,' she says. 'Being naked, being a disappointment, that I won't know how to do it anymore, I'll fuck it up — excuse the pun — I'll misread the situation, I'll have to be intimate with someone again. Everything, everything, everything.' And then she laughs. 'I can't believe I'm saying all this. I sound like a sixteen-year-old.'

'It's perfectly understandable to be nervous,' Victoria replies. 'But you also need to realise there's no need to rush into anything that makes you feel uncomfortable. You can take your time with this.'

'But I'm excited, too,' Ester interrupts. 'I feel happy.'

She looks around the room as she says those words — at the school notes on the fridge, the pile of washing in the corner, the clothes on the rack next to the heater, and, outside, the rain, still coming down. The joy she feels, the fizz that dances over the surface of this sheer ordinariness, makes her smile. It's so long since she's felt such a spark.

'It's been so hard,' she says. 'But I feel as though there's a shift. At last. And I don't think it's just linked to this — to meeting someone I might like. I think it was happening anyway. It's good.'

'That's wonderful,' Victoria tells her.

'It is,' Ester smiles.

'Have you thought any further about whether you're ready to make changes in relation to April?'

Ester looks at herself in the window opposite, phone in one hand. She shakes her head slowly, and when she speaks, her voice is soft, her sentiment uncertain.

'I miss her, or I miss the idea of what family was, but when I think about letting her into my life again, I'm terrified.'

'But you still feel this is the place you'd like to reach — a place of reconciliation?'

'I suppose so,' Ester replies. 'But I'm not sure whether this is because I think I should reach that place, or because I genuinely want to.' She looks down at her hand, resting on the kitchen bench: long fingers like her father's, her olive skin pale, her nails always kept short. They have similar hands, she and April, but in the rest of her appearance, April takes after Hilary: fine and delicate, light and wiry, a body that never carries weight, and that sparks and flies and cracks and shimmers. She doesn't want to talk about April today. She doesn't want to think about her.

'You know,' she says to Victoria, 'I'd rather move on. I don't want this session to be about April.'

'Why?' Victoria asks.

'Because I don't want April in my head today. I don't want to go out this evening, to try and trust again, thinking about her.' She is surprised at the anger in her voice as she speaks, and she apologises before asking Victoria if they can talk about Lindsay for a moment.

'The client I told you about last week. The one with panic attacks. I was trying to locate a group session for meditation and relaxation techniques, somewhere local. She's willing to try this.'

Victoria listens, letting Ester jump from the personal to the need for professional assistance, although Ester knows she will want to take her back there soon, if not during this session, then at the next.

As she writes down a couple of names in her book, possible places for Lindsay to go, the phone beeps with another call, and she ignores it, knowing it won't be a patient (they only have her mobile number) or Steven (who also doesn't have her home number). It will probably be a poll, she realises with a grimace. Worse still, one of those new robo ones.

Outside, the rain continues, easing momentarily into a light mist, soft grey against the dull sky, sliding down the glass, the world outside a blur, and Ester listens to Victoria as she tells her about a similar case she had some months earlier, and approaches that helped.

APRIL IS THE ONE who gets the call from the school. Catherine appears to have sprained her ankle. The girls say they are with their father this week, but he's not answering, nor is their mother, and April is named as the second emergency contact.

They are in the sick bay when she arrives. Lara is the one with her foot up; Catherine is sitting by her side, looking suitably concerned.

'Are you all right?' April asks, kissing both girls, and then, holding Lara's chin in one hand, she looks straight at her. Something is up.

'I twisted it,' Lara tells her, pointing to an ankle that looks remarkably unswollen. 'It hurts to walk.'

'I'll take them both with me,' April says. 'It's almost the end of the day.'

The administration woman glances at the clock. Her only response is to pass April a note, which she completes.

As they head out into the hall, it's Catherine who is limping, Lara who is supporting her.

'Have you got your raincoats?' April asks.

'They're in the classroom,' Catherine tells her. 'Do you want me to run and get them?'

April glances from one to the other, shaking her head. 'Are you two scamming?'

'No!' they protest in unison.

She looks out across the deserted playground. Rain drips from the basketball hoops, a halo of silver, and the bitumen shines, wet and slippery smooth, like a sheet of satin. The roots from the Moreton Bay figs lift up great cracks in the surface, elephantine as they snake away from the smooth trunk of those giant trees, the only shelter from the downpour.

'Okay,' April tells them both, 'give me your bags. Catherine, you help Lara, or Lara, you help Catherine. We'll stop at the trees, and then my car is out the front.'

Of course they end up running.

'It's not that bad,' Lara says, pointing to Catherine's ankle.

'Well, that's excellent news,' April replies, winking at them. 'So no need for X-rays?'

Lara considers the offer for a moment. She doesn't mind a trip to hospital.

'Could we go to your house instead?'

April glances in the rear-vision mirror at them. 'Do you know where your dad is?'

They shrug in unison.

She leaves a message for him on his mobile and on his work phone, and then she tells them they are going to her place — 'for a feast'.

'What of?' Catherine wants to know.

'We'll see when we get there.'

It has been so long, and April starts to sing as she drives, silly made-up songs that slip and slide, until both the girls are giggling, and outside the rain drives down, the wipers going back and forth, back and forth, the demister loud, all of their voices rising and falling in unison as they skip from one song to the next with no need to name the tune.

THREE YEARS EARLIER

IT WASN'T LONG BEFORE Lawrence began to wonder whether he had gone temporarily insane.

Sleeping alone in his newly rented office, he couldn't let his mind alight for too long on any of his actions or words over the past week. Like hot coals, everything he had said and done was spread out before him — incendiary, molten, terrifying to witness.

He had a sleeping bag on the couch, the vinyl slippery and sweaty. In the middle of the night, he slid onto the floor, dragging a glass of water down with him and waking with a start from a sleep that had only ever hovered on the edge of any depth. Cold and wet, he sat up, back against the tin wall, which had now come to remind him of a prison cell, and the hollow inside him was vast.

'I want to go home,' he said to no one.

He stood, clutching the vinyl around him, and looked out the single window behind his desk to the emptiness of the street. Across the road, there was a light in the café, and inside he could see Leon, who lived upstairs, reading the paper. He ran the place alone, and lived by himself, his wife long dead. When he heard Lawrence was having 'home problems', he said he could use his shower in the morning.

'No worries by me,' he grunted each time Lawrence came

down the stairs and thanked him. 'You sort out soon.' He nodded when he said this, his eyes on Lawrence, an old man who knew the importance of a resolution.

But when all was burnt to char, there was no rebuilding, no return, no way home. Just waste, waste that Lawrence could never speak of, and shame that gripped his heart and his tongue, clammy and cold.

If it had been insanity — and who knows what insanity looks like or how it speaks — then he had been released from its clutches the moment he told April of his confession to Ester.

'Oh God,' was all she'd said. 'You don't love me. Why would you think that? Why would you say it?'

It was as though she'd pulled out a brick from the bottom of a pile, causing everything to tumble before his eyes. How could he have believed in the structure when it was so very flimsy?

The night before, he'd been bold. He'd put the girls to bed, and come back to the kitchen, where Ester sat, a half-finished bottle of red on the table in front of her, the grey-green of her eyes cool as she appraised him. She was the one who spoke first, her words the careful words of a therapist, all her solicitude useless in the face of the onslaught he was about to deliver, but she didn't know that. How could she?

'I feel we need to talk.'

'We do,' he agreed.

'I haven't been happy.' She looked across at him, about to continue, but he cut over her, his words coming out in a rush.

'I know,' he said. 'This isn't us. Or it's not me. I'm so glad you don't want it either —'

Her hand, which had been resting around the stem of her glass, withdrew. He wasn't observant enough to slow down, to let her take the lead. Exhausted and confused and afflicted by temporary insanity, he kept speaking, the words of a madman tripping over each other as he said he'd come to a realisation when he was at the river. He had loved her, oh how he had loved her, but they weren't right for each other. He knew that, and she knew that. He loved April. He shook his head with the wonder of it. Ester would be so much happier with someone else, someone who was more like her, and he too would be happier. They were alike, he and April. They were of the same spirit. It could work, he had even said. They could build a new structure, a different kind of family. It would be all right.

And there, at the edge of the precipice, he had foolishly failed to realise that the fall was calamitous. In those moments, she had been silent, confused, floundering, and then all the horror of his confession appeared to fill her, and she had pushed back her chair and rushed to the sink, where she had vomited.

Each morning, Lawrence woke wondering where he was. He opened his eyes to the corrugated tin, chalky grey, and the silence of his near-empty room. Sometimes he reached for Ester, certain that if he stretched a little further he would feel the smooth curve of her hip, and he would be able to curl in close to the place he now wanted to return to: one arm draped around her waist, breathing in the sweet lavender of her hair, the richness of her skin.

And if he stayed perfectly still, completely quiet, he might just will their footsteps, Catherine and Lara, both of them running down the hall, one skidding along the rug, followed by the slam of cupboard doors, the scrape of a stool along the ground. One pulling down every cereal packet from the cupboard, the other taking out bowls, glasses, spoons, milk, sometimes closing the fridge door behind her, sometimes not. And then he would shuffle into the kitchen, eyes still bleary from sleep, hoping his pyjama bottoms were tied up properly, telling them it was the weekend, a time for all sane people to 'sleep, sleeeeep little ones, go to sleeeeeeep, tick tock, tick tock' as he swung an imaginary chain in front of them, trying to hypnotise them, until one or the other obliged and pretended to collapse into a deep enchanted slumber, right there on the floor.

April was his only visitor in that first week.

She looked as bad as he felt.

'You fucked up,' she shouted at him, and she hit him, over and over again. 'It was a mistake. You should never have said anything.'

And he had nodded. Because she was right.

She looked around his room. 'How long have you been here?'

He told her.

She had cried. 'It's not just your life that's fucked up. It's mine, too.'

He pulled out a seat for her, letting her speak because it was a relief to hear someone else's troubles, even those so closely linked to his own, and it was a relief to see her, to see anyone. As she rolled them each a cigarette, he offered her a drink, which she refused at first, but then changed her mind about, pouring the whisky into a glass, the fire on the throat nowhere near enough to compensate for the heaviness in the pit of the stomach.

Ester hadn't spoken to either of them since he'd left.

'I need to see the girls,' he told April.

And he did. The ache was visceral.

'Have you called her?'

He shook his head. He had wanted to, lifting the phone to dial so often, but each time he had stopped, scraped bare by the knowledge of what he'd done.

'I'm sure she won't stop you.'

'I just feel so ashamed.'

And April stood up then, and told him she had to go.

It was two weeks before Hilary came to see him.

She was at the door when he returned from his morning coffee, and he almost went back around the corner, wanting to hide away until she was gone.

'Will you come in?' he offered, and she shook her head.

She had known for more than a fortnight. 'When Ester told me, I wanted to come around and set fire to you.' Her eyes were on his, harsh blue. 'I hated you for what you'd done to my girls. Imagine,' she said, 'if it were Catherine and Lara. Imagine.'

He could only look at the ground.

'I was incensed. I have never been so angry,' and she shook her head, wiping at the sting of a tear in the corner of her eye. 'Don't,' she said as he reached for her. 'I've been waking up most nights, imagining telling you how I felt. There were times when I thought I would drive around here at midnight, and pour it all out on you. All my rage. But I have to concentrate on helping my girls. That's what I needed to tell you. That's all I wanted to say.'

She looked straight at him, her fine-boned face fierce and sure, and then she nodded once, and turned and left, her walk brisk and erect, her back to him as he watched her go, alone in his doorway.

That night, he drove back to where he used to live, the place he still thought of as home although he knew he had no hope of ever returning. He sat in the car, two doors down, on the opposite side of the road. Inside the lights were on, but the curtains were drawn.

He could walk down the path now and open the door — he still had his key.

It was all a mistake, he would tell her. A brief loss of his mind. Surely she had to understand and forgive, surely this was what she dealt with daily — the mess we are all capable of, the possibility of an eruption always just beneath the skin? If she were her own client, wouldn't she suggest repair?

He imagined himself standing before her in the hallway,

uttering those words, laying himself bare, the eloquence he was capable of his to use, words unspooling like a ribbon to draw them both together again. And the vision was so strong, he let himself be carried by it, opening the car door without thinking, walking straight to the gate, past the frangipani he had planted when they first moved in, home again, key in his hand.

She had changed the locks.

It took him some moments before he realised this, the metal not slotting into the grooves, nothing fitting, and when the realisation had sunk in, he hammered on the door with his fists, a parody of a broken man, locked out of his own home, calling her name.

It was Catherine who opened the door, Lara right behind her.

'Daddy,' she screamed.

He knelt down low, arms wrapped around them, determined not to cry.

Ester stood in the hall, right behind them, back against the wall, eyes fixed on the ceiling.

'Can I take them with me?' he asked.

She nodded.

'We need to talk,' he said.

She nodded again.

When she eventually spoke it was to tell the girls that they were going to have dinner with their father, 'get your shoes on,' she said, waiting until they had run down the hall before turning to face him. 'Bring them back by nine,' she instructed.

He opened his mouth to speak, but she silenced him.

'Not now.' Her tone was curt. 'I will text you and set up a time. But I don't want to talk to you now.'

IN THE FIRST WEEK, Ester woke each night to find she had been crying in her sleep. She would sit up, the pillow damp, the silence of the house so suffocating that she was afraid of not being able to breathe.

It was just a bad dream, she would tell herself. But it wasn't.

He had fucked April, and he had gone.

She took everything he owned and put it in the garage.

'I'd like to set a match to it all,' she told her friend, Sophia.

Sophia had never really liked Lawrence, which was why Ester sought out her company in those first few weeks. She avoided most of her other friends, particularly those who would try to reason with her, or, worse still, might let her know they had seen Lawrence. Sophia was safe. She had worked with Lawrence briefly when she'd been between jobs, which she frequently was. Sophia was sullen and moody, according to Lawrence. She was rude to clients. He'd told her there wasn't enough work to keep her on, and she'd been furious, coming round to their house one night and declaring that Lawrence was a smooth-talking asshole, a nasty liar. She'd stood in the doorway, her long black hair framing her pale face, her voice loud, her skin and her breath reeking of booze.

'Look at you,' she'd said. 'In your comfortable life, not giving a shit about anyone but yourself. You used to be an artist.'

And so they hadn't seen her for a long time after that, but

when Ester bumped into her outside the local café, she'd asked her if she wanted to have a coffee.

'You were right,' she said. 'He *was* a smooth-talking asshole.'

And all that she'd once found repellent in Sophia — her dark intensity, her simmering anger, her snide remarks about everyone they knew — became attractive.

Sophia had been a dancer and a choreographer who'd never quite made it. She had a teenage son, who spent all his time locked in his room on the computer. She had very few friends. She came to visit frequently, happy to drink Ester's wine and voice her disgust at everyone and everything.

Ester showed her the pile of Lawrence's clothes and books in the garage.

'You should burn them,' Sophia encouraged her. 'Here, I'll help you.' She stepped forward, slightly unsteady in her high-heeled black leather boots, and began to pour the remains of the bottle of white wine she was holding over the lot. She took her cigarette out of her mouth and threw it on top.

Nothing happened.

She was about to bend down with her lighter when Ester stopped her. She scooped the clothes up in her arms, the smell of wine and Lawrence and her own tears pressed close as she told Sophia to just leave her alone. 'This is mine,' she said. 'I'll get rid of it in the way I want to.'

They were both drunk.

Sophia glared at her. 'You were always alike,' she said. 'Both of you thought you were better than everyone else. You deserved each other. And now look at you. All alone and clutching the clothes of a bastard who fucked your sister.'

That night Ester went to April's, barging through the door, sweeping everything onto the floor, trying to pull curtains off the railings, ripping pictures from the walls.

'Why can't I trash your life the way you trash mine?' she shouted.

And then, as April tried to contain her, to hold her, the fury of her anger so pure she could not bear to be touched, she pushed her sister away and told her she never wanted to see her again. Ever.

The next morning, Ester booked an appointment with Victoria.

Each day she called, oscillating between rage and sorrow, see-sawing up and down and up and down until, on the tenth day, Victoria stopped her.

It was enough. You could only burn out of control for so long. *Turn down the oxygen*, Victoria said. *Let's start focusing on the practical.*

The clipped directness of Victoria's tone silenced Ester, her words of fury and self-pity halted before she had a chance to utter them.

'Of course, you've been angry,' Victoria continued, her tone smooth, not dissimilar to the modulation Ester would use when she wanted to offer firm, detached sympathy laced with the implicit instruction that it was time to take those first steps in a different direction. 'But is that anger achieving anything other than very brief momentary relief?'

'No.' Ester sounded like a child. 'But it's bloody good.'

'There were times when you spoke to me about a desire to change your relationship with Lawrence. I'm sure you didn't want it to be changed in this way, but there's no reason why you can't take some control of the situation, instead of letting it control you.'

And so began the many sessions that Ester liked to term her 'lessons in how to talk to her husband'. There were even practice attempts, with Victoria pretending to be Lawrence while delivering techniques Ester could use to stay calm as they tried to negotiate all that needed to be divvied up: bank accounts, the house, time with the girls, means of communicating in the future, even the redrafting of wills. The business of dismantling a marriage was like the business of organising a funeral, a distraction for which she could be grateful.

And so she made lists, pages and pages of them, all saved in a file she labelled 'the end'. What she didn't tell Victoria was that she also saved letters in this file, long missives in which she let her anger off the leash again, sometimes her sorrow as well, correspondence addressed to both Lawrence and April, never to be sent.

She also didn't speak of the dreams she had.

She had loved him once, and it was to this love that she returned in her sleep. There was no conversation, just the deep slate of his eyes on her, his mouth warm and alive, his skin, the sensation of being wrapped in another. It was like she had submerged herself, and the sweetness of it was like a drug, a haze that she did not want to emerge from. But she did. She always did. Waking, gasping for air, the sorrow right there in her ribs, separating the cage that encased her, pulling her apart.

Sometimes she did not know if the heaviness of the loss would ever lighten.

'It will,' Victoria assured her, leading her back to the practicalities.

Finally, Ester was ready to talk with him.

As she dressed herself that morning, she remembered the care with which she would choose her clothes when they'd first started seeing each other, the shiny glitter of knowing he was hers, the desire to just take him home and get him into bed, and afterwards to lie there, the silkiness of his skin, the slow roll of their talk, all of her a-sparkle with him.

So long ago.

And so sullied now.

She brushed her hair, and told herself to be brave.

Courage, Maurie used to tell her when she was in a panic about having to give a speech at school, or present her work for a crit. 'You have far more strength than you ever give yourself credit for.'

It was not that she feared he would argue with her about all they needed to discuss. He was ashamed, and would agree to what she wanted. It was the threat of falling apart again — the fierceness of her anger, the blackness of her sorrow still too present.

And so she walked to the café she had chosen, wanting a public place to meet, somewhere she was less likely to shatter. She had her list in her bag, carefully worked out arrangements that would be unlikely to cause dispute. As she felt for the piece of paper, she wondered whether she would vomit, the nausea so high and dense she realised she might not even be able to open her mouth and speak.

So she stopped, her skin clammy, her throat dry as she tried to utter a simple word, a practice 'hello', her voice, when it eventually came, harsh and grating.

I can't do this, she thought.

She caught sight of herself in the shop window, a stranger she didn't know. A woman about to try and meet up with someone who had once held her safe and loved, only to betray her in a way she could not forgive.

I don't have to do this, she realised.

And she sat on a low brick wall, the realisation that she could just turn her back on this meeting both light and terrifying.

I'm not ready, she told herself.

At the end of the street, she could see Lawrence's car. He was already there. She tried to imagine herself walking in, staying upright, opening her mouth, uttering adult words, looking at him, eyes clear and open — and it was all so impossible to visualise that she knew she had no choice.

Have had to cancel, she wrote, fingers trembling as she tapped on the letters, frequently missing the one she wanted, the predictive text quick to make sense of the jumble she was writing. *Will email this evening with proposed arrangements.*

She pressed 'send', relieved as the message turned green.

It was going to be a long time before she could talk to him.

Perhaps it would never happen again.

And the solid weight of that sorrow pressed down, bruising and ugly, cloaking the shape of her, close.

NOW

THE LAST TIME ESTER saw Steven was a fortnight ago. She had gone into the city to complete the second part of the mediation course — a half-day workshop. She hadn't known whether he would be in this group, or another.

'Ask him,' her friend Marta had encouraged. 'I'm sure you could find him on the internet and email him.'

Of course she could. She'd found him already, googling him the day after their drink together, surprised by his picture on his website. It wasn't how she recalled him. It was a black and white studio photograph, a bit like a magazine shot, showing him in a grey T-shirt and jeans, sitting on a chair and leaning forward, eager to listen. There was something fake about it, and, embarrassed, she closed the page immediately, only to reopen it later that night, a glass of wine by her side.

She read his bio with the same degree of discomfort.

'Steven Lansdowne works closely with clients to help them achieve their full potential. He provides individual coaching sessions for executives and runs highly acclaimed leadership courses.

'Steven began his working life as an actor, appearing in films, commercials, and on stage. In his late twenties, he completed an

MBA, with a major in psychology, and commenced a successful career in change management consultancy, working with companies in the finance industry. During this time, he discovered the importance of tapping into people potential, harnessing the full creative power of the individual to fully realise success.'

Hilary would hate it.

Maurie would have hated it too.

She trawled though old entries under Steven's name, digging up short films, television series, and plays he'd appeared in years earlier. A couple were on YouTube, and she sat back, slightly embarrassed, as she watched — his roles usually those of a pretty boy, a minor love interest at the sideline of the story. He was someone who'd been just a few shades away from becoming a recognised actor at the same time as she'd been letting go of painting. Feeling as though she was spying, she shut down the computer.

Ester remembered the period of giving up painting. Her work was formalistic, strong architectural shapes that repeated themselves with an order that never varied, very different to the seemingly chaotic riot of her father's canvases. Hilary had never been a fan, but she had nonetheless been dismayed by Ester's decision. Maurie had been more sympathetic.

'You can paint,' he'd told her. 'But so can a lot of people.'

She had waited for him to continue.

'You're always going to battle with being my daughter. Sometimes you'll be lauded for it, at other times you'll be pilloried. In order to overcome that, you'll need a certain "fuck you" temperament, and a real desire to be known for your work. I'm not sure that you have either.'

He was right.

She'd glanced across at him. 'I'd like to do something completely different,' she'd confessed. 'Something that's just mine.'

He'd understood.

'It'll mean I'll be a Sunday painter.' She'd smiled at him, knowing that he had little time or patience for weekend artists.

He'd grinned. 'Ah, but you'll be different to all those other Sunday painters,' he'd told her. 'You're my daughter.' He'd folded her close, and told her he'd keep a space for her in his studio, whenever she wanted to use it.

He didn't, of course. The area that she'd occupied was soon filled with his work, and she would laugh when she came to visit him, referring to her ever shrinking corner — a space that he would hastily clean in embarrassment, telling her he was just using it temporarily.

Marta continued to urge her to ring Steven.

She'd been a friend of Ester's and Lawrence's, and, like so many of their friends, she'd chosen to stay with Ester during the split. She looked at Steven's bio on his website but was quick to dismiss Ester's unease. 'A little cheesy, yes,' she'd agreed, pouring herself another wine, 'but he'd have to present himself in a certain way to get work. I mean, look at you —' and she flicked over to Ester's homepage. 'All caring and sharing.'

'Which I am,' Ester insisted.

'I know. But you're more than that.'

Ester tried to articulate her fear a little more clearly. 'What do they call them now? "A player?" That's what he looks like — a player. Smooth and charming.' She shook her head, her words barely audible as she uttered them: 'Like Lawrence.'

Marta looked at her. 'Does this mean you'll dismiss anyone who's handsome?'

'I probably should,' Ester smiled. She remembered the man she'd met on the internet date so long ago, and how quick she'd been to write him off. He was the type she should be considering, she told Marta. Someone safe. She sat on the floor, and looked up at the ceiling. It had been so long, and she was terrified.

Marta slid down the wall and sat next to her. She took Ester's hand in her own and squeezed it. 'Of course you are,' she said gently.

Ester sent him an email in the end — carefully worded, asking him if he was going to the second part of the course on Friday, and if so, did he want to have lunch afterwards?

He never replied.

And so she turned up on the day, hoping he wouldn't be there because she felt so foolish. They took their seats at the round table, the moderator in the middle, and just as she began to speak, he arrived. Seeing her, he raised a hand in greeting, a smile on his face as he tried to squeeze a chair in next to her.

She nodded, hoping she wasn't blushing, and then looked steadily at her notepad as she continued to write. At the end of the session, he asked her if she wanted to have lunch.

'Oh.' Her confusion was obvious.

'You can't?'

She shook her head. 'When I didn't hear from you, I thought you weren't coming today.'

And now *he* looked confused. He'd never received an email from her. He checked his junk mail on his iPad, and there it was — her carefully worded invitation. She couldn't watch him open and read it.

'Love to,' he said.

They talked over a bowl of soup, her nerves soon gone. He asked her if she was religious, or voted Liberal. 'Possibly insurmountable problems if you say yes to either.'

She shook her head. 'What about you? Do you go shooting for a hobby? Maybe we need to give each other a questionnaire.' She smiled, and told him she'd lived with a pollster.

'He came to hate it more and more.' She was about to

continue, to talk about the corrosive effect it had on Lawrence, but she stopped herself, wary of being one of those people who talked too much about their past relationship.

'I've never voted Liberal. I had a teenage flirtation with Jesus that ended when the guy who ran the youth group was outed for kissing just about every girl over thirteen. I thought about Buddhism briefly, but never seriously.' She narrowed her eyes. 'Do I pass?'

He nodded.

'Be careful,' she added. 'I could now do something just as bad as vote Liberal or go to church. I could bring out an iPad covered in a pink fluffy case with "Princess" written on it.'

'Possibly worse,' he agreed. His phone beeped but he ignored it. 'And I've never owned a gun, or used one,' he promised.

She broke herself a piece of bread, and asked him to tell her more about himself, hating her words as soon as she uttered them. She sounded like a therapist. 'Not your problems, of course,' she hastened to add. 'Or at least not the real, real, real ones.'

His eyes were direct, a gaze that she tried to meet. 'Do you want me to start with my childhood, or leap straight to my first marriage?'

She didn't mean to cough into her water, and then it was like a choking sound, embarrassing and foolish. 'Can I ask how many marriages you've had?'

'Are you worried I'm one of those hopeless romantics who gets married on a weekly basis?'

She nodded.

'I've only been married once. And it was to a friend of mine who had a girlfriend in Australia and wanted to be able to stay. What about you?'

She held up a finger, still chewing on her bread.

'Is that an "up yours"? Or a one?'

'One marriage — the pollster. We have two daughters — twins. But you know that.'

'Did it end a long time ago?'

She nodded, not wanting the conversation to veer back to Lawrence.

He asked if she wanted a coffee, and she said yes, relieved at the chance to shift the talk in another direction.

'I didn't know your father was Maurie Marcel.' He looked embarrassed then. 'I did a bit of research,' he confessed. 'I'm sorry. I feel foolish now.'

She smiled, although she didn't confess to her own internet trawling.

'I actually have one of his paintings. I bought it when I got my first paid work as an actor. I've always loved it.' And then he shook his head and smiled again, laughing slightly. 'I almost made a worse fool of myself,' he told her, holding two fingers up, touching. 'This close to saying you'd have to come over and see it sometime.'

'The old etchings line,' she grinned. 'Got used in art school far too often.'

'I can imagine.'

She liked him. Even more than she had the last time she met. Her skin rushed with effervescent sparks of joy and nerves; it was as though each sense had been turned up a notch.

Strange, she thought, *how readily we forget the intensity of attraction, how impossible it becomes to recall.* She'd felt it once before with Lawrence, and years earlier with Matthew, who'd been a sculptor in the year above her at art school. She'd adored Matthew, plotting and planning what she did and where she went in the hope of bumping into him. She took him home several times, back to the share house she'd lived in in Redfern, her bedroom up the top, two French doors opening onto a dust-caked balcony and the constant hum of traffic. They would lie on her bed under the swinging rice-paper lightshade and kiss for hours, his mouth like silk on hers, his pale hair sweeping across her cheek. And then he would fall asleep. Always.

'He's a junkie,' her housemate told her. 'I can't believe you didn't know. Everyone knows.'

She was right. Ester saw the marks on his arms the next time, the tiny black pinpricks of his pupils as he smiled lazily at her before once again drifting away, fast asleep next to her. He'd stolen her rent money twice. She hadn't wanted to admit it to herself, but it was hard to deny. And still she'd loved him, sure that he would change, furious with her housemates when they said they didn't want him round anymore (the kitty had also disappeared).

He didn't even tell her when he checked into Odyssey House; it was a friend of a friend who explained why he was nowhere to be found. He moved to Melbourne soon afterwards, and it wasn't until years later that she learnt of his overdose, the news saddening her more than she would have expected, the memory of her feelings for him enough to take her back there, briefly.

She looked at Steven sitting opposite her, and told him that she'd never had any regrets about giving up art. 'I thought I would have. Which only goes to show I wasn't cut out for it in the first place. I guess Maurie knew that.'

Steven's father had been a used-car salesman.

'Of the worst type,' he confessed. 'He even sold clapped-out pieces of junk to friends of mine, and then refused to give back their money when they wouldn't start. We were always going from boom to bust — living in a mansion one week, fleeing creditors the next. He died of a heart attack two years ago.'

Ester looked at him. 'And your mother?'

'Family life sent her to an early grave.' He grimaced.

It was strange shaping your life for someone else, she thought.

Here they were, both in the business of extracting such stories from clients, spinning tales across the table, tossing them forth to snare each other.

In the days following her lunch with Steven, she resisted the urge to contact him again.

'But what if he's lost my email, or thinks that I wasn't keen?' After four days of waiting, she told Marta she couldn't do it any longer. She felt embarrassed by her eagerness. She'd seen clients ruin new relationships by rushing in, giving too much too soon, and she feared behaving like that because it had been so very long since she'd felt this way.

Marta was the only friend she'd told. She'd come over to help Ester put together an Ikea chest of drawers for the girls' room. She'd worked as an assistant for a sculptor who made public art pieces, and had developed a practical competence that most of Ester's other friends lacked. Lawrence used to call on her too, asking her to help him rehang doors and fix window sashes on their old house, always determined to do it himself, only to find that he didn't have the skills he pretended to have. Marta would take over, dismantling his initial work and teasing him mercilessly as she started from scratch.

She had the instructions laid out on the floor, and was reading through them as Ester spoke.

'Perhaps I should just send him an email?'

'No.' Marta insisted. She tapped the hammer gently on the side of Ester's foot. 'No. No. No. Subliminal messaging from me to you. If you try to send that email you'll feel those hammer blows, and they'll stop you.'

'I don't think so,' Ester told her. 'Although, I will feel foolish and wish I could retract the message as soon as I've pressed send.'

She counted the bolts in her hand. 'Have you got the other one?'

Marta did.

'I had a client once who told me that finding a man was like finding real estate.'

Marta rolled her eyes.

'You have to put in your offer straight away or someone else will come and nab it.' Ester chewed on her bottom lip. 'What if she was right?'

'So what is he?'

Ester didn't understand.

'In real-estate language?'

Ester laughed. 'Harbourside. Off-street parking. Custom joinery. Seamless indoor-outdoor flow.'

'An infinity-edge lap pool?'

'Oh god, I hope not. Far too common.'

She stepped nervously from foot to foot, unable to keep still, her heart too quick, all of her on edge with the potential for disappointment, the potential of not hearing from him again, of finding out he wasn't interested after all. The potential that she had fucked it up. She looked down at the ground and took a deep breath. 'I'm sorry,' she said. 'I will rein it in.' And she picked up the hammer and tapped the back of her hand three times lightly. 'Time to try and let it go.'

'And Lawrence?' Marta smiled at her. 'What was he?'

Ester shook her head. 'One of those new developments that seems so good on the prospectus — and then turns out to be nothing but trouble.'

She bent down to hold the side and the back of the chest together, trying to keep the edge steady while Marta bolted one into the other.

'And what is it you want?' Marta put the drill down and looked at Ester. 'Holiday cottage? Flashy city home? Rustic? Modern?'

'Something where the work's already been done,' Ester

eventually said. 'I really don't want to have to renovate.'

'Can't say I want that for you either. I'd be the one doing most of the work.'

Behind them, Ester's phone beeped. She'd put it on alert so that she could hear emails when they arrived. 'Can I look?'

Marta wagged her finger in admonishment, and then shooed her away. 'Go,' she told her.

And she did, her squeal ringing out from the kitchen to the girl's bedroom, followed by a peal of laughter — loud, embarrassed.

'I am so sorry,' she apologised, leaping up and down, phone in hand. 'I'm behaving like an adolescent. I know I am. I seem to have no control.' She held the phone out to Marta, the message open on the screen.

Lovely having lunch last week — want to have dinner on Friday?

Marta took the phone from her. 'You can reply when I'm gone,' she told her. 'Not until then.' And then she leant forward and kissed her on the cheek. 'I'm glad for you,' she said. 'I really am. Just don't buy without getting all those reports — pest inspection. Building. All of them.'

And Ester had nodded solemnly, eyes wide, as she looked at the phone lying on the floor, all of her a-wonder with the human capacity to fall again and again and again, clutching fast to the sheer beauty of hope in the faith it would somehow stay buoyant.

Today, the rain falls steadily, and she sits in her kitchen, her phone call to Victoria finished, wanting to hold in the incandescence of joy and excitement, to let it burn off the last vestige of the shame and sadness of Lawrence.

It glows.

BEING A CHRISTIAN underpins all of Edmund's actions. It is the foundation for who he is and how he should behave. It obviously takes precedence over any employment contract he may have with Lawrence, including any confidentiality obligations under that contract.

Lawrence reads the email several times.

Edmund does not wish to punish Lawrence — it is neither his role nor his intention. He believes Lawrence should be the one to confess to altering the polls. He has therefore decided to give him 48 hours to come clean to Paul. After this time has passed, Edmund himself intends to write to the editor — regardless of whether Lawrence has confessed or not — to assure him he had no knowledge of the numbers being altered. Needless to say, he no longer wishes to work for Lawrence, and he requests full payout of all moneys owing under their contract. In addition, he encloses the final poll figures.

Lawrence reads the email again.

Edmund is a sanctimonious fuckwit.

But perhaps there is a chance of salvaging other business if Paul can be convinced to stay quiet. After all, they are terminating their agreement with him anyway, and there is no reason why Paul would want to damage his own reputation. No one else need know. He just has to be careful about how he words his confession. He does not want Paul to feel that Lawrence has been making a fool of him. It is delicate.

He sits back in his chair and closes his eyes. Of course he can't confess. It would be professional suicide. He could lie, though. Why not? He does it well. Just pretend that Edmund and he have had a dispute, and Edmund is trying to bury him in a scandal. But what if Edmund sends through evidence? He stands up now, his heart beating like a hard stone in his chest.

He had never envisaged his life here. Middle-aged, divorced, unhappy with his work. It is a cliché of which he is ashamed. And now he is on the brink of being professionally ruined.

What was it he had wanted? He finds it so hard to remember. He opens his eyes to see himself reflected in the rain-streaked window, and flinches. He has fucked up, again and again, and he puts his head in his hands, wishing he could dissolve who he is, go back to who he once was.

He had loved music, but even he was wise enough to know he'd never had much talent. He'd loved drugs — still didn't mind them if the truth be known. Ditto women. He shakes his head. If he is ruined, there really isn't much to draw on in terms of setting up a new life.

Ester used to encourage him to quit. She'd make suggestions — politics, journalism, policy research — all of which he'd dismiss. Eventually, she gave up. What would she tell him to do now, he wonders, and he can see her, horrified at first by the mess he has found himself in, and then not surprised, because this is what Lawrence does: he lies, he cheats, and he fucks up.

As he glances down at his desk, the first thing he sees is Hilary's number scrawled on a piece of paper next to his computer.

He keys in each of the digits, and then hangs up before he presses call. Despite knowing it is unlikely she still wants to berate him (why now after such a long period of silence?), she makes him nervous. She always has.

The first time Ester took him home for lunch, Hilary failed to join them. Maurie cooked, grilling fish with his usual enthusiasm, and making at least four salads — far more than the three of them could possibly eat. He had discovered kingfish, he told them — 'is there any taste more perfect?' — and had decided he was going to eat it every day.

'Who knows, I might even trim down.' He stood, inspecting his girth in the reflection of the window, before turning to Lawrence to tell him that it was only in the last year he'd found himself unable to wear the same pants he had worn since he was in his thirties. 'Soft moleskin. They've never worn out — just become more pleasing with the years. Like your mother.' He winked at Ester, who rolled her eyes before asking where Hilary was.

'She knew we were coming.'

Maurie pointed up at the studio, and then bellowed her name out loudly.

There was no answer.

'She's tetchy,' he eventually explained, his voice loud enough for Hilary — perhaps even the whole neighbourhood — to hear. 'She seems to think I failed to tell her about today. Which of course I didn't.'

'I'll go up.' Ester beckoned Lawrence to follow her, which he did with some trepidation.

Hilary was at her desk, headphones on, unable to hear them until Ester lifted them from her head and asked her if she was going to join them.

'This is Lawrence,' she'd said, slightly shy as she introduced him.

Hilary had turned to look at him. Her blue eyes were sharp, her pale hair escaping a tangled knot at the back; she wore no make-up, and little jewellery, just a startlingly large silver ring, heavy in his hand as she reached out to greet him.

'I'm too busy,' she told them both. 'He knew I was planning on working all weekend, so I'm afraid you'll just have to eat without me.'

'Just for half an hour?' Ester asked.

But Hilary had already put her headphones on and turned back to the screen.

Ester sighed. 'I'm sorry,' she told Lawrence loudly, 'my parents seem to be locked in some childish fight.'

The headphones came off again, and Hilary turned to face Ester. 'I have a film to finish by Wednesday. I'm sorry I can't eat with you — but if he stays around,' she nodded briefly in Lawrence's direction, 'which remains to be seen, there'll be plenty of other opportunities for lunch.'

On the way home, Ester apologised for Hilary's rudeness. 'It was nothing to do with you. It's part of a long, ongoing war she's been having with Maurie about the lack of respect he gives to her work. Which isn't entirely true. Although if he'd had an exhibition to finish, he wouldn't have been there — and no one would have questioned it.'

Lawrence had grown used to Hilary over the years, although he was never entirely sure of how she felt about him.

Shortly after he and Ester had returned home from Paris with the girls, she'd taken him aside and told him he needed to 'change your act — pronto'.

She was worried about Ester not getting enough time to work.

'You earn enough to pay for extra childcare,' she told him.

Ester was quite happy working part-time, he replied. There was no need for her to go back full-time.

Hilary narrowed her eyes. 'Is that you saying this, or her?'

He lost his temper then, asking Hilary a similar question. If Ester was unhappy with the arrangement, she hadn't expressed it to him. And if it was simply Hilary who was unhappy with how they were living, then it was none of her business, and he had no interest in listening to her complaints.

She hadn't flinched. 'Fair enough,' she agreed.

He'd shaken his head. 'You're incredible,' he'd muttered.

She smiled then. 'She's my daughter. And I don't want to see her, years down the track, with regrets.'

'We all have regrets,' he countered.

She looked at him, surprised by his response. 'I don't,' she'd said, and she had seemed completely genuine.

She doesn't, Ester had agreed when he'd relayed the conversation to her later that night. 'She loves Maurie, her work, us — she doesn't hanker after anything or wish she'd lived a different life. She's genuinely happy with where she's at.'

'She's possibly one of the only people in the western world who could lay claim to that,' he'd replied. And he'd raised his glass. 'To Hilary.'

He dials her number again, knowing he should have called back straight away. What if something is wrong with Ester? It has been so long since they have spoken. If she was sick, she might even not tell him, he thinks — although surely she would for the sake of the girls? He is suddenly overwhelmed by a desire to see her, to have her centre him, right him, and then he shakes his head. Ester wouldn't want to know about putting him back on track. Not anymore.

Outside, the sky is low, darkening as another downpour builds. He glances across and sees Leon closing up, pulling the blind down on the front door of the café. He struggles for business most days of the week — the neighbourhood is now home to four or five fashionable new cafés — and today is hopeless. Lawrence wonders how he survives.

And then, after four rings, just when he is about lose his nerve, Hilary finally answers. Her voice is less certain than usual, the faintness heightening his anxiety so that he speaks without waiting for her to say any more than his name — 'Is Ester all right?' — his words cutting through any awkwardness.

'She's fine,' Hilary assures him. 'Unless there's something she's been keeping from me?'

And now it's Lawrence's turn to reassure, telling Hilary that if there were, he wouldn't know. She, Hilary, is far more likely to have heard. 'You called me,' he says. 'Asking me to ring you. I'm sorry I took so long. It's been one of those days. Terrible.'

She doesn't feign interest in what's been happening for him. Even if they had been on friendly terms she may not have asked him, assuming he would tell her if it mattered.

'I need you to help me,' she says. 'I don't want to discuss this on the phone. I need to see you.'

The next downpour has begun. Everything heaving with the weight of it, slanting sheets of rain, and across the road, a man tries to shelter under the awning over Leon's front door, but it is hopeless. The rain drenches him, his jeans darkening, his coat sodden. The drumming against the tin is so loud, Lawrence isn't sure if he has heard her correctly. He doesn't know how to respond.

'This is important,' she tells him.

Of course it is. She has never been one for just calling him to have a chat, and he laughs nervously as he tells her he gathered as much.

She cuts over him. 'I'm dying,' she says.

And he is appalled as he wonders why she needs to tell him — what does this have to do with him? He stands now, trying to move somewhere where he can hear more clearly, but also because he cannot sit still, he is feeling ill, and he doesn't know why.

He begins to utter a response, words of 'how awful', or something similarly pathetic, when once again she stops him from continuing.

'If you could come to my house and we could talk?'

He is shaking his head, mouthing the word 'no' and pressing the phone to his ear, when she utters the word that surprises him most of all.

'Please,' she says, and in that instant, the rain stops, as suddenly as it began, the clarity of her plea sharp and sudden, the only word he has truly heard.

'Of course,' he tells her, his panic dissipating as quickly as the downpour. And in the silence that follows, he looks out at the sky, still again, and asks her if she is at the same address.

She is.

'Do you want me to come now?'

She does.

And he is not to tell Ester or April. Not yet.

He stands alone at his window, his face reflected back at him, older than he ever expects — lines across his skin, greying hair, mouth drawn — and he watches himself as he tells her he will be there soon.

APRIL HAS PLAYED the record six times now, but they want to hear it again: 'I Can't Stand The Rain', louder each time, all three of them singing with the chorus, Catherine abandoning herself to the performance, wailing with the sadness of the refrain.

'Again,' Lara demands.

But this time, April shakes her head.

'I think we need something a little happier,' she tells them, searching through her old vinyl, the record covers a smear of colour across the floor. *It's on an old hits album, later than 'Ripper',* she thinks, and then there it is — an eighties disco collection she used to love.

'Now this is a good one,' she tells the girls.

The needle crackles, sliding round and round the edge. She lifts it and places it right in the groove this time, the music building and building until those first words take it to its crescendo —

Hi, Hi — We're your weather girls and have we got nooooos for you!

They love it — and of course they want it again and again, each of them familiar with all the words by the third hearing, Lara throwing her head back and singing to the sky, Catherine taking her pretend microphone and working the room.

When it ends for the fifth time, Lara wants to know what it means.

'Who'd want it to rain men?' she asks.

April shrugs. 'Sex-starved women?'

'That's gross,' Lara tells her. 'Really gross.' She looks out the window, a huge arched pane of glass looking over grey rooftops, the heavy sky low over the charcoal sliver of harbour, a strip of metal shimmering dully. 'Imagine if they were coming out of the clouds,' Lara says. 'They'd squash everything.'

April can only agree. 'But some of them might survive. And they might be fun.' She sniffs the air. 'I believe a cake may be cooked.' There's a warm sweetness, the scent of molten chocolate, and it's good.

'Perfect,' she says — and it is.

Her capacity to cook is something that always surprises people. She used to make the meals with Maurie, neither of them afraid to experiment, both of them with a nose for balance — 'when it comes to food,' April would add ruefully, 'but nothing else.'

Lara hovers, ready to stick her finger right in the centre, but April slaps her away, tickling her under the arm as she does so. 'Let it cool,' she says. 'Just a bit.'

It's 3 o'clock. She needs to call Lawrence again, but her phone is nowhere to be found.

'Here it is,' Catherine tells her, pointing to the landline long since disconnected.

'Doesn't work,' April replies.

'Then why do you keep it?'

She shrugs.

'Okay,' she tells them. 'Our mission is simple. Locate the communication device. If you find it, you win an extra piece for yourself and your sister.'

'What happens if *you* find it?' Catherine asks.

'I'll have to cut an extra piece for Ester.'

Lara rolls her eyes. 'What would be the point? It's not like you could give it to her.'

This is true. 'Maybe one day,' April tells her. 'I could put it in the freezer until then.' She looks around the room, hands on her hips, practiced in quickly scanning the chaos as a means of finding what she's lost. Sometimes it works immediately.

'Ah ha.' She had left it in a sensible spot. Hall table, next to her keys.

Lawrence answers on the third ring. He is in the car, he tells her, static making it difficult to hear as she asks him whether he got her message. 'I have the girls,' she tries to explain. 'It's complicated, but they are totally fine. I can bring them to you when you get home.'

He is heading in her direction, he replies. He can pick them up — if she doesn't mind keeping them for a little longer.

Of course she doesn't. 'It's lovely to see them again,' she says, but the call has disconnected, or at least this is what she'd like to presume, and not that he's hung up on her.

'There's no need for you to avoid me,' she'd once said to him, and she'd meant it, once her horror over his confession had subsided, and the cold chill of shame passed. 'We may as well try and be friends.'

The sadness of knowing they might have loved each other was always present, and even now there were times when she would wake from a dream of him, surprised by the intensity of her longing. But she was always quick to push it aside, to give it no air, trying for a more pragmatic assessment of their relationship. If there had been no obstacle — and when they first met, there had been none — would they have chosen each other? And would they have lasted? Of course not, she would tell herself. They would have enjoyed a period of drug-and-alcohol-fuelled days together, only to eventually sicken of the excess towards which they both tended to drift.

She'd had brief affairs with men like him. She knew what

happened. They were often drawn to her, sure that she would let them be who they wanted to be, that she wouldn't try and constrain them. But after an intense period of wild unadulterated fun, there was no net holding them together, no substance to anchor any connection between them, and it was over.

April stands in the doorway to her kitchen, where the girls are leaning together, both tall and slender, long limbs in school tracksuits smeared with flour and cocoa from the baking, tangled hair escaping pigtails. They concentrate as they serve up the cake, carefully cutting even slices — one for each of them, two for April, and an extra plate also with two slices.

April used to have them to stay when they were little. Ester would drop them off, each with a carefully packed bag containing neatly folded pyjamas, clean underpants, and toiletries. Her instructions were lengthy — bed times, number of stories, toilet routines, tooth brushing, hair brushing, sugar rationing. After the first time, April simply pretended to listen.

'And I'm trying to get them to sleep on their own,' Ester told her as she'd left. 'So if they get into bed with you, it'd be great if you could take them back to their own room.'

April had nodded earnestly, failing to tell Ester that she didn't actually have another bed for them to go to. The one in the spare room was covered with old guitars and clothes she'd been intending to donate to someone whenever she could figure out who might want them.

She always slept with both the girls. One on each side. Lavender shampoo and sweet milky skin, warm arms and legs tangled around her own. She would wake to them chattering, sometimes to each other, sometimes to her, and she wanted to drink them up, all of them — their little white teeth, clear eyes, and their breath, as fresh as water.

No longer seeing them had hurt.

She clears the records to one side of the lounge room floor and spreads a deep red blanket across the ground, scattering cushions around the edge so that they can have a picnic.

Ester had once asked her if she wanted to have children of her own. April had told her how much she loved them, that looking after them was never a chore — and she had meant it. It had been a rare moment when they had sat and talked, the girls still having their mid-morning nap when Ester had come to pick them up.

April said she found it hard to imagine herself as a mother. It had never been a vision for herself.

'But you'd be good at it,' Ester had replied with what seemed to be genuine enthusiasm.

'Really?'

'Yes,' Ester had continued, and she had looked around April's apartment — last night's dinner dishes still in front of the television, papers scattering in the breeze through the window, brilliant yellow daffodils stuffed into a vase with half-dead roses, a pile of clothes by the front door. 'You're so good with chaos.'

April shakes her head as she remembers.

Now, as Lara carries in two plates, one for herself and one for April — with two slices on it — she asks April if they should put Ester's pieces straight in the freezer. She has milk around her mouth, a slender line of white fur across the pale pink of her upper lip, and chocolate crumbs along her fingers. Behind her, Catherine also waits for April's answer.

'Or we could just take it home with us and give it to her?' she suggests.

April smiles at them both. 'It might be a bit silly to freeze it,' she eventually says. 'Besides, I'm not sure if your mother even likes my chocolate cake. And as it was me who lost the phone, I probably shouldn't win a prize for finding it.'

'So can we eat her pieces now?' Catherine asks.

April nods, her mouth full of cake.

'Is Daddy going to pick us up?' Lara wants to know.

He is, April tells them.

'So we can't stay the night?'

She shakes her head, knowing the questions are heading in a direction that should be avoided. And so she reaches behind her for a record and tells them that they are going to play a game. 'It's called disco queen,' she says.

They wait for her to continue.

'Follow me,' she tells them, standing and beckoning towards the open door of her bedroom. 'Your wardrobe and make-up await you.'

ESTER HAS BEEN seeing Sarah and Daniel for almost six weeks now, and yet she has surprisingly few pages of notes. Reading over the little she's written just confirms what she knows. They're stuck — the three of them, really — wheels grinding round and round, mud splattering on all of them. If she is truthful, she dreads these sessions. She doesn't particularly like Sarah. In fact, to be more honest, she actively dislikes her.

It was Sarah who contacted her first, booking a session for herself and Daniel. Ester chatted to her on the telephone for some time, trying to get an indication of what it was they were wanting from counselling. Sarah talked a lot, breathlessly skipping from topic to topic, leaping from Medicare details to the intimacy of her sex life with no pause between the two, her words rapid, the link between each sentence so tangled that Ester felt like someone had upended a basket of toys in front of her.

'We met in India. At an ashram,' Sarah told her, turning up alone for the first session. 'The attraction was like, how can I describe it? Red-hot? I mean, he was gorgeous, and we were both young, free spirits. You don't have a herbal tea, do you? Love a tea when I chat.'

He was a recovering alcoholic learning to become a yoga teacher. She was a student. 'A lot slimmer then.' She laughed, adjusting her skirt in the chair, the cotton crushed up against the side of her legs to reveal the paleness of her thigh, white and dimpled.

She was nothing like the person Ester had pictured, imagining someone small, too light to settle anywhere, the rapid speed of her endless talk burning up whatever physical substance she might have had. But Sarah was large, dressed in bright, fun clothes, her hair hennaed scarlet, jewellery covering her neck, her fingers, her wrists, all clanking loudly each time she moved.

She was pregnant, she declared in the first session. 'My fourth. I'm one of those women. Fertile as. You just have to look at me and I'm knocked up.'

Daniel wanted her to have a termination.

'We live off a yoga teacher's salary.' She brushed a curl out of her eyes. 'Doesn't leave much after feeding all those hungry mouths. But I'm a mother. That's what I am. This is what makes me sing. It's what I love.' She ran her hands through the air, following the shape of her own breasts, her belly, eyes widening as she leant forward. 'He knows that. Telling me he wants to kill it,' and she leant forward here, her words almost a hiss, 'it's like he's striking at the very heart of my being.' Her breath smelt of peppermint, her skin of musk.

Ester had to control herself from recoiling. She actively leant a little closer to counter all in her that wanted to pull away.

'Do you feel you need my help in talking this decision through?'

Sarah laughed loudly. God no, it had to be her choice. It was her body.

By the end of the first session, Ester still found it difficult to determine whether Sarah wanted counselling with Daniel or to see a therapist on her own. Were there issues in their relationship that she wanted to address? There are always issues. That's love. Was there a reason why Daniel hadn't come?

Sarah began then to talk about a rebirthing therapy Daniel had been doing. It was through an American who ran courses in the States and set up online support groups. Daniel had been three times. He spent a couple of nights a week talking to his group. He was very into it.

Was it causing tension?

It was why he didn't feel he could come to see Ester. They weren't meant to do two types of therapy at the same time.

Why did she want him to come with her?

Sarah paused for a moment then, her intake of air audible.

'He has anger issues.' She shook her head sadly. 'And he needs to take responsibility for them.'

As she stood to leave, she paused, putting her hand on Ester's arm, her voice hushed as she spoke. She had been abused as a child. A family friend had let himself into her room while her parents were downstairs having a party. She was fifteen, and he was forty. It had gone on for a year.

'I thought I loved him and he loved me. But I was young, vulnerable, foolish.'

Ester hated it when patients did this at the end of a session. It forced her to dismiss the issue, to tell the client that this was something they could discuss at the next appointment.

She used to tell Lawrence that she had to find the 'self of calm curiosity' to do the work she did. A client would come in, and Ester would always feel that moment when an array of selves, each responding differently, would jostle for position. There could be compassion, anger, judgement, fear, boredom, frustration, very rarely indifference — though occasionally even that was there — and they were all possible.

'I'm like a pack of cards,' she said. 'And with each client there's an immediate response. I have to take a deep breath, push that response to the back, and draw the same card every time.'

'Calm curiosity?'

She nodded.

If Sarah was without bounds, Daniel was tightly contained.

He came to the next session, sitting on the other end of the couch to Sarah, silent as she talked.

She had lost the baby, she declared. A miscarriage after she came home from the session with Ester. She'd reached for Daniel's hand to take it in her own, having to shift her entire body to get to where he sat. Her eyes were glassy as she looked at him; he remained staring at the ground.

Ester outlined her rules for working with both of them, one of which was a session with each of them on their own.

As soon as they were by themselves, Daniel told her Sarah had been lying. She was never pregnant; she made up stories all the time.

What made him think that?

They hadn't had sex for months. He looked straight at Ester, his grey-green eyes cold, his pale skin dusted with freckles. *He looks like a young boy*, she thought for a moment, like a Daniel you might see in the playground. He shifted nervously on the seat.

'She believes it completely,' he said.

Ester asked him why he was here — what did he see as the key issues in his relationship with Sarah?

He shrugged.

Could he talk a little more about the lack of sexual intimacy in their relationship? Did he feel this was a problem?

He no longer loved her. He hadn't loved her for years.

Then why did he stay?

He met Ester's gaze for a long time before he spoke. 'I don't know how to leave,' he eventually said. 'I mean I do. But she won't let me. It's like she's some kind of sinkhole, and I'm stuck.' He almost sneered as he uttered the words, his loathing for himself, Sarah, and the situation they were in naked on his face.

Another time, Ester told Lawrence that she felt she spent most of her days talking to frogs in boiling water. 'They come in, and I can see they are boiling,' she said. 'The water is bubbling. But they have been immersed for so long, and the temperature has been going up and up and up — it's only when it reaches critical that they try and leap out. And I have to help them do that.'

'Well, they're idiots,' he'd replied, putting his headphones back in so he could continue listening to music.

She'd remembered that conversation a month later, when he'd come home and told her he was in love with April.

She sits in her consulting room now with Sarah and Daniel, trying to banish all selves other than the calm and curious Ester. Sarah is crying, alone at her end of the couch, while Daniel remains impassive, looking only at the ceiling. He has been inching further away from her, his whole body pressed into his side of the couch, as she accuses him of not really trying, of not participating in these sessions.

'What do you want from me?' He glares across at Sarah.

The silence in the room builds, all the more pronounced with the steady hum of the rain outside. Eventually, Sarah tells him she doesn't deserve his anger. 'Jesus, darl, I love you. I do everything for you.'

'You don't fucking listen,' he mutters.

She seems relieved he has finally spoken, her words coming out in a torrent. 'Of course I listen to you, darl, but I've got a lot of people to listen to, what with the kids demanding attention all day. If you want to be heard, you've got to speak up,' she turns and smiles at Ester. 'It's chaos in our house. No one could be heard, really. Even I have a hard time being heard above the din, and that's saying something.'

Daniel's skin is even paler than usual, the tension in his jaw revealing the sharp line of the bone. Ester knows she should intervene, but Sarah keeps on talking.

'We need to make more time for each other. Get a babysitter, go out one night a week, talk about what's happening in our lives. I know I could try and arrange a swap with some of the other mothers at kindy. Give you a chance to be heard?' She turns to Daniel, reaching for him and smiling as she does so.

He presses further into the side of the couch.

'Do you feel that would help?' Ester looks at him. His hands are clenched in his lap, his top lip pressing down hard on his lower lips, the flesh white.

'No. It wouldn't help.'

Sarah shakes her head, mouth pursed. 'You see? This is the problem,' she says. 'Every time I try and come up with a solution — and it's always me doing that — you just reject it outright. Like the time I told you to go and have a holiday. When you were so depressed and miserable, which you probably don't remember because you're depressed and miserable most of the time. It's hard to be around. Honest. But I told you to take a week off, get away, I'd take care of the kids, I even found you somewhere to stay, but no. You just told me that a holiday wasn't the answer. Fine. But how am I meant to help if I don't even know what the problem is?' She crosses her arms across her chest and shakes her head.

Ester wonders whether Daniel will shout; she can feel it, the great bulk of all those unsaid words right there, the danger of them being dumped all at once in a truckload. She turns to him, breaking the silence before it builds any further.

'How do you feel about Sarah's response?' She keeps her voice low, even, and she focuses her gaze straight on him, willing him to lift his head and look her in the eyes.

'I don't want a holiday. I don't want a night out. I don't want to be here.' He stands, shaking.

Sarah tries to pull him down, her hands reaching up, her bangles jangling as he shoves her away.

'I don't love you. I don't fucking love you.'

Sarah's eyes widen, and the whole world flickers across them: disbelief, anger, denial, blink, blink, blink, grief, horror, fury, each so fast, and then, last, there is the need — bottomless in its depth, rapacious as it swallows all else.

He doesn't love her.

I don't love you.

The love has gone.

Every time those words are said, there is so much pain, Ester thinks. She has seen it before in this room — the utterance ripping through lives like a gunshot, a bomb, hollowing out the centre and leaving an all-consuming ache. You go to sleep to it, you dream of it, you wake to it; food is dry and tasteless, air is difficult to breathe, colour bleeds away. She knows this.

But there is also relief and the possibility of change, waiting just off centre-stage, hovering and ready to be allowed to tiptoe in. Not straight away, never straight away — in fact, those emotions cannot even be acknowledged for quite some time. But they are there.

Daniel is still standing, leaning against the wall now, and Ester talks, knowing she needs to bring this moment to some kind of resolution so that they can step out of her room and face each other alone.

She offers the box of tissues, but Sarah doesn't even see them. She puts her head in her hands, and her whole body heaves. *This is what's been at the edge of all of Sarah's talk*, Ester thinks. Sarah has known that it was there. It is always there. The layers and layers of words, even the fantasies, if that is what they are, had done little more than cover the knowledge that love would soon be ripped away.

Ester turns to Daniel, who has one single tear, perfect in its form, building slowly. He wipes it away.

'What you've just said is very difficult to say,' Ester tells him.

She looks at Sarah. 'And what you've just heard was very difficult to hear.'

She talks to them calmly about the impact of this moment, and the need for them both to navigate through this with an awareness of their children.

As soon as she mentions the kids, Sarah loses the last semblance of control. She sobs loudly, she says she can't bear it — *we're their parents* — her plea is to Daniel, and it's terrible in its despair.

'We're still their parents,' he says.

'No, we're not,' she replies, and she begins to hit him, beating him across the shoulders with her fists, shouting that he is a liar, he has always been a liar, they are a family, he has to love her, and as Ester tries to reach for her, to get her to stop, Daniel stands.

'Fuck this,' he tells them, and he is gone, the sound of the door slamming behind him followed moments later by his boots on the gravel as he walks off through the rain and around the corner.

ALONE IN HER HOUSE, Hilary knows that once she speaks to Lawrence, she will have begun to put into place a plan that grips too tight each time she lets her mind alight on it. The call to Henry, or perhaps the visit, could also be seen as first steps, but articulating her decision to Lawrence will be harder. She's scared he will lose his nerve and talk to the girls; April, most probably. And then they will beg her, and that's something she could not bear.

She has to stay calm. She has had to break it down. Step by step. Moment by moment. And if she falters, she only has to contemplate the alternative — the failure to act — and she finds she can lift her feet again and move that little bit closer.

She opens her bag, wanting to see the packet of heroin one more time: fine white powder in plastic. She holds it for a moment, surprised by its lack of weight. And then she puts it away.

She sits on the lounge, a faded forties couch covered in deep-red cotton, and sinks into its softness. She has never appreciated the comfort, she thinks, the joy of just sitting here. This is a beautiful room. The kauri boards are a deep honey, scratched and worn in places, covered in rugs that she and Maurie had bought over the years. There are bookshelves on either side of the fireplace, with paperbacks jammed up against each other, some in small piles on top of others, many of their covers now yellowing, the cardboard dog-eared or torn.

She has always been the reader — no one else in the family is that interested. She had carted her books from house to house as a student, the boxes growing in number each time, keeping them because she could not imagine doing otherwise, and because she thought that there was something permanent in a book, that it lasted forever. But now, when she takes an older paperback out to reread or loan, she is surprised at how fragile it has become, the paper threatening to tear in her hands if she turns the page, tiny black specks embedded in its tissue pages; bugs, probably. She should have cleared them out, she thinks. Packed them up in boxes for recycling. No one would want them when she was gone.

She comes from an era that has passed. Books, films, theatre, the art world — all are in an extraordinary shakedown. The films she makes no longer have any place in the currency of culture; they are meditations on fragments that take hold of her, often rambling, looping round and round and round an idea, using images, words, and sounds to play with notions that surface and sink, surface and sink. They would never show on television, they would never get a cinema release, they would not be watched by anyone on YouTube. They screen in festivals, mainly overseas, where she is often invited to talk, and where the few devoted followers of such work know and admire her.

She has never been sad about this, or bitter. She regards herself as exceptionally fortunate, actually. She found her niche at the tail end of this particular incarnation of cinema, and she was able to keep making work. She didn't want fame, although some notoriety ensured her work was screened and she received the occasional funding to produce another film. She also didn't want money. Maurie's success meant they had enough to live well.

He had more ego invested in his work than she ever did. He pretended it wasn't the case — he always said he painted for himself, and to an extent, he did. But the truth was — and she shakes her head at the memory of the tirades he would go into (or worse still, the slumps) whenever he was passed over for a prize or didn't receive a prominent enough review — he wanted mass adoration.

His paintings cover the walls of this house. Many of them are now quite valuable. She looks around her, letting her gaze settle on each of the ones in this room, trying to assess them without his presence. His work never changed. In all the years of painting, he stuck to one style: strong, thick brushstrokes, harsh lines of colour criss-crossing each other, almost as though they had been smeared on with the back of his fist, the effect striking, energetic but — and she smiles again — also perplexing.

She has never understood his paintings.

Once when they were very stoned, she admitted as much to him.

'I mean, are you thinking anything at all, when you do this?' She had begun to giggle as she waved her hand over a canvas. 'You call it "Terrain", but you could call it anything, couldn't you?'

Maurie, who had always had a sense of humour, had laughed, the great sonorous delight of his amusement filling the studio. 'I'm changing its name,' he pronounced, 'to "Hilary".'

'Oh no,' she protested. 'I'm not that one.' She looked around the room, her eyes finally alighting on a larger, more dramatic canvas, one that threatened to spill over onto the walls. 'That's me.'

She presumes he too had been exploring ideas, within his own language, although that was not a language she spoke with any eloquence. She responded on an aesthetic level only — the nature of the colours and shapes either arresting, or pleasing, or too ugly for her to want in the house. She was the one who selected which of his works they kept, aside from the few paintings he gave her, which she had to like.

She had contemplated sorting through the collection, calling the State and National Galleries to talk about keeping them together, and then she hadn't. *The girls can deal with it*, she had thought. She looks up at the ceiling and bites her lip. This is her sadness. Leaving them and knowing they aren't speaking to each other. Not that her being here has brought them closer to mending the rift.

Fuck Lawrence.

She rubs her temples slowly, wanting to ease the pain that is beginning to creep through the pills she took this morning, its sharp nails scratching at her brain. She is not meant to take any more medication until this evening — but what does it really matter? And she looks through her bag for the canister, her hand shaking slightly as she opens it, the smooth capsule falling onto the floor.

She is alone.

She takes slow, deep breaths, steady, steady, steady, picking the pill up and swallowing it without water. She has to bring everything down to the moment, to stay right in the present. She must imagine she is in a bubble of the immediate, able only to see, hear, taste, smell, and contemplate the world that is right next to her. Nothing beyond the boundaries.

She takes her shoes off and lets her toes rub through the carpet, the silky softness of the wool soothing against her skin. She runs her hands along the worn patch on the arm of the sofa, feeling each frayed edge of cotton, fine and delicate. The curtains are open to the courtyard, and she looks at the moss growing in the brick, jewelled green, luminous, velvety, so beautiful as it creeps, determined life in its growth, along the cracks and across the surface of the stone.

The rain is pouring over the gutters in a translucent sheet, bringing with it the occasional leaf or twig. *They need clearing*, she thinks. Another task to be completed — or not — by someone else. Because, conceivably, she could go, and all of this — her house, the remnants of her life — could remain, left to slowly rot away, back to nothing. The couch, the paintings, the books, the rug, the walls, roof, and floors — all disintegrating.

There is a slight break in the clouds, a piercing of light through the sombre darkness, and she stands to see if the day is clearing, but the vision is gone almost as soon as it has appeared, and a new sheet of grey covers the gap, bringing only more rain. What a day. She opens the door and steps out, wanting to feel the moss underfoot and the sweetness of the rain as it falls, cold and constant, soaking into her hair, beading on the surface of her skin, saturating her clothes. It is extraordinary that it can keep doing this, raining and raining and raining. And she stays where she is until she is too cold to bear it any longer, bringing a trail of damp mud and twigs into the house as she heads up the stairs to dry herself and change before Lawrence arrives.

When Maurie died, she took all his clothes to the Salvation Army, packing them up the day after his funeral.

'You don't need to rush,' Ester told her.

It was the smell of him each time she opened the wardrobe. It made her tremble.

He'd had a ridiculous amount of clothes. Jackets, pants, shirts, belts, all no longer worn, but kept in the certainty that there would come a time when he would be as trim as he'd been as a student, and he would put them on and look as handsome as he had in his youth. Some she remembered as she packed them. A beautiful worn green leather coat, soft to touch; an op-shop suit of heavy navy wool, double-breasted and stylish; a steel-grey sweater that his mother had knitted him. He hoarded.

'You might want to keep something,' Esther had suggested. She'd looked at one of the boxes, taking out a fat buttercup-yellow silk tie. 'Lawrence might like this,' she'd said.

And Hilary had told her to take it, to take anything she wanted, but to do it now because the boxes were going down to the car as soon as they were packed.

When she'd finished with the clothes, she went to his studio. That was easier. She took the paintings, and the rest she left, calling friends of theirs and asking them to clear it out. 'And please keep whatever you like,' she'd urged.

When she saw the 'For Sale' sign, Ester had said she needed to slow down. 'Maybe you'll want to convert it into a museum? You don't know.'

It was sold to a developer who remodelled it into a warehouse apartment, realising more than three times the purchase price. She never went to the open inspection, but Ester did, showing her the brochure afterwards. She'd been angry.

'How could they just wipe him out like that? Don't they know what that space was?'

Hilary had told her it was good. 'He's gone,' she said.

Because that wasn't him. Not the studio, not the paintings, not the clothes. They were all nothing without the flesh and blood of him, the warmth and bristle and laughter, the curve of his hip, the beautiful line of his back, the sharp focus of his gaze, his hand warm on her skin. That was her ache and her pain, even now, and she closes her eyes to the memory of him, the physical sense of his presence enveloping her.

He's gone.

She doesn't know what she believes, but she certainly has no faith in being reunited with Maurie in any kind of afterlife. That is not what this is about. If she expects anything at all — and she cannot let her mind rest for too long on any consequences flowing from her decision — she supposes it is the peace of absence, the calm of non-existence, that awaits her. Which isn't to say that she would regard herself as atheist. To deny the possibility of mystery is abhorrent to her, although to claim any knowledge of that mystery is equally repellent.

She dries her hair slowly, the steely white of her curls coarse in her hands. In the mirror, the age of her skin, the droop in her eyes is, as always, a shock to her. The towel is soft beneath her fingers, and she breathes it in deeply. She can smell April, and she presumes that this is the towel she used this morning. There is a milky sweetness to April; beneath the alcohol and cigarettes, the fear and the sadness, there is the hint of frangipani, and she holds it close.

When April had told her what had happened with Lawrence (and she hadn't done so until Hilary had gone over to her house, furious and sad and unable to comprehend how she could have been so stupid), the anger she had felt had been knotted, a squall as dense and dark as any she had known, but it had quickly dispersed.

She had so often seen April's tears, her drama and her capacity to hijack the emotions of others. But on that morning, she had been different. Hollowed out, unable to speak, she hadn't responded to Hilary's anger — and in the face of that silence, Hilary had stopped as suddenly as she had begun. Shaking her head, she had simply held April and told her that this was a mistake that they would all need time to recover from, aware as she uttered those words that the time required could extend beyond what they had.

She changes into dry clothes: a dark-grey cotton top and loose black trousers. The few clothes she owns are all similar; they always have been. She is a practical person, someone who finds a style that suits her and is easy to live in, and then stays with it. If she wears colour, it is usually a discrete flash — a bright scarf or her enamelled ring. And she puts this on now, the red like a crimson petal, concentrated in its beauty.

Sitting on the edge of the bed, she looks out the window to the last magnolia blooms, the first pale leaves of spring unfurling cellophane-fine along the branches, soon to crowd out every petal with a luridly healthy display of green.

Hilary loves this tree. She planted it when they moved to this house shortly after Ester was born, and it grew strong and beautiful, so perfectly sure of its place. In winter, when the leaves are gone, the sun shines through the window, and she delights in the beauty of each flower. Port-wine petals, smooth and waxy, cupped open to the sky. And then, as the summer sun increases in intensity, the foliage provides a cool green shade against the heat of the day.

She won't see it bloom again.

She bundles her damp clothes into her arms to put in the laundry. Conceivably, she could just leave them where they are, on the floor outside her room. Or she could throw them out. They should go to a charity shop, where they will be put on racks with the rows and rows and rows of other pants and tops without an owner — a decision that may just be a delay of the inevitability of contributing to landfill, but one that she likes to think is less wasteful than going straight to the bin. However, this is not the only reason why she takes them downstairs. She is committed to the choice she has made. That much she knows. But it doesn't mean she can bear to take steps that prematurely signal the finality of all she must do. Not yet. And so she holds them under one arm as she walks through to the laundry where the rain drums, ratatatatatat, on the tin roof, on and on and on, while she hangs them on the rack as though she will need them again.

But she won't need them again.

Enough. It is so hard trying to keep this voice at bay.

In the kitchen, she takes a pear from the fruit bowl, and holds it in the palm of her hand. It is firm and round, the brown skin rough, furry enough to send slight shivers up her spine. She slices into it, not because she is hungry, but because she needs to calm herself, absorb herself in a close examination of something, anything. (*It was so much easier when she was finishing off her film.*) The flesh is creamy-yellow, crisp, the sweetness of the pear almost almond-like, a sugary granulation to the juice along the edge of the knife.

There. And as she sits and takes a bite, disliking the sensation of the skin against her tongue, she focuses her mind on the experience only, her sense of calm returning, cautiously, like a whipped dog creeping back to its master.

LAWRENCE DRIVES IN the rain, the windscreen wipers clicking back and forth, back and forth. He has the demister on high, and it cuts a hole through the fog, but the noise is too loud. He turns it off and opens the window, the cold and the wet forcing him to close it again moments later.

He's glad April has the kids (even though he knows she shouldn't). In this weather, he wouldn't get back across town to collect them from afterschool care until much later than usual, and they would complain — no doubt telling Ester as soon as they could, painting him as the neglectful parent.

He takes a wrong turn and swears loudly. *This is not a day to be out*, he thinks, and he cranks the demister up again, the rattle loud as it clears the windscreen to show him what he already knows: it is raining heavily.

Pulling over to the side of the road, he stops. The corrosive acid of worry is making his gut ache, and the truth is, it's his own predicament that's the principal cause of this. He glances at himself in the rear-vision mirror. Hilary's news is terrible. Terrible. But deep inside, he is glad for a diversion from his own trouble, and he is ashamed of how appallingly pervasive his own self-absorption is.

He will be a national scandal.

No, he won't.

He shakes his head. The paper isn't going to want his confession to go public. They won't want to look like fools. He will be fired — which is happening anyway. But he will get no good word for the work he has done. He will spend the next years of his working life scrabbling for dull jobs measuring customer satisfaction, brand recognition, product loyalty — all the while getting less and less work as his name sinks into oblivion.

Perhaps it won't even be that bad. Paul won't want anyone to know. And it is not as though he needs any kind of reference from the paper. His name has been out there for long enough. He will tender for other political jobs — internal party polling — something that doesn't have a public profile, so Edmund won't be tempted to salvage Lawrence's conscience with another confession.

Perhaps everything will continue as it has been?

He winces slightly.

On a scale of one to five, where five is extremely satisfied and one is extremely dissatisfied, how do you feel about your life?

He used to do the odd bit of direct phone polling, just to keep his hand in as to which questions worked and which were problematic. It was years ago, when he still had days in which he could fool himself that he liked his job, that it even mattered.

Sometimes the respondent would argue.

'Are you talking about how I feel right this instant? As I'm wasting my time answering your questions on the phone? Or are you talking about five minutes ago, when I was enjoying a peaceful drink at the end of a hard day?'

Fair enough.

Every question had so many potential nuances, and for each there were so many responses that could be given at any moment, influenced by something as simple as having just heard a song that irritated the shit out of the person, or having eaten a delicious meal.

It was the horrifying conclusion of democracy, an attempt

to capture and measure the extraordinarily infinite range of our desires, beliefs, thoughts, dreams, and hopes. Everyone had the chance to speak. Worse still, the dross of it was actually being listened to; extracts of sludge were being drawn out, held up as truth, and it pained him more than he could bear. Was that why he had done it? Perhaps that was part of the reason. And because he *could*. That was the strange thrill of it — knowing he could tweak a little here, tuck a little there, kid himself that he was making the voice of humanity sound just that bit better.

Sometimes, late at night, Lawrence would go out. He would walk the streets on his own, thinking he was going to find a bar and have a drink, thinking he might even take someone home and lose himself momentarily in sex.

He would open the back gate onto the laneway, the smell of the jasmine that grew over the rotting wooden palings sickly sweet, the air dark and soft against his skin, the sounds of laughter in other houses, sometimes shouting or arguing, the lights in the rooms framing all the lives within — lonely, messy, hopeful — television screens glowing, dishes being done, heads bent over desks, a young girl dancing on her own in her bedroom, a child asleep on a couch, a dog barking relentlessly. And he would know he was not going to stop at a bar; he was just going to walk and walk, letting it wash over him, the great chaos of it all, impossible to contain.

And so, at the end of the laneway he followed the maze of streets until he was out on the oval — empty except for the occasional midnight walker like himself — and he would sit on a bench and look out across the expanse of green, floodlit by the lights that bordered the path in the distance, a spill of brightness under the sky.

He felt at peace then. Tired and empty, but at peace. Yet sadness was inevitable. As soon as he realised that he was content, it would dissipate, the awareness breaking up any stillness of his soul, stirring it into a thousand particles that floated away, only to be replaced with a gnawing dissatisfaction, a sorrow that this was not his usual state.

This was the way it had always been.

As soon as he finally held what he wanted in his hands, he lost it.

ACROSS TOWN, ESTER has her next client for the day.

She had had no break after Sarah and Daniel. Sarah had sat and wept in the waiting room for ten minutes after the session had ended, and then Ester had told her she would have to leave, another client was due to arrive.

'How am I meant to cope?' Sarah had asked as Ester had shown her the door. 'What am I meant to do?'

'Do you have a friend you can call?' Ester had suggested. 'Someone you might go and sit with until you feel a little calmer?'

Outside, the rain slanted down towards the house, and with the door open, they were getting wet. She asked Sarah if she'd brought an umbrella with her, a raincoat? Sarah didn't respond.

'I have to get home to the kids,' she said. 'I have to face the kids after that.'

'Perhaps you could see if someone could come over?'

But Sarah wasn't listening. She was buried deep in the darkness of rejection. She looked blankly at Ester and shook her head, and then she walked out across the street and into the rain, letting it soak into her, darkening the purple of her top, bleeding into the crimson of her skirt, her hair dripping as she headed towards the main road, where she would wait for the bus, oblivious to anything that lay outside the circle of her misery.

Ester looked across the street to see if Chris had arrived, relieved his car wasn't there yet. She had a few moments to clear out her bin (there were a lot of tissues), to plump up the cushions on her sofa, and to jot down one or two key points she wanted to remember so that she could write up her notes in the few hours left at the end of the day.

The room felt dank. It was the gloom and the perpetual rain of course, but — and she didn't like to admit this to herself — it was also Sarah. It always felt this way after she left. Gardenias and sweat. She wished she could open the window wide and let the air in, but the rain was too heavy. She smiled as she stood in the corner and waved a wad of paper around — a useless attempt that was more for herself than for any practical purpose.

It was strange, this blank slate you presented to each client. You existed only for them. Nothing else happened in this room, before or after. They came, they went, and then the next one arrived. None would know how much sorrow and shame and grief and fear this room had seen, from small ordinary madnesses to great howling despair. When the day was finished, she didn't like to open the door. She locked it behind her, grateful for the warm evenings when she could leave the windows open to the night air, letting the outside world in to cleanse, so that, in the morning, the space felt a little better for having breathed. But on nights like this, she had to leave it closed up, hoping that somehow the misery would disperse, seeping under the cracks and out the front door.

There — the room felt better.

Across the road, Chris had pulled up. He was turning off his phone, and she watched as he walked across the street. He too was oblivious to the rain.

His daughter had died 18 months ago.

He had told her the story during their first session, sitting upright, chin lifted, voice level. Her name was Zoe, and she had been eight years old. Completely healthy, happy, ordinary — not a child that either he or his wife, Marina, worried about.

At first, she had simply complained about a pain in her shoulder. It was just one of those things. Marina wanted to take her to the doctor. He thought she was being overly anxious. The GP, who was new and young, couldn't see anything wrong with her. She'd probably just slept in a strange way. It would fix itself.

Three days later, she went back to school, determined to run in the cross-country.

She dropped dead 400 metres in.

These were the hard stories. As he uttered the words, Ester had to steel herself.

Zoe had a blood clot. It had gone to her brain.

'It's unusual for a young girl,' he explained. 'It's not the kind of condition that a doctor would normally look for.'

He was silent, staring out the window, breathing slowly before he continued.

Marina had wanted to sue the doctors. He hadn't. Marina had raged and ranted, and called lawyers, and screamed at him and everyone — *how could he have told her she was over-anxious, how could he have made her doubt herself? How could the doctors have missed something so obvious? They should have given her an ultrasound.* She had downloaded article after article about the condition, underlining the symptoms, showing him how simple it should have been to detect. Next, she took to parking outside the GP's rooms for days on end, waiting for any doctor to come out, wanting to shake each of them, to tell them of her anguish, but never doing it. Sometimes she was there well into the evening. He knew when he called her, the sound of the traffic behind her as she lied and told him she was somewhere else.

And then she had become silent.

The house had been quiet. The pair of them barely talking, barely eating, slowly being swallowed by the emptiness that followed her rage.

He should have tried to reach her. He knew that now. But he'd been lost in his own pain, unaware of her pulling away until it was too late.

'I can't stay here.' Her voice was flat, stripped bare, as she told him she had applied for a job in London. She needed to go. She had arranged everything without his knowing, and he had done nothing to stop her.

The next day she was gone, and Chris had looked at the emptiness of their house and known how perilously close he had come to losing all hold on his desire to live.

His GP had prescribed antidepressants and anti-anxiety medication, both of which he took.

'But I need to talk,' he had told Ester during their first appointment. And he had put his head in his hands and wept. 'I need to talk.'

Ester knows that this is often the case with people in grief. She has seen this in her practice, and she reads about it in the literature debating the effectiveness of bereavement counselling. There are many articles about whether talking is of any assistance in the healing process. She doesn't know, but her instinct with Chris was strong. He needed to speak.

For the first few sessions, he wanted only to talk of Zoe, alternating between remembering her as she'd been and the despair he felt at her death. The stories he related were like snapshots, an album of a life he had loved beyond compare. He would open a certain page and tell Ester small stories. When she was about two, Zoe had loved dandelions, the ones you could blow into the breeze. She called them blowflowers. *I hope so the blowflowers*, she would say each time she went anywhere. She didn't like girls called Maya. There had been cruel Mayas at daycare and at school. She was shy, but she pushed herself, entering the public speaking competition at her school. *She got to the State finals*, Chris told

Ester. *I have never seen anyone so nervous.* She woke up in the morning convinced she couldn't speak, and he and Marina had to get her to sing her favourite song, trying to show her that she hadn't lost her voice.

She shouldn't have died.

He should have been more alert.

He should have known it was serious.

She read voraciously. When she was little she had favourite books for months on end: *Madeline*, *Where the Wild Things Are*, and a fairy tale she loved about a young girl who wanted a man to marry her, but he ignored her. He and Marina had to read those tales, no others, over and over again.

She had a trampoline and she bounced on it, morning and night, every day, making up stories in her head. If he went out to the garden, he could sometimes hear her, her whisper slightly louder as she came to a dramatic place in the tale. Chris thought it was the rhythm that she liked; it helped her to create the narrative.

As he spoke of her, his eyes became brighter, he sat up straighter. It was as though he were bringing her back to life with his tales.

He wished they'd had another. He was the one who'd put a halt to the idea when Zoe was young. Marina was keen, but he wasn't. It was money, he'd told Ester, staring up at the ceiling. He hadn't wanted them to be managing on one income again. But if they'd had another child, they would need to go on. They would be forced to continue.

She'd died at school.

Away from them.

No one had listened to her when she complained of pain.

They had failed her.

Sometimes he woke up, anxious that his own heart was stopping. He couldn't breathe, he told Ester. It was as though he had forgotten how. He had to concentrate, to think about taking air in and letting it out, because if he didn't, it wouldn't work. And at other times, he would think that maybe he shouldn't try; maybe he should just let himself die. Maybe that was what he deserved. But that too became a question of effort, of trying to stop, his body forcing him to inhale each time he came close to the edge.

He is always polite and gentle, apologising when he talks for too long without pausing, rarely crying since that first session, reasonable when she suggests ways in which he might begin to allow himself to move through the pain of what has happened, appearing to listen to her when she speaks. His surface rarely ripples, only occasionally revealing a tremor across the smooth darkness, a moment in which there is a glimpse of the eternal lack of light below.

She has talked to him about there being no 'correct' way to grieve, no 'normal' coping strategies. They have discussed letting go (an idea that he found abhorrent), and choosing to keep the relationship alive. They have talked about ritual, ways in which he can continue to honour Zoe's life. And in the last session, they began to discuss ideas for how he could learn to be more gentle towards himself, more forgiving, allowing himself to provide some comfort to his grieving self. She had suggested that he write a letter to himself. As though he were a friend who had suffered a similar loss many years ago — words that he wished he'd heard at the time.

He sits opposite her, on the couch, hands neatly folded in his lap, shoulders slightly hunched forward.

When she asks him whether the exercise had helped, he becomes agitated. He tried, he says.

Ester waits for him to continue.

'But each time I sat down to write, it felt so false.' He scratches at his wrist, pushing his sleeves up and then pulling them down again. 'I'm not that person.'

'Which person?' she asks.

'The comforter, years down the track. If I knew his words, I'd be all right.'

'We can know the words we need to hear. We can know how we would like to lead our lives. And we can know what we would like to say to others, how we would like to be in this world, yet it doesn't mean we are able to live that. But sometimes attempting to articulate those words can help bring them closer. Make them a little more real.'

He takes a single sheet of paper out of his coat pocket, clutching it tightly.

'You did write something?' she asks. Her smile is gentle.

He nods.

He has his shoes off, a habit he has had from the first session, preferring not to wear them inside. He had asked her if she minded, and she told him it was fine. His toes inside his socks are scrunched tight, digging into the softness of the carpet beneath his feet.

'I wrote to the man I was, before — ' He cannot continue.

She looks at him holding the letter, the paper damp from the sweat on his fingers. 'What did you want to say to him?'

'Not much,' he tells her.

She waits for him to speak again, but there is silence for a moment and then, to her slight surprise, he clears his throat, an awkward cough, and begins to read.

Dear Chris.

He isn't looking at her. His eyes are fixed on the letter, his voice steadying as he continues.

You were such an ignorant idiot. And then you lost everything. I can't bear to look back on you.

'That's all?' she asks.

He nods.

She is curious as to why he is angry with his former self.

'Because he had everything. He was blessed with an ordinary life. And he didn't even know.'

Outside, a delivery van has pulled up, beeping as it reverses into the neighbour's driveway; it is almost the only sound, that mechanical beep, and then the rain starts up again, pouring down on all the blessed, and Ester waits until she feels she has her composure, until she can open her mouth to speak, while opposite her, Chris folds the paper in his hands, carefully pressing down on the creases. He puts the letter back in his pocket, one white corner still showing.

And then he looks up at her.

She meets his gaze. 'It's how most of us live, paying so little attention to the good fortune we enjoy. Perhaps we have to stay ignorant of our blessings. Perhaps we can only carry our good fortune with us if we don't know that we are doing it — otherwise we would be overwhelmed by anxiety at the possibility of its loss.'

She waits for him to speak.

'Will I ever come back?'

She leans her head to the side slightly, unsure of what he's asking.

'To the world. To ordinary, everyday, shitty stuff that makes you forget just how lucky you are. All of that.' He lifts his arms half-heartedly, as if to embrace life, and then he lets them fall again. 'I don't even know if I want to. I don't want to be that stupid.'

He turns to the window, hands once more clasped in his lap, unadorned apart from his wedding ring, which he still wears.

Ester would like to reach for him, but she can't, and so her own hands are also clasped, her wedding ring long discarded, and she listens, aware of the truth and beauty in his words, and that here in this room, she too is blessed — an awareness she doesn't have enough, she realises, as the rain continues to fall, sweet against the soft grey of the sky.

It's been a long time since Lawrence has seen Hilary, even longer since he has been to this house.

He brushes against damp new leaves unfurling on the giant magnolia, the last of the flowers dropping their petals to the ground, where they lie bruised and bedraggled. He tries to shut the iron gate, but one of the hinges is rusted, and he gives up, bending low beneath an overhanging branch, the drops shaking loose and running down the back of his neck, cold, as he hurries to the shelter of the front verandah.

Hilary is there at the door moments after he knocks — the same, and not the same. She stands, shorter than he remembered, her face like April's but stronger, her gaze more focused. And yet there is a frailty in her eyes that he hasn't seen before, a slight twitch at the corner. But perhaps he just imagines this.

They are awkward in their initial greeting. In the past, he would always have kissed her on the cheek, but now they each lean hesitantly towards the other, unsure of how to say hello. Then she takes charge. Taking his hand in her own, only for a moment, she tells him to come in, out of the wet.

With the front door shut behind him, there is quiet. No birds, no hiss of distant traffic, just the faint tapping of the rain. The house seems empty, but then he has only ever experienced it at family gatherings, with Ester, the girls, sometimes April, and, in the more distant past, Maurie as well. There would be noise, disagreements, family frustrations, and joy as well. He had usually witnessed more than participated — this is how it is, he presumes, when you are not blood. Part of the family, but not. Definitely not now.

Ester used to worry about Hilary being lonely after Maurie died, but she had always seemed so busy to him, so capable, so self-contained that he'd found it difficult to imagine her experiencing anything as aimless and frail as loneliness. Yet now, as he follows her past the living room — hushed, neat, too large for one person — and down the hall, he recognises the emptiness he experiences in his own place when the girls go back to Ester; everything packed up, cleaned up, waiting, waiting for people to make each room exist again. Because that is how it feels sometimes — as though both he and the house in which he lives are not real when he is by himself. Who is to say they exist, other than himself? — and he smiles at the thought, the ludicrous existential spiral his mind is following because he is nervous about this meeting.

The kitchen has floor-to-ceiling glass windows on two sides — one looking out at an ivy-covered wall, the other across a courtyard. He remembers this room well; April and Maurie making salads, terrines, casseroles, marinading meat, all to be brought to the outside table. Which is still there, the wood sagging, damp and rotten in places, its surface covered in leaves, the legs laced with spider webs, glittering with perfect raindrops. What was the French phrase for a web? The star of the spider? Something like that.

There is a dining room as well, just behind them, but they rarely used it. He glances through there now, and it is like the rest of the house: empty, waiting, the large Victorian table pale with dust, one of Maurie's earlier paintings hanging on the wall behind it. He and Ester had once had sex in that room — and he blushes at the memory.

Opposite him, Hilary pours them both a glass of water. Her

hand is trembling. He opens his mouth to speak, to say something foolish like *how are you* when she has already told him she is dying, but she cuts over him, fortunately, taking charge once more.

'You look older,' she tells him.

He laughs. 'It's been a bad day.' He speaks without thinking, aware of how puny his complaints are in comparison to hers as soon as he utters the words, and he grimaces. 'Although not so bad — in comparison.'

There is almost a smile on her face. She clasps her hands around her glass, and asks him if he would like a coffee, a tea, or perhaps even a stiff drink.

'I'm tempted by the last one,' he says. 'But I have to pick up the girls and get them home.'

'I'd have one myself, but I'd probably pass out with the pills I've been taking.' She meets his gaze, and there is, in that instant, so much sadness in her eyes. 'I need your help,' she tells him. 'And I figure if there is anyone in the world who owes a debt to me and my daughters, it's you.'

Lawrence bristles. He shifts in his seat. He is pushing the chair back now, suddenly aware that he is quite ready to leave if she begins to berate him for the past, but she stops him.

'I haven't asked you here for us to argue. I've asked you here because I'm hoping that you will hear me out, understand, and ultimately help me.'

She tells him she has cancer.

He is sorry, he says, but she waves his condolences away with her hand. 'It's life. And I genuinely mean that. I would like to go on living, but it seems I can't.'

How long has she known?

'I will tell you everything,' she says. 'And I'm sorry if I'm a little slow or I repeat myself, but it's becoming harder to focus. My head hurts and I get terribly tired.'

He nods, waiting for her to continue.

'I went to the doctor about three months ago. I was getting blurred vision and aches,' she touches her temples. 'I've never suffered from anything like that so I was anxious. They sent me for scans and various tests — it seems I have a brain tumour, the most aggressive kind.'

He is silent as she breathes in.

'There is only one other person that I have told this to — apart from various doctors, of course. His name is Henry, and he is an old friend. He is helping me too, but more about that later. What I'm trying to say is that I'm not accustomed to speaking about this. It's far more difficult to voice than I expected.' She shakes her head slightly, bemused by her failure to rise to the occasion with as much strength as she normally displays. 'We all know we are going to die. It's all we know with complete certainty, but it's still an extraordinary shock when you find that your time has come. Even for me — and by that I mean, it's not as though this has come to me when I am still young. I'm not very old,' she smiles, 'but I'm at an age where death is less of a shock.

'I had to sit with the news for a while. It's the kind of person I am. I don't really want to discuss things — although if Maurie were here, I would have talked to him. In fact, I might even have asked him what I am going to ask of you. Although I'm not sure. He was always so optimistic, it is likely he would have fought me, convinced there was hope.

'The doctors have told me that there's not much they can do. It's inoperable. There's a new drug that they are trialling, and I could have taken part in the tests. But it was of so little benefit. If you are given it — and you might just be given a placebo — it can make you very ill — vomiting, diarrhoea, there's even the possibility of internal bleeding — and at best you will get another six months. I simply couldn't see the point.

'The time that they've given me isn't long, and I would say that I'm right at the end of the best of it. The headaches will become unbearable. I'll lose control of my bodily functions, and I'll be delusional. I'll go into palliative care, and I will die.'

Lawrence is silent. He does not know what to say in the face of this news, and she's made it clear that she doesn't want sympathy.

'I don't want to put myself through that kind of misery, and I don't want to put others through it either.' She stands now and looks out the window at the rain.

He can see the reflection of her face, fogged in the glass, and for a moment he thinks she is crying, but it's just raindrops, sliding down the pane. He waits for her to turn to face him, but she doesn't.

'I decided early on that I was going to take my own life.'

This is what he has been expecting, and he dreads her telling him the role she wants him to play in this. He coughs awkwardly, and he is aware of sweat on the back of his neck, clammy against his skin.

'I looked into finding a doctor that could assist me. I even spoke to my own GP about it — sounding her out, I suppose. But it's so difficult. I don't want her or any other doctor to have to carry the consequences of my decision. I really don't.'

Or me, Lawrence wants to add. *I don't want to have to bear the consequences either*. To go to court or, worse still, to jail for this.

She has turned around now.

'Don't worry.' She smiles. 'I'm not going to ask you to kill me.'

Lawrence laughs nervously, and he is too loud in the quiet of the kitchen. 'I wasn't thinking you were,' he lies.

She shakes her head, amused. 'I might have disliked you a lot over the last few years, but not that much.'

She can't resist, he thinks. One more go at him. And it won't be the last. But this time, he says nothing. It doesn't really matter, not in the face of this news.

Hilary picks up her bag from the floor and comes to sit at the table again. 'I find it difficult to stay still,' she apologises. 'It makes me more aware of the pain.'

She reaches into the zippered central compartment and brings out a bag of white powder, placing it in front of him.

He looks at it and then up at her.

'It's heroin,' she tells him matter-of-factly.

Lifting it in his hands, Lawrence turns the bag over. 'You know I've never tried it,' he says. 'In fact, I'm not sure I've ever seen heroin. And I know that may seem hard to believe, given my reputation, but it wasn't a drug I sought out, and it never seemed to come my way.'

She reaches across for the bag. 'Well, it's not for you.' There is a spark, flinty humour, in her eyes. 'It's mine.'

He hands the powder over to her.

'I did my research,' she continues. 'And it seems that an overdose is the least painful way to go. But obviously it's a matter of making sure you have the right dose. That's where my friend, Henry, came in. He's had a controlled habit for decades. He bought this for me, he's shown me what I have to do, and —'

She is silent then, swallowing, the ripple down her throat revealing the difficulty she has in uttering her next words. 'Now it's up to me.'

'Are you sure?' he eventually asks.

She nods. 'It's not like I haven't thought about this. I've thought about little else. The alternative terrifies me to such an extent that —'

She glances out to the studio. 'I wanted to finish my last film. And I've done that. I now have nothing left to distract me. And it is so hard to remain resolute, to hold onto my nerve. It is so hard.'

He takes her hand in his and says nothing. He knows her well enough to recognise that she does not want to cry. Her skin is cool against his, her touch loose, but it is almost as though he can feel her pulse, the determined, desperate life beat, there in the palm of her hand, and he is momentarily overwhelmed by the vastness of what awaits her. But he knows this is not the time or the place. His role is to listen and to find out what she wants. Whether he will be able to do as she asks is another matter.

'So,' she removes her hand from his and stands again. He watches as she fills a glass with water from the tap and sips it slowly. 'Why have I asked you here?'

'I don't know,' he smiles. 'I would think I'd be one of the last people you'd want around.' And then he starts to tell her how sorry he is. 'I shouldn't have made such a mess. I really shouldn't. And I wish I'd never caused such hurt. It was terrible. I can only apologise, so deeply and truly.'

She shushes him. 'I know,' she says.

The softness in her response almost brings him undone.

'I need you to deal with finding me.' She looks straight at him. 'I don't want a stranger to find me. I don't want the girls to find me. I hoped you would be able to do this for me.'

He can't say anything.

'And I want you to try and help the girls understand my decision.'

'You won't tell them yourself?'

She shakes her head vigorously. 'There's a lot I can do. But not that. Not that. If they begged me not to go ahead, I would cave in, completely. But it's not what I want. I mean, I don't want any of this at all — of course I don't — but I want to at least spare myself and others the indignity of what's to come. I want to choose how I'm going to go. And I know there is considerable arrogance in that — it's something I've grappled with, I still grapple with — but surely I can take some control?'

He looks down at the table, at the backs of his hands, hairier now in his middle age, liver-coloured spots appearing on his skin. He does not know if he's up to this.

'Perhaps it would be easier if I just told you my plan?'

He nods.

'I am going to go to the river shack tomorrow. I have written letters to Ester and April, explaining what has happened and why. I will have them with me. When I get there, I want to go for a walk and a last swim.' She looks out the window and grimaces. 'Although it's hardly swimming weather. But things can't be just how we want them, can they? And then I plan to text you and take the overdose. I would like you to come up. I don't want a stranger to find me. I don't want the people who have bought the place to find me. Just come up and call the ambulance.'

He has never seen a dead body before. He does not know if he can do this.

'Why can't I just call the ambulance from here?'

'You could,' she tells him, and he realises she has thought all this through. 'I suppose I just wanted to know that there would be someone there to check that everything went as it should. I wanted someone who knew and understood what I was doing. I hoped that you could tell the girls that you saw me and that I was peaceful, and that this was what needed to happen. I hoped you could watch over my body until the ambulance came.' Her gaze is direct and clear.

'And what happens if you don't take enough? If I arrive and it hasn't worked?' He can hear a slightly shrill panic in his voice, probably audible only to himself.

'It's up to you, really. I don't want to you to put yourself at risk, but if I seem close to gone —'

'Oh, I can't kill you,' he tells her, suddenly struck by how surreal this conversation has become.

'No, but you could take your time in calling for help. If I

seemed peaceful. If it seemed close. But I have to leave that up to you. And I have to assume that Henry is right. The amount is correct. And if you can't do this, if you can only call the ambulance for me from here, I understand.'

Lawrence rubs at his cheek, the palm of his hand against his skin. He pushes his chair back slightly, also finding it difficult to sit still. He goes to the tap and pours himself a glass of water. He tries to swallow.

'Why me?'

She is sitting again now, and she turns to where he still stands, at the sink.

'There's enough distance and enough closeness. And as I said, I feel that you owe me. But I don't mean that in an angry, vindictive way. I suppose I saw this as a way of making amends all round.'

'And you think April and Ester won't be angry that I didn't alert them to this, that I didn't try and change your mind?'

'They probably will be initially. But then they'll be glad that you helped me do what I needed to do.'

'You haven't given me long to think about this,' he protests.

'I couldn't. I was afraid you'd tell the girls if there was too much time, that after a few days, your doubts would grow and maybe ebb again, only to grow once more, and then, eventually, you would just cave in and tell them everything. I really don't want them to know. You must promise me that much at least.'

He is silent. The tap drips, and he tightens it. Maurie would have fixed this in the past.

When he eventually speaks, it is to ask a question, his voice feeble at the shame of confessing his potential cowardliness: 'And what if I can't do this?'

She looks at him. 'Then I suppose I just go there and don't return. When they notice, they will call the police, or maybe someone will find me before then.' She scratches at the kitchen table, her nails tightly clipped, her fingers fine and square-tipped. 'I'll be gone.'

'And they'll find your letter, explaining why you did this?'

'I hope so,' she tells him.

'Does it mention me?'

She doesn't understand what he is asking.

'Am I woven into this scenario, even if I don't want to participate?'

She nods. 'I tell them that I explained my decision to you, and that is why you found me.'

'And then I have to explain to them that I chose not to help you? That I wasn't there. And that I didn't warn them of what you were going to do?' Lawrence shakes his head, the full ramifications slowly seeping in. 'And when you don't come back from the river, I'll either have to tell them that I know what happened to you, or I'll have to lie.'

She is standing again, looking out the window at the courtyard; the pattern of wet leaves across the bricks is a patchwork of brown, gold, silver, green, and russet. 'If you don't want to do this, I can change my letters. But you need to let me know your decision.' She looks tired. 'I can't talk a lot more about this. It's up to you, really.'

No matter what he chooses, she has told him of her plans. Even if he says he can't be part of this, even if she changes her letter, he will see their anxiety when she fails to return from the river, when she doesn't answer their calls. How can he remain silent then? He sits at the table, hands clasped in front of him and looks up at her, still standing by the window.

If only she hadn't asked this of him.

'I wish I could see them grow a little older,' Hilary says.

Looking out at the rain, he thinks for a moment she is referring to a plant, something she is growing in the courtyard, before he realises that she is, of course, talking of Catherine and Lara.

'They'll miss you,' he says.

'For a while.' She smiles. 'And then life goes on, and I will be someone that they remember occasionally, with fondness, but with no real substance to the recollection. And that's the way it should be,' she says. 'You get a brief time, and it's so vivid and wonderful and not to be wasted, but of course you only know that when it's about to be snatched away. And then there's a fainter imprint left behind, a period in which you are remembered. After that you are gone.'

The rain stops and the silence is sudden, broken by the fall of drops from the gutter. He looks out the window. They are hitting the edge of a metal pail, the sound loud in the new quiet. He is exhausted. For an instant, his mind returns to the mundane, the practicalities of picking up the girls, the weariness he feels at the thought of cooking dinner. They will get takeaway, he thinks. And then, as quickly as he had veered off on a tangent, he is back again, here in the silence of this room, unable to grasp what Hilary has asked of him. He thinks he might cry. And he is appalled. He stands then and walks to the door, opening it so he can smell the sweetness that follows each shower.

'I'll help you,' Lawrence tells her.

'I knew you would.' She looks at him. 'You're not all bad, you know.'

He unclasps his hands, eyes still fixed on her. 'If you weren't dying, I'd tell you that you could thank me.' He laughs, a strange sound, tugging between tears and anger and frustration and sadness, and then he just shakes his head.

'Thank you,' she says to him, and she holds her hand out.

He takes it.

As he holds her in the silence of the kitchen, he is emptied completely, the frailness of her, the impossibility of imagining the line she is preparing to cross so much bigger than his own self, his worries and anxieties.

And then she pulls away, telling him he'd best get going. She is tired now and she needs to be alone.

Ester's last client for the day has never had a sexual relationship.

'Which you think might mean she's never had any issues either,' Ester once joked. 'I was tempted to congratulate her on her wisdom.'

The friend she was with raised an eyebrow, and Ester smiled. 'Well — imagine how simple life would be.' She shook her head. 'It's probably something I don't even need to imagine — it may be the life I live from now on.'

She never used names, but there were times when she talked about her clients. How could she not? She was immersed in their lives all day, the intensity sometimes blanching her own of any colour or substance.

Hannah was forty years old. Tiny, dark-haired, pale, she wore all black, her make-up equally dramatic: white powder, dark mascara, and a deep-plum lipstick. Her clothes were expensive, Belgian designer, deconstructed to make them look they hadn't been stitched properly, with tiny signifiers to let those in the know see that they were the real deal: a white cross on the back of the neck, or a small square near the hem. Ester used to try clothes on like this in Paris. She even bought a coat once, and then felt ashamed at never wearing it. But the truth was, she found the look ugly, hard; or perhaps she just didn't get the language of high-end designer fashion. What were they trying to say by making them look like they had been roughly made?

She had tried on a few identities during that time, unsure as to who she was, alone in an apartment with the twins while Lawrence went off to an office job each day — both of them unhappy. On the good days, he would assess her with amusement on his return, or when they met for lunch, eyes narrowed as he tried to pinpoint her latest look — 'It's *Breakfast at Tiffany's*?' 'A lesbian golfer?' 'An uptight academic?'

She'd feign innocence, shrugging his comments off and denying this loss of self — until he came home late one night, drunk and dishevelled, to find her sitting on the floor, crying. She was lonely. She didn't know who she was anymore. She wanted to go home.

He'd held her, kissing her softly, sweet and boozy, as he'd told her he would quit, he hated it as well, they would go home, the four of them would live in sharp white light so harsh it hurt; they would wake to salty skies and the lazy drone of insects, perhaps they would buy an inner-city house that would seem spacious and bright and almost bucolic, he laughed. And she might get back to just being Ester.

Whoever she *was*, Ester thought, but she didn't utter the words out loud.

Hannah, too, has lived in Paris, and New York, and London, and even Brussels, briefly. She is a corporate counsel for a major international brand, but she wishes she were an architect.

'I'm good at my job,' she told Ester. 'But I don't enjoy it.' She reconsidered her statement. 'That's probably not entirely true. I get satisfaction from doing it well, and there are times when it's intellectually challenging. But if I tried to explain what I did most days, you'd stop listening.'

Ester smiled. 'I'd try not to.'

Hannah's laugh was tight. 'You're paid to, regardless of how dull. Essentially, it's work that benefits wealthy shareholders by putting more money in their pockets. I don't create anything, or make anything. I don't help people. I don't have any belief in the necessity of what I do.'

'And do you want to change this?' Ester asked.

Hannah contemplated the question for a moment. 'There was a time when I wanted to. Very much. But I'm pragmatic. I'm used to earning well. And I wouldn't cope with being at the bottom of the pile. Not at this stage of my life.'

Work is not the reason she came to see Ester.

She was frank from the outset about her failure to have a relationship, her words clipped and direct, almost daring Ester to look startled as she uttered the words: 'I've never had sex. I haven't even kissed anyone since I was in primary school.' On her wrist she wore a leather cuff, and she turned it, too loose on the white skin. 'It's not that I don't want to have a relationship, although I probably am fussy.' She pressed the cuff tighter. 'And if I met someone, how do I explain who I am? That I'm this age and I've no ...' she paused, 'experience?'

Ester asked her to tell her a little more about herself.

Hannah was adopted. She hadn't been told this. She had discovered it when she was 17, after her mother died, the papers in a neat folder at the bottom of her underwear drawer. She'd tried to find her birth mother, lodging a request for contact with various agencies, but she never received a response.

'How did that make you feel?'

Hannah shrugged. 'Disappointed?' She glanced at the fireplace. 'That's a beautiful painting. Is it a Maurie Marcel?'

It is, Ester said.

'Are you related?' Hannah asked.

Ester said they were.

She had to be quick; she learnt that within the first hour. Hannah would talk in a seemingly open and frank manner, and then stymie any attempt to analyse or investigate a little deeper. The third time she did it, Ester smiled, gently pointing the habit out to her.

'I don't think there's anything further to say about the matter,' Hannah replied, and she looked genuinely bemused.

Her childhood was neither happy nor unhappy, she said. 'Colourless.'

They lived in an outer-northern suburb, and Hannah went to an ordinary suburban public school. She studied hard, she had few friends, and in her final year, she became ill. 'Glandular fever. I had to work from home. I took the exams and did well enough to get into law — not as well as I would have done otherwise, but well enough. And then my mother died. I was on my own.'

'And was that hard?'

'Not particularly,' Hannah said. 'We were never close. I was self-sufficient.'

Hannah just doesn't know how to meet someone. Doesn't know how to fall in love, to have sex, to be normal, and she asks these questions during most sessions with the persistence Ester has come to know during their time together, wanting this to be just another problem that can be solved with a logical and determined approach.

Today, she wears slim-fitting black pants, boots with a strange lacing system that makes them look a little like orthopaedic shoes, a loose black knit, and several silver discs around her neck. Her hair is damp from the rain, and she musses it with her fingers to dry it, beginning the session with her usual barrage of talk. She is late — as she often is — and she has excuses banked up: meetings that went over time; the need to get something off layby on the way here (she is a compulsive shopper who puts everything on layby, stretching the terms of the agreement to breaking point); taxis that didn't come.

Ester has told her that failing to be on time only sabotages the session for herself. 'It's very hard to do effective work in under an hour.' She has also made rules with Hannah. More than ten minutes late, and the session will be cancelled. Hannah usually arrives moments after the ten-minute cut-off. Late twice in a row, and the therapy will come to an end. They have come perilously close to this point several times.

Over the last month, Hannah has commenced internet dating.

'Browsing actually,' she always says.

She finds it demeaning and demoralising. 'I don't think this is something we should shop for. You reach a certain level of income and you can buy most things — cooked meals, a clean apartment, someone to do your chores — but I'm not sure you should purchase a relationship.'

'What makes you think of it as purchasing?' Ester asks.

Hannah considers the question. 'I realise there's no exchange of money, but it's still like a display of goods, an advertising of the wares.' She rolls her eyes. 'And most of the wares aren't that enticing. I knew there were a lot of dull men out there but to be reminded of this — en masse —'

Ester smiles, remembering her own experiences of internet trawling.

'But I've decided this is a mountain that needs to be climbed.' Hannah leans forward, her words becoming more rapid as she confesses her decision. 'I need to have sex. I've picked one of them — the least offensive I could find — and I'm meeting him tonight, for a "date",' she puts inverted commas around the words with her fingers and raises her eyebrows, 'so I can go to bed with him. I can't put it off any longer.'

Then, sitting back in her chair, Hannah asks whether Ester has changed the room around. 'I like it,' she says, appraising the space, which hasn't altered since Ester moved here, let alone in the fortnight that's passed since Hannah's last session.

Ester tells her no, following up with her own question before Hannah gets another chance to divert her, aware that these sessions are sometimes like a sprinting competition. She has to be on her toes.

'So you see the problem as being simply one of not having had sex? That this has held you back from having a relationship?'

Hannah nods earnestly, and there is something childlike in her desire to believe that such a simple solution is possible. 'Once I've had sex, I won't feel so anxious. Will I?'

Ester tells her it's one approach. 'But perhaps it's worth also looking at why you haven't had a physically intimate relationship — or encounter — until now. There are fixes and there are fixes,' she says. 'It's a little like the difference between a quick surface clean of a room, or a thorough clean. The band-aid or the operation.'

Hannah nods. 'The surface clean shouldn't be dismissed. It can make a difference.'

Ester crosses her legs and smiles. 'If you decide to take this approach,' she says, 'will you promise me one thing? Look after yourself. Don't be afraid to back away if you feel uncomfortable.'

Hannah nods, and then laughs. 'Actually, I can't promise you that. It's inevitable I'm going to feel uncomfortable.'

Ester smiles. 'Fair enough. But don't push yourself into a place that feels completely wrong. And, perhaps more importantly, be prepared to accept that this may not provide the miracle cure you're looking for.'

Hannah looks down at her hands. She has delicate, slender fingers, the first signs of age on the paleness of her skin, the back of her hands dry and papery, livery age-spots freckling the blue of her veins. She scratches at one of her nails, shaping it. The silence is rare.

When she looks up again, her eyes glitter. She turns to stare at the rain on the window, the film over the darkness of her pupils gone as soon as she glances back to Ester.

'All my life, I have been lonely.'

Ester remains silent.

'I knew it, but I didn't know it. When something is constant, you're often not aware of it. The house was quiet with just my mother and me. She went to bed by nine, and I spent most nights in my room, studying. I listened to the radio while I worked. People rang the late-night show. Love songs and dedications, it was called. They would talk about their husband who'd left, their first love, their partner that cheated on them. *And what would you like to say to him?* the announcer would ask. *I forgive you,* they would say. Or: *Come home, I miss you.* And then they would play a song for them.

'One night, a woman rang. She had no one to make a dedication to. And so she was making it to a man she was yet to meet, a man who would love and cherish her. *I'm sure he's out there for you,* the announcer said in his smooth, deep voice. *I know you will cross paths one day soon.*' Hannah stares at Ester. 'Who was he to make that assurance?'

Ester smiles.

'I've become so used to being alone. I find it hard to imagine this will ever change.'

Ester nods. 'You have learnt to be extraordinarily self-reliant, and to do without people. This was probably very necessary as a child. It helped you survive. But the survival skills we develop as a child often don't work so well for us when we are older. And breaking down patterns, habits, ways of being that are entrenched, can be a slow process.'

The rain drums down, down and down and down. Ester looks at Hannah sitting opposite her — intelligent, original, fierce, determined — and she is seized by a foolish desire to give her something more than this careful response.

They all come in here, day after day, session after session. Loneliness, heartache, despair, anger. Most of her clients are there at the uncomfortable edge of one of the darker facets of life. She could stand up now in her room and open the window, let the rain pour in, across her desk, onto the beautiful carpet, her papers curling up, ink smudging, the sound of the downpour uncomfortably loud and close, and she could look at Hannah and tell her to just go for it — have sex, have it often, throw herself into life with no reserve.

But she does not utter those words to Hannah. Of course she doesn't.

This temptation often creeps in at the end of the day. And she always resists.

Opposite her, Hannah is picking up her bag, a large, soft, leather pouch.

'I understand how you could feel that having sex will break down the barriers quickly.'

Hannah grimaces.

Ester smiles: 'Apologies for the unfortunate choice of words.'

'I know what you're saying,' Hannah interjects. 'You're telling me to be careful. To not expect too much.' And she stands, tiny, delicate in her black, bag swung onto her shoulder. 'I like your skirt by the way. Is it a Paul Smith?'

At the end of day in her room, Ester sits for a moment. She would like to do a little talking herself. This is how she feels at the end of most days, actually.

On the afternoons she picks the girls up from school, she tests out her voice when she is alone in the car, sometimes venting her frustrations with particular clients out loud, sometimes reminding herself of tasks she is meant to do, or even expressing her own feelings to the dashboard. The sound of her words is strange after sitting in a room alone with other voices washing over her — woes, joys, and grievances layered and twisted and knotted, and dumped, one after the other.

She used to ring Lawrence for this purpose, and the beauty of it was that she didn't even care that he was — as he so often was towards the end — non-responsive. She would simply talk, chatting about what she would make for dinner or her plans for the weekend, or about a movie she wanted to see, an issue in the news, or her own anxieties about Hilary, or how difficult she found April.

Often she could hear the music he was listening to in the background: the low hum of a guitar, or the steady beat of drums. Sometimes, he was in a café, and there would be other voices around him, a clatter of plates. He would grunt in response, only occasionally asking questions or contributing himself. She didn't care. She just wanted to talk and talk and talk.

It must have been irritating, she thinks now, smiling as she does so, because her thoughts towards him are not unkind, and this surprises her. It's happening more frequently, her mind resting on Lawrence momentarily, alighting with a well-accustomed wariness, only to find that the landing is softer each time.

'Perhaps we *will* speak again,' she says to herself, because this is one of those days when she is at home alone and the easiest solution to that immediate need to talk is to bore herself with her own words, which she does.

Opposite, she can see her reflection in the window. The desk lamp is still on, a pool of light in the glass, revealing the pale lines of her face, her dark eyes, brown hair pulled back, the lipstick on her mouth faded now. She imagines facing this woman in this room and talking to her.

'My husband cheated on me with my sister, and, for over three years, I have been unable to forgive either of them.'

The words are bald when she utters them, and she glances up at the Ester in the window, eyes a little too wide for the calm and curious self who usually listens in this room.

'Almost three years. And I have not uttered a word to either of them.'

And now that other Ester responds. 'What are you afraid of?' she asks, leaping several steps ahead because they know each other well, this client and this therapist, and there is no need for the cautious steps she would normally take.

'What am I afraid of?' Ester repeats the question.

Letting go of that anger and hatred. She tries to imagine it, while knowing that the remnants she hangs onto now are tattered scraps, frayed and symbolic only. What would she have left without it?

Ester closes her eyes. It is April she sees. They are in their early twenties, and they are at a party. April is dancing, oblivious to everyone around her. Men and women drift in and out of her orbit as she moves under a hazy night-time sky, the few stars obscured by the sea-spray fog, the air warm and humid, so salty she can almost taste it. It's 'Sign of the Times' by Prince that she's dancing to, and she's lost in it.

Ester's boyfriend of the time is off trying to buy some ecstasy. The plan is for the three of them to go and take it before the night gets any later. But the truth is that Ester doesn't really want to. She never likes taking drugs when she is with April. Ester knows what will happen. She will sit removed, watching the evening from a distance, judging April, judging her own boyfriend, telling herself that it's just the drugs making them have such a good time, as though they are cheating. As though, somehow, this is a game with results, and they are cheating. And she doesn't want it to be like this. She wishes they had never decided to buy any.

She stands, slightly unsteady in her new heels, and weaves her way through the bodies. She has drunk too much, and, in the heat, she feels vaguely ill. These are April's friends — she doesn't know many of them — and she takes her sister by the hand and tells her she needs to go home.

April runs her fingers down Ester's arm, her touch surprisingly cool despite the warmth. 'Dance with me,' she says. Ester shakes her head, but before she knows it, she is moving with her sister, as they used to do when they were young, the music loud in their bedroom, dressed up in a strange array of clothes they had stolen from Hilary and Maurie's wardrobe, and she feels all her self-conscious anxiety slide away, tumbling like silk to the dance floor where she kicks it off to the side, out of their orbit, both of them aware of nothing more than the music and each other.

She is having fun; beautiful, bright, fizzy fun, and April is right there with her, the pair of them sparkling in the joy of it.

Opening her eyes again, Ester is surprised to find herself crying.

'I miss her,' she says out loud to the other self, who is a terrible therapist because she is crying too. They smile at each other.

'The truth is really very simple,' Ester the client says to Ester the therapist. 'And also very complicated.' They laugh.

Lawrence should have been with someone like April, but all the time he would have wanted to love someone like Ester. He'd known that. And so he'd fallen for Ester because that was what he'd wanted to be — a man who fell for a woman like Ester. And yet, wanting is not enough.

She'd loved him. But sometimes she wondered whether part of her love came from being so amazed that someone like him had chosen someone like her.

'He picked me over my sister.'

'And then he didn't,' the therapist says. Or is it the client?

She leans forward and switches off the lamp, the darkness of the day seeping in now. She stacks her papers neatly on the desk and powers down the computer. Lifting each of the cushions off the two-seater couch, she shakes them, the feathers fluffing up; they are full again, as though no one has sat here all day.

Last is the bin. Still empty after Chris. Hannah doesn't cry. Ester remembers this as soon as she looks at it, and she pushes it back under the desk, ready for next week's tissues.

Closing the door behind her, she steps out into the house, the corridor dark, the silence heavy. She needs to work out what she is going to wear, and she flinches from the prospect of trying to decide, because it is not something she is good at. Lawrence had an eye for clothes. He would often advise her if she couldn't choose, knowing what would suit her and what wouldn't. She shakes her head at the thought of ringing him now.

'Help me,' she would say. 'I need an outfit for my first proper date.'

And he would tell her to avoid black, and the librarian look or the lesbian golfer, unless, of course, this date was a man who went for a more uptight get-up.

'Which you do well,' he would say, one eyebrow raised, the old Lawrence again, the one from their early days, teasing her as he used to, such a long time ago.

HALFWAY TO APRIL'S HOUSE, the nausea that Lawrence feels gets the better of him. He has the heater on too high, and he winds down the window, the chill slap of the rain on his skin a relief. Sticking his head out, he breathes in deeply, only to quickly recoil as a truck passes, the fumes and oil and rush of wind sudden and fierce.

He doesn't know how he will act as though everything is normal. He doesn't know if he should. He wishes he could ring Ester and ask her advice. She was good at listening and guiding him to a decision. But eventually he began to recoil from that, wary of the therapist in her, and feeling that she was turning their relationship into client and counsellor, which made him behave badly.

'Red rag to a bull,' he would say when she accused him of drinking too much, and he would pour another wine without flinching from her gaze.

He turns the news on, the results of a rival poll making headlines. The issue is climate change and whether the government should do more to combat the effects. He switches to music, not wanting to hear the tedium of the analysis, knowing that if he does, he will pick holes in the questions. Besides, what does it matter what people think? What does it fucking matter? The world is dying, and we are still asking the opinions of every person on the street while failing to listen to what our experts are telling us. He finds he is crying, his eyes as blurred as the windscreen, everything awash, wiping the tears with the back of his hands as the blades go back and forth across the glass.

By the side of the road, he winds the window right down and puts his head out to vomit. The hazard lights tick, a steady rhythm over the hiss of other cars as they rush past. The music is off. When he closes the window again, there is only silence, and he sobs, the salt of his tears diluted by the rain, everything fogged up so there is just him and his terrible sadness.

'Okay,' he says to himself in the rear-vision mirror. 'Enough.'

He puts the key in the ignition and turns back onto the road, wipers flicking back and forth, back and forth, breathing slowly to calm himself before he gets to April's.

Catherine has always been the artist. She lies on the floor, sheets of newspaper spread out in front of her, crayons and textas to choose from, her legs swinging behind her in rhythm to the music as she contemplates which colour to use next.

Lara is on the couch reading, although her boredom is evident; half her body has slipped down toward the ground, and he can see she is ready to start causing trouble.

'Daddy,' she calls out, and she jumps up, Catherine right behind her.

He hugs them both tight.

'So who hurt herself?' he asks, and they look momentarily confused — the whole accident at school forgotten — and then they point at each other, while he shakes his head in mock disapproval. 'Have you been good for your Auntie April?' He grins at them.

'Angelic,' April says, and she sits back on the old leather couch, feet up on the coffee table as she asks him whether he wants a cup of tea.

'And a piece of cake,' Lara adds.

'Or something stronger?' April glances at the clock. 'It's getting to that time. Besides, it's so bloody dark and miserable outside it might as well be night.'

Why not, he thinks, and he tells her a whiskey and cake is just what he needs.

'Lara, you be the barmaid,' April points to the cupboard where the bottle is. 'And Catherine, you serve the cake. I'm shagged.'

Lawrence shakes his head. 'I don't think you're meant to ask young children to serve alcohol,' he says, aware that in the absence of Ester, he becomes very like her.

April smiles. 'I'm not asking her to drink it. Just to make it. Ice and a dash,' she adds to Lara. 'Pouring a drink is a useful skill.'

'For an alcoholic.'

April raises an eyebrow. 'Shitty day at the office?'

He smiles at her, aware of how like a parody of a married couple they are, and then he looks down at his jeans, still damp from the dash across the street, and steadies himself because he remains perilously close to tears. 'Thank you for getting them.'

Catherine has two plates of cake on a tray. She curtsies and giggles. 'May I serve you, oh lord and lady?'

Behind her, Lara waits with two very large glasses of whiskey in her hands. She inhales deeply and then curls her lip. 'Disgusting.'

'This lady is going to renounce her cake and give it to the serving girls,' April says. 'Why don't you take it through to my bedroom and watch some television?'

'I'll come and get you soon,' Lawrence adds. 'We need to get home for dinner.' He knows he is saying this to April really, to let her know he won't be staying, and he takes a long gulp of the whiskey, ice cold, burning in his throat.

'What's up?' April's pale eyes are focused on him.

He shrugs, lying badly. 'Just tired.'

She doesn't buy it. 'I've known you for a while. In some very trying circumstances. Is it the girls being here?'

He shakes his head. 'They shouldn't be here, but I appreciate what you did.' He takes another slug of the whiskey and then puts the glass down. 'I've got to drive.'

In the soft light from the lamp next to the window, April's long, fine arms are golden, her fingers delicate, two heavy silver rings on each hand. The glass is sweating in her grasp, and she too puts her drink down, running her damp palms through the curls in her hair before standing slowly and coming over to where he sits. 'I'm not going to bite you,' she says, and she leans down and kisses him gently on the cheek, her touch warm and kind. 'Nor am I going to try and make you stay. You just look sad.'

He shifts in his chair, wanting to pull her towards him and hold her close, to cry and tell her everything; he doesn't know what he wants, really. It's been so long since he's had any idea; he can't even remember when he knew, or what it was he desired. It's all shifting, and he is seasick with the motion, so he closes his eyes, letting in the sound of the rain, the low hum of the television from the other room, the softness of the couch. There is a velvet smell — roses — heavy and funereal above the richness of the cake and whiskey, and, last, the touch of April's hand resting warm on his arm.

'Has something happened?' she asks. 'Are you ill?'

He shakes his head.

'Ester? Is Ester ill? Is no one telling me?'

No, no, no.

And then he tells her — not about Hilary, not that — he tells her about Edmund and being caught out, and he probably does it to avoid relaying the news of her mother, and because it's all too much now. He says it all — how he fiddled with the last three polls, just slightly, why, he didn't know. He hated the government? He was bored witless with what he did? Did it make any difference? No. It was a puny misdemeanour, really. There were many legitimate ways he could, and did, meddle — the questions he chose, the timing, the slant on his interpretation of the responses. As he talks, he finds it hard to understand his actions. He finds it hard to understand anything.

'Fuck me.' April looks at him and grins.

He doesn't know whether to laugh or cry.

He doesn't mean to kiss her, but he does; it is like a default mechanism, kicking in as a response to desperate floundering; her mouth is soft, whiskey-warm on his, and it is like hovering above the edge of a deep pool, only to be stopped by her hand on his shoulder, pushing him away as Catherine asks what they are doing, her voice clear above the rain and television.

'Nothing,' he says too quickly and loudly.

'Why are you kissing April?'

'I wasn't,' he lies.

'Well, you were, actually,' April responds, the only one keeping her head, and she is laughing now. 'Which was stupid of your father, but sometimes too much rain and whiskey makes idiots of us all.'

Catherine just stares at them.

'Come over here,' Lawrence says, and he pats the arm of the chair.

She turns and runs out of the room.

In April's bedroom, he tries to sit Catherine on his lap, but she continues to resist him.

'It's all right,' he tells her. 'There's nothing happening with April. It was a mistake,' he says. 'I had some bad news today, and I'm not behaving how I should.'

'I don't want to talk,' Catherine says, fingers blocking her ears.

Lara is transfixed by the television.

'Okay.' Lawrence sighs. 'We'll head home in a few minutes.'

In the lounge room, April looks up at him. 'She'll be fine,' she says. 'Just don't make too big a deal of it.' And then she picks up her glass and shakes her head. 'You need to grow up,' she tells him. 'And stop falling onto whoever is closest when the shit hits the fan.'

That's rich, he thinks. *Coming from her.*

'So what are you going to do?'

'Confess,' he eventually says. 'I don't have any choice.'

'I would have thought you'd have dreamed up something more interesting than that. Tell them Edmund has lost his mind. Or that you've fired him and he's seeking revenge.' She pours herself another glass. 'Or go brave. Tell them the polls create their own truth.' She smiles. 'Become a political rebel.'

He's had enough.

'I'm not a kid anymore. This is my work.'

The clock chimes behind him. She doesn't shift. 'You hate it. You're miserable. You have been for years. If you're going to fiddle the results, at least have some guts about it, shout it out loud. You've got nothing to lose.'

She doesn't get it.

'And live off what?'

Her eyes remain fixed on him. 'What else is going on?'

He ignores her, standing to leave, calling out the girls' names as he does so.

'So I presume I won't see you again for a while,' April says. She begins gathering the twins' bags, putting them next to their raincoats by the door, and then she scans the chaos of the room one last time to see if there's anything she's forgotten.

He, too, surveys the mess. Records and newspaper spread out across the floor, cake plates on the carpet. The rain is soft against the windows.

'Do you think we could have been happy together?'

The question is without rancour or sadness. Her voice is soft so the girls won't hear, but still he looks quickly to the closed bedroom door.

He doesn't know the answer.

'Maybe,' he says.

'I'd like us to be friends. I'd like to see the girls. But more than anything, I want to have Ester in my life again.'

He can see the need in her eyes, and he looks away.

'I'm going to call her tomorrow. And if she won't answer, I'm going to go to her.'

He doesn't reply. But in that instant, he wants, more than anything, for her desire to be realised.

He calls the girls, loudly now: 'Come on, you two,' his voice too harsh, startling enough to make them both obey, Catherine still refusing to look at him as she picks up her school bag and waits for him in the hall.

HILARY DOES NOT know why she has always felt a greater vulnerability around Ester. She is afraid for her, and slightly afraid of her. And yet, by all measures, she's the more sensible of her daughters, the one who considers before she acts, who listens and usually responds with reason. She doesn't fall into great drama over an event of little incident, nor display a lack of interest in an important moment.

Perhaps it is Hilary's sense that this calm simply covers all that Ester hides, a shield to cloak her frailty, just as Hilary hides behind a stern facade. They are alike, and that is what makes her more afraid for her younger daughter.

Ester sits at the table now, the smooth sheen of her dark hair rich in the softness of the lamplight, her skin pale. She looks beautiful this evening, dressed in a silvery-grey sweater and black jeans; she is also wearing make-up, which for her is unusual, the dark around her eyes and the red on her lips bringing out the delicacy of her features. Like Hilary, she wears little jewellery — just a fine gold bracelet and a beaten-gold ring that has a dull shine.

She is translating the program notes, reading them aloud, head bent in concentration, one finger running along each line of text, but Hilary is not listening. All she can hear is the stillness of the evening — the rain has eased — and, floating above the silence, the gentleness of Ester's voice darting over and around the steady beat of a drip drip drip, the last of the previous downpour earthbound from gutter to ground.

Ester looks up, waiting for Hilary to comment, to demand certain changes — which is what she usually does — or to signify her approval.

'It's fine,' Hilary tells her.

'Even being called "elderly"?'

Hilary just nods. She no longer cares about the film or the program. She just wants to drink in Ester, take her fill. 'Where are you off to this evening?'

Ester hesitates before answering, and then a smile escapes the corners of her mouth, and she folds up the translation. 'I think I've met someone,' she says. 'We're going out to dinner.'

Hilary holds her daughter's hands in her own and lifts them slowly, kissing the smooth skin, and squeezing them a little before she lets them go.

'He's a lucky man,' she eventually says. 'You are a beautiful young woman, and so easy to love.'

Ester blinks and stares up at the ceiling.

'Don't doubt it for a minute,' Hilary leans closer, about to continue, but Ester shifts back. She never wants to talk about this.

'Listen to me,' Hilary continues. 'I'm elderly so I do know some things. I forget others, but what I remember has some value. You've been hurt, I know that. And your anger was understandable. But now it's time to let it go and enjoy your life. It's so short. Don't waste it.' She stands because the throbbing pain is too much. Her hands shake as she pours herself a glass of water. 'Shall we have a wine to celebrate?' She shouldn't drink on the painkillers, but what does it matter? She could down the whole bottle if she chose. She could do anything tonight — and with that realisation comes a strange vertigo that makes her clutch the fridge door a little tighter to steady herself.

Ester notices. 'Are you all right?'

She is tired of lying. 'I haven't been feeling well,' she says.

'You should see a doctor.'

And there she is, balanced on the point — *I have*, she could say. *And I don't have long to live*. But as she opens her mouth, her throat dries up, and fortunately Ester is too distracted by the evening ahead to press the point.

'Just one glass,' she tells Hilary.

'Are you nervous?'

Ester always avoids discussing herself. And so she too stands and looks out the window at the courtyard, glistening under the light from the kitchen. 'Didn't you want to show me your film?'

Hilary no longer cares. But if it means she can keep Ester here for a little longer, she will.

She has tidied the studio, cataloguing all her stills and working drafts into neatly labelled boxes. April hadn't noticed this morning, but Ester does. 'God, you've been busy. Why the big clean-up?' She walks around, reading the notes on top of several boxes, and then she turns to Maurie's drawing of the horse. 'I think that's my favourite work of his.'

Hilary looks at it. She smiles. 'Mine, too.' It is the arch of the neck that she has always liked best. 'No one will be able to keep it when I'm gone.'

In the silence that follows, she can feel Ester watching her for a moment, hesitating, and so she turns quickly to the computer and loads the film. 'Here,' she pulls out a seat for her daughter and dims the lights.

She had been nervous at the prospect of showing Ester the footage of her and April, but she no longer cares. There's nothing she can do. It's up to Ester now. And so she presses play, and the first of the images floods the screen, starting with suitcases, her own from when she was young, her school satchel with her name written on it, and the bag she took when she came to Australia, leading down to the story of all she chose to keep from her past when she began her new life here.

It wasn't much.

Clothes, a diary, two novels, and a camera.

Cracked leather, frayed cotton, yellowed paper, and a hard Bakelite shell.

She stands, washed out by white sunlight, hair like fairy-floss in the stiffness of the sea breeze, that camera pressed to her eye.

And the images build — negatives, prints, too many to contain, kept in files, digitised, catalogued, weightless and yet so very weighty — until, finally, they settle on a photo of Maurie, a man without suitcases or bags, just paints and pencils and turpentine, canvas and wood, colours waxy and oiled, palettes overrun with hues, splattered floors and walls, and paintings stacked up against walls, in storage, digitised, catalogued, and valued.

Hilary glances across at Ester, who is leaning forward, listening to her mother's narrative, her voice weaving a tale of a life, of all that is amassed in such a short period of time, all that is purchased, created, swapped, gifted, lost, and forgotten.

And now the sisters sleep — two young girls, one dark, one fair, lying next to each other in a hammock by the river. Hilary would like to touch the downy hair on those legs again, feel the curl of a small, sticky finger in her own, and breathe in the sugary sweetness of milk teeth and plump cheeks.

They are older now, in dress-ups from one of the suitcases, dancing on the verandah of the river house, behind them a hazy drone of insects buzzing in the grass and the sky, everything wilting under the summer heat.

Suitcases again — dress-up clothes tumbling out across the floor, and the images melt into carefully folded pants and shirts, jackets, ties and sweaters, shoes in rows, socks curled into each other, underpants; the sadness of clothes without flesh. Hilary puts them all into garbage bags, talking to the camera the whole time, saying that this is not what she wants to hold onto. Not at all. And then she sits there on the empty bed, her hands open on her lap. She has nothing she can grasp.

The footage shifts now to other tales, memento mori, keepsakes — dandelion wisps of hair in lockets, pressed flowers, jewellery, even a clipping about a woman who kept fur from each of her cats. Slowly, these images dissolve to the floor of the river shack, belongings spread out across the bare boards.

Hilary has filmed herself packing up.

She glances across at Ester now, who is still watching, chin cupped in one hand, eyes focused. Hilary knows Ester has not been there since she learnt about April and Lawrence. But she does not flinch at the footage.

The camera flickers off and then on again, the images blurred by the rain that had fallen on the lens, the focus now on the swollen river seizing debris with its furious pace, the swirl and then the stillness as all the force of that water rushed up against a small dam, everything left behind as the flow moved on.

Hilary reaches for the light and then stops.

Ester has her head in her hands.

'Has it upset you?' Hilary eventually asks.

'No.' Ester looks at her mother. 'It's a beautiful film. The best you've made. You should be very proud of it.' She picks up her empty glass and turns it around in her hands. 'You're not really elderly.' Her words are slow, considered. 'You're only seventy — and look at your work.'

In the darkness of the studio, Hilary doesn't move.

Ester turns on the desk lamp, a pale pool of golden light spilling across the room. *She has on that face*, Hilary thinks, *that therapist face.*

'Is everything all right?' Ester asks.

Hilary stands up briskly and comes over to the computer, leaning forward to log off. 'Absolutely fine.'

'I know it's been some time since Maurie died.' Ester's words are hesitant. 'But you know people can be depressed after the loss of a partner … well, for many years.'

Her head hurts and she does not want to snap, each word slapping the next towards an argument. 'I'm not depressed,' she replies. And then she tells Ester that they should get inside to the warmth. 'You'll need to get going. For your date.'

Fortunately, this is enough to distract Ester from the conversation she has been attempting.

'I'm glad you showed me,' she tells Hilary.

The air is sweet outside, damp and cool, a scattering of crushed leaves and twigs and petals covering the path from the front door. Hilary throws her head back. 'Sometimes I think how extraordinary it would be to be a dog — to be led by scent.' She picks up a small branch of red-and-gold eucalyptus, astringent and cold, and inhales deeply.

'I'm fine,' she tells Ester, who is still looking at her.

Ester's gaze stays fixed for a moment longer, and then she lets it go. 'Wish me luck.'

'I wish you all the luck and wonder and beauty in the world.' Hilary holds her close, breathing her in, warm and soft, the dampness of her hair, the faint perfume of her lipstick, the musty smell of rain on clothes, all of it, and then because she is terrified of letting go, she laughs with a little too much gaiety, and steps back into the emptiness of her house. 'I love you,' she tells Ester. 'With all of my heart.'

Her declaration floats off into the night, unheard by her daughter who is already out on the street.

Ester raises her hand. 'I'll ring you tomorrow.'

'Look forward to it,' Hilary replies.

It was an ordinary hour together, she thinks. Which is what it had to be.

All of her is stretched, taut. She looks down at her arm, the flesh and muscle, the living, breathing being that she is, warm blood pumping, pumping. Her own heart too loud. Her head thumping. And so she closes the front door, standing pressed against the wall until she is steady again, steely inside and out, focusing only on the alternative, because the horror of *not* doing what she has resolved to do is all she has left to propel her forward.

IT IS TEN O'CLOCK.

April was right. There are so many ways in which Lawrence could respond. He could fight, lie, and cheat, wait until Edmund has written to Paul and then deny everything, say that Edmund is going through a personal crisis, perhaps a mental illness. He could go public, be loud about all that is wrong with surveys, polls, focus groups, be the rebel she laughingly urged him to be. Or he could just confess in an email to Paul. A message that isn't long or difficult to compose. He altered the results. Not significantly. But the fact remained that he had done this. There were a number of reasons why. He was happy to explain, if Paul were interested in hearing, but at this stage all he wanted to do was tell him the truth. He wished him luck with the robo polls. He had enjoyed the work they had done together.

Perhaps not that last sentence. He won't lie. He deletes it, writing his name before raising his glass to his own reflection. 'To Hilary,' he whispers, pressing 'send' before he can change his mind.

And so he is done. Ruined. Fucked.

Tomorrow, Paul will ring him and ask him what in God's name he thought he was doing. Perhaps he will think Lawrence's email is some kind of drunken joke in response to his contract ending, perhaps he'll delete it before he even reads it.

He forwards a copy to Edmund with one word in the subject line: *Done*.

The response is almost immediate: Edmund is glad Lawrence has confessed, he hopes this will represent a fresh start in his life, the first steps towards being a better person. He has every confidence it will.

Lawrence deletes it.

Outside, it is silent, quiet after hours and hours of rain. The peace wraps around, soft and heavy, and Lawrence sits with it, the bottle of whiskey by his side. Somewhere in the distance, he hears a car alarm, and then a harsh beep, followed by voices, the sound of people saying farewell, laughter, and a door slamming shut. He wonders about topping himself — isn't this what people do, professional suicide followed by the real thing? He contemplates the quietness of this moment: he hasn't lied to cover it up, or gone down screaming dragging others with him, he hasn't been a rebel. He has simply confessed and said he is sorry. And he feels nothing.

Paul will bury it. No one will know. And life will carry on, with him doing shitty jobs for not much money, never quite becoming the better person he could be. *That's the truth of it*, he thinks, and he reaches for his glass, warm to the hold now, all the ice long since melted, and drinks — water with just an insipid touch of alcohol. And so he stands to pour himself another, surprised that he is slightly unsteady on his feet because he usually holds his booze with the practiced skill of a seasoned drinker.

The bottle is empty.

Outside the girls' room, he presses his ear to the door, wanting to hear their breathing, and then he slowly turns the handle.

They lie side by side in the bottom bunk, pale hair knotted, cheeks waxy, Lara's eyes closed, Catherine's open. She does this sometimes — sleeping like she is wide awake — and he bends down and shuts her eyelids gently, fingers light on the smooth skin, not looking because he has always found it disconcerting, too like the sleep of the dead.

'I love you,' he whispers, but she doesn't stir.

She hasn't spoken to him all night. And he knows he is going to have to talk to her about the kiss with April, somehow resolve it in her mind, make it seem like nothing and yet also make her realise she shouldn't tell Ester. How, he doesn't know.

Back in the lounge room, he shuts his laptop. Lawrence the pollster is done. Tomorrow he will be Lawrence the guardian of the dead, the keeper of a promise. Hungover on the job, but true to his word.

How can she bear it? Will she be lying there awake, knowing that this is it?

Against this, all the rest is just noise.

He has had too much alcohol. He knows that, but in the midst of the haze there is a clarity, and he acts on impulse, picking up his phone and ringing Ester, the switch to message bank quick.

No need to call me, he texts. *Girls are fine. Just thinking of you, and wanting all the best for you.*

She will think he is drunk — which he is — but he is glad he sent it. Tomorrow he will call her, and his heart sinks with the weight of the news he will bear.

THE RESTAURANT THEY are in is crowded, their table right at the back, out of the worst of the noise but still loud enough for them to need to lean close. Ester's knee occasionally touches his, and she can see the veins on the inside of his wrist as he reaches for the water.

Can I just kiss you? This is what she'd like to say. *Can I just take you home now?*

But of course she doesn't; she is telling Steven about her mother's films, the strange, ordered chaos of them, the beauty of the images she chooses, the way in which she weaves a story from a seemingly random selection of ideas, and, as she speaks, she is enjoying this moment of being new to someone, a whole lifetime of tales that have not been told, each one shiny and unsullied, ready to be unwrapped and marvelled at.

'I'll have to look at them,' he tells her, and he offers her some of his meal.

She shakes her head, too nervous to trust herself with the simple act of taking his fork and getting it to her mouth without spilling the lot. It is ridiculous. And then she knocks her knife to the ground, only just managing to stop her wine from toppling in the process. She laughs as she looks at him.

'I'm a klutz when I'm nervous,' she confesses. 'It's my curse. You'll just have to excuse me in advance for the many accidents that may occur before dinner is finished.'

He grins. 'Fortunately, I'm a sucker for slapstick.'

It is then that she feels her phone in her pocket, and she apologises for quickly checking. 'Just in case it's the kids.'

But it isn't. It's Lawrence.

She shakes her head in wonder at his timing.

And then puts the phone away immediately.

'It's nothing,' she says.

Steven is asking her about her sister now, and it takes a moment before Ester answers. 'I have a complicated relationship with her,' she eventually says. 'It's not great.' She looks at him, grimacing slightly. 'You might have to wait a while before I go into the details.'

He tells her he had a brother. 'My twin.' He pauses for a moment here. 'We're identical, but there was an accident during the birth. For some reason, he didn't breathe for a while. He was on life support. And there was some trauma. In any event, he had a lot of problems.'

Ester is not sure if he is going to continue. She sits back a little.

'He killed someone.'

He utters the words without stumbling, his voice remaining even, but as he swallows, she can see how hard it was to say out loud.

'So I guess I know about complex sibling relationships.' His smile is tight.

She asks whether he ever sees this brother, if they have stayed in touch.

He shakes his head. 'I did for a while. He's in a psych ward. It's so difficult. I used to try and tell myself he couldn't be held completely accountable for his actions. He's struggled with psychosis and addiction — but in the end I just didn't know what I thought. I still don't. And I stopped seeing him.'

She is about to speak, but he cuts over her.

'It was a brutal crime.' He narrows his eyes in shame, and then meets her gaze. 'And I guess I just don't know if he has ever felt that what he did was wrong. Not that I am his judge.' He looks down at the table. 'We had a difficult history, and it was just too painful.'

She waits for a moment longer, but he is finished now.

'I can't imagine,' she eventually says.

He waves his hand. 'Maybe we should move on from siblings. I'm sorry if I was clumsy in telling you this. I suppose I felt it was important for you to know.' Steven nods as the waiter offers him another glass of wine. 'Perhaps there's something about him being my twin that makes me feel responsible.'

Ester puts her hand over her glass as the waiter offers her the bottle.

'I'm a cheap drunk,' she tells Steven. 'Particularly after a day of clients.' She shifts slightly in her chair, awkward now. 'I appreciate you telling me,' she says. She looks at him directly. Her mouth is dry, but she wants to speak. 'I've been by myself for a while now — and I mean really by myself.' She bites on her top lip, barely daring to keep her gaze fixed on him. 'I don't want to drink any more because I fear I'll just make a fool of myself. I have a tendency to just crash out on alcohol.'

'We can't have that,' he winks.

She picks up her napkin and glances across to where the waiter stands, ready to come over and ask if they want dessert. 'Can we skip the next course?' she asks.

'And go home together?'

She nods.

And he leans across the table and kisses her, red wine lips, his hand on hers.

APRIL SITS UNDER the open window, face turned to the night sky, and plays her guitar softly, teasing out a combination of other people's melodies and her own.

On the wall behind her, she has tacked up Catherine's drawing: a deep swirl of black, streaked with colour.

'It's called "Joy",' she'd said when she'd finished. 'It's for you.'

She has never regretted not having children, and supposes she still could if the urge overwhelmed her, but the truth is she's never wanted it enough.

But she loves those girls.

She remembers Lara singing this afternoon, and she smiles.

Picking up the phone, April calls Hilary without checking the time. She does this often, oblivious to the fact that it may be late.

Hilary answers, wide awake. 'I knew it was you,' she says. 'You do realise it's almost eleven?'

April apologises.

'It doesn't matter. I couldn't sleep,' Hilary confesses.

'I saw the twins today,' April tells her. 'It was so lovely. Like there'd been no time apart. They're beautiful girls.'

Surprisingly, Hilary doesn't ask if Ester knew, or how the visit came to pass. She doesn't want details, she just agrees. 'They look like you did when you were their age,' she says. 'Golden, a streak of sunlight. You were such a treasure.'

'Not always,' April adds.

'Nobody said anything about always,' Hilary agrees.

'I'm going to talk to Ester,' April tells her. 'I miss them, I miss her, I hate that we can't all be together. It's enough. Surely there has to be an end to punishment.'

Hilary is silent for a moment. When she speaks, her voice is soft. 'Oh, my brave one,' she says.

The slight slur in Hilary's voice makes April wonder whether she has been drinking. 'Are you okay?' she asks.

Hilary tells her it is the painkillers she takes. 'I've been getting headaches, I haven't been well …'

'Have you been to a doctor?'

'I've been,' Hilary says.

April switches back to Ester. 'I've decided I'm just going to go round there. Maybe tomorrow. I will stay at the door until she talks to me. I'll camp there,' she laughs. 'Maybe even take placards and a tent. A camp cooker and a stool.'

Hilary is silent.

'I'll call you tomorrow,' April says.

'I'm going to the river,' Hilary reminds her.

'When you get back. I'll let you know how I went. Sleep well,' she adds, hanging up and standing by the open window.

She thinks about going out. She can see the first of the stars, a smattering in the one patch of clear sky. She could walk down to the wine bar on the corner, she might see someone she knows. She looks around the lounge room, wondering where she left her bag, and then she changes her mind. She will try to sleep. Face Ester tomorrow with a clear head.

She stands tall, breathes in deeply, and wishes herself good night, her voice clear and sweet as she replies with a grin. 'A very good night to you, too,' she says. 'I'll see you in the morning.'

But it is just her and her reflection in the darkness of the glass doors that divide the living room.

THE DAY AFTER

This is it.

Hilary drives with complete focus on the road, aware that the painkillers have made her slow, her vision slightly blurred. She has all the windows down, the freshness of the afternoon streaming in, each leaf, each blade of grass, each particle of air washed clean and new.

She does not stop until she reaches the turn-off that leads to the top of the river, pulling over where the orchard flats stretch under the sunlight, rows and rows of glossy-leaved orange trees pressed close to each other.

This is what she wants. To smell an orange.

Leaning over the fence, she reaches into one of the branches, through the mass of foliage, and plucks a perfectly formed navel. The peel is waxy, its scent sweet and sharp. She closes her eyes and breathes it in, breaking through the rind with her thumb, the juice cold.

'This is private property.'

The harshness of the voice makes her jump, and she apologises. 'They just looked so beautiful.'

He continues to glare at her.

She holds the orange out to him, but he doesn't take it.

'I'm dying, you know.' She utters the words without thinking. 'I wanted to smell one of these before I …' At a loss for words, she shrugs. 'Get to the other side.'

She is just a loony old bat. She can see it in his eyes. And in a strange way, it is a relief.

'Well, now you have.'

She nods at him, and walks to the car without looking back.

He'll feel like shit, she thinks, *when he hears about them finding me,* and she almost turns around to tell him not to feel bad, that it's okay, but the exuberance of the moment is rapidly fading. She needs to get back into the car and drive, to keep propelling herself forward before her nerve fails and she collapses, weak, pain-riddled, and at the mercy of others.

The rains have been here, too. When she reaches the low wooden bridge that takes her onto the last stretch of road, she sees the swollen down-flow rushing over the boards, dirty brown and fast. Strange how she pulls up to see whether it is safe to cross — but then to be swept away, injured and even worse off than she is now, is not a possibility she wants to bring into this very small orbit she is spinning around in. She leans out and looks closely at the depth.

Maurie wouldn't have paused.

There had been times late at night when she'd told him it wasn't safe, when she'd insisted he let her and the girls out.

He never did.

She follows his lead, foot steady on the accelerator, the rush of water spraying up against the side of the car and through the window, icy on her arms, smelling of dirt and leaves, both rotten and sweet.

On the other side, the road pulls steeply upwards beneath overarching branches, patches of washed blue sky like tattered holes in fabric.

She drives until she reaches the gate, the 'For Sale' sign hanging off the wire, one end loose, the lock rusty.

At the bottom of the dip she can see the house, the crazy angles of the roof and the golden, dappled sway of the new leaves on the poplars beyond the clearing. Her heart lifts, beating too fast, as she looks down.

This is the place she has loved more than any other, she realises. This is Maurie, and the girls, and the sweetest moments of life.

She is here.

In her bag is the white powder.

She runs her fingers over the plastic.

First, she will swim in the river.

Under the shade of the desert oaks, Hilary takes off all her clothes.

Strange, this body of hers. Old now. Knotted veins on her legs, a stomach that droops, small breasts, pale skin. She unties her hair, white-grey, like wool, and lets it loose. Her feet sink in the cold sand, and the touch of the water is like an ice grip, solid around her ankles.

She has had a good life, she thinks, and she lets herself sink down, her breath caught tight in her chest as the chill takes hold. A good life. Floating past her. The girls in the river, her and Maurie drifting on their backs under the light of the full moon, making love on one of the small islands, the grit of the sand against her legs, the sweat on his skin, and she scoops up a mouthful of the water, pure and sweet, and drinks it down, eyes closed to the darkening sky, skin alive to the cold.

Oh God, she whispers.

Perhaps she could just stay here forever, naked in this water, the cold slowly squeezing the life out of her. She looks up now, inhaling deeply as she does.

Her clothes are in a bundle, and she dresses slowly. She does not want to be found naked, and she smiles at her own vanity, her hands shaking as she tries to clasp her bra. Smoothing down her hair, she ties it back again, and then she begins the walk back up to the house, feet slipping in the mud, hands grasping for branches, using her arms to haul herself up to where the grass stretches, pale and long beneath the poplars, crumpled leaves of bronze and gold and silver scrunching underfoot.

Maurie once painted this grove, the metallic lines of the trunks slashed across the canvas. She has filmed it. She remembers the footage — the girls are skipping beneath one of the trees — but she doesn't think she ever used it. Why not? She shakes her head. It doesn't matter.

The verandah boards are rough beneath her feet, scattered with twigs and dirt, dry and swollen; they creak beneath her, and she sits for a moment, trying to breathe calmly.

All around her it is quiet and still. *It is that hour*, she thinks. Where day turns to night.

Her bag is on the ground where she left it. The white powder still inside.

She has written letters. She has told her daughters she loves them. She has urged them to make up. She has told the twins that they are beautiful and special and she adores them. She has asked them all not to be angry with Lawrence, but to remember that he is just respecting her wishes, and that she is grateful to him, more grateful than she was able to allow herself to express at the time. She wrote with her black Artline pen, her script round and clear; words, words, and more words.

Here, far from them all, it no longer matters. In another place, April is standing on Ester's doorstep, knocking until she is let in; or perhaps she is already inside and they are talking, really talking; or maybe she is at home, her courage having failed her. Ester is smiling; it is her best self she is showing to someone, a man Hilary has never met and will never meet, it is all her hope and promise and goodness unfurling once more. And the girls, those girls; they will live and stumble and fall, and pick themselves up and shine.

The strangeness of imposing last words of advice and wishes now seems ludicrous. At most, her letters will give them some ease about her decision.

She has the spoon, the needle, a cigarette lighter, and the heroin.

Henry has shown her what to do.

As the daylight slides away, Hilary picks up her phone, the text written: *I've gone*, the message reaching Lawrence, who is driving to be with her, behind him a mauve light, deepening like a bruise, the cold breath of the wind a low moan in his ear as he heads out along the highway, on the road already because he knew she wouldn't falter, and he, too, didn't want to falter, but to be there, just as he'd promised he would be.

ACKNOWLEDGEMENTS

Thank you to all the team at Scribe, and particularly Marika Webb-Pullman. Your work on this book was so much appreciated. I'd also like to thank John Stirton for sharing his years of polling experience with me.

This book is dedicated to the four people whom I hold most dear in my heart: Rosie, Anne, Odessa, and Andrew. You have provided joy, counsel, and love, and I am blessed to have had you in my life.